THE

COLLECTOR

OF WORLDS

ALSO BY ILIYA TROYANOV

FICTION

The World is Vast and Everywhere Salvation Lies in Wait
Autopol

NONFICTION

Mumbai to Mecca
Along the Ganges
To the Holy Sources of Islam
Zimbabwe
Kenya and Northern Tanzania
Custodians of the Sun
East Africa—Nature's Wonder
In Africa

"In *The Collector of Worlds*, Iliya Troyanov has turned Burton's unbelievable life into believable fiction, achieving a rounded and satisfying portrait that traditional biography could never match. . . . Troyanov's novel is itself an act of brave exploration, setting out to chart the unknown and unknowable by filling in the blank spaces of Richard Francis Burton."

— Ben Macintyre, *New York Times Book Review*

"I was thrilled by this book. One could compare it to *Moby-Dick*, narrated in a masterly manner. . . . This is a novel that entertains as well as informs, and this is the best that one could say of any book."

— Günter Grass

"Troyanov recounts with gusto the three big adventures in Sir Richard Francis Burton's oversized life. . . . But the book's most satisfying adventure is the African explorations. . . . Troyanov (*Mumbai to Mecca*) is intimately acquainted with the Indian Ocean world, and this book has the cool virtuosity of one explorer saluting another."

— *Publishers Weekly* (starred review)

"When I was an impressionable school kid, my mother told me about Sir Richard Francis Burton. She portrayed him as an exemplary adventurer who wandered around the world at a time when almost no one traveled beyond their own borders, disguising himself to enter exotic, forbidden cultures, then writing in lavish prose about his encounters and discoveries. . . . So it was thrilling to come across *The Collector of Worlds*, Iliya Troyanov's newly translated fictionalized re-creation of Sir Richard's exploits in British West India, on the hajj to Mecca, and in East Africa. This mesmerizing novel illuminates the iconic explorer and the world he wandered; it's the perfect present for wannabe explorers, or their irrepressible moms."

— *National Geographic Traveler*

"A sprawling, densely imagined historical novel, the life of Richard Francis Burton—by turns disgruntled colonial administrator, spy, mystic, and explorer—is one more profoundly affected by forms of unknowing and inexpressibility. . . . Troyanov offers a rich meditation on the many layers of a character whom a reader is invited not to like, but to recognize as 'true to his disguise.'"

—Bharat Tandon, *Daily Telegraph*

"Troyanov . . . is an excellent storyteller, and his intensively researched tale contains vivid scenes of enchantment, erotic encounter, and horror. His prose at times comes close to poetry and it has been well translated by William Hobson."

—Robert Irwin, *Times Literary Supplement*

"An entrancing novel. . . . The adventures could gallop along, but Troyanov writes with the sort of specificity that makes his readers savor each detail and each line. From the novel's first line . . . words explode with meaning, descriptions shimmer in new light."

—Rose Jacobs, *Financial Times*

"Such expressiveness is typical of the novel as a whole, which marshals its many voices in perfect pitch. . . . With its radical code-switching, shifts of perspective, and ahead-of-his-time hero who himself knew how to turn barriers into throughways, *The Collector of Worlds* triumphantly shows us one method. But we will need others, too. I would not be surprised if Iliya Troyanov were to show us some of those in subsequent books."

—Giles Foden, *Guardian*

"Curiously . . . there have been no major novels based on Burton's extraordinary life. Iliya Troyanov, in a remarkable German novel *Der Weltensammler*, has corrected this omission. The English translation of his work, *The Collector of Worlds*, has created a sensual adventure, and an exploration of Burton's behavior. . . . Troyanov's sympathetic novel is the product of immense research and understanding. . . . One of the great values of this absorbing novel is that we are allowed to discover for ourselves the passionate curiosity that shaped Burton's entire life. . . . Troyanov's scholarship has given us a new understanding of Burton's world. It is an intensely passionate journey, and a wonderful piece of storytelling."

— Christopher Ondaatje, *Spectator*

THE
COLLECTOR
OF WORLDS

∽

Iliya Troyanov

Translated by
William Hobson

ecco
An Imprint of HarperCollinsPublishers

For Nuruddin & Ranjit,
who truly cared

Originally published in Germany in 2006 by Carl Hanser Verlag.
First published in Great Britain in 2008 by Faber and Faber Ltd.

FIRST ECCO PAPERBACK EDITION PUBLISHED 2010.

Library of Congress Cataloging-in-Publication Data
        Trojanow, Ilija.
    [Weltensammler. English]
    The collector of worlds : a novel of Sir Richard Francis Burton / Iliya
Troyanov.
        p. cm.
    ISBN 978-0-06-135193-8 (hardcover)
    ISBN 978-0-06-135194-5 (trade paperback)
    1. Burton, Richard Francis, Sir, 1821–1890—Fiction. I. Title.
    PT2682.R56W45513 2009
    833'.92—dc22   2008034363

10 11 12 13 14 OFF/RRD 10 09 08 07 06 05 04 03 02 01

This novel is inspired by the life and works of Sir Richard Francis Burton (1821–90). In following the outline and, in many respects, the detail of his career as a young man, it does not hesitate to depart from – or to elaborate on the gaps within – the historical record. Despite occasional direct quotation, its characters and plot are predominantly the product of the author's imagination and make no claim to be measured against biographical fact. All individual lives are mysterious, particularly those of people one has never met. This novel is intended as a personal approach to a mystery rather than as an attempt at definitive revelation.

Do what thy manhood bids thee to,
From none but self expect applause:
He noblest lives and noblest dies
Who makes and keeps his self-made laws.

Richard Francis Burton, *Kasidah VIII*, 9

The Final Transformation

He died early in the morning before you could tell a black thread from a white. The final prayer ebbed away; the priest moistened his lips, swallowed his spit, aware now that the doctor, who had been silent since the pulse under his fingertips had failed, stood unmoving at his side. At the end the patient had hung on out of sheer stubbornness, but had finally been defeated by an embolism. A woman's liver-spotted hand rested on the dead man's folded arms. Now it drew back and placed a crucifix on his bare chest. It's far too big, thought the doctor, outlandishly Catholic; as baroque as the man's scarred torso. He sensed the widow facing him across the bed, but couldn't bring himself to look her in the eye. She turned away, moved calmly to the desk, sat down and began writing something. The doctor saw the priest put the flask of oil in his pocket, and took this as a signal to pack away the electric battery. It had been a long night, he reflected, and now he'd have to look for a new position. A damn shame, the whole thing. He had grown to like the patient and it had been extremely agreeable living in this villa high above the town with its view over the bay, far out into the Mediterranean. He felt himself blushing and that made him blush even more. He turned away from the dead man.

The priest, the doctor's junior by a few years, glanced surreptitiously around the room. On one wall a map of the African continent, bookshelves crowding in on it on either side. The open window made him anxious – everything made him anxious at this point – and through it came rustling noises that reminded him of other sleepless nights. A drawing to his left, beautiful and incomprehensible, which had disturbed him the minute he had set eyes on it. It reminded him this Englishman had roamed in godless parts where only the ignorant or the arrogant would venture. He had been a notoriously wilful character, but, apart from that, the priest knew virtually nothing about him. Yet another unpleasant duty the bishop had wriggled out of! This was not the first time he'd been called on to administer extreme unction to a total stranger. The bishop had offered him only one piece of guidance: Trust your common sense. Strange advice. But, in any event, he hadn't even had time to get his bearings. The fellow's wife had caught him off guard, pressing him so insistently, demanding so categorically that he give the dying man the last sacraments – as if it were his simple duty as a priest – that he had bowed to her will. He regretted it already. Now she was standing in the open door, giving the doctor an envelope, talking urgently to him about something. Should he speak his mind? The priest accepted her quiet yet determined thanks – what should he say? – and with the thanks the unspoken request that he leave. He smelled her sweat, said nothing. In the hall she held out his coat and her hand. He turned, then stopped – he couldn't go out into the night weighed down like this. He swung round abruptly.

'Signora . . .'

'You will forgive me if I don't walk you to the door?'

'It was wrong. It was a mistake.'

'No!'

'I must inform the bishop.'

'It was his last wish. You must respect it. Please excuse me, Father, I have a great deal to do. Your worries are unfounded. The bishop is quite aware of this.'

'Signora, so you say, but I lack any such assurance.'

'Please pray for the salvation of his soul. That will be best for all of us. Goodbye, Father.'

She spent two days at his deathbed, occasionally interrupted in her prayers and conversations by people coming to pay their last respects. On the third day she woke the maid earlier than usual. The woman threw a shawl over her nightdress and felt her way through the woollen darkness to the shed where the gardener slept. She called but got no answer until she gave his door a clout with a shovel.

'Anna,' he cried, 'has something bad happened again?'

'The mistress needs you,' she told him, adding: 'right away.'

'Have you laid in firewood yet, Massimo?'

'Yes, Signora, last week, when it turned cold. We've got enough . . .'

'I'd like you to make a fire.'

'Yes, Signora.'

'In the garden, not too near to the house, but not too far down either.'

He built a small bonfire, like the ones in his village at solstice-time. The exertion warmed him a little but the heavy dew and his sodden toes made him look forward to a good blaze. Anna came out with a cup in her hand, her hair tangled like brushwood twigs. He smelt the coffee as he took it from her.

'Will it burn?'

'As long as it doesn't start raining.'

He bent over the cup as if he were trying to make out something in the liquid, and took a loud sip.

'Should I light it?'

'No. Who knows what she wants. Better wait.'

The bay grew light; a three-master dropped its sails. Trieste awoke to the sound of one-horse carriages and porters. The mistress strode across the lawn in one of her heavy, full dresses.

'Light it.'

He obeyed. Burn, burn, bride of the sun, blaze, blaze, consort of the moon, he whispered to the first flames. His father's solstice song. The mistress came over and stood so close he found it hard not to flinch. She held out a book.

'Throw this in!'

She had almost touched him. He sensed something helpless in her order; she wouldn't throw it in herself. He ran his fingers over the binding, the worn patches and the stitching, and stepped back from the flames a little, stroking the leather, searching for a memory, until he realised what it felt like – the scar on his eldest child's back.

'No.'

The fire darted in every direction.

'You will do it. This minute.'

The flames righted themselves, but still he didn't know what answer to give her. Anna's voice flickered in his ear.

'This isn't anything to do with us. If she goes now . . . what sort of testimonials will she give us, what about our leaving presents? What's this book to you? Give it to me. What's so special about it?'

He didn't see it spin through the air, he only heard a crash of embers, flames flaring up, and by the time he saw the book in the fire, its cover was already curling in on itself like an overgrown toenail. The maid squatted down, a sooty birthmark on her bare knee. The camel skin catches light, a grimace cracks, page numbers burn, baboon sounds flicker, Marathi, Gujarati, Sindi evaporate, leaving only scribbled letters that float up as sparks and sink as cinders. He, Massimo Gotti, a gardener from the karst near Trieste, recognises the late Signor Burton in the fire, as a young man dressed in old-fashioned clothes. Massimo stretches out his arm, singeing the hairs on the back of his hand, and the pages burn, the notes, the stitching and the bookmarks burn, the hair . . . the silken black hair, the long black hair burning as it spills over the front of the bier and blows in the keening wind. A wall of flames and there, just the other side, is a dead woman. Her skin peels away, her skull splits open; she starts to shrivel until all that's left of her weighs less than her beautiful long black hair. The young officer doesn't know what she is called, who she is. He can't stand the smell a moment longer.

Richard Francis Burton strides hurriedly away. Imagine – in his mind he begins his first letter home about the new country – after four months on the high seas you finally arrive and there on the beach, the firewood piled up right in front of you on the bloody sand, they're burning their dead. Slap bang in the middle of this filthy stinking dump called Bombay.

British India

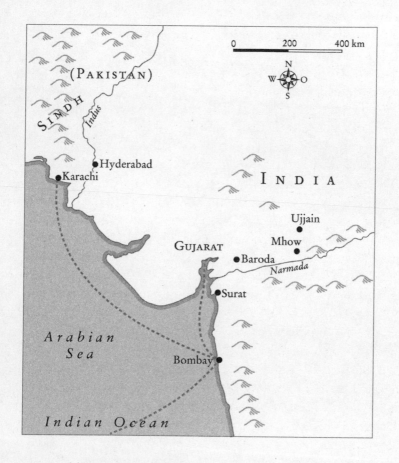

The stories of the letter-writer of the servant of the master

○

FIRST STEPS

After months at sea at the mercy of chance acquaintances and interminable chit-chat, his reading rationed by the swell, taking every opportunity to barter port for vocabulary with the Hindustani servants – *aste aste* in the doldrums, what a brute of a hangover that was; *khatarnak* and *khabardar* in a storm off the Cape, the waves attacking in sheer formation, the ship pitching so hard no one could keep their food down; and plenty more he had the devil of a job pronouncing. After months of this, the days began to grow even stranger, everyone started talking to themselves, and still on they drifted across the Indian pond.

Then there it was! The bay. Bulging sails scooped up air like hands scoop water. The passengers finally glimpsed scenes that the ship's binoculars, with their smell of oil of cloves, had long since conjured up in their imaginations. Distinctions blurred – were they striking land, was land coming aboard – as the deck became a thronged viewing platform, a stage echoing with excited comment.

'It's a tabla!'

Interrupted in their conversation at the ship's rail, the group of British turned to find an elderly Indian simply dressed in white cotton standing directly behind them. He was somewhat smaller than his powerful voice, with a white beard hanging down to his belly offsetting a high, smooth forehead. He was smiling at them in a friendly way, but he had stood very close all the same.

'A double drum, playing a bol of *Bom* and *Bay*.'

The man produced two arms and two hands and began moving them in time to his deep voice.

'Left hand the blessed bay, Bom Bahia, right hand Mumbai, the goddess of the fishermen. A tintaal of four syllables. I'll show you, if you like.'

He had already pushed in among them and began to drum on the rail with his index fingers, shaking his mane of hair.

Bom-Bom-Bay-Bay
Bom-Bom-Bai-Bai
Mum-Mum-Bai-Bai
Bom-Bom-Bay-Bay

'Harsh and rough as a rhythm that has rung out for centuries should be: Europe on the one hand, India on the other. It's simple, really, if you're one of those people who can hear it.'

The man's eyes laughed gaily, as a call went out for the more select passengers to seize land. The sloop awaited; India was only a few oar strokes away. Burton helped one of the women, beside herself with excitement, down the ladder. When she was safely seated, her hands clasped in her lap, he looked back. The white-haired, white-bearded drummer was standing on the deck, stiffly upright, his legs splayed, his arms folded behind his back. His eyes rolled behind thick spectacle lenses. 'Go, go! But keep an eye on your bags! This is not Britain. You're entering enemy territory now.' And his laughter flew away as the sloop creaked on ropes down to the sea.

Landing revealed how their binoculars had deceived them. The dock rose over mounds of rotten fish, coated with urine and a slick of acrid water. Sleeves were hurriedly clamped over noses. The quay itself was accumulated centuries of putrefaction, trodden into a solid mass by bare feet, up and down which now marched a man in uniform, sweating and yelling. The new arrivals looked timidly around, their curiosity suspended until further notice.

'Leave everything to us; we'll be relieving you of all labour!' Richard Burton parried the agent's viscous English proudly, in measured Hindustani. He called to a coolie standing off to one side, who was ignoring the commotion, and having questioned, listened and negotiated, supervised the loading of his trunks onto a succession of backs and their transfer into a waiting cab. It was not far, the driver announced, the fare was modest, and with that the carriage moved away into the mass of humanity like a barge under tow; caps and bald heads, turbans and topis bobbing in its wake.

Burton couldn't make out a single face in the eddying press around him. It was a while before he could see something that made any sense at all: a shopkeeper's paws resting on some sacks of rice outside a shop. Then the cab escaped the harbour and swung into a broad street, and he leant back in his seat. A youngster darted out of the way of the hooves at the last split second, testing his nerve, and rewarded himself with a grin. A man was being shaved near whirling wheels. A child without skin was thrust towards him. Burton was horrified for a moment, then forgot about it. The driver seemed to be telling him the names of the buildings on either side of the road: 'Apollo Gate, behind this, Fort, Secretariat, Forbes House. Sepoy!' He pointed to a cap perched on a mop of greasy hair and, below, a set of thin, hairy legs sticking out of a pair of khaki shorts. Appalling, thought Burton, there's the native soldiers I'll be commanding. Damn it, those clothes are nothing but window-dressing. Even the expression on the man's face looks copied.

The carriage curved past a cluster of women with tattoos on their hands and feet. 'Wedding,' beamed the driver, as the elaborately adorned guests vanished round a corner. All the buildings, most of them three-storeyed, seemed afflicted by gangrene. A man on one of the wooden balconies coughed freely and spat his malady onto the street. The few upright constructions looked like attendants in a leper colony. Burton kept catching glimpses of grey-headed crows between the crowns of the palm trees. At one point they were wheeling round a marble angel whose feet a veiled woman was kissing. Then, just before they arrived at the hotel, he saw a handful swoop down on a corpse. 'Sometimes', said the driver, turning round to him as they barrelled along at full tilt, 'they don't wait for death.'

The British Hotel in Bombay bore all but no resemblance to the Hotel Britain in Brighton. In Bombay higher prices were charged for less comfort, and guests were required to find their beds, tables and chairs themselves. In Brighton, you also tended not to get drunken cadets with scrubby hair and swampy breath clambering on chairs in the middle of the night to goggle at you over a muslin curtain. Burton, no nearer sleep after hours of trying, snatched aside his mosquito net and pelted his neighbour with the first thing he could find under his bed. A direct hit, in the face. The fellow toppled off his chair and cursed softly until a candle was lit and a scream rang out; he had identified the missile, a rat Burton had killed with his boot a while before. In the ensuing volley of abuse, the fabric partition was the only thing protecting the lanky cadet from his own threats, as Burton reached back under his bed and pulled out a bottle of brandy. Lizards were auspicious creatures, rats loathed, which explained why the lizards hung on the walls like colourful miniatures and the rats hid. Not always successfully.

Burton's neighbour on the other side was a medical orderly on his first posting. He liked to sit on the windowsill and look out to sea until the wind changed, when he'd call through the dormitory: 'Watch out, roast Hindu coming this way.' His shouts of 'Eyes and hatches shut!' would ring down the narrow stairwell onto the forehead of the dozing Parsee hotel manager, who treated the guests with exaggerated servility. The Parsee would look up and shake his head irritably. These damned goras could only take the view if there was a tailwind.

The medical orderly refused to go to the cremation grounds with Burton. 'One must guard against wanton curiosity, you know,' he explained, the dutiful son of his father's sermonising, taking his first steps away from the maternal fold. Burton attempted to sing the praises of an enquiring mind, but, as he soon realised, his account of his childhood in Italy and France as the son of a restless father, punctuated by the years 'at home', at boarding school, made almost no sense to the young man. He did, however, after a few days manage to talk him into crossing Carnac Road, the thoroughfare that formed the border between the Empire's brains and its bowels.

Burton had heard all about Carnac Road at dinner with the magniloquent officials who governed entire districts, the provincial shopkeepers' sons and bailiffs' descendants who, perpetually ferried on heathen hands between the shade and the cool, found themselves richer and more powerful than they could ever have imagined in their most brazen dreams. Their wives had meticulously drawn up the map of prevailing prejudices for the sake of their new guest. Every one of their sentences was a danger sign, framed with a 'Listen here, young man!' Having thoroughly surveyed the terrain, they were now convinced of the most appropriate ways to describe India. The climate: 'deadly'. The staff: 'simple'. The streets: 'septic'. Indian women: all of the above. Which is why – 'now listen carefully, young man' – they are absolutely to be avoided, even if, with the passage of time, certain bad habits may take hold (as if a little morality and self-control were too much to ask of our menfolk.) All in all – 'now you won't hear a more honest piece of advice than this' – your wisest course of action would be to keep well away from anything foreign.

They plunged into the clogged lanes, brushing up against something at every step. Burton was always jumping out of the way, his attention caught up by the bearers, the luggers, the shovers. Only the loads were fully visible in that human sea, huge blocks hovering and rolling on a swell of bobbing heads. Lines of rag-and-bone shops. One identical workshop after the other. Merchants sitting on mats, fanning themselves, in front of narrow entrances that led to bulbous, flyblown caverns.

Burton practically had to beg these traders to sell him something, and when they had finally come round to the idea, they offered him the worst of their wares, tirelessly swearing to their excellence and vouching for them on their word of honour until he accepted the particular small dagger or stone divinity in question. Then began a tug of war over the price, accompanied by renewed volleys of sighs and grimaces. At the conclusion of one of these bouts, the orderly remarked somewhat reproachfully, 'You speak these fellows' dialect awfully well.'

Burton laughed: 'The women from yesterday would be horrified. I'm sure they think sharing a language is the same as sharing a bed.'

This black city. Suddenly up ahead a temple and a mosque appeared side by side; a patchwork of colour hard by white monochrome walls. The orderly was repelled by the misshapen goddess, with her grotesque head many times the size of her body. 'Oh, but you can enjoy the element of surprise at least,' said Burton. 'The city's home to a multitude of tongues, and yet it has her, a mute goddess, as its patron saint.' They passed a tomb. A line of clubs hung on a wall above the corpse, which was draped in embroidered green cloth. The Holy Baba's magical tools, an attendant explained. Calabashes from Africa.

The throng grew denser. Human strays and untouchable dogs. Beggars with withered appendages painted a sacred colour; a deformed cow swishing away near by, its short fifth leg smeared orange. Then a limbless figure on a blanket in the middle of the lane leading to the rear of the great mosque, coins scattered around him like smallpox.

A naked, dark-skinned man was holding up the traffic. He was covered in fat from head to toe and had a red handkerchief tied round his forehead and a sword in his hand. His disoriented screams drew a huge crowd. 'Show me the right way,' he yelled, slashing at the air with his sword. An elderly man near Burton mumbled something in the flat monotone of a prayer, as the naked man started cracking his sword like a whip. The crowd gradually turned hostile. 'What is happening here, I don't understand, what is happening here?' The orderly cowered behind Burton's back. The naked man spun with his outstretched sword in a slashing circle until he lost his footing, the sword slipped from his grasp, and the men in the crowd fell on him and began to beat and kick him. 'Don't get involved,' the orderly begged, 'you're tall and you may be strong but you're no match for these wild beasts.'

'But what if they kill him?'

'That's none of our concern!'

'Two monsoons, Dick,' the orderly said on the way home. 'That's the average life expectancy for a griffin.'

'Don't worry,' Burton reassured him, 'that's only for the sort of over-cautious people who die of acute constipation.'

'Obstipation,' whispered the orderly; 'I'm not ready for that at all.'

I

THE SERVANT

No one's going to come and see the lahiya at this hour. Not in this month of drought. In the temple they'll be imploring the gods for rain again, but is there a vow he hasn't made to Ganesh? Of course, he could just pack up, shut his office and flee the dust but it's a long way to his bed. Paper and quill stand ready . . . not that anyone's going to call on him. Not at this hour of the day, not in this month of drought.

He's too restless to have a midday nap. It's become a habit of his never to let any of the other letter-writers, those jackals, out of his sight. The way they scramble for a customer before he's barely even turned into the street; the way they size up his insecurities before he has squatted down and presented his order as a request; the poor soul never even realises how those ignoble wretches have gulled him. They still respect the lahiya, though, even fear him a little. He doesn't know why but his voice, more robust than his body, sees they keep their distance.

His dignified appearance, his good name, his venerable age – he still has a few strengths he can depend on. Oh, but this time of day, this time of year drives a man to despair. The earth swelters and nothing moves.

The lahiya stretches out his legs. The heat melts over the street and clings to the hooves of an ox, which refuses to budge. Wearily the drover lays into it, a lash for every step of the way until the pair of them turn the corner.

That man there, in the middle of the street. A customer? He's been ambushed instantly. A tall fellow, slightly stooped, who bows and lifts his head, whose body offers no resistance to the hands tugging at him. He seems rooted to the spot. Wait, now he's lifting his head again. One of the jackals peels away from the pack, then others follow. They're leaving him be, this figure who towers above them. The lahiya sees the other scribes pointing his way with their know-all fingers. The tall man comes towards him, his face wearing a look of stubborn pride and a dull grey moustache. It's obvious the other scribblers haven't got a look-in this time, however much they casually tie their dhotis and act as if the world holds no secrets for them. This character clearly has a desire only he can fulfil.

'Letters to officials of the British Empire are my speciality.'

'It won't be a normal letter . . .'

'As are letters to the East India Company.'

'Does that include officers?'

'Naturally.'

'It won't be a formal letter.'

'We'll write what you wish. But certain formalities have to be observed. The authorities insist on form. The slightest mistake in structure, the slightest lapse in forms of address and the letter isn't worth an anna.'

'There's a lot to explain. I took on responsibilities that no other . . .'

'We will be as detailed as the occasion permits.'

'I stood by him for many years. Not just here in Baroda; I moved with him when he was transferred . . .'

'I understand, I understand.'

'I gave him loyal service.'

'I would not doubt it for a moment.'

'He would have been lost without me.'

'Of course.'

'And how has he rewarded me?'

'Ingratitude is nobility's reward.'

'I saved his life!'

'May I ask who the correspondence is to be addressed to?'

'To no one.'

'To no one? That would be unusual.'

'To no one in particular.'

'I see. You wish to use the letter a number of times.'

'No. Or rather, yes. I don't know who I'll give the letter to. All the Angrezi in the city knew him. It was a long time ago – perhaps too long, I'm not sure – but some of them are definitely still in Baroda. I saw Lieutenant Whistler only this morning. He drove past in a carriage, one of those new carriages with a leather half roof, a beautiful vehicle. He almost ran me over. I recognised Lieutenant Whistler straight away. He came to visit a few times. I ran after the carriage and it wasn't long before it had to stop. I asked the driver.'

'And?'

'"No," he said, "this is *Colonel* Whistler's carriage." I knew it. My master used to make fun of his name.'

'Then we'll write to Colonel Whistler!'

To demonstrate his readiness, the lahiya opens his little inkwell, takes his quill, dips it in, makes a few trial scratches, bends several inches forward and then freezes. The dust raised by the newcomer has settled. Out of the tormenting light into which the lahiya can no longer bear to squint the tentative voice begins to tell its story. Intimations give way to suggestions, suggestions to silhouettes, silhouettes to individuals; anonymous figures to people with names, qualities and faces. The lahiya grips the quill firmly in his fingers but he can't make out where this man's life story begins, or what it means.

17

There's no sense taking down these muddled outlines.

'Listen. This is getting us nowhere. Let's start with some thoughts, some notes, some sketches, and then I'll suggest a way to order the letter.'

'But . . . I have to know. What will the cost be?'

'Pay a deposit of two rupees, Naukaram bhai. Then we'll see later what sort of outlay is required.'

2

OF A SINGLE SYLLABLE

Stuffed to bursting, the city let out a belch from time to time. Everything smelled as if it was being eaten away by gastric juices. Figures lay by the roadside in the last throes of a fitful, half-digested sleep. A spoon sliced through the flesh of an over-ripe papaya; feet sweated coriander on their way back from market. Burton didn't know what revolted him more, the breeze coming off the sea at low tide, rank with seaweed and washed-up jellyfish, or the stench of goats' innards, the staple Muslim breakfast, as they sizzled on tiny stoves. Mankind's path was indeed paved with bizarre temptations.

'Sir, it is not in my nature to disturb you, an important gentleman like you . . . I see you are, I am seeing it immediately, you must not think I'm just . . . Ah, I am a simple man, sir, I could not fool you. No, sir, I do not want to take up your time, no . . . but if you will just be so kind as to listen, I can be of assistance to you.'

Burton strolled along, letting the streets take him where they pleased, a flâneur casting an appraising glance at every building he passed. He caught the eye, this young British officer who wore his beard full and carried his head straight.

'You have surely just arrived. Difficult days. It is the same everywhere. After you arrive, there is no one to stand by you. Difficult difficult . . .'

'*Aapka shubh naam kyaa hai?*' asked the officer.

'*Are Bhagwan, ap Hindi bolte hai?* Naukaram is my name. At your service, Sahib, at your service.'

After a week, Burton knew the city was teeming with ingratiating Indians who saw in every officer – every white man – an unholy cow they looked forward to milking at their leisure. Their hands were in your pockets before they'd even finished bowing.

'What sort of service exactly?'

'You have learnt our language quick, Sahib, *bahut atschi tarah*. You are only recently arrived, just on the last ship from England.'

'You're well informed.'

'Only a coincidence, Sahib. My brother . . . I am meaning my cousin, is working in the harbour, you see.'

What did this precocious-looking young man want? A bundle of embarrassment, he was tall, slightly stooped, surprisingly light-skinned, with a responsive, if not particularly attractive, face.

'The quicker you are finding a servant, the better.'

'What concern is that of yours?'

'I, Ramji Naukaram, will be your servant.'

'What makes you think I'm looking for a servant?'

'You have a servant already?'

'No. I haven't got a servant. Nor a horse.'

'Every sahib needs a servant.'

'And why should I choose you . . .?'

They stopped at a crossroads where further propositions lay in wait for Burton. Leaving the hotel early that morning, he had resolved the day's lesson would be how to say no, how to remain unbending, at least until the afternoon. He wanted to expose himself to every temptation to prove to himself he could resist them. And then be able to yield to them later.

'. . . Only the best will do for me.'

'Ah, Sahib, what does best mean? There is man and there is woman, and the man who doesn't take a woman because round the corner a better woman, a more beautiful woman, a richer woman is waiting, at the end that man is left without a woman. In the hand today is better than a promise of tomorrow. Today is certain – no one knows what tomorrow is.'

A couple of days later Burton had an idea.

'I want to see the city at night.'

'Go to the club, Sahib?'

'The real city.'

'What is that, real?'

'Show me where the natives go to enjoy themselves.'

'What do you want in those places, Sahib?'

'The same as the regular guests. Whatever passes the time for them shall pass it for me.'

This time Burton didn't take the orderly, whose nerves would have given out before they'd even arrived. There were no lights; every figure they passed was enveloped in a solitary shroud of dust. The streets grew progressively narrower, forking so frequently he would have been lost on his own. After a while, they had to get out and continue on foot. He felt an unexpected jolt of tension, and wondered whether he would hear the footsteps before the knife pierced his skin. The thought excited him; the evening had got off to just the sort of start he liked. Ahead of them glimmered a row of buildings, which, as they drew nearer, revealed themselves to be freestanding houses, each three storeys high, with a balcony running the length of every floor. These were filled with women leaning over the railings, calling to him, *Hamara ghar ana, atscha din hae,* far too stridently and greedily to tempt him into any of the ground floors, with their open frontages like shops, where an elderly woman sat poised to take over proceedings. The courtesans' make-up was even louder than their voices. Apart from these painted faces, all there was to be seen on the first floor was billowing saris.

'Ah, they are not beautiful, Sahib. Am I right?'

'Do many people come here?'

'The ones having little come here, but here is not good. Now we will be seeing better, Sahib.'

They passed a building where according to Naukaram you could smoke opium. The gold of my employers, thought Burton – the source of all silver and gold, in fact. The haze he, as a military officer, was here to protect. He was tempted to go in but a group of men standing paralysed by the entrance like waxworks disconcerted him. 'They can't move,' said Naukaram, 'too much smoking.'

It wasn't far to the appointed establishment, which stood in a street like the others of buildings several storeys high, with balconies on each floor, but here fresh flowers, rather than courtesans, twined themselves round the railings.

'Come on, in we go.'

'No, Sahib, you go, I'll be waiting outside.'

'Nonsense, you're coming with me. Don't forget, you're still on probation.'

A slim man greeted them so obsequiously Burton could have sworn he bowed, despite him standing facing them, perfectly upright, throughout. He assured them at great length how welcome they were, all the while casting doubtful looks at Naukaram's threadbare kurta. 'See you treat my companion decently,' Burton ordered, and he sensed what a struggle it was for Naukaram to step over the threshold. They followed the welcomer into a lavishly decorated room that was appreciably cooler than outside, with thick carpets on its floors. There was a group of musicians off to one side, resting, and a sweetish fragrance that hung over everything. They sat in a corner heaped with cushions, and the slim greeter had barely retired before a woman served them cold drinks and sweetmeats. Burton registered a beautiful navel, a black pigtail reaching to her waist. 'These women write poems,' Naukaram whispered; 'they are wearing beautiful clothes other women never do.' A second slender, graceful figure drifted over to join them and, just as Burton was about to surrender himself to the enchantment of her appearance, she fired off a volley of questions at Naukaram, as brusque and off-hand as if she were throwing darts, while looking Burton over as if he were a fish on a market slab. This done, she sat down next to him and smiled. Her green eyes wore an expression of indefinite promise, like a pearl oyster slowly opening. He instantly forgave her the crude cross-examination and shameless sizing-up.

'He says you understand our language.'

'Only if you speak it very slowly and smile after every word.'

'Would you like me to sing for you?'

'If you explain the song to me.'

She nodded to the musicians, stood up, took a few steps back until she was suddenly looking into Burton's eyes and then began to sway to a weaving melody, slowly at first, like a swing gaining momentum, until she clapped her hands and sang:

'He who does good in this life
Will be reborn as a drop of water,
As a dewdrop on my lip.
He who is virtuous in this life
Shall rest in an oyster shell
In the soft cup of my mouth.
But of all, count him most blessed
Who shall hang, a white pearl,
A white pearl between my breasts.'

The whole song she stayed close to him, a tremor running through her lips, her green eyes half-closed as if they needed to be restrained. At one point she spun in a circle and froze inches away from him, close enough for him to kiss her navel, her spine arched, her head thrown back. Every fold of her dress was quivering, as were her breasts under its threaded gold. Then two little cymbals appeared in her hands and she began to play them as she resumed her dance. When the music finally died away, he had the impression he was more exhausted than she was. She froze once again, her face full of expectation.

'You must give her money.'

'I don't want to insult her.'

'Oh no, Sahib, the insult is not to give her.'

Burton held out his hand, a note between his fingers. The

amusement in the woman's eyes was unmistakable. She took the note as if reluctant to wake his fingers, then spun on her heel and vanished behind a curtain.

'I had the feeling she was laughing at me.'

'No, Sahib. You are just giving the money wrong.'

'Too little?'

'No, enough, but you have to play with the money, like this, you see . . .'

'That looks ridiculous. I will not be anybody's puppet.'

The sweet smell in the air came from hookahs, which, as one of the women explained to him, contained Persian tobacco mixed with herbs, unrefined sugar and spices, and filtered through fresh water. 'Try it; you'll like it.' She produced a wooden mouthpiece from a hidden pocket of her robe and drew on a pipe herself.

He couldn't have said afterwards how long the women danced and sang for him, soaring songs, each trumping the last, the rhythms rolling out, one after the other, taut, pounding, pulsating waves, the lyrics hiding nothing. He drank some sort of milk – Naukaram said it was soma, the draught of inspiration, the miracle-working drink, guarantor of prayer and progeny – and felt it suffuse his body as he gazed at the glittering, glimmering, glowing jewels, the chains on the ankles and arms, the bare waists; his eyes lingering on a belly's gentle curve, the divine hollow of a navel, a stunning smile that seemed to burst out of nowhere, a hand running through loose-hanging hair again and again, shaking it free. He couldn't have said afterwards if he even chose one of the women of his own will. She took him by the hand – a room on the first floor, a high bed – undressed him and carefully washed his body with warm water. She held a flower to his face. 'Remember this scent,' she said. 'It will bring back happy memories, like all flowers.' Everything smelled of flowers: the doors, the panelling, the portraits of ancestors, the roof beams, the woman's hair as she took off her clothes, cloud by cloud, and he became hard as the barrel of a gun. She gently bit his earlobe and whispered something that he only grasped when, flickering her tongue over his throat, she moved round to the other earlobe. *Rath ki rani*. The words were easy enough to understand – Queen of the Night – but what did they mean? Her name, her courtesan title? She inspected his body inch by pleasurable inch, not taking him by surprise until she made him shudder and began savouring his erection, measuring it out in doses – that moment was never to end, neither when she trailed her breasts over his face, nor when she sunk down and took him into the depths with her and he allowed himself to utter a few stifled cries. She raised her pelvis, he saw the flower in her hand again, and then her hand disappeared under her buttocks, and he couldn't control himself any longer. He thrust into her with a last, loud, convulsive delight, crushing the petals of the flower, as he supposed, because when he was lying next to her, exhausted, he smelled a faint, beguiling scent. The scent of the Queen of the Night.

He would have liked to stay in that high bed for hours, but as the scent faded, he sensed impatience in the naked body at his side. My time is up. No, he corrected himself, my time has just begun. And what a beginning, he reflected, as he and Naukaram left the scene of his first enchantment and walked the short distance to where they had left the carriage.

'Where are we going now?'

'To your hotel, Sahib.'

'We'll take you home first.'

'No, Sahib, no need. All fine.'

'But you don't want to walk halfway across town.'

'I am not walking far, Sahib. From here, I am walking half an hour.'

'If you insist. Good night then.'

Naukaram got out. He had already slipped into the shadows, when he heard his name being called again.

'You've passed the test, Naukaram. I'm going to hire you. But you have to be ready to move north with me, four hundred miles or so, to a place called Baroda. I found out yesterday I'm being transferred there. I'll need a servant.'

The answer came out of the darkness.

'Everything is written, Sahib; everything follows a plan. I know where Baroda is. I know where it is exactly, because I am coming from Baroda. Everything is as it should be, Sahib; I am going home with you.'

3

NAUKARAM

II *Om Ekaakshara namah* I *Sarvavighnopashantaye namah* I *Om Ganeshaya namah* II

'I'm ready.'

'I met my master, Captain Richard Francis Burton, in Bombay. I'd been recommended to him. He had just arrived from Anglestan, he was looking for a reliable servant. He hired me on the spot.'

'No! Not like that. Do you think you're Sayaji Rao the Second, just jabbering away from the word go as if everyone knows who you are? We have to introduce you first; your background, your family, so people who read the letter will know who it's from.'

'What should I say about myself?'

'Do I know your life story? Am I an expert on all its ins and outs? Just talk normally, don't hold back; anything superfluous I can leave out later.'

'I should say something about myself?'

'Away you go!'

'All right. I was born in Baroda in the palace. In the wrong half of the palace. I was a sickly child, the source of much anxiety. Perhaps I should say first that I didn't grow up with my father and my mother and my brothers. I only got to know them later . . . well, actually I never knew my parents. They came to visit me once when I was young . . . but maybe that's not so important. My family has been in the Gaekwads' service for generations, since the days when a Gaekwad was Shivaji's right hand. One of my ancestors fought at his side in the great battle . . . but no, that doesn't matter, I'm sure it's just part of our family lore, a beautiful story we can be proud of. Anyway, I was the youngest son, I think. Before my mother became pregnant with me, she had already given my father six sons. Healthy, strapping boys, every one of them. My father was overjoyed at the birth of his first son; he was very proud of his second son; he was pleased with his third son – and after that, every son was a matter of course to him. But blessings can never be a matter of course, at least I don't think so. You have to appreciate every one of your blessings. When my mother felt the first contractions, my father went and found the jyotish in the palace. He was an impatient man, I suppose, my father, and he couldn't wait to know whether the day was an auspicious one. That was a mistake; he got a nasty shock. The position of the stars, the number seven, the number nine, the date and my father's age, my mother's age, and . . .'

'Enough. Spare me this gibberish.'

'Gibberish? Don't you believe it? He was the maharajah's jyotish.'

'I am a member of the Satya Shodak Samaj, if that means any-thing to you. We have renounced such primitive superstitions.'

'The constellation of the planets really was very ominous, though. A bit like drought and flooding at the same time. Too much good fortune, the jyotish explained, could turn into its opposite. The child's health was in danger, the family's future at risk. My father was very worried. He wanted to know what he could do about it. "There is only one hope," the jyotish said. "Your wife" – my mother, that is – "has to give birth to a daughter. Then order will be restored." The jyotish sent my father away with a little bottle of neem oil and a sheaf of mys-tic formulas, which he was to recite while the midwife rubbed my mother's stomach in a circle, clockwise, once every hour . . .'

'All right, all right. We're not compiling a magic handbook here.'

'My birth drew nearer, and all the maharajah's servants who weren't working at that moment gathered outside my parents' box room, all praying heartily for a girl. My mother's labour was drawn-out; the prayers grew more and more fervent. One person fetched a pujari; another took up a collection for coconuts and garlands. I don't know whether the priest really knew any prayers for a girl, or if he just quickly thought some up.'

'A virtuoso extemporiser.'

'I'm sorry?'

'Never mind. Don't let me put you off.'

'In the middle of the night the door opened – the pujari had left long ago by then, only a few friends were still with my father – and the midwife came out, holding the newborn in her arms. "It's a beautiful baby," she said happily, "hale and hearty, doing well."

'"Doing well, what does that have to do with anything, doing well?" shouted my father. "Is it a girl?" And in her exhaustion the midwife completely forgot the reason for all the carry-on and answered, "No, thanks be to Krishna, it is a boy." My father smote his forehead and screamed so loud that the guards came rushing up. His friends gathered round, trying to comfort him. No one paid any attention to the midwife, who took me back into the room and put me down next to my mother. There was such a commotion, they forgot to put the piece of wet cotton on my tongue.'

'All right, now that you've finally been born, do you think you could enlighten me as to why you've told me all this? Do you think Col. Whistler wants to know it would have been better all round if you had been born a girl?'

'I got caught up in my memories.'

'We have to include everything that reflects well on you. We have to demonstrate your extensive experience as a servant, set out your strengths, list your successes, detail your abilities. No one wants to know about the bad luck dogging you. You can share that with your wife.'

'I don't have a wife.'

'No wife? Are you a widower?'

'No, I never married. I was in love, once. It didn't turn out well.'

'You see. That's important. You were always a servant, so devoted that you couldn't even find time to marry.'

'That wasn't the reason.'

'Does that matter? Are you sure of the reasons why you did or did not do something? Who can ever know that exactly? Go on.'

'My father didn't want to wait until Vidhata wrote my fate; he preferred to save on fabric and sweetmeats. So he took me straight to his relatives in Surat. He gave them the gold pieces the diwan had slipped into his pocket the morning after my birth – my father had looked so mortified the diwan presumed he had been burdened with a daughter – and in return for this dowry, if I can call it that, the relatives agreed to look after me. The jyotish had assured my father that misfortune would be averted, if I lived far enough away.'

'Have you finally reached the end of this unspeakable story? You are trying my patience even more than this heat. Let's pause here. This is going to be harder than I thought. And a good deal more expensive! We're going to need a few days.'

'A few days? As long as that?'

'We mustn't be in too much of a rush drafting this letter. There's no harm in you telling me more than we need. Leave it up to me to choose. But I'm afraid two rupees won't be enough. It will cost you more than that.'

4

BESTOWER OF SUCCESS

No one had warned Burton the wooden house he had been allocated had stood empty for months – in India, an unoccupied house is defenceless against the seasons. There was no sign of damage from the outside, apart from a few broken windows, but when they pulled open the creaking door, they regretted it immediately. The stench of monkey excrement was overpowering, bestial. Burton decided to wait until Naukaram had organised help and cleaned out the place, and stayed by the door, looking out at the jungle. He had been assigned a bungalow at the furthest corner of the cantonment, the regiment's quarters less than three miles south-east of town; untamed vegetation came right up to his plot. So much the better, he thought; it would be easier to keep his distance from his fellow officers out here. Naukaram wiped down a wicker chair and dragged it onto the veranda so that he could sit facing the meagre garden: not exactly large, nor exactly lush, and hemmed in by a stone wall, but at least there was a banyan tree and a few scattered palms. He could string a hammock between a couple of those.

Of the natives' quarter in the valley below, all he could see was what projected against the sky: towers and minarets. Otherwise it was just a big stew, totally indigestible, according to the old hands who had taken him into their confidence in the regimental mess that morning. 'Our main street', they had explained to him, 'leads straight down into that swill. But luckily it branches off to the parade ground first, so there's no need actually to ride down the hill. We have to defend the high ground – metaphorically speaking, of course.' Burton didn't join in the conspiratorial laughter. 'Now, ride out as early as possible in the morning fresh, steal a march on the heat – that's the great secret of health, believe me – and head in the other direction. The jungle is far less dangerous than the town, far less dangerous. All our life is here, in the cantonment. We get up early and we finish early too. The prince is perfectly decent. Doesn't harbour any secret ambitions to mount a rebellion, quite the opposite. Quite the opposite. Morning roll call, then patrol, after which we've earned our breakfast, I can tell you. You play billiards, don't you? Bridge at least? Ah, we'll make a splendid player out of you yet!' At which everyone – they had all gathered round, presumably to bolster esprit de corps – had laughed, and he could tell from their peeved faces that they had expected him to join in. He had disappointed them. 'Don't worry, messmates,' he'd have liked to say, 'it won't be the last time.'

Burton heard the window being wrenched open. He stood up and peered through the mesh into his new home. It seemed roomy enough. There were no floorboards, the ceiling wasn't panelled, the walls were as bare as a pilgrim's skull. The exposed roof truss was a novel sight, but not unappealing. Thick cords curled from the beams, from which heavy fans would evidently soon hang.

'Naukaram, the little hut in the corner there, that looks unoccupied and even less enticing than this cowshed, what's it for? Tools?'

'Bubukhanna, Sahib.'

'Perhaps you'll explain what that means.'

'House where the wife lives.'

'Your wife?'

'No. Not my wife.'

'Well, definitely not my wife.'

'Maybe, Sahib. Maybe your wife.'

The air of homeliness pervading the mess was so exhaustive – the walls with their dark, heavy panelling, those comforting carpets, sapphire blue, medallioned, imported from Wilton, and already buckling in places – it was as if he hadn't sailed halfway round the world. His first evening 'at the Club'. A new chap. He mustn't adapt, not one iota, just try to overcome the worst of his repugnance. It was Oxford and London all over again, repeated down to every last detail. He recognised every-thing – the pictures, the frames, the particular horses painted in aspic, the garden parties with their swarms of children, as heavy going as Christmas cake. All of it was so familiar to him – the low tables, the deep armchairs, the bar, the bottles, even the whiskers. Here it was, everything he had run from. He felt it caving in on him like a collapsing building.

'If you don't have fans, you'll simply shrivel up and die when the heat gets really fierce. A khelassy is an absolute must.'

'Or several.'

'For the fans?'

'Naturally. And make sure the khelassy does a regular check-up of the ropes holding the blessed thing. Time has a way of snipping away at those fellows.'

'We're confusing our young friend with details. Now listen: in these latitudes, what you're dealing with is a bunch of canny layabouts who spend their whole time thinking up excuses to skive off work.'

'The purity line is particularly cunning.'

'It's no laughing matter, I can tell you.'

'If you don't see through their games, they'll twist you round their little finger.'

'Let's say, just for example's sake, that you want to read the paper and have your feet washed at the same time. In a lovely big chilumchi.'

'A chi-chi, as we call it.'

'Now, it wouldn't even cross our mind, but to this lot, if a fellow washes your feet, that makes him impure. Because feet are impure and because you're Christian, hence impure per se.'

'Hard to believe, isn't it?'

'Ergo, he can't do any work in your house that'll involve contact with any other servants. The higher-caste ones won't even touch the chi-chi. So even for such a simple job as this, you need one fellow to pour in the water and another to dry your feet. But that's not the end of it, not by any means. The boy who cleans the lavatory – how impure do you think he is? There isn't a single other job he can do.'

'You come across these sorts of excuses at every turn, and believe me, after five, even ten years, you're still nowhere near hearing the last of them.'

They observed him intently in between their impassioned briefings, this gathering comprised almost entirely of bachelors. They were assessing him, his eligibility to make a fourth, to play billiards, to be an advocate of bad jokes. To be a member of the inner circle.

'The nub of it all, really, is who you get to supervise the whole lot.'

'A tricky business for bachelors, you can imagine.'

'There's no two ways about it, you just have to face up to the fact that these fellows are no good. Once you've accepted that, then you can never be disappointed again. All this talk about education's a joke. Have you ever known one of them to show any improvement at all? At best, the whip may stop them stealing.'

'If you ask me, I'd set exceptional store by the sircar.'

'The sircar? What's his indispensable role?'

'You have to be able to trust him. You can't entertain any doubts, not even a flicker. He carries your purse, you see.'

'A sircar? These days? My goodness, thanks to the silver rupee, we do now have a standard currency, you know. Our good Dr Huntington is still living in an age when there were so many different coins to juggle, one had to be something of a circus strongman.'

'I can't carry money myself. Am I supposed to count it openly? And where am I going to wash my hands afterwards?'

'Let's order another bottle in our griffin's honour.'

'I tell you something, Burton. You'll only have an orderly household if now and then someone shows the boys what's what. You don't want to wield the strap yourself, do you? It's far too strenuous and no good for the health in this heat. Get yourself a servant who'll discipline the others.'

'Hasn't he got a title as well?'

Silence fell for a moment. Burton couldn't bear to look at these tenacious prophets, their grimacing faces. He was the pilgrim they were called on to lead astray. The intolerable outdoors had been repotted, and it was only here, in this mess, this greenhouse, that one could survive it. At least it would make it easier to ignore their proselytising.

'Follow our example, Burton. Have a go at whatever takes your fancy, enjoy yourself without a qualm, but do not, under any circumstances, forget to do one thing: drink port! A snort a day keeps the fever away.'

5

NAUKARAM

II Om Siddhivinayaka namah I Sarvavighnopashantaye namah I Om Ganeshaya namah II

'Go on.'

'Soon after his arrival, my master, Captain Richard Francis Burton, was transferred by ship from Bombay to Baroda. And because I had already made myself useful in the weeks he spent in Bombay . . .'

'Indispensable sounds better.'

'Indispensable. Because I had made myself indispensable, he took me with him. And so I returned for the first time to the city of my birth.'

'Where you were welcomed like a king.'

'No one knew me. I appeared out of thin air. But I was well dressed – Burton Sahib had given me money for new kurtas in Bombay – and I was very much in demand. After all, I was hiring servants for an officer of the Jan Kampani Bahadur . . .'

'The Honourable East India Company. You see how vigilant I have to be? If those sorts of mistakes creep into your letter, the best you'll be able to hope for is latrine cleaner.'

'My relatives didn't give me a moment's peace once they had found me again. My parents were dead, but all the others decked themselves out in me, their new finery. The day after I arrived they started looking for a wife for me. I tried my best not to think about how I'd been given away all those years ago, in that vile Surat.'

'Are you trying to bring tears to my eyes?'

'Everyone wanted a job. My brothers were first in the queue, naturally, as soon as they'd recovered from the surprise I existed, that is; because my parents' story – this I have to tell you – had been that I'd died at birth. They were off, trying to worm their way into my affections. "How many years have we missed, brother of ours? We must make up for them all. We cannot be parted again; we cannot lose each other ever again." They looked me in the eye when they were talking, and I could almost have believed them for a moment: people get so caught up in their play-acting. "We want to honour you; you are our delight, the present we have finally been granted after years of waiting." On and on they went like this, frothing away, my six brothers and all the cousins. I accepted their attentions. It was a sort of compensation, a ridiculously small sort. Oh, the lengths they went to make a good impression. But I had a good hard look; I made a sober judgement of who was any use and who wasn't. I'm good on people . . . Good judge of character, write that down. When I had decided on twelve, I let each of them know they had to obey me. The sahib too, of course, if he spoke to them directly. But otherwise, me. I was the only one who had any influence on the sahib, and if they didn't obey me, at any time I could see to it . . .'

'Twelve servants, two masters.'

'In all those years, Burton Sahib never once had any trouble with his servants! That was my doing.'

'How much did they pay you?'

'Who?'

'The lackeys you call your relatives.'

'What do you mean?'

'You milked them. You would have had to be very stupid to have just given them such a lucrative position.'

'Burton Sahib gave me a fixed sum for expenses. I paid them out of that. They were satisfied. Everyone was satisfied. I had the whole household in hand. It was a lovely bungalow, although unfortunately right at the back of the cantonment. Everywhere was a long way away. Burton Sahib quickly settled in. The other officers called him a griffin, a newcomer, but that wasn't true for long. He was the sort of person, my master, who, wherever he went, would in no time get to know the place better than people who'd lived there their whole lives. He adapted very quickly. You wouldn't believe how fast he could learn things. If I'd had that ability, then none of it would have ended anywhere near as badly.'

'You fell out of favour?'

'I was sent home without a testimonial, without a letter of reference. After all those years! Just a small redundancy and the clothes I was wearing. It wasn't all my fault. More was expected of me than of anyone else. It was like that from the start.'

'Of course, of course.'

'But the end can't overshadow everything else, can it? The end can't be that important.'

'Listen, I'm not going to mention any of your weaknesses, the more awkward sides of the story, but I do have to be aware of them. The more I know, the better – you understand. Go on.'

'He wasn't used to lots of servants. I was surprised at the time, until I found out many years later how modestly he lived at home, how simply. Just with a manservant and a cook. I only found that out when I went to England and France with him . . .'

'You were in the Feringhi's country?'

'I was sent home from there.'

'You didn't say that.'

'He took me with him to his country. That's how important I was to him.'

'Why didn't you tell me that earlier? You are a man with experience of the Feringhi's country. That boosts your stock.'

'Well, now you know.'

'I've never met a servant who's been to England.'

'I was more than just a servant.'

'A friend?'

'No, not a friend, you can't be their friend.'

'Confidant, perhaps. That sounds good. Naukaram, confidant of Captain Burton! Go on.'

'Captain Richard Francis Burton. Perhaps it's better if you write the whole name.'

'Of course. But it would be even better if you didn't hide anything from me. The more tiptoeing around I have to do, the longer it will take.'

'This letter has to be good, as good as it can possibly be. I have to take service in another Angrezi's household. That's what I was born for. I haven't forgotten any of my mistakes. The first time he had a shave, it almost ended in murder. He was asleep – dozing, really – while his beard was soaped. The hajam already had the razor in hand and was just about to start shaving him when Burton Sahib opened his eyes. I don't know what he thought he saw, but he rolled over the bed, his face covered in foam. The hajam's things went flying. Burton Sahib crashed to the floor, grabbed his pistol and he'd have fired, I am absolutely sure, if I hadn't yelled: "Everything's fine, Sahib, no danger, everything's fine. You're just having a shave!" He waved the pistol about in my direction, and warned me that if he was jumped like that again he would shoot me.'

'Did you believe him?'

'He was capable of it, I think, when the evil spirits took him over.'

'Then you really did a great service with your courage. You saved a barber's life.'

6

DESTROYER OF OBSTACLES

'I can't organise the household with fewer than a dozen servants,' Naukaram had insisted, so a dozen servants was the complement Burton had given him permission to select and present for his inspection. Heaven knew how or where he had got them. It didn't interest him; Naukaram was to have free rein until further notice, he had decided. He just accepted them, these twelve unknown, dark figures who stole into the room, wordlessly went about their work, then froze in an attitude of all but invisible subservience, one palm laid on top of the other, their gaze fixed on their master. Sometimes he would forget about them and start with fright when they made a noise. Together they passed their days in the bungalow, glaring days that grew

36

ever hotter and more glutinous, which he spent at his desk behind drawn blinds that screened out the world completely. He could read and write more or less comfortably like that; it made the day more or less bearable. What else was he supposed to do anyway? In the hours immediately after dawn, he inculcated the basic alphabet of drill into an arbitrarily recruited, miserably motivated body of men. Prodigious reserves of self-conceit were needed to consider the training of these 'Johnny Raws' an important activity. Nor was security a matter for concern in the area covered by this outpost: the natives were peaceful, and the last casualties had been some years previously, when an elephant had gone on the rampage during a parade at the maharajah's palace and trampled a number of the sepoys to death.

Otherwise it was so quiet, he thought he could hear the pulse of narrow-mindedness throbbing. It nauseated him, the clammy apathy of that life devoted to bridge and billiards. He was damned if he was going to see out his time slumped in armchairs as deep as they were musty, staring blankly at his fingernails and the sand and dust gathering under their rims. There was only one way for him not to fritter away his life: learn languages. Languages were weapons. With them he could throw off the fetters of this tedium, give his career a fillip, put himself in line for some more challenging commissions. He had picked up enough Hindi on the boat to find his way around, broadly speaking, without making a complete fool of himself in front of the natives, and that was more, as he'd realised to his amazement, than even Hind's most seasoned officers could manage. One of them spoke solely in imperatives. Another used verbs exclusively in the feminine form: everyone knew he simply repeated parrot-fashion whatever his native lover said. A Scot, meanwhile, had been so incapable of adapting his darting tongue that his compatriots only understood him with difficulty and the natives not a word. If he tried Hindustani, they answered with polite regret that unfortunately they didn't speak English. If the sahib could just wait a moment, they'd fetch someone who could translate.

After completing his regimental duties, Burton would sit at his desk and immerse himself in grammars picked up in Bombay until late into the night. He was rarely disturbed: word had soon got around that the griffin was an eccentric. But that didn't make it any the easier to remain sitting quietly. It was less than six months ago that he had left Greenwich, fully expecting to pass from the mercantile everyday into a realm of glittering heroism and lightning advancement, there to cover himself in glory and honour. Men his age were commanding three thousand Sikhs conquering territories bigger than Ireland in her majesty's name.

Drops of sweat rolled down his forearms, his back; flies buzzed around him. Afghanistan was miles away and already pacified and there was nothing left for him to do but to say words out loud, repeat them a hundred times. The moment he fell silent, he heard the drone of the mosquitoes; no matter how often he beat the air and yelled the word he had just learnt, he couldn't get rid of them. There was only one tactic that worked against that scourge: he had to sit perfectly still in his chair, his eyes fixed on the grammar open in front of him, on the next English word for which Hindi, as so often, had two counterparts – 'the natives' duplicity is there, plain for all to see, in their language,' the feminine-conjugating officer had volunteered. He was a cunning victim, his hearing calibrated to the insect's approach as he slowly enunciated the first equivalent, *pratiksha karna*, every syllable a glug of water, then the next, *intezaar karna*, which he repeated over and over until he felt the mosquito land on his arm, felt it bite him – and then squashed it.

'Naukaram!'

'Yes, Sahib.'

'I'm not going to get any further just with grammars. I need a teacher. Can you get your hands on someone who'll pass muster?'

'I can try.'

'In the town?'

'Yes, in the town.'

38

'Another thing, Naukaram.'

'Yes, Sahib!'

'I forbid you to say another word of English in my presence from now on. Speak Hindustani! Or Gujarati, or the devil knows what, but not a single word of English.'

'What about when there are visitors?'

'The minimum. The bare minimum.'

7

NAUKARAM

II Om Vignaharta namah I Sarvavighnopashantaye namah I Om Ganeshaya namah II

'On you go.'

'Where did we leave it yesterday?'

'Ah! Now listen – because I take my responsibilities seriously, I read through everything we'd written last night, checking for mistakes, to see if there was anything I wanted to ask you. But you can't always rely on me. From now on, you have to remember what you've told me and what you still want to say.'

'What a tyrant, worse than Shivaji! You can't talk to me like that. I need your services, yes, but that doesn't mean I'm your servant.'

'Come on, we shouldn't waste time. By the way, when I was reading your story, I found myself wondering what your master looked like. I should know that.'

'Why? The Angrezi know what he looked like. They'll all remember him, I'm sure. No one could forget him.'

'You don't understand this whole business very well, do you? How am I supposed to come up with the appropriate language if I can't form an image of this Burton Sahib in my mind?'

'He was tall, almost as tall as me. But sturdier, like one of those black buffaloes that can toil in the fields all day. And untirable, just like them. His eyes were very dark, you noticed

39

that immediately, but they also looked very naked, that was the odd thing. I have to tell you: I've never seen eyes as naked as Burton Sahib's. You could be trapped in his gaze. I saw him mesmerise people so often, as if his eyes had cast a spell on them. When he was angry, he'd look at me as if I was a complete stranger, as if vicious yakshas were going to leap out at me. It was terrifying. He would often fly into a rage all of a sudden, for some reason that seemed insignificant to us, completely insignificant.'

'You already told me that yesterday. Did he beat you?'

'No! Beat me? How could he? Of course he didn't beat me. I get the feeling you haven't understood my position in that house, the role I played. You haven't understood it at all!'

'Well, tell me more about your responsibilities then.'

'I did everything, took care of everything for him.'

'Everything?'

'Everything he asked of me. All the things that had to be done and sometimes what he secretly wanted.'

'Examples! Give me examples.'

'Doing up the house for a start, the broken windows . . . I got new panes put in and blinds hung. I found some lovely Kobbradul for the curtains, very reasonably priced. I wasn't in the habit of squandering my master's money. They were so beautiful, the brigadier's wife sent word asking where I'd bought the material.'

'I'll make a point of that: an authority on Kobbradul.'

'I did the shopping, I got the ganja; he liked smoking in the evening when he drank his port . . .'

'Port?'

'Yes, port wine. You know what that is, don't you?'

'Of course. I just had to make sure I heard right.'

'Ah! I get into a muddle when you interrupt me, I lose track of what I was thinking, there's no need . . . port . . . ah yes, and I got books for him – he wanted to read everything – and herbs and henna and the monkeys, those wretched monkeys, I got hold of them. That wasn't easy . . .'

'Monkeys?'

'And the teacher, who meant so much to him. I found him.'

'Monkeys and teacher? Wait.'

'And Kundalini, even Kundalini . . .'

'Wait, wait, wait! Who's Kundalini? What are you talking about?'

'You asked me for examples.'

'Well, explain them.'

'I can't imagine why you'd need to know about that.'

'Which of us has more sense, you or I?'

'The whole idea of this letter is ridiculous. The heat has gone to my head.'

'Not at all, Naukaram-bhai, not at all. You are mistaken. It makes perfect sense, you have to do it! This is the best idea you have had for a long time. You've found your way to me, that's good, and now we have a long road ahead of us, we must be patient. I'll see you to your destination, though, trust me. Now tell me something else, something you're proud of.'

'It wasn't easy finding a halfway decent teacher. Burton Sahib came to me after he'd tried himself. He had asked his people about a munshi. They couldn't help him. They only knew simple munshis who have nice handwriting and can quote a few sacred texts.'

'Of course. Who really wants to learn anything these days?'

'Burton Sahib wanted to be taught by a real scholar. "I don't want to be sitting opposite someone", he said, "who can't answer every third question I ask." I enquired at the maharajah's library first. They pointed me towards a brahmin who they said was famous throughout Gujarat for his learning and could speak the Angrezi's language wonderfully. I went to see him at his home. He didn't live far from the library, in a corner house with little balconies on both sides. It was beautiful, but very small, barely wider than a cow. The door was on the main street, and it was open, because a barber had his premises on the ground floor by the stairs. A long, narrow barbershop that left the barber just enough room to stand behind his customers.

41

I couldn't help smiling when I saw the teacher. He hadn't had his hair cut for decades. Or his beard. He kept me waiting at first, even though I'd told him what I was coming about. Ah, the arrogance of these people: that annoyed me. He was very messy, books everywhere. I could see through the open door into the next room: piles of books, books lying open; I could hardly see the floor. His wife was friendly, though. She offered me chai and freshly made puranpolis. So I got my own back on that conceited teacher: I ate them all.'

'How many?'

'How many what? Puranpolis? Why do you or anyone else care how many puranpolis I ate eight years ago?'

'This was eight years ago?'

'Well, how many puranpolis did you eat? Last year? What do you want of me?'

'Calm down. I just wanted to relax you a little.'

'I am relaxed. I'm trying to tell my story and you keep knocking me off my stride.'

'My question wasn't as pointless as you think. I learnt something important, something I should have known from the start. You said eight years. Does that mean you served this sahib for eight years?'

'Almost. I had to come back from Anglestan. That takes months. Didn't you know that? Or did you think I flew back on Garuda's wings?'

'Eight years, excellent. I'll put that piece of information, that figure, at the start of my letter; it sounds impressive: Naukaram, for eight years loyal servant and close intimate of the famous officer of the Honourable East India Company, Burton Sahib . . .'

'Famous officer? Famous for what? He was sent home in disgrace, just as I was later. His people thought of him as an untouchable.'

'That wasn't the impression I'd got so far.'

'Are you writing down what I tell you – exactly what I tell you? Or are you adding whatever comes into your head?'

'I spoke off the cuff just then. Calm down, I just used that sentence as an example, that's all. You're too on edge, you're not breathing properly.'

'Ah! No! We're not going to talk about my breathing now. We're going to carry on. Half the afternoon has gone already, I haven't got time for this, we have to make headway. So – I was shown in to see the teacher. Eventually. I had to be careful not to step on one of the books. He was a small man but little by little he grew taller as he started talking. He quizzed me as if I was the one asking him a favour. He wanted to know everything about my master. I felt like telling him he had no right to ask such questions, but something stopped me. He was a venerable gentleman. The pay didn't seem to interest him at all. I offered him twenty rupees a month, but he didn't show the slightest emotion. I didn't know if he'd even heard me; I thought he'd be thrilled. Ah, really, I have to tell you, these people are presumptuous and arrogant. He wouldn't even agree to teach Burton Sahib there and then. He just said he'd meet him. I was even afraid he'd say Burton Sahib would have to pay *him* a visit. Sometimes these people forget themselves; they think because they've got brains, they have power. He mulled it over for a while, but then he remembered the rightful order of things. We arranged for him to come in a couple of days.'

8

AN OCEAN OF KNOWLEDGE

Burton couldn't believe his eyes. Before him, legs sturdily spread, stood a small man with a luminous face, long, white beard, greying eyebrows, the hair at the back of his head gathered up in a pigtail – it was the odd customer who had accosted them in such a forthright way at the ship's rail just before they landed in Bombay. He was virtually a gnome, his forehead smooth with age. A roguish wisdom glinted in his eyes. Respect everything, it counselled, yet take nothing too seriously. An imp playing the part of a court jester. He would have been perfect as a figure on a bas-relief of a Hindu temple. When it rained, the water would have purled over his rounded belly.

'How's enemy territory agreeing with you?' – the fellow had been equally quick to recognise him. 'How often do you curse the commanding officer who sent you to Baroda?'

'That's the reason for our meeting today,' answered Burton. 'I want to escape the ennui here by learning.'

'Ennui? You like unusual words? Then you must learn Sanskrit. The world is created out of the syllables of this language. Everything comes from Sanskrit. Take the word "elephant": in Sanskrit *pilu*. Where is the similarity there, you may ask? Follow me to Iran, where it becomes *pil*, because the Persians ignore short final syllables. In Arabic the *pil* becomes *fil*, because, as I'm sure you know, Arabic doesn't have a "p". The Greeks like to add an "as" to all Arabic words, and so, if you couple it with a consonant shift, we already have an "elephas", and from there it's only an etymological hop and a skip to the "elephant" you know. I see we will enjoy ourselves. Incidentally, what does ennui mean?'

He didn't allow silence to settle, this old man. Almost before the last syllables of Burton's explanation had faded away, words were pouring out of him again.

'Upanishe is my name. You've heard it before, now write it down – Up-a-n-i-sh-e – in Devanagari script so I can see the extent of your knowledge.'

What self-assurance, Burton thought irritably, as he slowly wrote out the letters that twisted up and down like the skeletons of dead fish. This was the first native who hadn't behaved in a craven fashion towards him. Anything but: there was something almost imperious about this teacher's manner, the way he clicked his tongue as he examined Burton's forlorn show of learning on the piece of paper. He did so three times, without indicating whether he was applauding or criticising. Then he grabbed the quill from Burton – shouldn't he ask permission? – and wrote a line on the paper.

44

'Can you decipher that?'

Burton said he couldn't.

'No command of Gujarati,' pronounced Upanishe, as if he were marshalling the elements of a diagnosis. 'What is it you want to learn?'

'Everything,' said Burton, judging it was time to regain lost ground.

'This lifetime?'

'This year! A few languages in particular first: Hindustani, Gujarati, Marathi. I want to put in for the exam in Bombay. It will be good for my career.'

'Haste', said Upanishe disparagingly, 'is something to be overcome. That is the first thing we have to be clear about.'

'We should agree on teaching times and salary,' said Burton.

'I will test your hunger for a week,' Upanishe decreed, 'each afternoon until it is time for your evening meal. After that we will see. And as far as money is concerned, I cannot accept any from you.'

'Because I'm a mlecha?'

Upanishe burst out laughing.

'I see you've already acquainted yourself with a few commonplaces. I have had many dealings with the Angrezi; to me you are neither a pariah nor an untouchable, you needn't worry on that score. No, it's an old tradition; we brahmins do not sell our learning in the marketplace. We do, however – never underestimate the brahmins' ingenuity – accept gifts. At Guru Purnima, the day pupils honour their teachers, we are given sweets: little sesame balls in which are hidden a modest coin or an expensive piece of jewellery, as the case may be. When we're alone, we split them open with our fingers, like ripe guavas. You can see the advantages of this practice. The pupils feel under no obligation: they have no cause to be ashamed if they're in need and have little to give. And we gurus in turn give some of these laddoos to our own teachers, and to our fathers if they should still be alive. The question, therefore, of who gets what present is left up to a higher power. You would call it chance.'

Upanishe spoke like an actor, exaggerating his phrasings so that the distinction between stressed and unstressed syllables was extremely marked, and emphasising every point with dynamic, decisive gestures. It seemed impossible to imagine anything ruffling his confidence.

'The dematerialised gift,' Burton interjected, 'an extremely interesting concept.'

'Ah, you've understood. Good. With us, gifts are not opened the moment they're given; we avoid awkward situations. A gift ought not to solicit the recipient's goodwill in full view of everyone. May I bid you farewell now?'

Upanishe had barely uttered his rhetorical question before he was already on his feet. Burton accompanied him to the door.

'I look forward to our lessons, Upanishe Sahib.'

'As we have come to an agreement, you may call me Guru-ji. Oh, incidentally – this is something I haven't told you – for us a shishya has to submit unreservedly to his guru's authority. The guru is owed shushrusha and shraddha, obedience and blind faith. In the past pupils used to go to their teacher with a log as a symbol of their readiness to burn in the fire of knowledge. They may walk their own paths when they have come to the end of the teacher's.'

An amanuensis was waiting in the shadow of the canopy, a young boy carrying a bundle, which Burton presumed contained the master's writing things. He rushed forward to hold a sunshade over his master's head.

'Now for your first lesson in Gujarati,' said Upanishe. 'In the day-to-day, we take our leave by saying *aojo*, which literally means: come and go. I go, so I can come back again. Do you understand? So, Mister Burton, until tomorrow, *aojo*.'

'*Aojo*, Guru-ji,' said Burton, and deep in his new teacher's eyes he saw the seed of a possible friendship.

9

NAUKARAM

II Om Vidyavaridhi namah I Sarvavighnopashantaye namah I Om Ganeshaya namah II

'One thing I don't understand. Your master was an officer, yet he seems to have spent his days exactly as he pleased.'

'He had to go to Mhow a few times. That was his only duty, apart from drilling the sepoys, of course. Every morning, except Sundays, when the Feringhi gathered for prayers. Burton Sahib didn't join in, though. He had no time for his people's faith. That amazed me. He was more interested in Arti, and Friday prayers, and Shivaratri, and Urs. It was strange. I asked him later, when I was allowed to ask the questions a servant normally doesn't ask his master, why he felt closer to foreign rites than his own. He told me that to him his own customs were just superstition, hocus-pocus . . .'

'What was that?'

'Empty words, *yantru mantru jalajala tantru*. Magic . . .'

'Maya.'

'Yes, if you like. But the foreign traditions fascinated him because he hadn't seen through them yet.'

'Did it take him that long to see through our superstitions? You should have brought him to see me. The mantras are stones the brahmins produce from their mouths while we stand there, totally dumbstruck, as if they're giving us something valuable. Have you noticed magicians often wave torches to distract us during a trick, just as the priests do at Arti? Same sleight of hand. Same illusion.'

'I am not such a big man as you; I can't make a joke of it.'

'I was being serious.'

'*Oim aim klim hrim slim.*'

'Is that meant to be an insult?'

'No, not at the prices you charge. I cannot afford insults. I want to carry on with my story. We shouldn't talk about ourselves.'

'The main thing you shouldn't do is forget who you owe respect to.'

'His regiment had only one duty. All the time we were in Baroda, it was only brought out once a year. To guard – no, to honour, more like – the maharajah at Ganesh Chathurti. The three hundred sepoys and the officers marched to the palace in full uniform, led by the regiment's band. Then they accompanied the procession to the river Vishvamitra. The band played as loud as they could, so that everyone would hear them above the din of bells and cymbals and seashells. And when the maharajah walked over the bridge, the soldiers fired a salute. It was the loudest tribute he received all day, and everyone was extremely satisfied.'

'Yes, all right, I don't need all that, I've been there. I know what sort of displays the Feringhi put on of their power. So – he had time, he was curious and you found a teacher for him. The right one too, it sounds, someone of great learning.'

'The best teacher in Baroda. Under his instruction, Burton Sahib quickly learnt our languages. A year later he went to Bombay and shone in his exams in Hindi and Gujarati. He earned more money after that too.'

'Did he tell you that? He must really have trusted you.'

'Otherwise things didn't change much. He sometimes translated at court – knowing him as I do, I am not sure how accurately. He spent most of the day sitting at home, as before. He had no duties except to learn. He was industrious, toiling away like an ox in an oil mill. And the next year it was the same all over again: he sat more exams in Bombay, this time in Marathi and Sanskrit; he passed with distinction, and then he came back to Baroda to sit at his desk and be looked after by me. He'll run out of languages one day, I thought. He was a young man. But then in the third year we had to leave Baroda. Unexpectedly. That was a terrible blow for me. His masters had obviously noticed how little he had to do. Burton Sahib was transferred – it couldn't have been worse – to Sind, to the wilderness, to the other end of the Thar desert.'

48

'Wait, wait, wait. We don't know enough about your time in Baroda. You skip too much. We need to know how the teacher, what was his name again . . . Upanishe . . . how he taught Burton Sahib.'

'What does the teacher have to do with my work? Why should we waste our time on him?'

'Well, you did find him after all, so, apart from anything else, it is down to you that the Angrezi learnt so much.'

'The teacher, Upanishe Sahib, as I have already said, wasn't a usual munshi. He said Burton Sahib wouldn't be able to learn to speak like a Gujarati if he didn't eat like a Gujarati. Then he suggested he should give up meat, eat more vegetables and nuts and fruit, and eat less at a time, but more often, rather than just a few heavy meals. The Feringhi thought they had stomachs like elephants, he used to say. Burton Sahib adopted these foreign habits; he changed what he ate, and told me to instruct the cook accordingly. The cook was not happy at all. He was so proud to have learnt some of the Feringhi's dishes.'

'I have never heard of an Angrezi being so conscientious. In the old days – I don't know if you remember this – they were known as "I don't have to work".'

10
HE WHO SITS LIKE A ROCK

At last, an assignment that broke up the routine, which had already settled into a numbing daily round after only a week. He was detailed to escort a representative of the East India Company to Mhow, where the rest of the regiment was stationed. Hardly taxing, but at least it would allow him to get out of town while the weather was still cool. Before setting off, the fellow said a prayer, one of those prayers that give the impression God has taken personal charge of this member of His flock, not that he mentioned his work – perhaps as a trader licensed to ship opium from Malwa to China, he'd had to loosen the belt of his conscience as it was. They headed east towards the Narmada river, a herd of goats trotting on their left, and came first to a village called Kelenpur and then Jambuwa, a waterless river.

'Why are the rivers hereabouts all feminine? All goddesses, to be precise.'

Burton's attempt to strike up conversation was met with a disapproving stare. Families of nomads sat near the road's edge, cooking on campfires. They reached Dhaboi, an old fort . . .

'. . . You know its architect was buried alive in those walls.'

A grunt was the only response this piece of information elicited. A boarded-up house, this character, Burton thought and gave up casting around for a suitable conversational gambit. The Vindhyachal chain appeared in the distance, then they crossed the Narmada at Garudeshwar.

'Holiest of all rivers,' remarked Burton, damned if he was going to put up with the silence any longer. 'Did you know that the remission of one's sins takes seven days at the Yamuna river and three at the Saraswati, but that the sight of the Narmada alone is enough to absolve one of all guilt? Ingenious myth, don't you think?'

'Filthy water,' said the opium dealer.

'With cleansing properties,' replied Burton.

The opium dealer spurred on his horse.

'I'm afraid', Burton said, soon catching up with him, 'you don't know the way. And you will have trouble communicating with our guide. He speaks broken Hindustani and only one word of English: shortcut.'

'Damn cheek,' muttered the opium trader.

'Another fascinating detail about the Ganges. Because so many people wash in it, in time it becomes impure itself. Once a year it assumes the form of a black cow and walks to the Narmada to bathe, not far from here. The village is called . . .'

'Keep your composure, fellow,' snapped the opium trader, raising his voice for the first time.

'You're right, I'm getting bogged down in details. Much more important is that when the cow gets out of the water it is white, entirely white. Figure that one out.'

Whereupon Burton urged on his horse.

The next day, after climbing into the mountains, they rode for hours at a gentle trot between vast fields of poppies. This was the high plateau from which the Honourable Company orchestrated the debauch of the Middle Kingdom. An elegant remedy to the foreign trade deficit, according to a columnist in *The Times* the previous year, when the fighting in China had been resolved. The opium trader only spoke to Burton once. They were trotting up to a cart when he asked, 'What's in there, do you think?' as if he knew considerably more than met the eye.

'Hay would be my guess,' answered Burton.

'That's what it looks like, but looks can be deceiving.' He clearly had privileged information. 'Recently we picked up a fellow: he had his whole cart full of contraband, under the hay.'

'Contraband,' Burton asked innocently, 'what sort of contraband?'

'Best quality, we seized a small fortune.' And that was the only thing the trader had to say until a muttered farewell in Mhow.

Burton gave the major in command a message from the brigadier in Baroda, and then feigned a slight attack of dizziness to get out of lunch in the mess, which would have put paid to the rest of the day. Instead, he slipped out to reconnoitre the little town.

The sun was pitilessly high. A few men were enjoying the shade under their carts. Cows munched. Other than that, nothing was happening at the meridian hour.

'Come!' A boy had tagged on to his heels. 'Come with me! You must meet the judge. No one can leave this place without meeting Judge Ironside.' Burton was dragged along through the clayey lanes, the lad running next to him, constantly tugging at his sleeve and bragging about the dignitaries he had taken to see the judge. He was enumerating their titles for the third time when they reached the court building. It was surrounded by a garden, which afforded justice protection from the dirt of the streets. Tugging at his stained belt, the chowkidar at the gate saluted with his left hand and worked his lips without any sound coming out, only a trickle of spit that crept along his moustache.

'Perhaps the judge is not in court today?'

'The judge is always here. Where else should the judge be?'

They followed a gravel path, once elegantly bordered with shrubs and now completely overgrown. The lawn in front of the portico was covered with squatting figures. Between the columns, clerks sat scratchily taking down whispered dictation, then stamping the petitions with scrutinising looks. The boy marched confidently into the building without asking permission, although in fact there was no one to be seen whose permission he could have asked. They walked unchallenged past a row of sternly frowning marble busts and came to a chamber that reminded Burton of a basilica, its steepling ceiling holding up a vast dome from which revolving fans hung down on long stems. The air was alive with flurries of birds, their fluttering wings louder than the fans' blades, countless tiny green birds that must have flown in through the holes Burton could see all over the dome. In the middle of the room, surrounded by files, cages, candlesticks and an enormous inkwell, sat a man in a wig, engrossed in a pile of documents. A group of petitioners squatted on their heels at a considerable distance from his desk, while between them and the judge – for the pale man with the goatee beard couldn't be anybody else – stretched a gleaming expanse of floor. The boy seemed to hesitate for the first time. Burton observed the judge's wig, the front of which a breeze was ruffling, while it hung down at the sides like a wet flannel. He continued reading with unbroken attention, not moving even when a canary landed on his right shoulder. And the plaintiffs remained equally silent and unmoving, as if their patience were an offering they were making to this alien idol. Suddenly, without any clearing of his throat or preamble, the judge delivered his verdict. He didn't conclude by looking up or sending the petitioners on their way with a final remark or gesture. Instead they awkwardly got to their feet in stifled silence and withdrew.

'Now!'

'Judge-ji! Visitor. I'm bringing you a visitor. At last, another visitor for you.'

The judge waved them forward and, as they approached his desk, a little man with a bucket scurried into the room, mopped the floor to an even more brilliant shine, then stopped at the spot where the petitioners had previously been squatting, as if it marked an invisible boundary. The boy motioned to Burton to stop there too.

'You've come on a wild-goose chase. I am afraid I can't offer you anything today. Coming unannounced as you do. Most regrettable. I could perfectly easily have laid something on for you, but as it is, you'll have to take pot luck, that meagrest of fares.'

'I didn't know what would be expected of me in Mhow. At least we were able to visit the Buddhist caves on the way.'

'Did you meet the hermit?'

'Today was his day of silence. We inspected one another for a while.'

'Precisely! Unfortunate. Most unfortunate. Nothing must be left to chance. That is the first rule of civilisation, I've had to learn it by heart here, believe me. The birds defecate on my files. Do you think there's any design to that? I can't get rid of them. We lure them into these cages and they're sold in the bazaar – although now that's getting harder; glut of the market, you know – but there's too many that get through those holes. You have no idea how long I've been waiting for authorisation to have the whole place renovated. It's a miracle it hasn't rained properly here for years. God is on the side of justice.'

'Justitia is His favourite daughter.'

'I've developed my own system. I concentrated entirely on areas I can control. Do you want to know how?'

'In fact I just wanted . . .'

'I asked myself: what is the greatest nuisance? The dirt? Yes.

The importunity? Oh yes. The lack of punctuality? Merciful Lord. So I resolved to eradicate these scourges. I introduced the notion of an inviolable precinct that no one is allowed to enter. You must forgive me, I know it's impolite but exceptions are a sign of weakness. I tried to introduce a uniform. There has never been anything like that: one uniform for prosecutors, one for the accused, one for witnesses. But that was too ambitious. I thought about it all for a long time, and then I realised that the voices of these people were driving me to despair. That shrill babble that sounds as if the words are tossed out at random, on the throw of a die, as it were. It drove me to distraction. So I banned all talking.'

'The clerks outside . . .'

'Every petition must be presented in writing. There is no talking in court. The sentence is the only thing said. Silence reigns here every day. I try to impress upon these people how important it is to keep talking in check.'

'An old . . .'

'But that wasn't enough! I had to put an end to the constant unreliability. What a colossal job, though. How many people have come aground on those shoals? Do you know what I did? I introduced strict time regulations. I consider that my greatest achievement.'

As he said this, nodding his head for emphasis, the tip of the judge's goatee slipped into the inkwell.

'Our day consists of half-hours. I devote twenty-three minutes to every case, leaving me seven minutes' break. You'll see, the next ones will appear in a minute. As punctual as Big Ben. The point being that if they appear too early or too late, their case won't be heard. No right of appeal. They can go and join the back of the queue again.'

The tip of his beard was still dangling in the inkwell, slowly changing colour. Strand by strand blue veinlets rose towards his chin.

'Perhaps you think my mind is whirring with all these birds . . .' He laughed. His teeth were blue, as was his tongue.

'You may think what you like, but you may be sure I will acquit my responsibilities better than any other godforsaken court in this godforsaken country. I must prepare for the next case.'

He picked up a file from a low pile next to his chair, brought it to his mouth and blew off a few invisible specks of dirt.

'There's dust everywhere. It helps to take turmeric daily. In the evening, mixed with a little honey, then the dust can't do you any harm. Stay if you like but I'm afraid this case will prove dull. Irredeemably dull.'

The judge immersed himself in his papers before Burton could say goodbye. The boy tugged his sleeve and steered him to the rear entrance at the far end of the room. Before they reached it Burton couldn't help asking a question. His voice curved around the room, loud and echoing.

'Your honour. What was this building before?'

As the birds flew up under the dome, startled by the noise, the judge fixed him with a joyless stare.

'A Muslim mausoleum. Now out you go!'

II

NAUKARAM

II Om Pashinaya namah I Sarvavighnopashantaye namah I Om Ganeshaya namah II

'Yesterday wasn't a productive day. I looked through my notes in the evening and found hardly anything usable there. It was a waste of money.'

'A waste of money? How can that be? I paid you and gave you something to write down.'

'We need to put in more about Baroda. After all, Baroda's where you'll be looking for a new post. Sind is a long way away.'

'I've already told you everything about my time here.'

'You left out Kundalini.'

'On purpose.'

'Such a display of shame is unnecessary, really. Everyone in town knows that the Angrezi without wives take concubines; they all have a bubu. So – you got a lover for the Feringhi.'

'How do you know that?'

'The poet finds his way where even the sun can't reach. So, what are you trying to hide from me?'

'It was different in my case.'

'I'm sure it was. That's why I want to pin down this story. It makes you special. It does you credit, I'm sure, even without knowing what happened.'

'No. Not necessarily.'

'How often have I told you: anything that doesn't show you in a favourable light won't go in.'

'Better not to speak about it at all.'

'You're not only as stubborn as a mule . . .'

'I don't have to talk about everything.'

'But you also think you can justify your obstinacy.'

'I don't want to talk today. I'm going to go.'

'Without my blessing . . .'

'*Aojo*. We will see each other tomorrow.'

'You're a fool. I am the only one who can help you disguise your stupidity. Do you hear me, you fool?'

12

SPORTING A CRESCENT MOON

Suddenly there she was, and he wasn't prepared at all. The first thing he saw was her back, like a bay. A tan-coloured dupatta was draped over her shoulders; her neck looked like the bay's mouth, and her blue sari was the colour of deep water. She was sitting in the garden on a stool, which he thought – was that right? – came from the kitchen. He saw the back of her head, the nape of her neck bisected by a cord-like plait, woven with red and silver threads. A thin gold chain rested on one of her vertebrae, like a hanging thought. She sat perfectly still as he stood at the window, watching her in silence. Of course, Naukaram wouldn't let her in the house – whoever she was, a sister perhaps, or his lover, no, that was very unlikely – without asking his permission first. The tips of her hair touched the grass. He envied the natives this hair that gleamed like lustrous coal when it was motionless. Blond hair was an aberration of nature, an expression of a rash urge for diversity. Her blouse was a lighter blue, like seawater close to shore. A faint swell of muscle showed under the sleeves – or perhaps that was wrong, perhaps they were just too tight. Silver bracelets hung at her wrists.

There was a knock at the door. He moved away from the window and sat down at his desk before asking Naukaram to come in.

'Sahib, sorry to disturb you, but I'd like to introduce someone to you, a guest.'

'In what regard, Naukaram?'

'No regard, Sahib, just someone for you to get to know. You won't regret it, I assure you.'

He noticed the bindi on her forehead first, a dot of concentrated blue that matched her sari. Her face was dark, narrow. Naukaram introduced her in English, extolling her merits as if he wanted to sell her. The situation was embarrassing and exciting at the same time. Once her lower lip slipped under her front teeth and then out again so quickly he wasn't sure if he had really seen it. He asked her polite questions, and only after she'd given several answers did she lift her head. The look in her eyes was less submissive than her posture; they were black on white, like onyx stone, rimmed with kohl. Her perfect face had only a single flaw: a curved little scar high up on her forehead, close to the hairline, like a new moon. He didn't understand what Naukaram was saying, he wasn't listening, and he just nodded his head once when she turned and followed Naukaram out. She left behind a smile as small as the folded-down corner of a page in a book. Naukaram came back immediately.

'What was all that, Naukaram?'

'I thought you desired a woman's company.'

'And you presumed I wasn't capable of arranging that myself?'

'You are very busy; I didn't see why you should burden yourself with this task on top of everything else.'

'I see.'

'Don't you like her?'

'She is enchanting. Besides, you're right, how would I find a woman?'

'Perhaps, if you'd like to try for a few days, see whether her company gives you pleasure?'

'I am not used to such arrangements.'

'Don't worry about anything, Sahib. I will take care of everything that could be awkward for you. You must just enjoy yourself.'

But there was more to this woman than simply the assured promise of pleasure.

13
NAUKARAM

II Om Bhalchandraya namah I Sarvavighnopashantaye namah I Om Ganeshaya namah II

'You should know about Kundalini. I've thought it over. There's nothing for me to hide.'

'Do you see me writing? No. I'll just listen.'

'I found her in a maikhanna. I saw her serving. She brought my drink – milk with bhang, my favourite. I've never drunk daaru: I hate alcohol. You may not know this, but the women there are very charming-looking and they're good at dancing. If they like a guest and the guest puts some money on the table, then they dance in front of him, for him. I watched her. I thought it would be wonderful if she could dance for me. I had the money so I went back and put it on the table. And then she danced. Just for me. When she looked in my eyes, she made me feel very close to her and at the same time as if I'd never be able to touch her. She was like the pipal tree in the middle of the village . . .'

'Aren't you exaggerating a little?'

'Maybe. It doesn't matter what she reminded me of. All that matters is that by the time she had finished dancing, a thought had taken root in my mind. She was a woman I could imagine with Burton Sahib; she would satisfy his thirst for the unusual. My master needed a companion. He never did anything by halves, so how were occasional adventures going to satisfy his desires?'

'He didn't just sit at his desk, then.'

'I talked to her; I went to a lot of trouble to say the right things. I didn't want to insult her. She had to know my offer was a mark of respect. She agreed immediately, which, I have to tell you, did surprise me. Then I took care of everything else.'

'Her pay, I presume.'

'Not just that. Such relationships are always for a set time. I asked around. I had to look after my master. I had to protect him from everything that could go wrong. I drew up a document, and she signed it.'

'How?'

'How what?'

'How did you draw it up? You can't write, if I may remind you.'

'You should be able to think of the answer to that. I went to a lahiya.'

'He was prepared to put such an arrangement down on paper?'

'Why not? It is common practice.'

'Really, we must clean up this country. These mlecha bring in such filth, they're corrupting the whole land.'

'Now you're exaggerating.'

'What do you know? You were in their midst, you were

59

their pupil, maybe you are just like them now.'

'Because I know them does that mean I am one of them? That's ridiculous. What about Burton Sahib? He was in our midst. If he dressed like me, he could be taken for one of us. Does that mean he is?'

'There is a difference between becoming another person and putting on fancy dress. A big one.'

'By the way, I know we've always had courtesans; they're even in the Puranas.'

'Who told you that?'

'It doesn't make any difference.'

'Who?'

'Burton Sahib.'

'Burton Sahib! You trust the word of a mlecha about our traditions? Since when have the foreigners been guardians of our knowledge? Courtesans in the Puranas, ha! What vile lies are they going to come up with next?'

'Are you sure it's not true?'

'Let's drop the subject. So what did this woman promise you, or the two of you, in writing?'

'She promised not to have any children.'

'She promised it?'

'She knew what to do.'

'Let me guess. Cashews? Did she eat a papaya every time she thought she might be pregnant?'

'No. She knew mantras that worked and she had a talisman. And she also made up a mixture of cow dung, herbs, lemon juice, the juice from some other sour fruits and a little bi-carbonate of soda, if I remember rightly.'

'And a chicken claw.'

'I beg your pardon?'

'Nothing. So, you arranged with her what had to be arranged. We could recommend your services as a procurer, why not? Oh, by the way, since the burden of work you expect me to shoulder keeps growing, we're going to have to agree a larger fee. I think I'll need at least eight rupees.'

A lucky few were allowed to die for their country. The rest spent their evenings in the mess bewailing the sacrifices asked of them. Eleven unbearable months, they chorused, and one worse than all the rest: May. Burton was paralysed by the heat. The thoughts drained out of his mind. He lay on his bed, incapable of anything except a bleary stare at the thermometer. The bed stood in the middle of the room, veiled on all sides by bright green raw silk. If he stretched out an arm, he could dip his hand in a copper bowl of cool water, which the servants changed every hour. Above his head spun a wood and canvas punkah, which he knew was connected by a piece of string that went through the wall to the big toe of one of those dark, quiet figures whose only job consisted of stretching and bending his leg so that air would be wafted towards him, the Sahib.

Outside, no one was going anywhere. He didn't need to leave his house to know the whole town was as paralysed as he was. A feverish, sweltering wind sweeps all life from the plain. The clouds are made of dust. The air smells like snuff. Baroda is sunk in lethargy in this, the last month before the liberating rains. The horses stand tethered with bowed heads and out-turned bottom lips, too lazy to shoo away the flies, while next door the stable boys snore, the tack they're meant to clean having fallen from their hands. Even the crows pant for breath. You have to reduce all your body's actions to a minimum. Avoid all unnecessary movement. Use the servants, think of them as your limbs and organs. He was right, the fellow who'd told him that; when he couldn't stand it a minute longer, Burton would follow his recommendation, call Naukaram, take off his loose cotton clothes and go to the bathroom, where some of the servants would pour water over him from leaky clay jugs. Then he'd be able to read.

He had already explored Baroda and the surrounding countryside. He had been everywhere, everywhere he could get to as a British officer, and had already seen more than almost all his colleagues, but still he was dissatisfied. From his horse the natives looked like characters in a fairy tale that had been translated into stilted English. And he could imagine what he looked like: a monument. That's why they were frightened when the bronze horseman said something in their language. As long as he was a foreigner, he would learn almost nothing and he would be a foreigner as long as he was seen as one. There was only one solution; it appealed to him immediately. He would cast off his foreignness instead of waiting for it to be taken from him. He would act as if he were one of them. All it needed was the right opportunity. The most exciting thing was that it wouldn't be hard. The distances to be bridged didn't seem that great to him. People attach such importance to differences and yet they are charmed away by a cloak, seen off by a good accent. Even the right headgear could establish some common ground.

A sandstorm blew up. Black clouds were soon roaring over the ground, hungry-mouthed. The sand forced its way in through every opening, every crack, leaving a thick layer on everything. The bed sheets were brown; he could have signed his pillow with his forefinger. The whirlwind sucked up rubbish, ripped tarpaulins, scattered grain until suddenly it abated, exhausted by its mad rampage, and allowed all the things it had swept up to fall back to earth.

15
NAUKARAM

II Om Vigneshvaraya namah I Sarvavighnopashantaye namah I Om Ganeshaya namah II

'Everything changed for the worse when we were sent to Sind. The people there are savage and brutal and they hate strangers with all their hearts.'

'I've got a few more questions about Baroda. We should deal with those first.'

'There were sandstorms all hours of the day.'

'I'm still not clear about a few things.'

'It was unbearable. Like May here. Meals were the worst; I had to cover everything. If the tiniest crack was left open, the food crunched when you bit it. And there was dust everywhere.'

'I haven't finished the previous chapter yet.'

'Chapter? What chapter?'

'Just an expression. Look at me. Notice anything? I'm not writing anything down.'

'We didn't have a bungalow any more. Only two tents pitched in the middle of a sandy plain.'

'All right. As you wish. We'll return to Baroda later. Why didn't you have a house?'

'Burton Sahib didn't have enough money. He got two hundred rupees a month. That wasn't enough to build a house, especially when someone spent as much on books as he did.'

'The officers had to pay for their accommodation themselves?'

'Yes, and organise it too. I'd have done that, of course. But it wasn't worth it, because Burton Sahib was soon assigned duties that took him all over the country. We learnt how to lead a normal life on the move. That was a big test of my ability to adapt, to make the best out of what's available. And don't forget, I was alone suddenly. I didn't have twelve helpers at my side any more. Write that down. There was only a cook and a boy who helped out. He was useless, in fact. Instead of a whole house, I had seven trunks, and out of seven trunks I had to make the sahib as comfortable a home as possible. I was alone in that wilderness. The only person I could talk to was Burton Sahib. You can't talk to the circumcised, even if you do have a common language. Their faces are like a fortress, their eyes two cannons constantly trained on you. It was a huge job but, I have to tell you, I was completely equal to the task. Burton Sahib wanted to read and write even during sandstorms. He sat

63

at a folding table, and I put a cool cloth on his forehead. I swept up the dust that came in through the gaps in the tent, otherwise it would have got in his eyes. That was so painful, like having chilli powder sprinkled in them. Writing was difficult. The ink turned into a lump on the tip of the quill, the paper quickly got dusty, I couldn't keep up. I stood behind him and every few minutes I bent over his right shoulder and ran a cloth over the piece of paper that he was writing on. Once he laughed and said I was like an assistant turning the pages for a musician. Did you know that the Angrezi read music from pages? When he stood up, I had to put everything away in the trunks. If a piece of paper was left out for a day, it looked like a paratha. Not covered with a layer of dough, no, just that bloody Sindhi dust.'

16
THE SMOKE-COLOURED BODY

Time to give the night a kick, send it and its last nightmare packing. Outside a solitary passer-by spat, his footsteps crunching on the path; he sounded in a hurry to be the first to meet the dawn. Crows rent the remains of the silence with their hoarse endearments. He went and stood at the window and pressed his forehead against the wire mesh. Someone lit a fire, a greeting, preparations for the first tea of the day. The smell of dung caressed the steaming fields like an unwashed hand. The air was cool, slightly damp. He heard Naukaram open the door and set down the tray. He felt his way to the pot, poured black tea into a cup and dripped in some milk. When he brought the cup to his lips, he noticed that dawn had stolen into the room, as if it were ashamed to have spent the night elsewhere. He savoured the warmth of the cup in his hands, then he felt her pressing her breasts into his back. That was her form of morning greeting.

'Do you want a sip?' he asked, although he knew she would decline. He could share a bed with her, but not a teacup. She never ate with him. She lived on the same floor but he had to take his meals alone. 'That's how it should be,' she had said. She refused his requests and invitations just as she had so far refused to spend the whole night with him. 'When you wake up, I'll be here again.' She kept her promise, as well as her distance.

Unlike the courtesans he had known before her, she asked him to put out all the lights before she undressed. She had made that a condition from the start. He complied, thinking of it as an expression of intimacy. The moon had given him gentle assistance the first time. His hands had envisaged her skin. When he tried to kiss her on the mouth, she had sealed her lips. It had excited him that she gave herself to him without opening herself. She proved skilful and experienced, like the other courtesans. He didn't have to think of anything or make any decisions; she satisfied his desires before he expressed them. I'm watching her at work, he thought, a sobering notion that muted his orgasm. Afterwards he hadn't even opened his eyes again before she had got out of bed, and he heard the sound of her bare feet fade away. She didn't come back.

After several such nights he informed Naukaram that Kundalini would be moving into the bubukhanna. Naukaram had been glad – genuinely delighted, Burton thought. He was touched Naukaram was so concerned about his welfare. One night, for it was only cool enough to bear the touch of another person's skin at night, he gripped her arm tightly as she tried to get up.

She protested. 'I have to go,' she said.

'Please stay, just for a little while.'

She leant back. He lit a lamp and set it down as she regarded him mistrustfully. He pulled away the sari covering her body. He wanted to see her, her skin the colour of dark smoke. He wanted to see all of her, but she immediately put one hand between her legs and tried unsuccessfully to hide her breasts with the other. Finally, helpless before his curiosity, she sat up and covered his eyes with both hands. He put up as little resistance as possible, just spreading his toes, and she began to laugh like water about to boil. Still blind, he put his arms around her, around her laughter. That's a start, he thought. If only he knew whether she enjoyed being with him.

It was difficult for him to ask her; he needed a few days to summon up the courage.

'You should like it, master,' she said anxiously.

'I did like it.'

'Then I'm happy too.' It wasn't the tone in which she said this nor the look on her face, but something else that aroused his suspicion. The words seemed rehearsed. He had to ask Naukaram. Not directly, of course not. What would be his expression if he called him in when he was having his bath, for instance, and demanded, 'Find out if I satisfy Kundalini'? It was almost a pity he couldn't allow himself this pleasure. Instead, he felt his way, hint by hint, to a coded phrasing. Despite all his circumspection, however, Naukaram was appalled. But then he did sometimes react out of all proportion. He fussed about like a governess. 'You are very prim for a panderer,' Burton almost flung in his teeth.

'Are you dissatisfied with her, Sahib?'

'No, not in the slightest. I'd just like Kundalini and I to understand one another better.'

'Doesn't she respond to your wishes, Sahib?'

'I would like to find out more about her wishes, that's the point.'

'It's not usual for her to have wishes.'

'I understand. You can't help me.'

'Yes, I can, Sahib, always. I can always help you.'

The next evening Kundalini remarked with tentative disapproval that he shaved where all women could see, but not where she alone directed her gaze. That was something, some dissent . . . Perhaps that's why the hajam had wanted to shave him when he was half asleep. Now he'd have to do it himself.

Another time, when he was lying spent on his back and she next to him on her side, she began casually, jokingly talking about her grandmother, who divided men into different animals. Which did he belong to? 'The hares,' she said. It didn't sound like a compliment.

'What are the other types?'

'There are bulls and stallions as well.'

'They're probably better, are they?'

'No, the hare's not a disadvantage in itself, just the quick hare.'

'Are there slow ones too?'

She nodded. 'Slow and moderate.'

'For the bulls and stallions too?'

'Yes.'

'What does the speed mean? Wait, I think I know: is it to do with prolonging pleasure?'

'Yes, it's about waiting for the woman, for her climax.'

'Women have a climax?' Burton blurted, regretting it immediately. She looked at him in dismay. 'What about you,' he asked tentatively, 'have you experienced that with us?'

She shook her head.

'Because I am a quick hare?'

'Yes, it takes time for me.'

'How long?'

'That depends if time is on your tongue's side. Have you never heard of ishqmak, the art of delaying climax?'

'No, I haven't. I know other noble arts, the art of foxhunting, the art of fencing, the art of knocking little balls over green baize, but the art of delaying the climax, no, that I don't know. It's not one we practise. With us one climax comes racing along after another.'

She didn't even smile. 'I will teach you,' she said seriously, ignoring his smirk, 'if you would like.'

He replied with a seriousness he had to force himself to assume, 'Yes, I want to witness your climax. I want to be its cause.'

He put his hand on her shoulder and observed the contrast between them. 'Why are you so dark-skinned?' She turned and looked at him sternly, as if he had asked an improper question, then bent down until she was so close he almost couldn't see her. 'Because I was born on the new moon,' she whispered, her eyes like fireworks.

The next time they were together she sat astride him, but just as his moans forecast the storm that was brewing inside him, she stopped. Her body became quiet, and straddling his still thrusting astonishment, she rested her hands on his chest and began to talk. She spoke in measured sentences, in an intimate voice that expressed itself calmly and yet demanded his full attention. He had to stop moving to hear her story: the story of 'cobra courtesans', women whose bodies, over the years, had been habituated to cobra venom; a drop at first, then a few at a time, the dose was gradually increased until they were drinking a teaspoon of poison a day. By the end they could drink a glass full of venom without suffering harm. But their sweat, their spit, their spendings were so poisonous that any man who slept with them was condemned to death. Even someone who wiped away one of their tears, and then put his hand to his lips, would be killed. 'You understand, they were only allowed to yield to their desire when they had to murder someone. They were just hired killers in their ruler's service. They poisoned everyone they touched, everyone they kissed, regardless of whether they despised or loved him. Can you imagine such misfortune?'

Burton lay motionless on the bed, his penis a statement he was retracting. She scratched his chest. 'The story's not over,' she said. 'There was a poet, perhaps the most gifted in the land, who, no sooner had he seen one of these courtesans, than he fell in love with her. He was no headstrong, infatuated youth. No, he was an experienced man, versed in the rules of the court and the laws of the heart. He suffered agonies of uncertainty, wracked with doubt as to whether he should confess his love. Just as he had resolved to do so, she approached him on the banks of the Yamuna. She desired him to teach her Sanskrit. This was the only one of a courtesan's arts she lacked. And so he obtained the ruler's permission to teach her every day.'

Kundalini bent forward, her hair stroking his face, and then sat up straight again; her hands vanished, and he felt her fingernail running along the inside of his thigh.

'Listen carefully,' she said. 'Over the years of studying together, the courtesan gradually fell in love with the poet, as slowly as once her body had become habituated to the venom. And then one day she made a double confession, a confession of her love for him and a confession of how she had been bred to kill. I often think of how the poet must have felt at that moment, when their mutual love was delivered stillborn. He didn't turn away from her. He decided to be united with his beloved, even if it was only to be for one time. Do you understand? He took it upon himself to make up for all the cruelty this woman had suffered.'

Burton shuddered.

'And then?'

'That is the strangest thing; there are countless versions of this story and they are all agreed on only one thing. He died, of course, but as he died the features of his face relaxed in an expression of that bliss known only to those who have seen the gate of liberation.'

Kundalini moved off him, stretched out at his side, and ran the nail of her index finger over his limp penis.

'That, master, was the art of delaying the climax. Once you have recovered from my story, we can start again.'

He looked at her through new eyes. He would have liked to have kissed her and forgotten who she was and why she lay in this room. But he was not like the poet. He had discovered cowardice in himself where he would least have suspected it.

17
NAUKARAM

II Om Dhoomravarnaya namah I Sarvavighnopashantaye namah I Om Ganeshaya namah II

'That's enough about Baroda, enough. We still have a lot to

say about Sind, about my service there. Those were years of constant toil for me and very little joy.'

'Fine.'

'Remember I went there with my master: that doesn't happen as a matter of course. And I didn't just serve him there, I served the Angrezi army as well. And I saved his life, you really must make a point of that . . .'

'We'll get round to all that. So, you went with him, but what about his lover, Kundalini . . . I can't imagine an Angrezi officer taking his lover with him when he upped and moved.'

'The question didn't arise.'

'Why not?'

'Because it didn't arise.'

'Ah ha, she left him. You chose someone who wasn't faithful. She ran off.'

'No, that's a lie!'

'Why do you always react so violently whenever she's mentioned? Your feelings are excessive, don't you think?'

'What are excessive feelings? Do you lay down the limits? Everything went wrong. I didn't make a mistake. If I'd had a woman like Kundalini . . .'

'Like Kundalini? Or Kundalini herself?'

'I can't describe her to you. I was glad to get up in the morning knowing that I'd see her, that I'd hear her voice. She used to sing when she was bathing – she knew many bhajan – and when she sang, it was as if she was decking the day out with jewels. She was often in high spirits . . . not at first, though. The other servants ran her down, those hypocrites; every one of them would have been overjoyed to have her as a wife. But they soon had to swallow their contempt. She was so lovely. Sometimes we all sat in the kitchen together, and she would make everyone laugh. Other times her mood was so black, it seemed as if the whole world was wearing a burkha. I wanted to cheer her up but what consolation did I have to offer? I wasn't the one . . .'

'You were in love with her; I should have guessed. She stole your heart.'

70

'It wouldn't have been so bad if he hadn't taken me into his confidence. I could barely stand it. He thought he was showing me his esteem, his respect, by talking to me about her. The things he found amazing, the things he liked. I couldn't stop him. Anything I said would have made him suspicious. The longer she stayed with us, the more open he was with me. I didn't want to hear a word of it, but there was worse to come. He didn't just want my advice; he wanted me to talk to her. He never gave me an order, but there was no mistaking his wishes. I was supposed to talk to her about him.'

'You were jealous of the sahib. Now I understand. He had so much already, so much more than you, why on top of everything else did he have to have the beautiful woman you were in love with? Wasn't that it? Didn't he feel your hatred?'

'I didn't hate him. That's a lie too.'

'Is that why she stayed in Baroda? Did you blacken her name to the Feringhi? Because you couldn't stand her presence any longer? Because she had sown strife between the two of you?'

'Be quiet! You're talking nonsense. She was dead. She'd been dead for a long time.'

'What? What did she die of?'

'You are excessive. You think I will tell you what I have never told anyone in my life.'

'I just asked a question.'

'You can't ask every question.'

'It was a perfectly reasonable question.'

'Do I pay you so that I have to tell you all my secrets? You have turned my life upside down.'

18

QUICK TO ACT

A week later Upanishe agreed to take on the new pupil, and Burton instructed Naukaram to pick out a big pumpkin every now and then and take it round to his teacher's house.

'What do you think of him?' Burton asked.

'I have noticed he is always punctual, Sahib,' Naukaram replied. 'He has his life under control. That is the sign of a great teacher.' And sure enough, every afternoon on the dot of four, they would hear the tonga's rattling wheels and the mule's wheezing and by the time Naukaram got to the door, the little white-bearded man would already be striding up the garden path with his amanuensis at his heels and a sunshade over his head. They would drink a cup of chai, which he liked spicy, and then sit down side by side at Burton's desk, Naukaram having first put three cushions on Upanishe's wicker chair.

For Upanishe, grammar was a dance floor on which he could perform his repertoire of pirouettes. Burton didn't take this amiss. One had no right to expect a lively mind to be satisfied with the subjunctive of the auxiliary verb. At first the digressions confined themselves to the boards of language in general.

'I'm sure you know our two words for "man": *admi*, which is derived from Adam, who, so the Muslims claim, came into the world in these parts, and *manav*, which comes from Manu, the other forefather in, as you would say, the Hindu tradition. By their language you shall know them, isn't that the phrase? Our language shows us to be the descendants of two races. What a source of strength that could be for us!'

'Wouldn't it follow from that, Guru-ji, that every Indian is both Hindu and Muslim?'

'We don't want to be too bold, my shishya, just glad they can live together side by side.'

But soon language wasn't enough. A somersault, whoops, and he'd land two-footed in jurisprudence – ancient Indian criminal law contained crimes against animals, you know. And then, three pirouettes later, he would be commenting on the caste system.

'You say high-born, we say twice born. Not such a great difference, don't you think?'

After explaining the vocative he rewarded his pupil with a saying: One should never lend a book, a pen or a wife. When they come back, they will be torn, broken or plucked.

'Is that one of yours, Guru-ji?'

'No, no, it's from a Sanskrit poem, from a – what would you call it – classical work . . .?'

'Astonishing!'

'Yes, good, be astonished. Astonishment is healthy.'

'Should we start another lesson?'

'No, that's enough for today, Mr Burton, that's enough.'

'A shishya wearing out his guru: has there ever been such a thing?'

'Now that's impertinent. You have to spare my strength. You'll need your Guru-ji for a while yet.'

Late one afternoon the tonga didn't appear to collect him, and Upanishe was forced to wait while Naukaram found a replacement. Although he sat comfortably on the leather arm-chair, his legs stretched out on a stool, he was distracted, clicking his thumb and middle finger as he answered Burton's questions about his career. Every second sentence, he listened for the rattle of wheels.

'Are you concerned about your wife, Guru-ji?'

'I will be very late, that's not good. I can't bear it. We are the inheritors of a meticulous civilisation. The cosmic order is reflected in every one of our seconds and with every one that is wasted it is fatally threatened. Take no notice of all the talk about the cycles of kala in which we allegedly so liberally think. We have to be precise.'

When Naukaram returned empty-handed, Upanishe drummed his fingers on the armrest and shifted around on the cushions. Naukaram hadn't been able to find a tonga anywhere in the entire cantonment. Burton decided to take the teacher home himself on the back of his horse. The amanuensis could walk.

'Oh my shishya, you ask too much of me. How am I supposed to get on your horse?'

'We'll hoist you up.'

'No, I don't like that; a teacher is not a piece of furniture.'

'All right, then Naukaram will bring out a chair, I'll hold the horse still, and you can climb up and sit down.'

'I have never sat on a horse, not even on a mule.'

'Just sit in the saddle, Guru-ji, a little further back please, so there's room for me in front.'

'What if I fall off?'

'Hold on tight to me, Guru-ji. Now you're dependent on me for once.'

'We're going to ride through the night, are we?'

'Like young lovers.'

'What if anyone sees us? Please don't take the high street; there are unlit side streets I prefer.'

Burton kept the horse to a gentle trot and Upanishe gradually grew calmer.

'This is an unusual evening. I should like to show my gratitude. Or rather, give you something that seems to me appropriate to this occasion.'

'What are you thinking of, Guru-ji?'

'A mantra. Perhaps the most powerful of all mantras. Think of this mantra as my toll. It will never fail you.

> *Purnamadaha*
> *Purnamidam*
> *Purnaat Purnamudachyate*
> *Purnasya Purnamaadaya*
> *Purnameva Avasishyate*'

'That sounds beautiful, Guru-ji. I could ride all night with you with such mantras in my ear.'

'Oh, we don't want to exaggerate. What have I taught you? Moderation at all times. Aren't you curious about its translation?'

'It won't sound as convincing as the Sanskrit.'

'You're right; just learn it off by heart for the moment. The meaning can come later. It works, you'll see. It works worlds.'

'It works worlds?'

'Set me down in front there, I'll walk the rest of the way on my own. Come to our house tomorrow, for a simple meal.'

'Thank you for the invitation.'

'Don't thank me. Thanks are like money. When you know someone better, there are more valuable things you can give. I have a request, in fact. I don't know how the neighbours will react if we have a British officer as a guest in our house. I would like to spare them the sight. Perhaps you could wear local dress. I know I am presuming a great deal, but think of it as part of your language studies. It will be easier for you to get into conversation with people. You'll just have to stand somewhere for a moment, and in a few minutes you'll have struck up your first friendships.'

'My Gujarati isn't up to it yet.'

'How could it be? You're a traveller. You come from . . . let me think . . . Kashmir! Yes, you're a brahmin from Kashmir. And if anyone asks you what sort of brahmin, say Nandera Brahmin.'

'Nandera.'

'And if someone asks you what gotra you belong to, then say Bharadwaj.'

'Bharadwaj.'

'And if someone asks about your family, then say . . .'

'Upanishe!'

'Why not? A distant cousin who has heard of this Guru-ji's fame and so has come to look him up. Excellent.'

'And what if I meet a Kashmiri?'

'Then you will let him know you are a high-ranking officer in the Jan Kampani Bahadur and threaten to have him thrown in prison if he exposes you.'

'Isn't it common knowledge that you associate with the Feringhi?'

'It used to be, my shishya, it used to be. But times are changing. Indifference is giving way to a new spirit of denunciation. I hear people speaking about the British with a great deal of hatred.'

'You're exaggerating. It can't be that bad.'

'Perhaps I am. Exaggeration can be useful in such matters. My intention is, I admit, the child of several fathers. I would also like to play a little trick on my neighbours. And the barber. I'd like to introduce you as a scholar from Kashmir so that I can see the stunned expression on their faces when, after they have explained at voluminous, flowery length why you're such a typical Kashmiri, I finally confess my guest was an Angrezi. Come early, we only eat a proper meal once a day. We will treat ourselves to a late lunch and you can set out for home at dusk.'

'*Aojo*, Guru-ji.'

'*Aojo*. Oh, and one other thing. Please don't bring any books.'

Burton thought this was a joke he hadn't understood. But, having leapt at the chance to dress up as an Indian now the longed-for opportunity had finally presented itself, he had barely entered the teacher's house before he realised books really were the last thing this household needed. Upanishe's wife, who was even shorter than her husband and blessed with a face of the utmost transparency and candour, greeted their guest warmly and served him and Upanishe drinks. For whatever reason she thought of this shishya as an ally in her evidently hopeless fight against her husband's countless books, which rose in crooked columns from among the cushions on the floor.

'All these dusty books,' she said loudly, the guest in her sights, 'can't you throw any away? You haven't touched them for ten years.'

'So what?' retorted Guru-ji. 'I haven't touched you for ten years either. Should I throw you away?'

Burton was appalled; he didn't know where to look. What on earth had he got himself involved in? He heard the two old folk laughing wholeheartedly and when he looked up, Upanishe winked at him.

'You sleep with your books,' Upanishe's wife continued.

'Are you jealous?'

'You should have married a book, not me.'

'Would the book have given me sons?'

'You haven't got a heart.'

'Just a big black book where a heart should be, I know.'

'It doesn't pump blood, your heart, just words.'

'Is that why you've learnt to read, mother of my sons?'

'I would have memorised its contents a long time ago if you weren't always adding new bits. I can't keep up. I stopped trying – ten years ago!'

Again they burst out laughing and this time Burton joined in. He suddenly noticed how comfortable he felt with this old married couple who kept up their closeness with merciless teasing.

'When are you going to serve us something substantial?'

'Can't you see I'm talking?'

'You're always talking. If it were up to you, our guest would starve.'

That evening Upanishe had no time for earnestness.

'One of our most famous poets had several wives. He is a paragon, who many people try to emulate, so some time ago I suggested to my wife that it was impossible for me to be a great poet with only one wife. Do you know her response? You become a great poet first, then you can take more wives!'

Burton heard the purling of her laughter in the kitchen. Upanishe leant back contentedly, drew his right hand slowly down his white beard, and then dispelled the silence with the next joke. They laughed at this in unison, both collapsing into such hysterics that Burton had to bend forwards, his hands clasping his stomach, his eyes inches away from his teacher's eyes, which promptly popped out of their sockets, rolled across the table, and began multiplying until Upanishe's gnarled fingers gathered them up like prayer beads.

'What was in the milk?' asked Burton, a grin draining from his face.

'Oh, bhang of course, my shishya. We wanted you to feel at home with us.'

The delicate figure of Mrs Upanishe appeared before them like a sprite, with two thali trays in her hands. She explained

77

what was in the five little dishes, and while Burton fished out lightly spiced pieces of steamed okra with a chapatti, Upanishe crept into the village of the girl he was to marry, a sprig of a lad hiding behind trees to catch a glimpse of his bride to be. That fleeting glance was the last he saw of her until the wedding day, until the moment they were sitting facing each other, surrounded by priests and relatives, and the shawl covering her head and shoulders was lifted.

'Were you appalled?' she asked.

'You'd impressed me from a distance, I have to admit. But seeing you close to, my heart fluttered up in my chest and it hasn't been still ever since.'

There was a knock at the door. The neighbours come to pay their respects to the learned gentleman from Kashmir. They praised his Gujarati. Later Upanishe took his pupil downstairs, introduced him to the barber and asked if his guest could stay a while because he had an important letter to write. 'I have not much room, as you see,' the barber apologised. Burton sat for a long time in the furthest, darkest corner of the narrow shop. He could barely talk to the barber amid the flow of customers. Shaves ended with a brief head massage and a few gentle slaps in the face. Burton dozed off until an overweight voice tore him out of his slumber and launched into a long diatribe. The barber sought to stem, or at least divert, the customer's torrent of complaint, but to no avail.

'In the past we only had to support one set of leeches.'

'Ah.'

'Now the Feringhi have come.'

'Ah.'

'And they are even worse leeches, the Angrezi.'

'Ah.'

'We can't feed two maharajahs at once.'

'Ah.'

'How right you are,' Burton echoed from the back of the shop.

'*Are Baapre*, you've got a guest.'

78

'An educated gentleman, from Kashmir. Visiting Guru-ji.'

'I agree with you. These Angrezi waylay us, rob us, take root like parasites and expect us to feed them until the end of time.'

'Very true, traveller. You Kashmiris are not so inured to slavery as we are. It is like any parasite. No matter how much we work, how much we eat, as the host we will always remain weak and emaciated.'

'Exactly. But what can we do?'

'We have to stand up for ourselves.'

'How?'

'We have to incite the ones with weapons, who can fight against the Angrezi. You know who I mean?'

'The sepoys.'

'Yes. We think the same. I noticed that immediately. We are brother spirits. What's your name?'

'Upanishe . . .'

'And your first name?'

'My first name, yes, I'm called . . . Ramji.'

'It is an honour. My name is Suresh Zaveri. You'll find me in the gold market. We should continue our conversation.'

It was already late when Burton left the house. After going a little way, he saw the district lamplighter coming towards him, carrying a ladder on his shoulder and with an oilcan in his hand. Burton greeted him effusively. The man softly returned his greeting, leant his ladder against a wooden pole and then climbed to its tar-covered tip.

19

NAUKARAM

II Om Kshipraya namah I Sarvavighnopashantaye namah I Om Ganeshaya namah II

'I have been thinking. I have been searching for something that will make even the stupidest Angrezi understand my worth.

Burton Sahib was a spy. Not in Baroda – later, when we lived in Sind. An important spy. One of the most important there was. He could go and see the general of the Angrezi any time he wanted. They had long conversations together. And do you know how that came about? I played a big part in it, with Guru-ji. We made him a spy.'

'Aren't you ashamed of that?'

'I didn't express myself properly. We didn't encourage him to lead a double life; we just suggested he wear our clothes, act like one of us. Guru-ji asked him to do it once. He borrowed a kurta from me.'

'If ever there was a sign of intimacy.'

'He was so excited after his visit to Guru-ji and his wife. I had been sceptical when he first put the kurta on. Seeing him standing there in front of me in his disguise, it was hard not to laugh. The trousers were too long; he looked like a scarecrow. But I had forgotten something crucial. I knew the man in front of me was Burton Sahib. I hadn't thought how people who didn't know that would see him. He rubbed some henna oil into his face, and onto his hands and feet, and then he took a tonga into town. It was dark when he came back, and he was thrilled. I'd hardly ever seen him so thrilled. He wanted to tell me everything. How everyone had taken him for a Kashmiri; how comfortable he'd felt playing his part; how he had sat in the corner, listening; how he'd forgotten for a moment that he didn't actually belong there. He talked and talked, and I realised I had misjudged his disguise. He just had to pretend to be someone from the Himalayas and, there you were, he already looked like someone from the Himalayas. Even his accent fitted the part. It didn't sound completely wrong, but just enough to be noticed.'

'Have you ever heard a Kashmiri speak Gujarati?'

'No.'

'Then how can you know that his accent fitted his disguise?'

'I've an idea of how they would sound. And that's what he sounded like. A few days later we went to the bazaar together.

He wanted me to play the master and him the servant. He told me before we set off not to show him the slightest respect; the whole thing had to be convincing. He insisted on carrying our purchases. I didn't say anything at first; I just played along, but that wasn't enough for him. He hissed in my ear in English, and told me to chide him at the top of my voice, loud enough for everyone to hear. I began berating him for his laziness. Tentatively at first, but then I began to enjoy it, so then I moved onto his untrustworthiness. I might have overdone it a little. Anyway, next moment a man standing in front of a jeweller's shop was calling us over. He seemed to know Burton Sahib, whom he addressed as Upanishe, and he was clearly very put out to find he was a servant. "Has it come to this in our Bharat," he cried, "that educated men have to sell themselves to traitors, knuckle under to turncoats?" And he looked at me as if he wanted to grind me to a pulp.'

'Very comical, I must say.'

'It wasn't funny for me. Not afterwards, anyway. Burton Sahib was furious, even though I had done exactly as he had asked. He hadn't counted on bumping into this acquaintance. Now he wouldn't be able to pay him a visit; he had lost his respect. How was he supposed to explain the fact that a proud Kashmiri like him was in the service of a Gujarati merchant? But still, this setback was part of the whole success. From then on Burton Sahib was obsessed with the idea of disguise. He got me to find a tailor to measure him up and make him a set of clothes, for everyday use as well as special occasions. He wore an ordinary kurta at home until it became frayed and torn. He wouldn't allow me to wash it. A piece of clothing for every caste, he said. He liked hanging around outside the regimental mess and begging from the other officers. When they shooed him away, he would raise his voice to the heavens in outrage and complain of his countrymen's heartlessness in perfect English.'

'What did he hope to gain from these masquerades? Was it just a game?'

'Yes, it was a game, definitely. But it was more than that too. At first he thought of it as a means to escape the boredom of his work. But it wasn't long before he recognised a greater value. I remember him telling me once that the resident had to pay hundreds of rupees every month for secret reports to keep him informed about events at the maharajah's court. He could dig up fifty rupees' worth of information in town in one evening alone. "It's a shame the resident is an idiot who doesn't deserve such help," he said. He saw it as a chance to rise quicker through the ranks.'

'A useful passion.'

'That's right. He got into a real state. Soon he was convincing himself he could think and see and feel just like one of us. He started to believe that rather than wearing a disguise, what he was doing was transforming himself. And he took it very seriously, this transformation. His working days grew even longer. He practised sitting cross-legged for hours until his legs were almost dead and we had to pick him up and carry him to bed. He wanted to be able to sit still for a long time, so as to appear as dignified as possible. And whenever he wasn't studying with Guru-ji, he would ask me to teach him something.'

'What could you teach him?'

'Oh, lots. Little things. Details I'd never have thought of. How to cut fingernails, how you talk about your mother, how to nod your head, how to squat on your heels, how to express enthusiasm. He wanted me to sit with him when I was showing him or telling him something, but I refused. Every time. Write that down: I knew how to set a limit to familiarity. I always refused his invitations to eat with him. That wouldn't have looked right in front of the other servants. Unlike him, I wasn't by any means convinced that you can change your role in life.'

A few days before she suddenly fell ill, he took her hand and tried in words that hid their true meaning to declare his feelings for her. It was a disaster. She cut him short, dabbed a quick, absolving kiss on his neck, undressed him and then, ignoring the measured sequence she had taught him, guided his penis into her with almost grotesque haste. He was about to make a plainer declaration of his love when she stopped. Her body became quiet, and straddling his still thrusting astonishment, she rested her hands on his chest and began to talk. She spoke in measured sentences, in an intimate voice that expressed itself calmly and yet demanded his full attention. He had to stop moving to hear her story: the story of a man in love. 'He was in love with a woman he didn't know, but who meant more to him than anything else in the world. He followed her whenever she left her house, he was her slave, he never let her out of his sight, he couldn't imagine the world existing without her; there she was, present in his every thought. One day, steeling his nerve and summoning up all his courage, he spoke to her in the street and passionately declared his love in a voice that kept cracking; in words that knew no end he professed eternal love until finally she cut him short. She smiled, and he thought it would never grow dark again. Then she said to him in a voice that was even more enchanting than he had imagined it, "Your words are wonderful: they fill me with delight, they do me honour, but I don't deserve them, because my sister, who is walking behind me, is far more beautiful, far more charming than I could ever be. I am sure that when you see her in a moment, you will award her the prize." Whereupon the man whose love was an imperishable fire averted his eyes from his beloved to cast a glance, just one short, appraising glance, at the vaunted sister. The beloved struck him hard across the back of the head: "So this is your eternal love! I hardly mention a more beautiful woman and you turn away from me to snatch a glimpse of her. What do you know of love?"'

How dare she? How could she provoke him like this? Burton tried to break free, but she resisted, pressing down on him with the full weight of her body, clasping him with her hips, resisting his every move, her long fingers forcing him to submit until he no longer knew whether he was furious or aroused again. His rage clamped itself around his desire: it couldn't erupt, it couldn't subside, his arousal was a torment driving him to such a pitch of turmoil until finally he had to beg for release, and then he screamed. That was a few days before she fell seriously ill.

21

NAUKARAM

II Om Manomaya namah I Sarvavighnopashantaye namah I Om Ganeshaya namah II

'He had barely learnt how to act like a Kashmiri before he had to forget he was one. He had to take on a new form, and in that one it was best he didn't even remember ever having been a Nandera Brahmin. That was what was hard about the task he set himself. He kept having to readapt. The Angrezi occupy so many lands, one disguise wasn't enough. His disguises changed like the seasons. It's as if I were to work as a khelassy in spring, a kedmutgar in summer, a bhisti in autumn and a hajam in winter.'

'I'm not sure if I should admire that.'

'It was bewildering, our time in Sind. We sailed to Karachi from Bombay. A journey of just a few days. A journey into the heart of the wilderness. From the day I set foot in that land, I knew I didn't belong there. It was plain for all to see that I was a foreigner. And that's what I remained: a foreigner. I needed all my strength not to forget who I was. Whereas Burton Sahib doubled the stakes. He wanted people to think he was a

Muslim. Can you imagine anything harder? Or more repulsive? He had to learn so many things off by heart. He muttered away all day. I didn't understand a word, but he still made me listen to him producing those harsh sounds. May every tongue that twists itself into such knots catch gout! But that was only the beginning. He had to walk with a hand on his hip. He had to give up whistling. Do you know those stupid Miya think the Feringhi are talking to the Devil when they whistle? He learned to hum quietly instead. He had to get used to stroking his beard with his right hand. He had to practise keeping silent for a long time, to let silence speak for itself, and that, I have to tell you, he found the hardest.'

'He can't have learned all this overnight?'

'It took time. He needed months to tie his turban properly. He was astonishing. He could devote his entire soul to patience and then fly into a mad rage because you hadn't done something immediately. He needed both these qualities, a sort of furious patience, to overcome the greatest challenge he was presented with: the camel. His first attempt to ride one ended in humiliation and, I have to admit, that gave me a great deal of satisfaction. He imagined that if you could ride a horse, a camel would be easy. He swung himself onto the back of one without finding out about its temperament first. The camel immediately started howling and bellowing and fighting with all its might. It was a pack animal; it wasn't used to having a rider. Burton Sahib had barely seated himself before it was snapping at him, at his boots. He drew his sword and jabbed the animal in the nose whenever it turned its head. They went on like this, the two of them, back and forth, until the animal suddenly trotted off without warning. At last it's obeying his orders, I thought. I was wrong. The next moment it galloped off to the nearest tree, raced under its thorny branches and if Burton Sahib hadn't been quick-witted enough to duck, he would have had his face scratched to bits and his eyes poked out. When that trick didn't work, the camel came to a standstill. Nothing Burton Sahib did could budge the animal. He tried everything – cajoling, digging in his heels, the whip, belabouring its flanks with his rapier. All useless. The camel alone would decide when it was going to move. When it finally did so, it seemed to have turned docile at last. It trotted off with its neck held high, apparently reconciled, apparently good-tempered, and Burton Sahib grinned at me with contentment. That grin didn't stay in place for long, though, because the animal promptly left the path and headed straight for the nearest swamp. From a distance, we saw Burton Sahib raise his sword, wondering whether he should kill the camel before it started sliding into the bog. But it was already too late. The animal skidded down the slope, sunk into the ooze, and then went over on its side with a crash. Burton Sahib was thrown off and landed in the muck, and when we rushed up we had to pass him a long stick to pull himself out. You can imagine what a sight he was. We had to stifle our giggles. We could only laugh about it properly later that evening.'

'I find your story hard to believe. Riding a camel and stroking a beard is a long way from making someone a Muslim.'

'I don't know if I've told you this. In Baroda, he had learnt quite a lot from Guru-ji about our Santana Dharma. Just before we left, they even went to a Shivaratri festival together, in a temple near the Narmada. He told me afterwards that he spent the whole night singing bhajan with the other Nandera Brahmins, and he accompanied the god when He was taken out of the temple on a litter. But the minute we got to Sind, he forgot all about Shiva and Lakshmi Narayan. He steeped himself in the castrated's superstitions as if that's what he had been waiting for all his life. I have no idea what it was about them that attracted him so much. At first he claimed he was only studying their beliefs to understand the locals better. But he couldn't fool me. I saw the devotion with which he performed the rituals, the time he spent learning off by heart things he barely understood. Then I realised he thought he could change the outer layer of his faith, just like he could that of his behaviour or his clothes or his language. And when that became clear to me, I lost part of my respect for him.'

'You are petty-minded. Every change of place brings a change of belief.'

'What do you mean?'

'Why do we have so many different forms of our own religion? Because the requirements of faith in the forest are different to those on the plain or in the desert. Because the spices of the place change the flavour of the whole dish.'

22

OLDER THAN HIS BROTHER

We eat sand, we breathe sand, we think sand. The houses are made of sand, the roofs are made of sand, the walls are made of sand, the parapets are made of sand, and the foundations are made of rock, covered in sand. For our sins, we are, yes, you've almost guessed it, in Sind. But we're fine withal, and you're not to worry. This diet makes for good camouflage. If we were to meet in the middle of the desert, you'd fancy an erect, uniformed fossil had hoved into view, although admittedly one with a certain resemblance to your son. Fossilisation, moreover, is the great secret of survival here; my health is thriving.

Karachi, the harbour lately anointed by our Imperium's beringed hand, is no more than a big village of about five thousand inhabitants (there may be twice as many, but who knows – it is not populated by bodies you can count, but by shadows that split apart and fuse together from moment to moment). Karachi – I love saying that name, it sounds like a Neapolitan curse, don't you think, Father? – is surrounded by walls perforated with nostril holes, for the purposes of pouring boiling water should we come under siege. But who is supposed to be doing the besieging? And can you scald a shadow anyway? Every house looks like a little fortress and, strangely enough, seems to merge into the next. There are no streets, just the narrowest of lanes.

The only open ground is the bazaar, a miserable specimen of a marketplace, its shops feebly sheltering under palm-leaf roofs that keep out neither the rain nor the sun. The stench is unendurable most of the time; sewerage is only the vaguest of notions. But don't worry, there is a prophylactic against cholera and typhus, which is equally effective against shooting and stabbing – and even stupidity and pig-headedness: it is called luck and I have got it in spades.

On good days we have the sea to thank for a little fresh air. At low tide a row of silt banks emerges from the harbour basin and jacks up the ships, which tolerate this intermezzo with cock-eyed resignation. The soil here is clay, as stubborn as the people, and we have to hammer in our tent pegs with a mighty heave-ho. Only a few bungalows have been erected, but no doubt the authorities, who blindly and stutteringly administer our fate, have the future mapped out. For now, a racecourse is our pride and joy. How will we be judged when Napier the Unyielding occupies as heroic a place in mythology as Alexander the Great? How will mankind view a civilisation that laid out a racecourse before it even gave a thought to a church or a library? Are we the West of Jesus or of Equuleus?

'Sind-Hind' was the Arab traders' name for this part of the world: Sind was the land this side of the Indus, Hind – the India of today – lay on the other bank. So I've gone from Hind to Sind; oh, if only I had stayed with my trusted initial. Begorrah, what a god-forgotten hole this is, dreary tenements of stone and lime rising over a mass of dirty hovels of mat and mud. Anything that grows runs wild here, a meagre yield of thorns and fire-plants just sufficient to feed the camels that can chew their way through anything. Dear sister, esteemed brother-in-law, I am not sure if this is hell (our superiors keep such information from us) but it is a land of glaring reflections, of brilliant light that annihilates everything and heat that reaches such a broiling pitch, the earth's face flays and peels until it splits and fis-

sures and breaks out in feverish blisters. As you can imagine, I am in my element here and my body daily cries out for new challenges. Sometimes all too vociferously.
Recently the corpses of fifty camels – no, sis, I didn't count them, that is an olfactory estimate – were rotting near the camp. When I passed them – at a distance, you understand – I was surprised by two fat jackals crawling out of their little dining room in the belly of the corpse, all sluggish after their ravening feast.

Make sure you're never posted here, brother. This country is made for war, I can almost smell the fame the likes of us could win, but in peace it's as exciting as a graveyard buried in a sandstorm. That's right, this country is as sandy as a Scotchman's whiskers. Stay in beautiful Lanka. But just in case against all the odds you do land up here, I'll report on the brothels in our oversized village. There are three. Amazing, don't you think? A racecourse and three brothels. What more does an Englishman need? One of the brothels is an exact copy of the pleasure houses – as my trusty manservant Naukaram is wont to call them – of Bombay and Baroda, a half-civilised place which puts on tolerable shows of dancing and is populated by creatures with whom one can have an excellent conversation, provided, of course, one has a command of Sindi or Persian. I am making progress in these, and in order not to jeopardise it, I have become a regular guest. There is little to be seen in the second brothel, which is just as it's meant to be. The place is veiled in clouds of steam and customers are covered with clay of various colours, hence allowing men of every background to mix. As long as they sit quietly, acting their parts in the pantomime, all differences between them are temporarily suspended. The clay is reputed to be healthy, and apparently, after a couple of hours in its embrace, not only one's body but also one's desires are cleansed. I will try it one of these days and naturally report back to you, my dear Edward. The third brothel is the most notorious – people only speak about it on the quiet. It's called, in good classical style, the Lupanar and is an establishment where boys and young men offer themselves for sale. Rumour has it that it belongs to a respected emir, and the local aristocracy make up the majority of the clientele. We call it the backgammon parlour, which I find uncommonly amusing – you know how I love that game. I haven't entered this temple of vice so far, nor do I feel any inclination to do so, although I assume one sees many sights there that never show their faces elsewhere.

Talking of brothels, I have got into an argument – whole evenings are spent thrashing it out – as to whether Hindu or Muslim women make the best courtesans. You can't believe how heated the debate gets, nor the elevated heights at which it is conducted. The most compelling argument, to my mind, holds the Hindus to be at an advantage because they have a tradition of ritual prostitution, and so the man's gratification derives directly from the performance of divine duty. Your experiences would add greatly to the discussion. Please tell us your verdict, I beg you.

23
NAUKARAM

II *Om Skandapoorvaaja namah I Sarvavighnopashantaye namah I Om Ganeshaya namah II*

'You are in an especially bad mood today.'

'My wife's always pestering me. She won't let me work in peace. I need time to myself in the evening; I have to work on your letter. I have to think, select, abridge, rewrite. Your job requires particular attention.'

'So I'm to blame for your arguments with your wife?'

'Let's carry on. So . . . you despised him because he disguised himself as a Muslim. Were you ashamed to be seen with him?'

'I never was. He put on his disguise and he was off. Sometimes he was away for weeks.'

'You never went too?'

'No. Think for yourself. Is someone going to go to all that trouble over their disguise and then take an unbeliever as their servant? A Gujarati? Out of the question. Those people only associate with their kind. I stayed in the camp, where I didn't know anyone. I mean, of course I knew some of the other servants by sight and reputation, but I wasn't keen on their company.'

'What about the sepoys?'

'They didn't have anything to do with us. They thought they were a cut above. Can you believe it? They're just servants too, and there's nothing dirtier than the work they do for their masters: robbing and murdering. And yet they still think they're better than someone who keeps a household running smoothly.'

'What about his comrades? What did they say about his transformations?'

'I don't know. I hardly ever saw them. We couldn't receive visitors in the tent. I only heard they'd started calling him the white nigger in the mess. They thought he was betraying his people, dressing up like one of the savages.'

'But it was for a military purpose. He was a scout for the Angrezi's army. Everything he did was for the good of the Honourable Company.'

'They still felt his behaviour was improper. Some people thought it was unhealthy to have too many dealings with the natives. Others felt they could easily do without the information he collected. He laid himself open to suspicion – heavy, rank suspicion. As if he had brought weeds into a beautifully planted and nurtured and tended garden. Everyone knows how quickly weeds can spread.'

'Weeds, oh, once they get through the fence, if they're not got rid of in time. Still, looking at that from the other side, that gives us hope, doesn't it? Incidentally, I forgot yesterday, but we have to talk about my fee. Naturally the money you gave me ran out long ago. I think you should pay another eight rupees.'

'That makes sixteen in all.'

'Yes, and? How many days have I already devoted to you? The half-moon has been and gone. And you're moaning about sixteen rupees.'

24
A VALIANT WARRIOR

When Burton or Naukaram or any other outsider looked at Sind, all they saw was a barren, hopeless-looking waste. The general, however, had immediately seen fertile country, and what's more, with a precision unusual for dreams, known how it could be brought to bloom. The farmers had to become self-sufficient. Control of the Indus had to be wrested away from the big landowners who owned the marshes along the banks and kept them for hunting. The overgrown, quicksand-clogged canals had to be cleared – so vivid was his dream, he saw the shovels on the workers' shoulders – the river dammed, new locks built, swathes of farmland and paddy fields created by extensive irrigation. He had commissioned a captain called Walter Scott to survey the country before the excavations could begin. His dream had even extended to the rents to be charged; as part of a fair, efficient system, farmland would be leased for fourteen years, the first two free of tax. He was extremely meticulous, the general, and having worked out his dream in every last detail, he had duly submitted it in triplicate. But the directors of the Honourable East India Company feared the costs of regeneration on such a scale when the balance sheets looked grim. It was only when he read the rejection letter that the general had been rudely awakened from his dream, and looking out of his window, he too saw only bald and dismal waste. Now the enterprise had changed. The country wasn't to be improved any more, merely surveyed.

The inhabitants of this desert knew the general by the name of Shaitan-Bhai, 'the Devil's Brother'. Naturally his compatriots knew his civilian name – Charles Napier – but they seldom used it. The general despised anyone who contradicted him, regardless of whether they were subordinates or superiors. He delighted in conquest and the bad conscience it gave him. He mistrusted everyone, and at the same time expected everyone constantly to try to outdo himself, even in the error of his ways. Hence his propensity to overestimate the intrigues of the native princes. To protect himself, he developed a strategy that added to his notoriety: he prescribed counterattack before his adversary had even decided to attack. He considered this strategy an art and didn't shrink, therefore, from any of the sacrifices all forms of art demand. He had achieved resounding triumphs in the battles of Miani and Hyderabad. Mighty victories, in which the gunner manning the Talpur army's only cannon had intentionally aimed way above the heads of the attacking British, while the cavalry commander had treacherously withdrawn his troops and then urged them to flee. Even the name of the former battle was of dubious parentage. It was actually fought near the village of Dubba, which translates, more or less, as 'Skin on the Fat', so a wounded officer had ridden through the area looking for a more elegantly named place to be the scene of this glorious victory.

Although the payments for such high treason were inevitably buried away in the accounts, it was obvious to any observer how well the secret service money was spent. But this art, like all arts, was not immune to contingency. General Napier was hamstrung without a constant supply of reliable information that would enable him to stay one step ahead of the future. He was an excellent shot and, as he explained when Burton asked him once about his strategy, it was like shooting from distance: a marksman always has to calculate where the target will be in a fraction of a second; he must be able to predict its movement to be able to aim perfectly. The steadiest hand is no use if the prey stumbles over the roots of a Lawson's cypress at the moment the bullet leaves the gun. General Napier was a pedant, even in his similes. The man responsible for providing this information was Major McMurdo, who had created a network of informants, agents, insiders and spies, and instilled such fear into them in the process that in private they knew him as Mac the Murderer.

Major McMurdo prospected for the seam of riches dreamed of by General Napier, and the desert gave up its secrets in a mass of tips, leads and background reports, which, as the informants were all locals, were then transferred from the language of sand and dust to that of hedges and lawns by a unit of translators. All of which enabled McMurdo to provide the general with extensive daily reports. But a sceptic like the general sees clouds looming in the bluest of skies; to him peace is no less untrustworthy than any perfectly functioning system. He was as paranoid as men that have taken too much bhang. He insisted on having a safeguard, another barrel, should his first shot, against all the odds, miss the enemy.

Burton was one of these second rounds, another trump up his sleeve. A pair of sharp eyes beyond the cantonment, in that supposedly peaceful foreign land. The general was convinced the calm was deceptive, so Burton was to keep a lookout and his ears open for his commanding officer in person. When he returned from his first ask around, he brought word of such an unusual affair that the general felt confirmed in his decision to single him out for reconnaissance duties, this young man with the difficult character and incredible knowledge of languages. Richard Francis Burton. Father also an officer. Both grandfathers vicars. Part of the family from Ireland. Which didn't explain why he was so dark. Perhaps the rumour that a gypsy had got into the family tree somewhere was true. This Burton had far too individual a mind to get ahead in the army. He was one of those soldiers you should either promote to general immediately or discharge.

Burton delivered his report with the panache of a leading man declaiming the pivotal monologue of a play. While formally well advanced, practically the introduction of the British legal system was still suffering hiccups. The first convictions for murder had recently been secured after due trial, and the general himself had signed a number of death sentences, which he had been told had been carried out. It now emerged, however, that the convicted men were still alive. The general, who could never sit still behind his desk, who had his subordinates report to him while he was inspecting the troops, riding out, practising fencing and limping from one building to another – the general froze and, looking down his aquiline nose, eyed Burton like a falcon through his wire spectacles.

'Are you bent on sowing confusion?'

'No, sir. The convicted were rich men. They hired replacements who were hanged in their place.'

'You are trying to provoke me, young man!'

'Not at all, sir. I am merely pointing out that man is an amazingly inventive creature when it comes to survival. The system even has a name: badli.'

'Who allows himself of his own free will to be hanged instead of someone else?'

'I don't know, sir.'

'Then find out. At once.'

Burton waited for the next hanging, and then intervened before the trapdoor could open. 'Stop,' he called. 'I have reason to suppose that this man is not the same as the one sentenced to death.'

'Really?' asked the bystanders with innocent surprise.

'As you know full well,' Burton said. 'I want to talk to this fool, then he can go home in peace. Do you understand?'

The man who had escaped the rope by a whisker showered Burton with abuse. 'May your nose fall off, you pig eater.' He couldn't give a hoot Burton had saved his life. Only much later, after he had calmed down and become reconciled to the idea of carrying on living, did he answer the question of why he had accepted such a trade. 'I have been poor all my life,' he said calmly. 'So poor I didn't know when I would eat next. My belly was always empty. My wife and children are half starved.

This is fate, but it is beyond my patience. I got 250 rupees. With a small part of this money I filled my belly. The rest I left to my family. They will be provided for, for a while. What better can I do on earth?'

Burton reported again. The general's eyebrows shot up as if on strings.

'How can we put an end to this deplorable business?'

'By eradicating poverty?'

'If I'm in the mood for wit, I read Lucian. Understand, soldier?'

'The *Alethon Diegematon*, or do you prefer the *Nekrikoi Dialogoi*?'

'The world is generally open to a man of your talent. But I fear your nerve may close a few doors for you, Burton. Have you any other suggestions in this affair of ours?'

'Not at present, sir. May I have permission to reimburse the man the money he spent on his last meal?'

'Hasn't the guilty party been executed?'

'Yes. And now his family are collecting his debt. The reluctant rescuee has paid the rest back, but the amount he spent before he went to the gallows, he has to . . .'

'How much?'

'Ten rupees.'

'A banquet!'

'He treated himself to something for once in his life.'

'At the public expense, as it turns out. Make sure it doesn't come out what sort of excesses Pax Britannica is sanctioning.'

'Yes, sir.'

25

NAUKARAM

II *Om Skandapurvaaja namah I Sarvavighnopashantaye namah I Om Ganeshaya namah II*

'Burton Sahib's life changed in Sind. And mine did too. His for the better, mine for the worse. Not that he was promoted, or earned any more money. The house we lived in was a tent. In Baroda we had twelve servants, now we only had two. From the outside, no one would have guessed his position had grown more important. Sind was governed by an old general everybody was afraid of, even people who had never met him. He sent for Burton Sahib one day – he needed him to translate something – and he was impressed. How could he not be? Burton Sahib was a man who towered over the other Angrezi. The general couldn't fail to see that. He sent for him again. A private conversation. I don't know what they talked about. But I know the difficulties that came later.'

'As a result of this conversation?'

'Yes. We were heading for terrible trouble. I had no idea what job the general gave Burton Sahib. Even his direct superiors and his comrades were kept in the dark.'

'He didn't tell you anything?'

'He was supposed to reconnoitre, he told me that much. It meant mixing with the Miya, which he seemed delighted by. When he came home – I say home, but that's not the right word for our dusty tent – he was in higher spirits than I had seen him for a long time. He announced with great fanfare: "We're going to have a look around the country, Naukaram. The empire is finally starting to recognise our talents." He was happy that day and I hadn't thought he could feel such a thing. Everything started off so well for him; I don't understand why the end had to be so bad. Anyway, his mission had no effect on what I did every day. I was as busy barring the desert entrance to the tent as ever; it always found a way past me. Burton Sahib went off in disguise more and more often. Somewhere. He never told me where. At first he would be gone for a day. Then he learnt people talk more frankly at night. So then he would be gone for a few days and by the end sometimes I didn't see him for a week. It made me uneasy, thinking of him at the mercy of those savages, those circumcised. For the first time since I'd been with him I couldn't be at his side. I worried about him. How did he feed himself, where did he sleep? I didn't know, he didn't take any bags. He disappeared, and I was left behind with my worries until he reappeared – exhausted, worn out, but beaming. I could feel the excitement coursing through him. After he got back, he'd tell me some of the things that had happened. Unusual customs he had seen. Crowded festivals at tombs. Little things like that. I was baffled. That couldn't be the information he was meant to collect.'

'He kept the most important of it secret.'

'He wasn't allowed to tell anyone. Not even me.'

26

HE WHO BESTOWS EXPERTISE ON HIS DISCIPLES

Captain Walter Scott – a relative of the writer, a direct descendant even – rammed a ranging pole into the ground. Its red and white stripes stood out against the barren landscape like prison clothes. The soil was a puffy skin stretched over black clay.

'You'll pick it up in no time. It's as easy as playing patience. All we do is join the unknown to the known. We catch the landscape like a wild horse, by technical means. We are the second advance guard; first you conquer, then you survey. Our influence is writ on squared paper. I know you're cut up about not seeing any action, but you shouldn't be. The cartographical work we are doing here is of enormous military significance. The compass, theodolite and surveyor's level are our most important weapons. Whoever is caught in our net of coordinates is lost to his cause. Civilisation has broken him in. Now, shut one eye and focus the other as carefully as possible. There's only one quality you need as a surveyor. You have to be accurate, absolutely precise. We surveyors are pernickety people. So be prepared for a certain amount of pedantry. The principle is simplicity itself. The fixed points form a triangle. Slowly we advance, triangle by triangle, polygon by polygon.

We cannot cover more than a kilometre a day, so we camp for weeks at a time in one place and extend our triangles in all directions. There are two values to measure: distance and altitude. As well, of course, as the angle between a position and an elevation. And what's the definition of an angle, Dick?'

'The distance between orthodoxy and heresy?'

'The difference between two directions actually.'

'So I was more or less right?'

'Do you know what it means to be "more or less" right in mathematics, Dick? Why do I find it difficult to imagine you as a surveyor?'

Burton isn't destined for a career with a ranging pole in his hand, Scottie's right about that. He has been assigned to this unit because he had to be assigned somewhere and because it will be easier for him to set out on his forays from the remote camps. He can make himself useful in the meantime behind a levelling tool. He shuts his eyes. It's that time of day when one's thoughts turn to silt. How are you supposed to determine the exact position of a point when everything is shimmering? When he opens his eyes again he sees a dervish moving along the horizontal. A black robe, a patched cap. I am the one who flies alone. His eyes are set deep in a trough of kohl, his hands adorned with monstrous rings. Burton shuts his eyes. When he opens them again, the dervish is dressed in green; the chains around his neck are alternately silver and brass, fabric and ivory. I am the one who flies alone. His hair and beard are dyed an orangey brown like henna. Burton shuts his eyes once more and keeps them shut for a long time. He repeats all the alphabets he knows. 'Did you see him?' he eventually shouts into the wind to his comrades. 'What's the value of the variable?' they shout back.

The dervish wasn't a solitary apparition. The closer they moved their triangles to the next village, the more often he passed, at a safe distance, before Burton's measuring gaze. The dervish was different every time; he seemed never to assume a form he had taken before. Strange the others didn't see him.

Once, when the day was almost done, Burton decided to follow him. He came to a mosque, at the side of which stood a mausoleum in a walled precinct with a narrow entrance thick with people and excitement. He heard a song that drew him in, scraping at the plaster of a secret chamber of his being. He felt touched by a sort of radiance; the place in front of him was ablaze with light and he was flooded with light as well. A festival was in progress; the saint's tomb was charged with an immeasurable longing. The crowd absorbed him as a friend, a foretaste of the throng outside the gates of heaven. Before he could reach the tomb covered with embroidered green fabric, his attention was distracted. Opposite the little door through which the stooping pilgrims were passing, a few men were sitting on the ground. They were singing the song that had touched him. It sounded like a declaration of love for every living thing. The singer's voice, an unusual instrument that imparted a shrill, almost clownish note to the most serious things, screwed itself up to a higher pitch, turning the song on a disc that rotated ever faster. Suddenly the dervish looked him full in the eye. The revolutions continued inside him. Sit here, the eyes said, tarry a while. We are all guests. We are all wanderers. Be one of us. And the song continued to cast its light into the night and over the dense, surging crowd.

27
NAUKARAM

II *Om Sarvasiddhantaya namah I Sarvavighnopashantaye namah I Om Ganeshaya namah II*

'Didn't you have a bad conscience about helping a Feringhi spy on your own people?'

'My people? They weren't my people. Haven't you been listening? They're all circumcised there, more or less.'

'Even so. They're closer to you than the Angrezi.'

'Anyone is closer to me than a Miya. Do you know what sort of nightmares I had there? When I wasn't afraid Burton Sahib might be getting his throat cut in an alley somewhere, I was scared this Gujarat of ours might become another Sind. In my nightmares only a few of us were left. Baroda was in mourning. There was no sound in my dreams. No songs, no bells, no arti. The women walked through the streets in black, as if they were on the way to their own funeral. The men laid siege to our frightened politeness, hunting for a reason to draw their daggers.'

'Your brain's to blame for your nightmares, not your neighbours.'

'We can't be neighbours with them. They'll always do their utmost to drive us out, just as they did in Sind. If the Angrezi hadn't come, who knows how long we'd have survived in their midst.'

'You're still dreaming even though you're awake.'

'We have to stand up for ourselves before this Gujarat of ours becomes another Sind.'

'What happened with your master's reports?'

'He delivered them to the general in private. I think they enjoyed each other's company, the general and Burton Sahib, although they still had their arguments. The general expected every soldier to accept orders, carry them out, and not express an opinion unless asked. But Burton Sahib never needed an excuse to give his verdict. He contradicted the general whenever the fancy took him. And that was pretty often. He thought the general wanted to change too much in Sind, too fast. His sense of justice is too rigid – that was Burton Sahib's favourite example – it's bound to put their noses out of joint. "Justice is an acquired taste," he used to say. "How long did it take us to get used to porridge for breakfast? And how long would it take if we had to change our habits to grilled goat's liver, say?" The general, for instance, had a man hanged because he stabbed his wife when he found out she had betrayed him. The trouble was that the man had reacted exactly as men there are expected to react. They chop their wives to pieces the first opportunity they get. If he had let his wife live, both he and his sons would have been dishonoured. The shame would have been enormous. Unimaginable. They would have been outcasts, the object of everyone's scorn. Their friends would have turned their backs on them. But the general wanted to set an example, show the times had changed. Burton Sahib cursed the general's pig-headedness. Not because he condoned what the man had done, but because he saw immediately the locals wouldn't understand the sentence. He anticipated trouble. Rightly so. Everywhere people were cursing the madness of the unbelievers, who now didn't even allow a man to restore his honour. Every day the general's headquarters was besieged by protesters with their objections and complaints. There was a tidal wave of rumours about what the Angrezi intended to do. One day even the cour-tesans sent a delegation. Burton Sahib had just arrived when they were shown in. They were all veiled, very proper. One of them stepped forward and presented their complaint. If adul-tery was no longer punished, married women would take all their work from them. They'd steal the bread from the courte-sans' mouths. If things went on like this, they'd starve.'

28

HE WHO HOLDS THE FIRST PLACE

It is Jehannum by day and Barabut by night here. Pretty impressive settling-in, eh? Loosely translated: the Devil takes the chair by day and Beelzebub by night. You have to have a very distinctive sense of entertainment to make time pass satisfactorily here, but I am adapting. I still miss some things. None more than the company of Guru-ji. I'm sure you remember, I described him once in detail. Language teachers are two a penny here, like midges in a stable, but find me one who can celebrate the sacred frivolity of life like the wonder-fully cranky old Upanishe. He made life in Baroda bearable, especially at the end. I'm not exaggerating. He had a gift of making one's despair seem unimportant. His mind kept one foot in the everyday, while soaring far above the human condition. Still, I'll probably never see him again. Hinduism is *passé, mon cher ami*, henceforth I'm devoting myself to Islam. It suits the country here better, hence the high concentration of dervishes. I think I'll replace Guru-ji with a team of teachers. A man is teaching me the limpid secrets of al-Islam on the riverbank. We sit on a felt rug under a tamarind tree, surrounded by sweet-smelling basil, and as he instructs me, this teacher, who is too settled for a dervish and too wild for an alim, he looks out at the river and the people gathered at the ferry. I have also already found a teacher of Persian, which seems to me the proudest of all languages now I have started to be led through its halls. And then a third teacher, a true dervish, a wild man who leads you to higher truths by sowing confusion. Unfortunately we only see each other rarely. But when we do meet, generally by chance, he slips me a poem as if I were a poor man who's too proud to beg. He has thrown my surveyor's level quite off true. I have followed his lead and he has drawn me, my dear fellow, into a song, or to be more precise, the form contained within it. We've never had such a trapdoor to ecstasy. Music and poetry – these are what this country is blessed with. Urdu, a language like song, is so opulent that a conversation about potatoes sounds like a rendition of *Childe Harold*. The change is doing me a power of good.

29

NAUKARAM

II Om Prathameshvaraya namah I Sarvavighnopashantaye namah I Om Ganeshaya namah II

'When we were in Sind, I have to tell you, I went from confidant to outcast.'

'Did you fall from favour?'

'He turned away from me. He hardly discussed anything with me.'

'Does that surprise you?'

'What do you mean?'

'Everything you say about Muslims is so disparaging, you are so full of hatred, how is he supposed to tell someone like you what exciting discoveries he made on his travels?'

'Why do you say full of hatred? I didn't feel any hatred. I hardly knew anything about the Miya when we arrived. You don't know what they're capable of. They force our people to become Miya too. The abominations they committed were unbearable. Is it hatred to say that? A banyan was wrongly accused of something – I think he'd had an argument with another trader.'

'A Miya?'

'Yes, of course. The accusation was obviously far-fetched. And what did the qadi decide? The banyan was taken off, his clothes were removed, he was washed the way the Miya think people should wash. Three times here and three times there, while they squawk something over and over. Then they dressed him in new clothes and took him to the mosque, where they spattered him with their prayers. He had to repeat that he believed what a Miya has to believe. And just because he didn't stumble over his words, listen to this, they were running round beside themselves, announcing there'd been a miracle. And then came the most terrible thing, the poor man was circumcised.'

'With a knife?'

'How else? He was maimed. A whole lifetime isn't enough to put that right.'

'I've heard it's meant to be cleaner.'

'Don't you have any sympathy? An innocent man, one of us, deformed! To force a person to take up another faith is a mutilation without end.'

'Of course, of course. But I doubt it happens that often. Stories such as that one are the sort you always hear but never actually see, and you never know anyone who has.'

'You are shutting your eyes. That's why. And when you open them again, it'll be too late.'

'That's enough. We already wasted most of yesterday on your tirades.'

'You see how the Miya are still doing me harm today? Why didn't you stop me?'

'I thought it was doing you good to talk about it. This poison is obviously eating you up inside.'

'You have to stop me if I go off the track. I don't have any time or any money left. I'm going to have to ask you to give me until tomorrow to pay as it is. One of my brothers still owes me money. He was one of the servants then.'

'Then let's call a halt here. And we'll carry on tomorrow, without hatred in our hearts, but with the money you owe me.'

30

MASTER OF THE WHOLE WORLD

Two veils divided them, the rulers, from the country's inhabitants. The veil of their own ignorance, and the veil of mistrust behind which the people hid. The general knew the veils couldn't be torn away but he was determined to make them more transparent. Like all the empire's administrators, he spent most of his days at a desk, always rode out with an escort, and was only shown what in the opinion of the local emirs, as well as his subordinates, would meet with his approval. The thought of how little he knew the country and its inhabitants nagged away at him constantly. His adjutants pored over endless documents with owlish absorption, but they'd never been to a circumcision, marriage or funeral. Knowledge of Persian, Urdu or Sindi was the exception. And the situation didn't improve with time either. The younger officials and officers cut themselves off from the locals to even greater degrees. They prized a perfectly groomed, uncompromisingly British appearance, so shut themselves in the vacuum of their own rooms. They exercised their right to regular home leave, and came back with wives. Their sense of morality became increasingly acute, which revolved essentially around protecting their customs from foreign contamination. Valuable though such a moral code may have been at home, here it simply blinded the officers and civil servants in his command. They were the unseeing tentacles of that monster that administered half the world from a London side street.

'Only our knowledge of our adversary makes us strong,' the general used to say. 'We must deepen it. This thirst for knowledge is what distinguishes us from the natives. Who has ever heard of one of them setting out to find out something about us? If they were to explore us one day, our weaknesses and our fears, then they'd be able to do us a lot of harm; they'd grow into opponents to whom we'd owe a great deal of respect.'

His exhortations had no effect. Everyone thought the general a bizarre, quarrelsome old man. And indeed no one would have said he was a contented ruler. Occasionally he flew into fits of frenzied rage, in which he provoked his staff with the bitterest of home truths. 'What is the purpose of our administration in British India? Conquest? The well-being of the masses? Justice? Absolutely not. Let's be honest. Its sole purpose is to facilitate robbing and plunder.' His subordinates had learnt to veil their gazes, freeze their expressions. 'All the killing, all the dying just so our trade has decisive advantages over our competitors'. All the suffering just to maintain the rule of idiots. We're serving in a galaxy of asses.' But the general kicked in vain against the pricks. The more openly he spoke the truth, the more mad his subordinates thought him. You could only get away with such a thing if you were commander in chief, they told themselves. The general's heading for retirement. We are the future.

There were a few people he could rely on, such as this Burton who submitted reliable reports on the doings of the natives. He enjoyed their talks together. Burton's view of things was so fresh, it was as if the world had just been created. But this young man had one failing, a fatal one. He wasn't content simply to observe the natives. He wanted to be one of them. They had completely captivated him, so much so that he even wanted to maintain them in their backward condition. Burton's position was the diametric opposite of his. The general was bent on changing, improving the native, whereas Burton wanted to leave the native to his own devices because any improvement would mean his obliteration. The general found that incomprehensible, especially because this young man didn't doubt for a moment that British civilisation was superior to native customs. Shouldn't the superior prevail? Wasn't that the natural progress of history? Logical thinking was not this officer's strength. He got infuriated by the ubiquitous stupidity and laziness and brutishness, like anyone else. He could pass vehemently disparaging judgement. Like the thesis he had recently insisted on: that envy, hatred and malice were seeds the native scatters wherever he can – not from any fiendish conviction, but simply out of an instinct which is fostered by weakness and cunning. A bit thick, surely. And yet the author of these sentiments wanted to abide by native laws! He was an enigma, this Burton. He usually held the view one least expected of him. Murderers shouldn't be hanged, he had argued the last time they talked. 'They should be tied to a cannon, as they used to be, and then you fire the cannon. Brutal, admittedly. But I think our compassion should confine itself to the tried and tested paths of the realistic. Let us not forget the value of deterrence. A body that's torn to pieces cannot be buried, and without burial no Muslim can go to paradise. If we hang them we should burn the body for the same reason. Equal rights for all doesn't work here. Our criminal law has lost effectiveness in its lengthy transit. You see, locking someone up may work in Manchester, but in Sind it is completely counterproductive. The entire male population of these latitudes thinks of a few months in our prisons as a period of rest and relaxation. A chance to eat, drink, doze and smoke their pipes in peace. Instead of that, we should flog the poor criminals and fine the rich ones. That will make an impression.'

No, logical he was not, this officer whose job it was to report to the general in person.

31
NAUKARAM

II Om Avanishaya namah I Sarvavighnopashantaye namah I Om Ganeshaya namah II

'I've only come here today for one reason. At long last I would like to hold something in my hands. Some proof that we have been sitting down together every day for a month. Something that looks as if it could be worth sixteen rupees. A sign that will give me hope again.'

'We are not finished yet. I can't help it if you've had so many experiences.'

'You can't help it? All I wanted when I came to you last month was a two-page letter of reference.'

'There was never any talk of two pages.'

'Or a hundred.'

'What is it you want?'

'I would like you to prepare a letter by tomorrow. A few pages containing everything important. I want to start looking for a new job as soon as possible. In the monsoon, there's a lot to do in any well-run household. And the Feringhi are almost always at home. I will find them in when I go around to introduce myself.'

'I can't abide half measures. We should wait until our work is done and you can introduce yourself with the definitive, best possible letter. The monsoon won't go that quickly.'

'I insist.'

'Oh, and when you insist there's no possibility of discussion? "I insist"? Where did you learn that?'

'A month is a long time. Then even someone like me starts to realise when the wool is being pulled over his eyes.'

32

LORD OF POETS

Report to General Napier
Personal

Following your instructions to gather information that will enable us to form an impression of how the natives regard us, I have spent many hours in the company of Sindis, Baluchis and Punjabis of all classes, in markets, inns and at the makeshift court of the Aga Khan. I have listened attentively to every voice and avoided passing judgement on the sense of what was said. I proceeded from the assumption that I saw the world in just as one-sided a way as the person expressing an opinion in front of me. I never feigned a reaction, because I'm convinced the Orientals see through all affectation. Nor did I either contradict or provoke opinions. I simply played the part of a listener and I have to say, without any false modesty, that I have seldom been so popular in my whole life. The hardest thing has been to summarise concisely the contents of innumerable meandering, muddled, bombastic or, as the case may be, stilted conversations. Generalisations are inexorable levellers which we should guard against as the Devil guards against holy water, but I cannot refrain from them entirely, if the information I've collected is, following your brief, to be of the greatest possible use. 'Get to the point, will you,' I hear you say, and so I will hasten to do so.

The natives see us in quite a different way from how we see ourselves. That sounds trite but we should always bear

109

it in mind in our dealings with them. They don't consider us brave, clever, generous or civilised in any respect; they see us as nothing more than rogues. They don't forget a single promise we have failed to keep. They don't overlook a single corrupt official who is ostensibly employed to see our justice is done. They consider our manners repellent and, of course, we're unbelievers. Many natives long for a day of revenge, an eastern Night of the Long Knives, one might call it; they cannot wait for the day when the stinking intruder is driven out. They see through our hypocrisy, or, to be more precise, in their eyes the contradictions in our behaviour amount to a single all-encompassing hypocrisy.

'When the Angrezi put on an especial display of piety,' an elderly gentleman in Hyderabad told me, 'when they stuff our ears with fairy tales about the rising sun of Christianity, when they invoke the spread of civilisation and the unending advantages we barbarians are being showered with, then we know the Angrezi are planning another robbery. When they start speaking about values, then we're on our guard.'

We could call this man a cynic but he is undoubtedly a clever, highly respected cynic. As an example is worth more than a hundred assertions, I'd like to report another incident. A few months ago, in a remote part of the country west of Karchat, a Baluchi was captured, a tribal chieftain, who was accused of organising raids on our supply routes. He was renowned as a cunning and experienced duellist, which gave the officer who had performed the arrest the idea of challenging him to a duel. No doubt he imagined that his victory would demonstrate our military superiority. The prisoner was put on a tired old horse, while the officer vaulted onto his battle-tried stallion. He flung himself with great bravura and clamour into the first charge, and a host of subsequent ones, but no matter how often he attacked, how many blows he dealt, the Baluchi parried everything with sword and shield. The frustration of this officer, who set great store by his fencing skills, mounted steadily. He could hear the natives' incomprehensible, mocking-sounding shouts; he wouldn't be able to prevail, he would lose his excellent reputation among his comrades. He attacked one last time, with his pistol drawn, and instead of landing a blow with his sword, he shot the Baluchi at point-blank range. This story is told the length and breadth of the country; it is rampant, producing poisonous blooms that inflate the injustice into a demonic act. There are many different versions going around, but they all have the skeleton I have outlined. More serious for the natives than the officer's behaviour is the injustice that this officer has not had to answer for his crime before a court martial. Quite the contrary: he has been promoted and now occupies a high position.

33

NAUKARAM

II Om Kavishaaya namah I Sarvavighnopashantaye namah I Om Ganeshaya namah II

The lahiya took out his portfolio, a folder of fine leather, which he had bought when he realised how many pages he had already covered with Naukaram's story. They needed to be kept safely – he had suddenly felt afraid of losing them, of endangering even a page – and so he had bought the portfolio with part of his fee, thereby naturally provoking an argument about unnecessary expenditure with she who kept the books. He opened the portfolio a fraction, enough to slide out a page between his fingertips, and read it through slowly and carefully. Suddenly he felt like a young man who, if confronted with the hill in town he had just wheezed his way up, black spots swimming before his eyes, would run to the top and then down the other side; he felt he was almost flying as he sped past this servant's pedantic narration. The fellow had given him the necessary impetus, of course, and he was grateful for that, but he now had to give the story wings. *Om Balaganapati*, seven syllables, seven sounds to bestow meaning and beauty on this failed servant's story. What sort of beauty though? Only a few were afforded the gift of magic. Was he entitled to use it? What a petty question. Was he allowed to distort another's life? Why such scruples? He had to shrug off this stiffness; it only suited the rigid poses of heroes in old miniatures. Movement! Limberness! Besides, Naukaram lied constantly: that was obvious. It wasn't his real life he set before the lahiya, it was a beautified version, like a bride on her wedding day: every blemish plucked out, made up, disguised; every graze bandaged sevenfold. Of course it was. No one tells the truth. Who has the courage to do that?

And that's where matters would have rested if he hadn't probed. He had been able to uncover some things; he had a nose for lies. But Naukaram would hide certain painful episodes to the end. So the lahiya had no alternative but to fill in the gaps. It was his duty to make everything complete.

Who was Kundalini? Who was she really? He had looked up a pujari whose pilgrimages had taken him all over the country. Their conversation had been extremely productive, confirming some of his suppositions. The pujari had been able to draw certain conclusions from Kundalini's background. Her birthplace, Phaltan, in Satara, raised the possibility her family were members of the Mahanubhav sect. They were commonly devadasi. 'I was always being offered one in their temples,' the pujari had said, 'but I refused. Someone the age of a grandfather shouldn't behave like a young man who wants to become a father.' Various things apparently pointed to Kundalini having been a devadasi; in which case, she must have served in a temple and then run away. Devadasi never receive permission to leave the temple in their youth, the pujari had explained, in the years of their bloom. Only when the priests have no more use for them are they released, but by then they are often so accustomed to the life there that they're afraid of its counterpart outside. If the pujari are lenient, the older devadasi are allowed to stay on to sweep the temple's floor and fetch water. Kundalini had been young. If she had managed to seduce both an Angrezi officer and his servant, surely her charms must have been considerable. So why had she run away?

Next the lahiya went to see one of his friends – his only friend in fact, the only person whose company did not irritate him. A poet and musician who knew many things about the world that had remained hidden from the lahiya, since all his life he had only ever discovered the world through his customers' eyes. He had actually only meant to mention Naukaram's letter in passing, but his friend had promptly folded his arms over his stomach, which was as big as the copper bowl he played with his rings while he was singing, and demanded to know all. Kundalini had interested him to an almost indecent degree. He was able to answer some of the lahiya's questions, but it was disturbing the way he prefaced his explanations with statements such as: 'Everyone knows women in maikhanna sell their bodies, that's why they're called "the beloved", not because of their charms, didn't you know that?' Or: 'Everyone knows that the ones who can dance, like the ones who can sing bhajan, used to be devadasi.' There it was again: devadasi. There couldn't be any more doubt. A concubine shared between God and priests. Not that his friend had put it like that. He had explained that the devadasi were not allowed to marry mortals because they were wedded to the god of the temple in which they served. They dressed Him and undressed Him and cradled Him on their knees and fed Him and worshipped Him and did everything a good wife should do. There was only one thing of necessity the stone or bronze divinity was denied, and that was why the priests had to perform the act of love with the devadasi. But everyone knew that.

Steam enfolded the lahiya, as if rain had fallen on the parched clay, as if the earth was breathing again. He quickly took his leave of his friend. His return home was like a first walk after rainfall. In his room he lit a stick of sandalwood incense, implored his wife not to disturb him, took out a new sheet of paper and wrote what he now knew about the devadasi called Kundalini who had fled from the temple, from the pujari, a loathsome man with foul breath who wasn't remotely her equal in cultivation. She knew all the principal divine texts off by heart, whereas he made up sutras and stuck sacred endings on random syllables, and because she noticed, he grabbed hold of her and hurt her as punishment. (Was that taking it too far? No – those filthy, half-educated brahmins, a disgrace to their caste, that was just their way.) She knew a huge number of bhakti songs, and when she sang them, an ascetic would be overwhelmed with the love of God and a roué driven wild by the promise of sensual bliss. No – the lahiya crossed out the last bit. It was true but inappropriate. He mustn't let himself be carried away by this woman in whose songs dharma and karma became one.

So, she had fled from the pujari who had assaulted her once too often, to Baroda. (Why specifically to Baroda? What matter, not every puzzle had to be solved. Perhaps she knew another devadasi here.) She started working in the maikhanna where she met Naukaram, a customer, whom she gave herself to for money and then he introduced her to his master. Of course – the realisation hit like a bombshell – how could he have missed it? Naukaram hadn't had his master's happiness in mind, he had just been thinking of himself. He didn't want to have to go and see Kundalini in the maikhanna; he wanted to have her near by. For that he had to make a sacrifice: he had to share her with his master. But why not? If gods and priests could share a beloved, then why not an officer of the East India Company and his servant? That's how it must have been, more or less. The lahiya was very satisfied. That is genuine scruples, he thought, distorting a story until it becomes true.

For days everything had been waiting for the rains. The clouds, swollen and black, shrunk the sun to a glittering coin. Waves broke higher and higher on the quay wall, bursting over it. The world was uneasy. Houses braced themselves against the mist; the odd bird roamed shrilly through the air, climbing steeply as if afraid of having forgotten how to fly. In Bombay, the *Gazette* reported, a wave had leapt out onto Colaba dyke like the tongue of a chameleon and claimed the monsoon's first victim; none of the fishing boats could find the woman in the churning sea. Scraps of newspaper flew up into the air, higher than the birds; trees buckled, their trunks flimsier than stalks of grass. Leaves blew into people's mouths like communion wafers. And when the rains' time finally comes, the smell in the air is unmistakable. The first drop is gentle; subsequent drops seem to be on tiptoe, innocuously warming up as they sketch delicate miniatures on the window. Dots that pause a moment before trickling down the pane, spreading a milky veil behind which streets, markets, houses, districts begin to disappear. Then comes the noise: drumming, shrieks, the ecstatic, know-all call of the wind echoed by the palm leaves. Who can tell despair from happiness now? And then the rain strikes, as if the earth needs a thrashing. Time recedes; the monsoon sets in. Find cover, if you haven't got sturdy walls to wait it out behind. Save yourself, if you can't rely on the promise of your roof.

Burton, stretched out naked on his bed after a fall from his horse, tried to follow Kundalini's fingers. I'd like to understand what they're saying, he thought. The only language he couldn't learn. Did it mean anything at all? Outside the sound of the rain sobered up. A few drops rolled from the earth's sated lips. Everything was under water now, like those roots and the hole that had done for his horse. Lying in the mud, he'd remembered the warnings in the mess: if you don't have to, don't leave your house after the start of the monsoon. Serves him right, he heard her fingers say behind his sore back. Even with his eyes open, he couldn't recognise whether they were doing more than just their duty. After the fat years, the lean. Or year in his case – a year of desires fulfilled followed by this one, with its recurrent dissatisfactions. It was quieter outside; he could hear the torrents racing pitilessly down the hill onto the town. The huts would be flooded. From his neck to his backside, she traced each of his vertebrae as if discovering them for the first time, encircling them with the same unvarying pressure of her fingers. Her hand never strayed. It was amazing how much she knew about the human body.

She left the room, and his mood blackened. She gave him so much, she was always so eager to please him; she wore her hair loose because he liked it that way and plaited it when he wanted something different; she heeded his moods and occasionally she was even playful. And yet. And yet. She held so much back. There were moments when she looked into a distance he had no knowledge of. Sometimes she left without saying goodbye or telling him where she was going. She never spent the whole night with him. She demurred when he asked her about her family, her youth, her past. She denied him any right to fall in love with her and he was sure she suppressed any feelings she might have for him, except for the gratitude she regularly expressed in a tone and manner that brooked no intimacy.

He had resolved to talk to her about it. These are the hard things in life, eh: how do I ask my beloved – my purchased beloved, mark you – why we don't love each other like a debutante and her beau at a ball? She evaded his questions until he forced her into such a corner that she reacted with a rage he would have never suspected in her.

'I am a pariah,' she cried, her voice a one-stringed instrument. 'I can please you or someone else for years until my body betrays me, until there is nothing left of my beauty, and then I'll have no choice but to throw myself at God again and my only consolation then will be that no man will want to take his pleasure with me. The closeness of death is the only protection I have against your lust.'

He said nothing.

'Do you think I wouldn't like to escape? It's what I want, but it can't be at the expense of another lie.'

He said nothing.

'You want love? For how long? How long will you be here? A few years and then you'll move on, and even if you do stay here, at some moment you will want to marry a woman from your people to have children with her.'

'No,' he interrupted. 'I don't want that, marriage, children, that isn't for me.'

Then silence fell, driving them apart.

The smell of oil caught him like a wave. She had come back. He felt the warm oil run over his skin. As he knew she would, she quickly stifled his temper, spurring his desire, faster and faster, until suddenly she stopped. Her body became quiet, and straddling his still thrusting astonishment, she rested her hands on his chest and began to talk. She spoke in measured sentences, in an intimate voice that expressed itself calmly and yet demanded his full attention. He had to stop moving to hear her story: the story of a wise king who was rewarded by a holy man with the apple of immortality. 'The king is overjoyed at first until he finds out that only he will become immortal and that everything in life he takes delight in will die. So he gives the apple to his wife. The wife accepts the present as a great honour, while secretly thinking the king has only given it to her out of habit. And so she hands it to an adjutant who has proved himself an exceptional lover. The adjutant in turn passes it on to a courtesan whom he worships and she, after long reflection, gives the apple to the king of the realm because he is her ultimate patron and the protector of her art. The king holds the apple in his hand and understands what has happened. Nothing can console him. He calls the entire court together and curses those who have betrayed him. *Dhik tam tscha tvam tscha –*' Kundalini began to move her hips again – '*madanam tscha imam tscha mam tscha –*' her fingers dug into his thigh.

'Tell me what it means,' Burton gasped.

She speeded up her movements. 'A curse on them and a curse on you –' her breasts swung heavily like wild geese in flight '– a curse on love and on the beloved too –' she breathed more heavily '– and may I be equally accursed.'

Afterwards she lay at his side, the two of them separated like water and oil, both drained from the struggle of their passions. All life seemed to be in that room, until he heard a cuckoo outside. Her fingers crawled over his chest, slow as a plant growing towards a window. Anything she said in that uprooted moonlight would have been a poem. He kissed one of her closed eyes, taking the eyeball between his lips. It was like a gemstone, something hard you couldn't swallow. Only his lips sensed it moving like a globefish just beneath the surface of the water or a marble before it comes to rest. The room was muggy, stifling. As he made to get up, she objected; he thought she didn't want to let him go, even for the minute it took him to get to the window and open it, and he felt appeased. He heard the frogs croaking and turned round to her with a diaphanous smile. 'Hurry up and shut it,' she cried, 'the insects are getting in.' Before he could comply, termites, moths, fireflies, grasshoppers, beetles and hundreds of birbahuti like scraps of red velvet had landed on everything, the bed and her body alike.

It rained almost incessantly for the next eight days and eight nights. There was no roll call, no regimental duties, no extramarital assignations. It was impossible to go hunting. There was nothing but the bed where they lay and from which they did not move.

35

NAUKARAM

II *Om Ganadhakshaya namah* I *Sarvavighnopashantaye namah* I *Om Ganeshaya namah* II

'You loved her.'

'Yes, I already told you that.'

'She was your lover. You were together, she lay in your arms, you were joined as one.'

'How do you know?'

'I have thought about it for a long time. Your story has burnt a hole in my heart. My wife even says I am neglecting my duties as master of the house.'

'In your heart? What does that mean? I understand when something's burning a hole in someone's pocket. But what money has the heart got to give?'

'Forget about the heart. The situation between you two was complicated, wasn't it?'

'This is not about the letter of reference any more, is it?'

'Did you possess her before you paired her off with Burton Sahib?'

'The words you use . . . they're not right.'

'I want to know!'

'Yes. I possessed her. Before and afterwards.'

'In his house?'

'Yes. In his house – in our house. Are you satisfied now?'

'When he was there?'

'Sometimes, at night, she was with him first and then me. But mainly when he was away, in Mhow or Bombay. Once he had to go to Surat.'

'Weren't you ashamed?'

'Why should I have been? He was the one who should have been ashamed. You don't understand. He lusted after her, he craved her. I loved her, really loved her. I won't lie, when she and I were alone I was like a buffalo, the same as anyone, it would have needed too much tapas to resist her. I admit that, but it's not the main thing. I honoured her; he dragged her through the mud.'

'What about the other servants?'

'They knew everything, how was I supposed to keep it secret from them?'

'What if they had said anything?'

'They were dependent on me. They wouldn't have dared.'

'So, you were delighted with the situation you had engineered?'

'No, I wasn't delighted. Something happened I hadn't expected. That I couldn't have predicted. The worst thing that could have happened.'

'I know. Do you think I could have forgotten that she died?'

'No, even before that. For me, she died several times. One day, totally out of the blue, she refused herself to me.'

'Physically?'

'She didn't give me any explanation. I hadn't done anything to her. At first she brushed me off a few times, she said she was ill or tired, I left her in peace. I respected her. But then she said she didn't want to be alone with me in a room any more, she didn't want me to touch her.'

'She loved the Feringhi more.'

'Love? You don't know what you're talking about. Her love was always just pretend love. Fake love.'

'Why did she spurn you then? Fake love knows no bounds.'

'She thought she could snare the sahib. He was dependent on her, and she had worked out how many jewels this dependency could be worth. She didn't want to risk the spoils. Such a woman loves only gain.'

'Did you think that before she refused herself to you?'

'She shouldn't have done that to me.'

'If she was as calculating as you make out, then she only gave herself to you because she had to.'

'I respected her.'

'As long as she loved you.'

'She wasn't capable of love.'

'You're judging her unfairly. I didn't know her but if it's right what you say, if both you and the Feringhi had such strong feelings for her, then she must have reciprocated these feelings, at least in part. Or were you merely in love with a chimera? It seems to me two blind men were sharing a woman who yearned to be seen.'

'Roughly nineteen centuries ago, in the glorious city of
Ujjayini, which today is known as Ujjain, a prince was born
who bore a name that conferred on him the authority to do
anything he chose, a name of far too great a magnitude for just
one man to bear. It had been bestowed on him in the hope that,
thus distinguished, he would outgrow himself and into his
name – a high expectation which is rarely answered, since the
name tends generally to consume its more diminutive bearer.
You're asking yourself what he was called, what was this great
name, aren't you? It was Vikramditya. You're a good pupil: I
don't need to translate for you. An illustrious name, rather too
illustrious for the everyday, it was subsequently shortened to
Vikram, not because his elders lacked time but because the
heroic deeds the young man was called on to perform by the
abbreviated form were of a rather more manageable nature.
Vikram was hailed as a hero while still a prince, and as King
Vikram his fame has been passed down from generation to
generation. You English would probably shorten his name
even further to Vik, and you would call the book I want to tell
you about today, my shishya, *Vik and the Vampire*, and it
would sound like a story for children when, in fact, it is a story
for people who fear nothing. King Vikram was not the heir to
Ujjayini's throne – that privilege fell to his half-brother
Bhartirihari – and he would probably have become a hermit
who travelled the land to avoid being tempted by the sins
attendant upon a sedentary life, if his half-brother had not pre-
empted him, if Bhartirihari had not himself set off on the
thorniest and stoniest paths because of a disappointment that
he could not shake off, a disappointment in love. Imagine, my
shishya: an apple is given to you, an apple of immortality, sufficient unto one person, and you hand this present to your
wife, and she in turn – can you feel the disaster looming – gives
the apple . . .'

'To her lover. I know the story.'

'Oh. Where from?'

'I don't know. I picked it up somewhere.'

'A lucky man who picks up such valuable stories somewhere. Even if it is just in bed.'

Burton said nothing, as his mind raced. How had Upanishe found out about Kundalini? Naukaram was bound to have kept quiet. The other servants wouldn't have dared say a word either. Was Upanishe in touch with other British officers? He couldn't bring himself to ask. He felt shy and, besides, he already knew the answer: nothing stays hidden from the guru, Upanishe would say. A pendulum pushed in jest and yet swinging in earnest. From that moment on he noticed the guru constantly introducing the subject of his and Kundalini's living together into their classes, in the subjects he touched on and the maxims he proffered. Once, in the middle of a conversation that ranged in all directions, the teacher said: 'The only true bodily pleasure is that which, at the cost of a great struggle, you find with a woman who is not your own.' Burton had become used to this sort of surprise by then; it was no longer such a shock hearing such things from the mouth of his venerable and venerated teacher. He enquired politely after the author of this pearl.

'That's a quote from Vatsayayana, my shishya, the author of a work that may be of great use to you. It's called the *Kama Sutra* and contains exactly what the title promises: a lesson in love.'

'Divine love?'

'If you are talking of the love God equips us for, yes. Not the love of God, however. That receives less attention in this work.'

'I didn't know you studied these subjects too.'

'You know very little. You have before you the world's greatest expert on the *Kama Sutra*.'

'Why didn't you tell me earlier, Guru-ji?'

'Oh my shishya, the road to knowledge is a long one. A

pupil of a miniature-painter is only allowed to draw lines in his first year – circles and spirals on boards – and once he has perfected this skill, then he is allowed to draw a few lotus flowers, a deer here, one or two peacocks there. And when the flowers and the animals have satisfied the master's strict eye, he is allowed to work on a few details of a miniature. But only after years, my shishya. Should I give you all our treasures at once? Won't such a surfeit overwhelm you? No, you will learn them gradually and some you will never know.'

'I am curious, Guru-ji. When can I read this work?'

'That will be difficult, my shishya. How am I supposed to find it among all my books?'

'I can help you.'

'There are thousands of books. The pages often stick together; the title page is sometimes missing.'

'I don't mind the work.'

'I've heard the dust from books left lying around is poisonous. It settles in the lungs, and once exposed to it, you cough for the rest of your life.'

'It can't be as bad as all that.'

'Oh and I forgot to say, the *Kama Sutra* is written in an antiquated form of Sanskrit.'

'What do you say to two days' Sanskrit a week?'

'In sutras which only reveal themselves to those who have a prodigious knowledge not only of the language but also of the period.'

'You don't think your best shishya up to the task?'

'I will have to reflect. The *Kama Sutra* is easily misunderstood.'

'Couldn't you teach me one sutra at least? As a foretaste.'

'One sutra can't hurt. Let me think, my shishya, which one will suit a man of your calibre. I will teach you something from the sixth chapter, the chapter about courtesans. These women, Vatsayayana says – in fact he is only summarising what Dattaka formulated before him in teachings, which themselves are clearly based on the writings of other predecessors – these women are never known in their true light. They always hide their feelings, never revealing whether they love a man or are indifferent towards him, whether they stay with him because he gives them delight, or so as to extract from him all the wealth he may possess.'

37

NAUKARAM

II Om Shubhagunakananaya namah I Sarvavighnopashantaye namah I Om Ganeshaya namah II

'You're late.'

  'I can't afford a tonga any more.'

  'Still not found any work?'

  'No, nothing.'

  'The letter must have made some impression, though?'

  'They chase me away before I can show it to them. Somebody – at least one of these Feringhi – has to read your wonderful letter first. I made a mistake because of my dealings with them. I became a little conceited. I'm ridiculous, I know. I assumed they would show an interest. Why did I think that? Because it's me, Naukaram, the man who has experienced so much, who has learnt so much, who has changed so much. And yet what do the Feringhi who don't know me see? Not me – they don't see anything. Of course they don't. Burton Sahib wouldn't have turned me away. My story would have aroused his curiosity. He would have at least taken a few minutes of his time to read it. I am in despair.'

  'Stop it, Bhai Sahib, stop it. One of these Feringhi just has to have a look at the letter, then his appetite will be whetted.'

  'Oh, one of them just has to pick up all the pages, is that right? Is that what you're saying? He just has to start reading. Then what? He threw it in my face! What was I thinking, he shouted, blowing up my time in service to an officer into a big fairy tale?'

'That didn't happen.'

'It did. The pages are all dirty now. They probably don't even clean properly in that house. He needed me more than anybody. It was the bungalow next door. Ours is empty now; the garden is overgrown. There's a rumour it's haunted by the ghost of a woman. We've come up with a big fairy tale, you and I. Who's going to feed it now? That was the only Feringhi I got to see. Otherwise they just sent word they didn't need me. Has this town become so full of good servants since I went away? You know those conceited Goans, those creatures who dress like Feringhi and wear a cross round their necks that gets in their way when they run? One of them kept me waiting in the sun. Apparently his master didn't feel like reading anything. It was too hot. And where would he be if he read everything every stray passer-by gave him. I couldn't believe the Feringhi had said all that. How often, I asked him, do you get someone standing with a letter in their hand at this door? The Goan got a thrill out of provoking me. Why didn't I make myself useful in the kitchen for a day, he suggested, then the housekeeper could see if I was any good. It was humiliating.'

'Don't lose heart.'

'It's all very well for you to talk. I know how easy it is to bear the cares of another man. I even went and saw the teacher, Sri Upanishe. I hoped he would remember me, though almost five years had passed. His son opened the door – a tall man. The teacher was so small. He was in mourning. His mother had died and he said his father had gone to an ashram. Somewhere on the Ganges. The son was friendly, like his mother; he offered to help. But I left quickly. How could he help? Help from people who can't help only makes the humiliation more painful. The barber down below, by the entrance, was still the same. He didn't recognise me. And what if he had? What was he supposed to prove?'

'These are hard times, there's no doubt about that. I do feel awkward bringing up this subject at this precise moment but we have slightly lost sight of my fee. It has built up a little; the balance due is not inconsiderable. Ten rupees. I added it up yesterday evening. If I may, I have a suggestion, which will suit both of us, I think. We should agree on a sum that will cover the rest of the work, however long it takes.'

'I'm sure you have also given some thought to the nature of this sum.'

'I suggest you pay another sixteen rupees. And then we won't talk about money ever again.'

38
HE WHO ACCEPTS THE SACRIFICIAL FIRES

She never told him anything about herself. He tried to make her open up in bed, but it was a mistake. She began arousing him as a way of keeping her distance. When she withdrew her lips, he couldn't tear his gaze from her mouth; he stared up at its promise as she pressed her hips down into him, the glisten-ing expression of her muteness. She flung herself into her desire – that was her recourse, it seemed to him, when the grief in her threatened to paralyse everything else – her pigtail came loose, she began breathing heavily, her necklace broke, the pearls rolled down her breasts onto him. He looked everywhere, at everything, his eyes racing over their reciprocal desire. Her breathing became heavier as he revealed where he was hasten-ing, and heavier – he was only a few sensations away – and then she stopped. Her body became quiet, and straddling his still thrusting astonishment, she rested her hands on his chest and began to talk. She spoke in measured sentences, in an inti-mate voice that expressed itself calmly and yet demanded his full attention. He had to stop moving to hear her story: the story of a wise man, a brahmin by the name of Auddalaka who had been initiated into every form of Vedic ritual as a young man, including the offering of the union between a man and a woman as a sacrifice. 'One day this Auddalaka, who could lecture so knowledgeably on the symbolic force of the female vulva, conceived of a desire for a student called Vijayaa and contrived it so that they were joined in the ritual. But this wasn't enough; he craved a union with her outside the ritual as well, and so they came together spontaneously, these two young people, and the pleasure and joy they gave each other surpassed everything else, and took on a far greater significance than the ritual by which humans maintain their access to the gods.'

Kundalini fell silent.

'And then?' asked Burton. 'You've always finished your stories up until now.'

She said nothing, her silence sinking teeth into him. He dropped his eyes to the fine line of hair that extended like a column of tiny ants from her pubic bone over her belly to her navel, and then up to the little hollow between her breasts. He ran his fingers over these downy hairs, her proud romavali that, so she claimed, magically joined heaven and earth – to her mind, the surest mark of her beauty. He didn't agree, but she would have killed herself rather than pluck them out. His hand followed this connection between her heart and her sex. When they looked at each other again, he thought he saw affection flare up in a deep pool of her eyes. He smiled at her, and she, probably inferring from his smile that her eyes had promised too much, began moving again, her hips forcing him into the realm over which she held sway, and she was more ardent than ever, ardent to scratch and bite, as if she wanted to hang on to the taste of his body when he left tomorrow, as if she could permanently adorn his skin. Eventually they fell wearily back, the struggle relinquished. That was the most beautiful time, the minutes when he wasn't encumbered by a single thought; the most beautiful moments are those that pass unapprehended, he reflected. And they were over already. He sat up and sucked her lips as if seeking some anaesthetising nectar. She grasped his left hand and began playing with his fingers, linking them in hers, pulling the tips until they cracked, and humming a melody, she drifted into a song whose meaning only gradually unfolded:

'On a summer's day
In a shady place
Down she lay, oh, there she lay.
Her sari high, in disarray
"To shield my face,"
I heard her say, oh, heard her say,
"From the moon's embrace."'

39
NAUKARAM

II Om Yagnakaayaaya namah I Sarvavighnopashantaye namah I Om Ganeshaya namah II

On the second day the lahiya began to worry. It wasn't as if Naukaram had never missed an appointment – he had been sick once, and another time he had been brooding over some supposed slight – but the lahiya had always known he wasn't coming. This time there was no reason for him not to appear. Recently he had seemed more despondent than usual, it was true: limp, almost without a will of his own. But that was the problem with these lower castes: they gave up without a fight at the first sign of resistance. Oh damn this sitting by the road all day, waiting, surrounded by these jackals who never missed a chance to mock him. They couldn't abide the fact that he had a customer coming to see him every day for weeks on end at a time of year when normally a job a week was considered a godsend. He had one overriding fear: what if Naukaram disappeared? What if his narrative were to end here, just like that? The whole story would be garbled. That was unthinkable, they were so near the end; it would be horrific to break off now. He was surprised by the intensity of his fear, which brought him to his feet. That afternoon, he decided, he would go and look for Naukaram.

It was no easy task. He had no idea where he lived, just that he was staying with relatives near the Sarkarvada Palace. 'Do you know a tall, stooped man who used to work as a servant for a Feringhi?' he asked in all the local shops, but no one did. When he finally found him, it was pure chance. He had stopped off in a maikhanna because he was excruciatingly thirsty and his feet hurt, but before he could order something, he saw a familiar figure: Naukaram, sitting by himself at a table, barely conscious.

'I thought you didn't drink daaru.'

'Extraordinary times call for extraordinary drinks.'

'What's happened?'

'Nothing. I've come to the end, that's all.'

'Why have you come to the end?'

'None of your business. Our collaboration is – how should I put it – terminated.'

'Don't you want to continue?'

'I can't continue. I am a worthless man. I haven't a single rupee to my name. Only debts.'

'Who with?'

'I've gone from brother to brother, from mama to kaka. No one will lend me anything any more, and the ones who might want the money they have already lent me back first. I owe money to almost every person there is in this town, do you understand? Because this letter – or whatever the hell it is, it's not a bloody letter – is taking so long.'

'You can't give up now.'

'Listen, you made me drag out my story for as long as possible so that you could fleece me. You've robbed me blind. I've had to borrow money. I pawned everything I brought back from Europe. I have gone begging to all my relatives to scrape together your fee. You've led me a mighty dance. I am in debt all over town and what have I got for it? Nothing, nothing I can put my hands on. Just reams of boring scribbles that no one wants to read.'

'You can't give up now. Listen to me: when you've gone this

far, you have to see it through. You remind me of a man some years ago who was caught stealing. The judge let him choose his own punishment – either to eat a kilo of salt, to have a hundred strokes of the cane, or to pay a fine.'

'Who's Mr Chatterbox now?'

'The thief chose the salt. He ate and ate, struggling his way through, and just when he'd almost eaten it all, he got it into his head that he couldn't eat another pinch. So he called out, "Enough, enough of the salt. I want the cane instead." So he was given ninety, or even ninety-five strokes, and then suddenly he got it into his head that he couldn't take a single stroke more, and so he called out, "Enough, enough of the cane, please let me pay the fine."'

'Oh clever lahiya. And stupid servant, who doesn't understand a thing. You can read and write, can't you. You're a brahmin.'

'If you don't have any money, that doesn't matter. I'll give you time to pay.'

'So generous all of a sudden. *But I'm afraid two rupees won't be enough* – do you remember that? *At least another eight rupees.*'

'Let's not rehash old stories. It's my profession.'

'And an honourable profession, if ever there was one. The honourable lahiya. So many needy souls he can take advantage of. It makes me want to scream.'

'Please, I beg you. It will be good for you to get the story, the whole story, off your chest. Let's forget about the money.'

'Are you giving me a complete refund?'

'I've really become attached to your story, as I've told you already. I'll supply the paper and ink; you just have to summon up a few more days' patience. And at the end of it I will give you a letter the likes of which a servant has never before held in his hands.'

'That's not enough. It's not good enough. You've got to offer me something better.'

'All right, listen. Here's my very last offer.'

'I'm on tenterhooks.'

The day she fell ill, Kundalini asked Burton to marry her. Ascribing her pale, gaunt face to nervousness, he had been taken completely by surprise, and when he recalled his pitiful reaction afterwards, he felt himself unworthy, unworthy ever to have deserved her. He tangled himself up in a mass of excuses, until she cut him short with a bitter laugh.

'Don't worry, master, we're not going to walk four times round the fire or go up to the altar. All I want is a Gandharvavivaaha, a simple ceremony for which you only need consent and a pair of garlands. It's just to say we are going to stay together for as long as we want to stay together. A ceremony for when things are obvious already. We don't even need anyone else's help; the gandharva, the celestial singers, will be our witnesses.'

'What is this nonsense?' he asked. 'What good is such an arrangement to you?'

'It is important to me,' she pleaded. 'I'm not allowed to marry a mortal.'

'Why not?'

'I can't tell you, it's religious, to do with being the devotee of a temple.'

He shook his head uncomprehendingly.

'It's as if I'm already married to a divinity, that's all I can tell you,' she pleaded dull-eyed.

'And yet you're still allowed to enter into this second marriage?'

'It would set me free. You can't understand it now, but if you trust me, you will.'

He should have reassured her, agreed immediately, cheered her dull, beseeching eyes with a 'Yes', but he was too obsessed with breaking down the stiffness in their relationship, too busy trying to make the most of the situation to see it for what it was. Afterwards he was consumed with remorse and doubt, wondering if she had known how ill she was, if he had made her illness worse by telling her he'd let her know his answer when it was already obvious. Would he have saved her life if they had got married there and then, with the celestial singers as witnesses? It was a mark of his confusion that he even thought such a thing possible.

41

NAUKARAM

II Om Amitaya namah I Sarvavighnopashantaye namah I Om Ganeshaya namah II

'I was the one who found her. That wasn't fair. I had to fold her hands on her chest. When I sent someone to fetch Burton Sahib, I had already cleared away the worst signs. He wanted to call the old doctor immediately. I don't know how often I had to repeat, "She's dead," until he understood. He sat down on the edge of her bed and didn't get up for hours. I had to take care of all the practicalities. Who would have taken care of them otherwise? It hadn't crossed our mind that might be a difficult task, but that's what it proved to be. They refused to cremate her.'

'Who?'

'The priests. Burton Sahib was stunned. He was so furious I thought he'd make them cremate her at gunpoint. I tried not to let him know the reason. I gave him evasive answers, but he kept backing me into a corner until finally I had to tell him it was a question of purity. Was she considered unclean because of her relationship with him? "Yes," I said, "that's a reason."'

'Did you think of a solution?'

'I met a man near the cremation ground. One of the outcasts who hang around there. Half his face was eaten away, and half his tongue too. You couldn't look at him. When he talked, it felt as if his voice was skinning you alive. "Lost your way, boy?" I wanted to hurry away but I stayed . . . don't ask me why. I even told him our trouble. "We'll help you," he said. "Bring the body here tonight, when everyone's asleep, and we'll do what has to be done. We've got a pujari, if such a thing's important to you. Even his spit is holier than those hypocrites who turned you away. The minute it gets dark, they creep off and feast on the day's pickings." I've never accepted help so reluctantly, but we had no other choice. It was a good offer, even though it was made in such an ominous voice. It took me a long time to convince Burton Sahib, for him to understand that there was no alternative. All his influence and power were useless. I wanted to see if any of the servants would volunteer to help us carry her body to the river, but he stopped me. "We'll do it," he said. "Just the two of us. It's our duty." We wrapped her in sheets, and then waited until everyone had gone to sleep. I opened the door of the bubukhanna and the gate onto the street, then we took hold of her, I had her legs, Burton Sahib her head, and we set off . . .'

The lahiya wrote everything down, covering page after page with Naukaram's account, and as he did so, his thoughts constantly darted between the lines, cutting loose from all this weight of turgid description. Storm and death and midnight and cremation ground – what a stage! And this dullard sounded as if he were checking items on an inventory. Where were the naked, shameless watchmen mounting guard over brimming pots of jewels, treasure buried by gnarled misers whose greed had made them impervious to fear? Where was the yogi playing upon a human skull with two shank bones, making music for the horrid revelry? By the end of the session, the lahiya was barely listening; he couldn't wait to say his goodbyes. He hurried home, brushed aside his wife's greeting, and immediately shut himself away in the back room, worried lest even one of his innumerable ideas should evaporate before he wrote it down. He hurriedly sketched the first image that had come to mind: bistre-coloured clouds, like the forms of unwieldy beasts, roll heavily over the firmament plain. In front of these, centre stage, we see two men, a master and his servant, both strangers to this place and this night, joined in more ways than they either know or care to admit. They are laboriously dragging a corpse: the dead lover, the lover they shared. The crescent of the moon is no brighter than an elephant's tusk protruding from a mudhole. The master stops and heaves the corpse onto his shoulder; it is a strong man that can carry the burden of lost love itself through a storm. The other figure, the servant, searches for the path, groping his way forward as if expecting to stumble at any moment. It starts to rain. The path glimmers a ghastly white. A distant ray of light breaks through the shadows, like the line of pure gold streaking the dark surface of the touchstone. Both men follow it, because it's the only light there is, and also because the servant suspects that those are the fires of the burning ground reaching out so questioningly into the darkness. They come to the smashaana, an expanse of open ground near the river, which people avoid even in daylight. At first glance, both men think it deserted, and the servant wonders whether he's been the victim of a spiteful joke. But there's no doubting the stench of death rising from the earth. He hesitates: how will he be able to rid himself of the pollution he will incur by treading such impure ground? Shielded by his ignorance, his master forges ahead, his back bent under the corpse's weight; he tramples on bones with a noise like an ogre grinding his teeth. The servant covers his mouth with his turban end and follows. Spectral, murky red fires loom up ahead, feasting on the pathetic human remains like jackals, gnawing them down to the white bones. Subtle bodies hover over the flames, watching to see if the corpses they have escaped have been reduced to ashes, while they wait for the new bodies they are supposed to animate to be ready to receive them. There are other spirits too, who count the smashaana as home. The ghosts of those who have been foully slain wander around with gashed limbs, followed by the skeletons of their murderers, whose mouldy bodies are held together by a few last bits of blackened sinew. The wind moans fitfully while the swollen river gurgles with the blood of these ephemeral creatures. The two men, who have already exhausted the courage of several lifetimes, realise they are not the only flesh and blood in the vicinity. At the other end of the cremation ground, a group of wretches shelters under a tarpaulin that affords them little comfort against the wind and rain. In the middle of the group sits the man with half a face, a staff firmly planted in the ground next to him. He is dressed in an ochre-coloured dhoti, his bare torso covered by long, matted, lice-ridden hanks of horse hair. His body is striped with lines of white chalk, and a girdle of thighbones encircles his hips. He sits unmoving, his eyes as fixed as a statue's.

'You're here,' he says, finally getting to his feet. It's not a welcome. 'And you want to get rid of that.'

'Don't talk about her in that manner,' the master interrupts, and the servant wonders whether he has taken leave of his senses.

'We have collected the wood. We're fond of flowers of the night, so we will add sandalwood to the pyre of someone we didn't know but consider one of us. Her farewell will be more fragrant than that of any Nagar Brahmin.' The master puts the body on the ground. 'That is all that's required of you. Except that you go. There's nothing you can do here, other than be witnesses to your own nightmare.'

42
WITHOUT OBSTACLES

'I was amazed to read the results of our missionary work in last week's *Bombay Times*.'

'Given the circumstances, Lieutenant Awdry, we're not doing too badly.'

'Not too badly. Ah. Well. Could it be any worse?'

'We shouldn't be impatient.'

'*Bien sûr*. Patience is the British subject's highest duty.'

'You don't seriously mean to doubt we're making headway? Of a slow, measured sort, I'll readily admit.'

'Reverend Posthumus, the results obtained seem to me utterly disproportionate to the methods employed. The Hindus would have made double the number of converts with half as much money and in half as much time.'

'Honestly, Mr Burton, that's the limit!'

'Don't talk nonsense, Dick. You know perfectly well the Hindus don't convert.'

A big dinner in the mess, presided over by two chairmen at either end of a long table, two old boys whose brains had been melted by the heat and could only retain what had been most intensively drummed into them, the arcana of drill. Normally they forbade any contamination of dinner by serious conversation, but on this occasion they found themselves unable to impose this stricture, since one of them had caught a heavy chill at the start of the rains and was monopolised by his sniffling, while the other could only hear if you yelled in his ear. He smiled vaguely at the animated conversation between Richard Burton, Lieutenant Ambrose Awdry and Reverend Walter Posthumus, and then popped another piece of boiled turkey in his mouth.

'Wise people, wiser than we are. Voluntary conversion? That's a *contradictio in adjecto*. Why were the Portuguese successful in Goa? Because the Catholic Church was better at convincing heathens than the Anglican? Not at all. There's only one explanation: force. Unwavering use of force. Vasco da Gama took eight Franciscan monks and eight curates with him, supposedly to preach, but the cardinals suspected sermons would bear little fruit. Experience breeds cunning, so they had decreed that conversion should be left to the sword. Even before landing in Calcutta, the good da Gama, who was renowned in his country for his conquests of land and souls, set fire to a ship full of Muslim pilgrims. Once ashore, he didn't dither: he had all the unruly fishermen executed. Within the twinkling of an eye, the Indians were adopting Portuguese dress, assuming Portuguese names, outdrinking the Portuguese and attending Mass more often than them too.'

'We, on the other hand, put our faith in the Word, the divine message.'

'You know better than I what you're doing, obviously, gentlemen, but perhaps you can enlighten me on something. I've heard the Portuguese missionaries disguised themselves as natives. Apparently they travelled the land dressed as unkempt hermits. Some say they even preached a mishmash of the Gospel and native legends.'

'The Masala Gospel.'

'And in their processions they are meant to have put a number of Hindu gods on the litters next to the saints. An extremely mysterious business . . .'

'Blasphemous, rather!'

'Not without art, nor success, I imagine.'

Passably interesting, this conversation. He's grateful for any flowering of conversational life. The agonies he had suffered at his last dinner in the mess when some fellow or other was being decorated and the brigadier had delivered the encomium in the stifling heat, running through every detail of a career as exciting as the flies crawling on the table. Occasionally one of the kedmutgars sporting a turban like a big trophy would step forward to shoo them away, and his cloth would whir past the sunken head of a guest who'd fallen asleep. When the brigadier had ploughed his way through to the end of his rigidly formulaic *laudatio* and called out 'Hip-hip' for the hero of the evening, his exhortation fell on slack ears. It wasn't just the usual culprits taking a nap; every single person at the table had dozed off. The brigadier stood there, his face bright red, until Burton leapt to his rescue, an almost empty glass of Madeira in his hand, and yelled 'Hooray!' at the top of his voice. All the heads jerked awake, facial muscles flapping like birds who've had a stone thrown in their nest, and Burton grinned encouragingly at the brigadier to proceed to the second 'Hip-hip'. When this failed to materialise, he launched into 'For He's a

Jolly Good Fellow'. The others looked for a moment to join in, scratching and coughing, as the brigadier stood at the end of the table like a commander in chief of a hopelessly routed army. Voices clashed raggedly, until finally – 'Whichhhh . . . nobody can deny' – the last line sprayed in all directions like a cork shooting out of the whole pent-up evening.

'What does success count if one sacrifices the pillars of one's belief?'

'You would rather the heathens laughed at you because the founder of our faith was the son of a badhahi?'

'Does Joseph's profession matter?'

'If we made him a warrior or gave him some other trade – it doesn't matter which, just not one that belongs to the lowest caste – it would definitely make preaching easier.'

'Thank you for your concern, Burton. Once we're at it, we could rewrite the entire Gospels.'

'Not a bad idea. Let's say Jesus was the son of a prince in Mathura, and the evil maharajah had all the children of the area killed, because a prophecy had foretold calamity at the hands of a saviour born at midnight . . .'

'You're taking it too far.'

'Gently does it, dear fellow.'

'The feeding of the five thousand's undoubtedly an impressive achievement. But we'd make a considerably greater impression if our Jesus of Mathura could vanquish some monster or other. Strangle an evil snake. That should be possible.'

There was always too much mutton eaten at these dinners. Beef was out of the question, for a simple reason: its consumption was a higher form of cannibalism. Roast pork was equally inconceivable: they'd all seen the pigs in the bazaar – wallowing in filth was not the word for it – and, in any case, all the apprentice chefs were Muslim. Occasionally a ham would turn up, like a beautiful, wildly desired cousin who has left the straight and narrow and thus has to be cloaked in exaggerated respectability – hence its name, Wilayati Bakri, European Lamb, or in other words, Innocent Lamb. Of course, many Hindus didn't touch meat at all, a curious habit for which the brigadier had a straightforward explanation at the ready which he trotted out for the honour, and edification, of every new guest: 'The Hindus believe in reincarnation, no? And they believe that anyone who hasn't lived properly will be reborn as an animal. With me so far? So, they're afraid that if they eat meat, they'll be polishing off their own grandmother, don't you know.'

'Why don't we use other methods?'

'Than the Gospel, Ambrose?'

'No, than preaching and force. We could increase the number of Christians by distributing free food. We could kill two birds with one stone by our generosity: give people a healthy diet and increase the number of Christians. What do you think, what would be a successful correlation coefficient between sacks of rice and baptisms?'

'It could work, but think of the distribution network you'd need to keep all the new Christians. Honestly! Why are you all so keen on making bad Christians out of good heathens? Do you think we only have to dress Hindus up as Europeans or Christians and coach them a little for their thoughts and feelings to become European and Christian? Nonsense! What about the sepoys? Don't they feel damned uncomfortable in the thick cloth we force them to wear?'

'The minute we go our separate ways, those lads take off their uniforms and put on a thin kurta.'

'What do we know about them? We'd have no right to be amazed if they turn their weapons against us one of these days. We wouldn't be entitled to be bewildered just because we delude ourselves we have treated them well and thereby earned their loyalty. How often do you see your flock, Reverend? Have you ever wondered how they spend the rest of their time? How they behave, what they say about us, what schemes they are hatching?'

'I fear I've heard enough of this drunken conversation. I will take my leave now.'

'Listen to me, Reverend. Our power rests solely on the fact

that the natives entertain a high opinion of us and a low opinion of themselves. The moment they get to know us better, which would happen if they convert in numbers, they will lose all respect. They will outgrow their feelings of inferiority. They will rebel. They will believe themselves capable of victory, rather than assuming they are vanquished for all time, as is now the case. Within a generation we could be on the verge of catastrophe. We agree about one thing: if the people of India could unite for a single day and speak with a unanimous voice, then they would sweep us from their country.'

'As long as they dread us, there are no grounds for concern?'

'Fear leads to mistrust, mistrust to deceit. The weakling and the coward know exactly why they don't trust their neighbours.'

'Absolute rubbish! Really, I am surprised. Even if you were right from a political and military point of view, we couldn't abandon the heathen to eternal damnation. Are we to withhold our civilisation from them for such opportunistic reasons? No – missionary work will continue, you'll see, and even if it takes a century, British India will become Christian, and only then will this land truly blossom. Now please excuse me, gentlemen, you have given me an excellent idea for this Sunday's sermon.'

43
NAUKARAM

II Om Avighnaya namah I Sarvavighnopashantaye namah I Om Ganeshaya namah II

'He didn't know she'd been a devadasi before?'

'No.'

'He must have suspected something?'

'No. Definitely not.'

'So nothing overshadowed his feelings?'

'I didn't realise until too late. I underestimated how much she meant to him. It only dawned on me when she was dead.'

'Did he mourn for her?'

'In his own lopsided way. He didn't do anything like other people. My first duty after the night of her cremation was to find him some monkeys. It didn't matter what kind – far from it, the more kinds and ages they were, the better. And they had to be both sexes. I thought he was going mad. I managed to get hold of a dozen monkeys, and, with a few of the other servants, we took them back to the bungalow on a cart. They barked and mowed and gibbered the whole way; all the gardeners from the other bungalows came out to stare at us. Burton Sahib's next order was proof positive that he had lost his mind. He told us to put the monkeys in the bubukhanna. Then he informed me he was expecting visitors that evening: I was to lay for six and have the same number of servants waiting at table. I was stupid, I didn't think of adding six and six. How could I have guessed what was going to happen? None of us had bargained on that.'

'The uncommon is only ever explained after the event.'

'At dinner he ordered us to bring the monkeys into the house. He stood at the head of the table and greeted them warmly, like old friends. He had never given any of the other officers such a welcome. He showed them to the chairs around the large dining table and announced that they would be dining together. Then he introduced them to us in English; the other servants didn't understand a word – anyway, they had their hands full catching the monkeys and putting them back in their chairs. The large baboon was Dr Casamaijor, the smaller baboon Secretary Routledge, both accompanied by their wives; a third monkey was introduced as Adjutant McCurdy and the ugliest monkey of all was Reverend Posthumus. I gave a laugh, as if I was scraping laughter out of a burnt pot, and the other servants joined in, but really I wanted to look away. I thought that if I appreciated the joke then all this nonsense would be over sooner. But he shouted at us, would we kindly serve our guests, he would not tolerate any insubordination. He threatened to throw us out on our ears if we didn't treat his guests respectfully and I realised from his voice how serious he was. I gestured to the servants to start serving dinner. Of course, the monkeys didn't stay on the chairs; there was always one that had to be picked up and taken back to his seat, but Burton Sahib acted as if he didn't notice anything. He was the perfect host, talking away, discussing the latest court intrigues; you could hardly believe your eyes and ears. He railed against the Nagar Brahmin clique, which at the time contained all the maharajah's advisers, or all his ministers at least. He described the Angrezi's attempts to undermine their supremacy at court. He asked his guests their opinion, and when one of the monkeys grunted or barked, he called out in raptures, "Hark, ladies and gentlemen, did you hear that – what an enchanting reply!" The monkeys threw the cutlery around, spilled their wine, paddled their paws in the soup, tried a few peas, and then took potshots at each other with the rest. Only when the roast arrived did they quieten down a little. "You enjoy it," Burton Sahib cried. "Hallelujah, may you enjoy it now and for ever!" We had to carry him to bed, he was so drunk at the end of the evening. We felt ashamed for him but we were glad to have survived that madness. We didn't know that it would be repeated every evening. And every evening Burton Sahib got drunk; he wouldn't have found his bed on his own. The sights I had to witness in those days were so hideous, I could hardly bear to look.'

'Worse than hideous, against nature.'

'And it got even worse. One of the beasts was a female monkey. He said he had stolen her away from Secretary Routledge. Now she was his sweetheart. He made her up, put earrings on her and a necklace round her wrinkled throat. She was so small that when she sat down, she disappeared under the edge of the table. He borrowed a children's chair from one of the other officers, and she was allowed to sit on that at meals. He started calling her "sweetheart", wooing her. He enlisted the kedmutgar in the charade. He kept asking him over and over: "Isn't she charming? Isn't she bewitching? Oughtn't I to ask her if she's got a sister for you?" It was so degrading the kedmutgar ran out of the room, even though he didn't have any other work to do.'

'What about during the day? What did he do with the monkeys in the day?'

'He claimed to be learning their language. He began to write down the sounds. One day he asked me what I thought. Whether Devanagari script or Gujarati or even Roman script was best suited to reproduce the monkeys' language.'

'I'm sure he didn't ask Upanishe Sahib that.'

'No, you're right. How did you work that out?'

'He wasn't that mad. He had a sense of proportion for irreverence. He lacked any self-control with you, but not with Guru-ji. What did you tell him?'

'I didn't say anything. I was silent all those days. "It seems to me", he said, "the Chinese characters would be highly suitable but what am I to do, I can't now learn Mandarin on top of everything else just because of some monkeys." He produced a little dictionary of their sounds and claimed he had collected sixty different expressions. He was proud of that. He claimed he would soon be able to talk to them.'

44
ACCEPTER OF ALL PENANCES

'Ah, Naukaram, we have distinguished guests. Why aren't you joining us?'

'I'm sorry, Burton Sahib, I can't sit at table with monkeys.'

'What the hell is wrong with you and your sense of hospitality, Naukaram? You really are no support to me. It's just not good enough today.'

'Let me go, Sahib.'

'Come here!'

'I'm in mourning too, Sahib.'

'Who for, Naukaram? We're all in the shit, as we have just established, we've all made a terrible mess of it, eh, Naukaram, but we are as chirpy as crickets, are we not?'

'For her.'

'For her? And who may this her, this mysterious female, be?'

'For Kundalini, Sahib.'

'What's that you're whispering, my dear man? I almost thought I heard Kundalini. That cannot be. You? Why you? For you she was only – what's an elegant way to phrase it in the presence of these ladies, let me think . . . a whore! How's that: a whore you could palm off on me.'

'I brought her into the house because she made an impression on me.'

'She made an impression on him. How touched we are.'

'I liked her.'

'As a woman, Naukaram? As a woman?'

'Yes, I did. And this liking grew stronger. When she was there, I felt happy, and when she went away, I was sad and looked forward to her coming back. You know what she was like.'

'I do, I do know what she was like, I know it better than you. You only looked at her, you heard her voice, and look what an effect she had on you. Esteemed guests, I give you: a man in love.'

'What did you know about Kundalini, Sahib?'

'Knowing everything is not an end in itself. But since you ask, I knew enough about her.'

'Did you know where she went when she left us?'

'On feast days, you mean? To her family, of course.'

'She had no family. Her mother gave her up to a temple as a girl and never saw her again.'

'You're wrong. You must have misunderstood. She would have told me.'

'Would she? Why? Why should she have told you? She was afraid you would misunderstand everything. She was afraid of you.'

'You're lying. Misunderstand? What would I have misunderstood? She would have had my sympathy.'

'Perhaps. Perhaps your scorn too. Who can predict such things before they happen?'

'Who was she then?'

'It's better I don't tell you.'

'Naukaram! I'll throw you out of the house this evening, I swear, in front of all these monkeys here. Where did she go?'

'She visited the temple she grew up in.'

'She grew up in a temple?'

'Yes, before she came to Baroda.'

'Did she live in the temple?'

'In a little room behind the temple.'

'And what did she do there?'

'Served God, Sahib. She was a servant of God.'

'And what is there to despise about that?'

'I cannot say any more.'

'On the contrary. You will tell me everything. Don't worry, I've almost completely sobered up.'

'I'm more afraid of you when you're sober.'

'What happened in the temple?'

'She didn't just serve God. She also served the priest.'

'Doing what? Cooking, cleaning?'

'No, served him in other ways.'

'You mean, as a wife? Do you mean as a nautch girl?'

'Something like that.'

'I'm supposed to believe that, am I?'

'It's the truth, Sahib.'

'How long for?'

'I don't know.'

'When she went back, did she and the priest . . .?'

'No, I don't think so. Definitely not. She ran away from him; he treated her badly. That's why she came to Baroda.'

'You kept all this from me?'

'She had to go back. It was the only place she felt safe, despite the priest. She missed the temple's halls; she missed sitting at the god's feet, fanning Him. It was strange. She only felt safe there, even though he had treated her so badly.'

'You never told me anything about this. I've a mind to give you a whipping.'

'How was I supposed to guess you didn't know about it, Sahib? You were much more intimate with her than I was. I only knew her from the hours we spent together in the kitchen. Sometimes we ate together. Sometimes we sat on the veranda when you were away. You know how rare that was. How could I have had the nerve to talk to you about secrets that you were closer to than I could ever be?'

45
NAUKARAM

II Om Devavrataya namah I Sarvavighnopashantaye namah I Om Ganeshaya namah II

'You have gone too far! It is unforgivable what you've done. How could you give away my secrets? They were only meant for your ears. Are lahiyas allowed to repeat everything they're told? Are they allowed to pay at market in the coin of other people's confidences? I was wrong about you; you are not an honourable man. And, as if that wasn't bad enough, you've also been telling lies . . . lies that will ruin me in this town.'

'What? What? I don't tell lies.'

'I can't believe that.'

'Someone has been slandering me.'

'You're lying again. I heard it with my own ears. The singer started with a bhajan. But then he moved on to his own songs that were anything but sacred; vulgar stuff, meant to make the audience laugh. He made fun of the Angrezi and the sardar-ji; he made fun of a lecherous old man who was so inflamed with love for a washerwoman that he gave her his clothes to wash every day. Silly rubbish. Then he started making fun of a servant who was his master's slave and in love with his master's bubu, a devadasi who took advantage of both men. I froze. At first I thought it was just a coincidence, until I realised that couldn't possibly be true any more. I expected the spectators to

146

turn around at any moment and stare at me. I felt awful. It was agony. But it was nowhere near as embarrassing and painful as what came next. The bubu – ah, the singer was so cheerful; he had such a loathsome, conceited voice – had had a child when the master was away for a few months. She killed the baby when it was born and the servant helped her bury it in the woods.'

'I never told him anything like that.'

'So you admit that it all came from you.'

'He is a friend; I asked his advice. I wasn't sure how to go on with your story. It is not as easy as you think. Sometimes I feel overwhelmed. But I never said anything about a dead child . . . No, wait, wait, now I think of it, the dead monkey, you know, that Burton Sahib buried in the garden himself . . . you told me that. Perhaps I talked about the monkey being buried; you have to admit, it was the insane climax to a great madness, and as a likeness, you understand, I said that he buried it as if it was his own child. Just a harmless likeness.'

'What about the other harmless likenesses? Who came up with those? Who's responsible for them?'

'Which ones?'

'The verses of that jackal you call your friend. The song ended – I've never been so ashamed in my life – it ended with the servant poisoning the bubu. Because she didn't return his love, and he was consumed with jealousy. He took her life because he couldn't bear to see her in the arms of his master.'

'No, I would never say something like that. I wouldn't even think it. You are getting things mixed up. This story my friend told wasn't your story at all. He might have been inspired by what I told him; I can't deny that. He was definitely stirred up, but he made his own story out of it.'

'At my expense.'

'What harm does a manbhatt's prattle do you?'

'Who can tell the two stories apart? Everyone who knows a little about me will mix their knowledge with the poison of slander.'

When Burton first heard of him, the man was already buried under his name, the name that encapsulated all the insults they heaped on him in that town. He was called the bastard of Baroda. It was the only name he was known by and it was hard to imagine he had ever had another. He was an outcast, with whom no one who thought himself of any consequence would have had any contact if his presence were not occasionally required in court to fill in for the official translators. This was a task the bastard carried off with aplomb. He appeared to have a calming effect on the defendants, unwilling participants in the whole performance, and could at the same time realise the judge's wishes with astonishing dexterity. Local dialects poured from him, while his grammatically correct English sounded as if it had been kept in quarantine for too long. For, except on these occasions, the bastard of Baroda had no dealings with the British. Court was the only place he used the English he had been taught by his Irish father, an army deserter who had fathered him to a local woman somewhere over the northwestern border. The contempt with which his father was once regarded had devolved upon him, with one, not inconsiderable difference. Whereas his father had evaded the universal condemnation and led, all things considered, a happy life, his son was its helpless victim. Burton met the bastard of Baroda by chance in the street. He recognised him by his clothes, a wild jumble people had told him about. No one else would have worn a tattered army jacket patched with rags of all colours over a long kurta of coarse material, topped off by a bowler hat full of holes. To keep his brain cool, so the joke went. Burton urged his horse into a slow trot, caught up with the figure and addressed him in Hindustani. The bastard replied in English without looking up. Burton persisted in Hindustani.

'Speak English to me,' the fellow said gruffly.

'Why?'

'Because I'm British. You?'

Burton was astonished by such impudence. Amazing who dares call himself British in this country. 'You are a bastard,' Burton said before spurring on his horse, not in an unfriendly way but one that precluded any contradiction. And like all bastards, he thought, you combine the worst of both worlds. That's the law of nature; the negative prevails.

The bastard seemed determined to confirm Burton's assessment through his behaviour. On the queen's birthday, he appeared outside the mess and demanded admittance. 'All her subjects have the right to celebrate the occasion with her,' he shouted. He might have considered himself lucky just to be grabbed by the collar and thrown onto the street, but the bastard didn't give up easily. A little later a loud expostulation was heard in the mess, then another voice seconding the noisy expressions of disbelief. 'Good God, that's incredible!' Everyone gathered around the scouts at the window and stared out at an absolutely diabolical show of insolence. The bastard was sitting by the side of the road, on the edge of the lawn. He had spread out a white tablecloth and was laying it with ceramic crockery decorated with an ivy-leaf pattern. God knew where he had picked it up. He poured himself a little tea from a pot with a swan's neck – they saw its dark colour, not light brown like the chai these fellows normally drank – picked up the cup between thumb and middle finger . . . 'my God, he's even cocking his little finger' . . . and, paying no attention to the guards who stood round shouting at him, took a first sip. The teacup was knocked out of his hand, the hot tea – innocently or intentionally – splashing a guard in the face. The cup fell to the ground without breaking, but was then crushed under the boots of the guards who threw themselves at the slight man. Burton had to rush out with a few fellow officers to prevent the bastard being pummelled to death. He lay among the shattered crockery, covered in blood. No one knew where he lived; carrying him into the mess was out of the question. Burton and the other officers who had rushed out stood around him for a while, then turned, one after the other, and returned to the day's festivities. But Burton kept squinting out of the window. He couldn't leave the man lying out there. Naukaram and some of the other servants were quickly sent for. They carried the bastard to Burton's bungalow and laid him on the bed in the bubukhanna; the monkeys' presence wouldn't disturb their unconscious roommate. The promise of a bottle of good port convinced old Huntington to see if any bones had been broken and put on a few bandages. The next morning the bastard had disappeared.

After that he didn't appear in court. He spent his days at busy crossroads, preaching a truth no one could understand. The locals left him in peace, calling him with suitable respect a qalandar, a fool kissed by God. Early one morning, on the busiest market day of the month, he climbed a tree by the road that led into town from the east and yelled at the top of his voice: '*Duniya chordo, Jesu Christo, pakro. Har har Mahadev.*' Renounce the world and turn to the Saviour. Long live the Almighty. Reports spoke disbelievingly of his lungs' stamina. He was still yelling his injunctions when the market traders returned to the surrounding villages in the afternoon. No one would dare anticipate the behaviour of a qalandar, so it was only the British who were surprised when the bastard of Baroda appeared one day in a suit with sleeves that swallowed his hands and trouser bottoms that dragged on the ground. The suit's pattern looked alarmingly like a Union Jack. Swathed in her majesty's flag, the bastard swaggered through Baroda for a day, loitering outside the mess for the first time since his beating on the queen's birthday. He was chased away, but not before calling out that no one could hit him: it would be an affront to the sanctity of the flag and the values that are flown with it. Astonishment turned to furious indignation when a report from Surat solved the puzzle. In the early hours a few nights before, the Union Jack had been stolen from the mast at the entrance to Surat's cantonment. It wasn't long before sepoys were sent out

– feelings didn't run high enough to drive officers out of the shade – and found the bastard. Not a minute too soon, since he was already tying a strip of the flag around the neck of a stray dog he regularly fed. The bastard was thrown in prison and there was no shortage of people who thought that was where he should stay until the face of the world had been relieved of his presence. Burton was the only one to stand up for him, to general amazement. The bastard should be released, he argued. It wasn't his fault he'd gone bad, it was the inheritance his parents had saddled him with, and instead of reviling the poor creature, they should all take this unsavoury affair as a warning – namely, that western blood shouldn't mix with eastern. 'It is an intermingling that leaves both parties in tatters, gentlemen, a truth to which our Union Jack has painfully had to attest.'

47

NAUKARAM

II Om Dvaimaturaya namah I Sarvavighnopashantaye namah I Om Ganeshaya namah II

He just had to cover up one last bare patch. Nothing worth speaking of, really. He was more or less there; the first part of his work as good as finished. Wasn't it time he allowed himself a little satisfaction? Hadn't he made Kundalini into a wonderful character? She shouldn't be afraid of comparisons with Sakuntala, nor he with . . . No. That was going too far. He felt dizzy. He wasn't used to such thoughts. They were so beguiling, these insights, so new. All right, what did he still have to get clear in his mind? Just the question of why Kundalini had been given to the temple. A vow must have been involved. When do people make such extreme promises? When they long for a child. Yes, that was it, the simplest, most elegant solution. Kundalini's mother was barren. She had clung doggedly to her prayers, swearing – not just once . . . no . . .

oaths like that are repeated a thousand times, as if the god is deaf or forgetful – that if she had children, she would give her first daughter to the god as His bride. The god who heard her prayers proved conditionally generous. He gave only as much as He would get back. He granted her an only child, a daughter, and this was the price she paid for the original gift. What a service for a god to do a mortal! What a notion! He felt even dizzier. He was exceedingly satisfied.

'Everyone's asking after you; where you are, are you all right. What am I supposed to tell them?'

'Didn't you understand what I said?'

'I can't face the neighbours any more.'

'Don't you ever stop talking?'

'You sit here the whole time with your papers and quills when we have a guest – why don't you ever come out?'

'Because I have better things to do.'

'A curse on your writing! You never have time for anything else now. You have traded your family for an alphabet. Is this it, the wonderful invention that makes men hermits, lonely when there are people all around?'

'You don't understand, you ass. I've always had to write what other people have dictated to me. They were always dry letters, dreary documents. Petitions, property transfers. I phrased them as skilfully as I could, sometimes I embroidered the letters a little, but I always remained the slave of other people's intentions. I was cleverer than these customers, and yet I had to copy down their nonsense. Now that's changing. It already has. Don't you realise how important that is?'

48
SON OF SHIVA

Upanishe waited until it was almost too late before he taught his shishya the most important thing he could teach a foreigner. He waited until the night of Shiva, until Burton's mind had been bent like a bow by sheer tiredness. He waited until worship of the god was almost complete. They had returned to the temple after carrying Shiva over three hills and begging for alms every time they set down the litter. The crowd had been at odds with itself in its feelings. The bearers resolutely clasped the poles of the litter, the youngsters transformed their devotion into a whirling dance, the alms-raiser used every means, even ribald jokes, to loosen the onlookers' purses, sweating like a master of ceremonies who enjoys his job although it overtaxes him; the rest of the believers rotated round the litter in a dense mass of ecstasy. Now Guru-ji was ready for sleep, in white vest and pyjamas.

'Have you ever heard of Adavaita, my shishya?'

The way he said it made Burton think of a mithaiwallah standing in front of him, offering him another sweet. But the tone was deceptive; he knew seriousness was poised on the tip of Guru-ji's tongue.

'Adavaita simply means "without second". Listen to me, my shishya, then tell me if you have heard anything more rigorous. According to Adavaita, nothing exists outside of a unique reality, the name of which is insignificant: God, the Infinite, the Absolute, Brahman, Atman, whatever we wish to call it. This reality has no single attribute by which it can be defined. To every attempt to describe it we must answer, no. We can say what it isn't, but not what it is. Everything that seems like existence, the world of our mind and senses, is nothing but a false conception of the absolute. The only thing that exists among the flood of the ego's delusions is the true self, the one. *Tat tvam asi*, Adavaita says. You are that! That is why, my shishya, and this is the last thing I will say before we go to sleep, any thought that sets at variance is an offence against the supreme order. That is why it is in itself a form of violence when we see one another as strangers, when we consider ourselves as different.'

Upanishe lay down to sleep. Cymbals clashed in the distance with a high ring; the bhajan would keep watch all night. Burton drowsed off and then woke without knowing why. He sat up and looked around. The bodies lay close together; the entire hall was covered with a light film of sleep. He was one of these bodies. An intake of the universe's breath. Virtually nothing. How much more comforting to believe he was everything and everything was in him. These people were always borne up by the multitude. They slept every night among a crowd of others, they were used to being one body among many lying on the uneven ground. He listened. The sound of a new bhajan rang out. Other voices joined in the singing, accompanied by cries of delight and hands out-thrust in the pause, the ninth beat of the tabla. A thin stream of water cooled the god, playing over Him so gently it could only be heard on the empty beat. For hours they had sat next to the stream. 'Repeat the name of God so you don't get cold in your head, my shishya,' Guru-ji had advised. But Burton didn't understand enough Sanskrit; the litanies tired him. Instead his attention focused on the surroundings. The god's favourite flower scattered on the floor. The calluses on the pujari's feet. A small hair on Guru-ji's skin that hadn't yet turned white. When the ceremony was over, six hours later, the priest distributed all the donations he'd received in the puja among the worshippers. The pragmatic in religion, more comprehensive than any other statute book. On the night of Shiva, last night, and the day before, he had felt such a sense of belonging; the idea of being part of this family, this place, this ritual for the rest of his life had captivated him. Now he was startled by such a desire. Bewitching at first, it became oppressive the moment he dwelled upon it. He stood up, walked round the temple and sat down among the waking worshippers. He joined in a bhajan, his voice the deepest under the temple's porch. At sunrise, as he washed himself in the river, he heard one of the young men ask a friend, 'Where is this Feringhi from? Who knows what he will say about us when he gets home.'

'What is his gotra?' the friend asked slyly.

When Burton got home and looked in the mirror, he didn't recognise himself. Not through any outward change, but because he felt transformed.

*II Om Ishanaputraya namah I Sarvavighnopashantaye namah
I Om Ganeshaya namah II*

'I have already spelled it out to you that they're all Miya in
Sind . . . well, most of them, anyway. Our shrines looked out
of place there because they were so few and far between. Being
the exception – this I have to tell you – is shaming. They look
so natural at home. They don't there. The only temples left
were in grottoes and caves; the garlands were all withered. The
goddess – she was called Singhuvani – looked like Durga, after
riding too far into the west on Her lion. I'm sure I'm not making much sense, but that's how it seemed to me. I wanted to
pack up those shrines and take them home. A crazy thought, I
know. Away from those Makli hills, riddled with all their
tombs. The circumcised claim a million saints are buried there.
They're exaggerating, of course. A million holy sulla? How
could that be possible?'

'As if we'd never exaggerate.'

'We exaggerate with gods; they do with people.'

'Is that so? Perhaps it's because Muslims don't have an entire
menagerie of divinities.'

'Whose side are you on exactly?'

'There are more than just two sides. We ought to find a way
out of this maze, you know. Anyway, what did you want to tell
me about these hills?'

'Signs of our Santana Dharma were visible everywhere. Even
after all these centuries of oppression. Standing stones,
between the tombs. When you got closer, you could clearly see
they were Shiva linga, smeared with vermilion, just like we do.
And water basins in the shape of yonis. Knowing the bones of
those circumcised were lying between Shiva linga and yonis
was some consolation; the thought of it filled me with glee.'

'If the Miya are as bad as you say, then why haven't they

destroyed the Shiva linga and yonis? What sort of people willingly leave such things lying around their cemeteries?'

'I don't know. They've dug a million graves in those hills; are you saying we should be happy they've left a few Shivas?'

'What manner of people were these saints? What did they do? How did they become so revered?'

Naukaram unrolled a fresh description as expertly as a textile dealer who knows the pattern of a fabric inside out while nursing no illusions of the customer instantly falling under his spell. There was something in his account that fired the lahiya's imagination. By late afternoon this spark had grown into an idea. Without even changing – luckily his wife wasn't at home – he got out a fresh sheet of paper, dipped his quill in the ink, and wrote:

Miracles begin with danger, with the overcoming of danger. With a blessing that's not understood, or only partially. Fishermen who've gone out, for instance, and been caught in a storm. Finding themselves at the mercy of elemental forces, their minds turn to prayer. Whom do they pray to, whom do they beg for help? Their village holy man, the only man they know whom these forces do not overawe. They toss the storm his name as a testimonial, an answer. And they are saved. The storm recedes. They are alive, thanks to the holy man. How are they supposed to assume it is God himself who has spared them when they think of Him so rarely? They return to their village. And what story do they have to tell? Of a storm that did not bring about their ruin. Of a miracle. The waves tossed their little boat, the wind rent its sail, all would have been lost had they not called out the holy man's name. And they swear his form appeared to them, his voice comforted them, his presence allayed their fears and appeased the storm's rage. They believe in his appearance. What other explanation could there be for the miracle of their survival? What of the holy man meanwhile? How does he react when he hears of his alleged powers? Does he drop his eyes with a rapt smile? Does he allow his disciple to say he heard the fishermen's cries of panic and reached out to them with his spirit? Won't the fishermen be grateful, and show their gratitude with gifts? The next time they put to sea, won't they invoke the holy man as a precaution? Won't fishermen from other villages in time come to copy them? When it is noised abroad that they always come home safe, always with a good catch? And so the saint has proved himself a miracle worker. Didn't you hear that the boat sank and the men were lost until the saint fetched them out of the deep with the mighty hand of his spirit? Didn't you hear that he sent out the dolphins and the shipwrecked were carried back to shore on their backs? Who would gainsay such miracles? What reason could there be to gainsay them?

The lahiya leant back in his chair. He sat quietly for a moment, then read over what he'd written. Could be useful, he thought. He'd show it to his fellow members of Satya Shodak Samaj; they'd be able to judge it. There was plenty written about miracles but very little about the origins of wonder. And yet this faculty was more wondrous than the miracles themselves.

50
WITH BIG EARS

These shops are confusing at first, a mass of little things. The wooden spoons and tin pans hang down, blocking your view; the boxes of matches and soap cover the counter, where they are shunted from side to side when the shopkeeper is looking for a pencil to tot up the sums he can't do in his head. Everything seems to get in your way, the bulging sacks of rice and lentils and chickpeas, the baskets of spices and, somewhere in between, where you wouldn't think there'd be any room, the piles of sweets stacked next to great jars of oil, which is dispensed directly into bottles of all sizes brought by the customers. The costly items, meanwhile, are kept on the roughly knocked-up shelves along the back wall: the fine tobacco, the good tea, the dates from Medina. No one can take in such an establishment at a first visit; they will return many times and ask, more out of politeness than conviction, if there's any molasses, and to their amazement, the shopkeeper will reach into a hitherto invisible nook and tip the item in question into his scales. The bazzaz, who owns the place, is not from this town; he has only opened up recently. But word has quickly got around that his dukaan is worth visiting, for its dates, its tobacco, its pickled ginger and sweetmeats, and for the bazzaz himself, a distinguished gentleman who is excellent to talk to. He's never in a hurry. He's not from these parts, you know . . . perhaps that's why he's so generous. He always errs in your favour when he's weighing out measures. And have you noticed how women consider him worthy of a smile?

Mirza Abdullah the bazzaz – that is, originally from Bushire, part Persian, part Arab – is a man who has grown up in so many different parts of the world, who has plied his trade in so many regions, that he knows a host of languages but is master of none. Sometimes he even gets them mixed up. If the shop's quiet, he plays chess with his neighbour. Generally he wins, although he prefers chatting to mulling over his next move. He likes listening, this bazzaz. His eyes reward you when you tell him something. You feel grateful he's given you his attention. He asks his neighbour's son to keep an eye on the shop – he pays him so handsomely the boy won't even step out of the door – and you take him with you to meet friends after the Tarawih. It's the season for serious conversation. You bring him along to the houses where they smoke opium and drink hemp. His company is a pleasure; it's kayf to sit somewhere with him and smoke time down to its last embers. If he has a failing, this new friend, then it's his hatred for the Angrezi. A man must be level-headed in his judgements. He must be able to gauge what is possible. He must know how to adjust. The bazzaz doesn't understand that. He curses the unbelievers who defile our land, the parasites who suck our country's blood. Nor is he in a minority. They keep close company and think of Afghanistan. Sixteen thousand unbelievers retreated from Kabul, they say, and only one reached Jalalabad.

'Those are figures I like,' says a man with dilated pupils, the words slopping around his mouth like overcooked dhal.

'Serves the Angrezi right,' adds another; 'they could have lost twice as many for all I care. What a gift from the Almighty, that they too should have to know what it's like to lose, to be humiliated, to be powerless for once.'

'That's it though,' the bazzaz spoke up for the first time. 'For them it was just a solitary calamity, an exception. We live mired in calamity.'

'If only Sind could be a second Afghanistan,' interrupts a younger man, pathos in his voice. 'If only we could cleanse our land with the Feringhi's blood. Perhaps then they'd learn their lesson.'

The bazzaz simply nods and strokes his thick beard. Everyone knows that the man with the dilated pupils talks drivel, but who can tell with this young man? There's something about him that remains to be fathomed. One of the company who has been silent thus far reminds them of the battle of Miani. He has only smoked a little; he's still nervous.

'We have five thousand dead to mourn. Fighting two and a half thousand Angrezi. How can the fallen of one side outnumber their opponents' whole army? The Almighty shouldn't allow such a thing; with those rules, the game is more than we can bear.'

Nostalgic hot air. The same as with most people. How few are prepared to act, to fight. The bazzaz is not very discriminating in the company he keeps. He goes as far as to frequent pimps, buying up a hoard of rumours with his gifts of fine tobacco. Mulla Muhammad Hasan, Kalat's highest-ranking minister, is on everyone's lips. Embroiled in a personal feud with the ruler, Mir Mehrab Khan, he has cunningly led the Angrezi to believe that the khan is intriguing against their interests in Afghanistan.

'Those stupid Angrezi . . .'

'Not that stupid, Janab Sahib, if they've conquered not only us but now also the Sikhs.'

'Well, they've fallen for this ruse. They've put pressure on Mir Mehrab Khan and he's retaliating. Hence the regular raids. He'll never challenge the Angrezi openly.'

'I've heard, Janab Sahib, the Angrezi are planning to take action against Karchat.'

'If the plan has worked its way down to you, it can't be that precious.'

'There can't be a single fighter left in the city. A foiled plan, certainly.'

'I've also heard Muhtaram Khan knows about the Angrezi's plans the moment they're thought up.'

'Why not? Did you think treachery spares any side?'

'No, I just wondered what they gave the Angrezi, what he was tempted with.'

That's what he is like, this Mirza Abdullah whom we spend our evenings with. Always the crucial question on the tip of his tongue.

51
NAUKARAM

II Om Shurpakarnaya namah I Sarvavighnopashantaye namah I Om Ganeshaya namah II

'You're constantly railing against the Miya. What do you gain by insulting them?'

'They circumcise themselves to be different. I simply respect this difference.'

'You made a point of saying Burton Sahib was like one of

them. I don't understand, how did he do that without getting circumcised?'

'Nothing gets past you. Sly as a lahiya, that's what the saying should be. Burton Sahib made many mistakes. He often behaved as a master shouldn't. But nothing was as unworthy as this. I couldn't believe it. He didn't even try to hide the ignominy from me. Imagine that.'

'Who circumcised him?'

'I don't know.'

'It must have been very painful as an adult.'

'Horrific pain. Absolutely. He didn't let it show though. He didn't move for a few weeks, stayed in his tent the whole time. Served him right. Stupidity doesn't deserve any sympathy.'

'Do you really change as a person when you're circumcised? Does it affect your character, your spirit?'

'I didn't notice anything. But his disguise worked to perfection. He was overjoyed. Farmers didn't run away the minute they set eyes on him. Young women didn't go inside when he rode up on his horse. Beggars didn't bombard him with their tales of woe. Even the dogs stopped yapping at him.'

'So the circumcision was worthwhile.'

'If you look at it like that. But what a sacrifice.'

'Why does it mean so much to you?'

'I have given it a lot of thought. I've had enough time. Circumcision is not just abhorrent, it also makes no sense. Why has Allah given them something that they don't need? Why has he endowed their body with something that they're going to have to cut off soon after birth? Does that make any sense? If the foreskin were something unnecessary, something bad, wouldn't Allah have got rid of it a long time ago? No. This is the best example of how ridiculous these Miya's beliefs are. And because they are so ridiculous, they have to defend them so aggressively.'

Report to General Napier
SECRET

I can today report a success, which should be the occasion
for a fair amount of pride. The practice of badli, that
plague spot on our Justitia's toughened skin, has finally
been stamped out. For the first time in the history of this
land, we have established the principle that the sentenced
and the punished are one and the same. From now on
Sind's rich will show greater respect for our legal system;
they will fear our death penalty. The successful resolution
of this problem should open our eyes to further misunderstandings. We should not sink into complacency, because it
will be a very long time before our conception of law has
become established in every native heart and every native
mind. As an example of the challenges that still lie before
us, a case from Upper Sind will serve, to which, by a stroke
of good fortune, I can personally attest. Five notorious
thieves were caught in Sukkur with part of the haul they
had taken from their victims before, purely for conven-
ience, they had stabbed them. The evidence was overwhelming; the men confessed. They were hanged and, so as
to be more of a deterrent, left hanging from the gallows
with strict orders to the guards that no one be allowed near
them on any account. The next morning the officer
returned to check if his order had been carried out. I
accompanied him. To our amazement, there were only four
gallows standing on the hill and yet, almost as if in compensation, from one of them two bodies were hanging. One
of the bodies was clearly different – in clothes, as well as in
another, less savoury aspect – from the others, the bodies of
the robbers. The guards were immediately taken to task.
They confessed that they had fallen asleep the night before,

and when they had woken up, they had seen that not only had one of the gallows been stolen but also one of the bodies. The body that had disappeared was the corpse of the leader of the gang, which was cause for various suppositions. In their confusion, and their fear of the consequences, the guards had seized the first suitable man who came down the road in the morning and hanged him without further ado. The commanding officer, like any normal person when he's confronted with something totally incomprehensible, flew into a rage. His fury was further inflamed by the behaviour of the guards, who displayed neither shame nor doubt. The officer delivered a mighty lecture that was admirable in its ardour, it has to be said, if almost completely ineffectual. He implored them to renounce their barbaric disregard for human life, now they were in the employ of the highest civilisation on earth. After he had appealed to morality and conscience, he stopped, exhausted, whereupon one of the guards indicated a desire to speak. 'Lieutenant, we're terribly sorry, but we found something in this traveller's possession we'd like to show you.' We were led to a cart that we hadn't noticed before and one of the guards pulled back a tarpaulin. Before us lay a mutilated corpse. Clearly the traveller who they had strung up by pure chance had committed a foul murder. I found it hard to begrudge the guards the pleasure they took in declaring, 'Now who is the supreme judge? God in His omnipotence and infallibility, or one of those sweating judges from your country who has to have every detail of a case translated by people for whom truth is a profitable business?' I'm not exaggerating when I say that at that moment the officer not only had all the wind taken out of his sails but also fell into a despair of immeasurable depth. He swore never to try to teach these fellows anything ever again and I fear he will keep his vow. I left him to his furious thoughts, not knowing what I could say to comfort him.

*II Om Uddandaya namah I Sarvavighnopashantaye namah I
Om Ganeshaya namah II*

'He did take me with him once. To Sehwan. He wasn't in disguise. Anything but. The trip was to find out how the circumcised would react to an Angrezi officer visiting one of their shrines. Burton Sahib was convinced the risks everyone talked about were only slight really. He thought – you see how sympathy can do away with common sense – that it was unjust, the way people thought of the circumcised as aggressive and intolerant.'

'Are you trying to spoil the ending?'

'I just want to guard you against stupid thoughts. Sehwan contained the tomb of the Red Falcon – that was the name of one of their dervishes – on the site of a Shiva temple. Such unbelievable shamelessness! It should be punished; we have to uncover what was there originally one day. This saint was a foreigner. He came from somewhere or other, settled in Sehwan, and spent all his time with whores. He's supposed to have done miracles.'

'Are you against miracles on principle?'

'No. I know many sadhus have powers we don't understand.'

'Many dervishes too.'

'Not this dervish. I only saw beggars at his tomb. Stinking beggars. Nine out of ten people there were beggars.'

'Like at our temples.'

'Our sadhus wait patiently for the alms we give them. With the circumcised, they tug at your clothes, they never give you a moment's peace. They were sitting everywhere, smoking . . . I know, like the sadhus, every one of them had a chillum in his hand. They called out in their croaky voices, and that's what I couldn't stand, those yells of *mast qalandar*, over and over. I won't be able to listen to that ever again.'

'I understand. I understand. I'm the same.'

'You are?'

'Absolutely. We live near a temple. *Sita Ram, Sita Ram, Sita Ram Ram Ram.* All day long. Even when I hear it in the distance, I start to feel sick.'

'I know what you're up to, your trick. You exaggerate the similarities and blur the differences. Is that meant to make everything all right?'

'It's not a trick. I just see through the delusion you've been taken in by.'

'You know everything, do you? What have we got left to talk about then? I'm going.'

'Calm down. It's all provisional. We're arguing as if there was something proven definitively. Let's go back to your story. I'll just write. But leave the circumcised alone. Such primitive hatred is unworthy of you.'

'Do you know something? You're not completely wrong. Some dervishes – this I have to tell you – carried weights around to make life more of a struggle. The ones who wear heavy chains on their bodies are called malang, the prisoners of God. That really did remind me of our sadhus. You see, the circumcised have adopted our nonsense.'

'What about Burton Sahib? How did they treat him?'

'As a friend. I hate to admit it: the circumcised couldn't have been more obliging. They showed him around; they were proud of his interest. The only thing he wasn't allowed was to go into the tomb. But that didn't bother him. He winked at me as they were regretfully informing him of this, and afterwards, riding back to the camp, he said, "Mirza Abdullah will have to give the shrine a visit. You see more when there are two of you."'

54
GIVER OF FAME AND GLORY

The muezzin coughed up a piece of kofta that had become lodged in his throat overnight, then addressed himself to the first syllable, and then the second, stretching them as if he were cocking a slingshot aimed at mortal sleep. Burton heard slapping feet on the way to the bath. He had had a bad night, plagued with vivid dreams. He had seen a man from behind, wrapped in a cloak, standing by a grave in a barren landscape. A dog with a leg missing had limped past. A name was engraved on the tombstone in a shaky scrawl, *Rich Barton*. Other people approached the grave and stared at it in silence, without moving. One asked, 'Who is this buried here?' No one knew the answer. 'Sad,' they said, and laid a cloth on the grave before turning round. 'Far from the dust of his forefathers,' one of them said as he left. Only the man wrapped in the cloak remained by the grave. He didn't even raise a hand in tribute to the dead man whom clearly no one remembered. Why did the headstone even have a name?

One of the young men of the house called to him, telling him he could perform his wazu. 'Praying is better than sleeping,' the muezzin kept exhorting the neighbourhood, 'praying is better than sleeping.' The first prayer of the day was a short one. The spiritual equivalent of the cold water he splashed on his face. Not just to wake you up, but also to make you stand upright, perform a sincere bow and assume the right attitude for the day. Afterwards he drank a cup of tea with his host, Mirza Aziz, a new friend. As Mirza Abdullah, he had been reaping the harvest of his charisma and patience for weeks now. He had been passed around from house to house. A man deserving of every honour. Did the Prophet, may God bless Him and grant Him peace, not advise: 'Be in the world as a traveller'? And Mirza Abdullah was just such a traveller from afar. He had learnt exactly how to ingratiate himself, which doses of what sort of humour had the requisite stimulant properties. Expert in the art of conversation, this noble traveller had already enjoyed many people's hospitality. The venerable Mirza Aziz, who had unhesitatingly sworn eternal friendship with him, had proved the ideal informant. Connected by blood to several of the most important families, he traded in everything, including knowledge. Burton admired him, whilst knowing that one day he would have to betray him. For Mirza Aziz was playing a double game that harmed British interests. He was always superbly informed about British plans – Burton still had to find out how – and everything suggested he sold the information to the rebels in Baluchistan. For the moment this remained supposition, although based on a mounting number of clues, and the general had no time for circumstantial evidence. So, until his suspicions had been confirmed, he would have to continue being Mirza Aziz's charmed guest. It made him uneasy. Mirza Aziz was not only a conspirator but also a patron of the city's finest musical soirées. At that evening's event, Burton drew on a hookah and closed his eyes the better to give himself up to the song. It would take a long time before he really knew everything that was happening. A verse reeled him in. 'You don't create the sun when you draw back the curtain.' The woman sang with fragile certainty. 'You don't create the sun when you draw back the curtain.' As Mirza Abdullah, the bazzaz from Bushire, Richard Burton felt closer to happiness than he ever had as an officer of the Honourable East India Company.

55
NAUKARAM

II Om Yashaskaraya namah I Sarvavighnopashantaye namah I Om Ganeshaya namah II

'The Miya claim this Muhammad of theirs has given them Divine Law, but you're not allowed to ask them why, if that's the case, there are so many gaps in it. Such gaps that they have to fill them with the customs of the country. And listen, now this is the limit, these are often repulsive and totally disregard Divine Law.'

'How could it be otherwise? After all, it is a human law.'

'They use the coarsest thread to repair the sacred cloth. How can that work?'

'What I don't understand is why, if everything about the Miya is so ridiculous, Burton Sahib, who you have often said was a man of learning and culture, felt so drawn to their faith? Or was everything he learned just for the purpose of spying?'

'No. He was really interested; he felt really connected to it. It is a mystery to me. His teachers were nowhere near as impressive as Upanishe Sahib in Baroda. He even prayed with the Miya, can you imagine? The proud Burton Sahib bowed down and wiped the floor with his knees and his brow. There's no explaining it. Perhaps it was because it was so easy for him. No one else could enter so easily into another person's world as he could. He could adopt the manners and values of the people in front of him without any effort, sometimes without even consciously deciding to do so.'

'Didn't he have any of his own values? No laws he believed in?'

'He had his laws he lived by, yes. He expected complete loyalty. He was incensed that when they left, the Angrezi abandoned the people who had fought at their side. "We have earned a reputation for using a man when we need him and discarding him when he has lost his expediency," he cursed. "If one concludes an alliance," he stormed, "one must stand by it. We can't abandon our allies to their fate, to exile and poverty or even torture and death."'

'He recognised the contradictions we all live by, and expressed them.'

'Anything was possible with him.'

'He was like monsoon weather.'

'Unexpected. Often totally unexpected. Sometimes he did the exact opposite of what he preached. He sneered at that which moments earlier he had treated as sacred.'

'Can you give me an example?'

'Haven't we talked about him enough?'

'Please, one last example.'

'When we were in Sehwan, some Angrezi were digging for old treasures near by, relics from one of Iskander the Great's camps. They were very dedicated and a little too trusting, and for some reason they got on the wrong side of Burton Sahib. That was that. I never knew when something would provoke his wrath. The local Miya sold the credulous souls fake coins within a week. But one day all those in the camp who had poured scorn on the diggers had to retract their poisonous barbs. A find had been made: bits of pottery decorated with designs from an old, lost country of the Feringhis called Etruria. The diggers came to our camp; they wanted to show off their triumph. I was ashamed for them, and I was ashamed for Burton Sahib, who had hidden these fragments in the ground before sunrise.'

'Were you there?'

'No, but I'm sure.'

'How?'

'He had a vase that disappeared at the time. His friend, Scott Sahib, suspected him as well, but Burton Sahib protested his innocence. He rummaged around everywhere himself, digging up everything he could. But still he saw no harm in playing his crude jokes on others who shared his passion.'

56
LORD OF THE PLACE

Although he was half crippled, the thought of pitying the general wouldn't have crossed anyone's mind, perhaps because he himself never showed any moderation in dispensing praise or blame. He was under attack from all sides, and the longer he ruled over Sind, the more violent the criticism became. Even his successes on the battlefield were questioned retrospectively. Those who had been present supported him as unreservedly as ever, but the vast majority who had only participated through hearsay contradicted every last detail of his version of events.

The general understood the elastic rules of political ethics – they were one thing – but he couldn't tolerate any moral equivocation. He didn't smoke, he didn't play cards for money, he didn't drink – 'Why are you alive at all?' Burton had once wanted to ask, but had bitten his tongue. And as a young man, he had already laid the foundation stone of his grim reputation when he cured his regiments' lance corporals' drunkenness with the whip.

'What do you have to report?'

'I've got to know one of the middlemen who keep the Baluchi ringleaders copiously supplied with information. But I don't know how he gets it yet. I need more time.'

'As long as the insurgency doesn't break out before you've finished your investigation.'

'The situation seems peaceful at the moment.'

'How are the messages transmitted?'

'Mainly through Sidis.'

'Sidis? Explain yourself, soldier, don't just toss terms around.'

'Descendants of slaves from East Africa. You see them everywhere with their huge water-skins on their back or carrying burdens fit for buffaloes. They are often called Sidi individually and Sidis as a group.'

'Why do the insurgents use them in particular?'

'They're outside the system. Not caught up in the web of family and clan and tribe that makes everything so complicated.'

'Well, stir your stumps, soldier. I'd like to crack this puzzle soon. I have a feeling I won't be here much longer.'

'In Sind, sir?'

'On this earth.'

'Such feelings are generally deceptive.'

'It's absurd I'm still alive.'

'What do you mean, sir?'

'I was hit in my right cheek by a bullet that bored its way up into the sinus above my ear. I lay on the grass as two army doctors tried to get it out. It had dug itself deep into the bone, and however much they pulled, they couldn't dislodge it. Even when they had cut a three-inch hole in my cheek. One of them put his thumb in my mouth and pressed, while the other pulled, and finally the bullet came out with a mass of bone splinters. Since then I frequently feel I'm suffocating. I broke my leg; my brother strapped it up good and tight, and it healed. So badly that it had to be broken again years later and re-set. Every step I take hurts. And at night I can't sleep because of my rheumatism. Where's the sense in any of that?'

'You are doing useful work.'

'If you say so, soldier. Most people appear to have written me off.'

'May I ask you a delicate question, sir?'

'Go ahead, soldier.'

'Doesn't the responsibility you have been given for such a complex, incomprehensible, various country trouble you sometimes?'

'No. It doesn't bother me in the slightest. The exercise of power is never disagreeable.'

57

NAUKARAM

II Om Pramodaya namah I Sarvavighnopashantaye namah I Om Ganeshaya namah II

'Today I'm going to tell you how I saved his life. You have deserved it, waiting so patiently. You must have been eaten up with curiosity. It started when I heard Burton Sahib was in prison. No, actually I heard that some followers of Mirza Aziz had been arrested. I knew Mirza Aziz was a close friend of Burton Sahib. He had planned to spend a few days with him. And when he didn't come back, I thought he might have been arrested with the others.'

'An Angrezi officer? How's that possible?'

'Exactly. That's why I talked to his captain first. He couldn't have cared less. "Lieutenant Burton is always disappearing," he said, "why should this time be any different?" Then I remembered he was disguised as a Miya, so he wouldn't have been able to come out with the truth in front of the others. Mirza Aziz would have lost face and Burton Sahib's disguise would have been ruined.'

'Couldn't he have revealed his identity in the prison?'

'I thought that too at first. But the longer I thought about it, the more doubts I had. If they were all in the same cell, and he had asked to talk to the duty officer in private, the others would have assumed he wanted to betray them. So it struck me as much more likely that he would simply wait until they were all let out. My master wasn't someone who was afraid of a night in jail. Quite the opposite: it would be another experience for him to make the most of.'

'But it wasn't just one night.'

'After three days I was seriously worried. I didn't know who I could talk to. Captain Scott was with the squad of surveyors in Upper Sind. Burton Sahib hadn't been working with them for a long time because his eyes had got inflamed. Apart from him, no one else knew anything specific about his activities, except the general. What was I supposed to do? Go to the Angrezi headquarters and ask to see the ruler of Sind? I waited another day, then I went to the prison. The Angrezi kept their enemies in an old fort on a hill east of the city. It was frightening just looking at it, I have to tell you – a building like a mountain range. You had to climb hundreds of steps. The gate that only stood half open robbed me of my last ounce of courage. It was studded with huge iron spikes that were meant for elephants. In the old days. A shudder ran through me as I passed them. I had to put my request to two bored sepoys on the other side of the gate. I asked to speak to the commanding officer. They wouldn't let me through; they told me I had to tell them what it was about. I refused and said I was the servant of an Angrezi, an officer. In the end they took me to see him. What an office he had! The windows were small but they looked over the whole land. I told him that an Angrezi, an officer no less, had been arrested by mistake. He'd know if anything of that sort had happened, the officer said curtly. "Perhaps not," I objected carefully. "He is a spy, in camouflage; you wouldn't recognise him." He didn't believe me. My perseverance impressed him though. I described Burton Sahib down to the clothes he was wearing when he set out. The commanding officer's curiosity was pricked; I lured him in. "We will see about this," he said eventually and stood up. He told me to wait at the gate. After some time, I was called back in again. When I stepped through the heavy gate again, my heart shrank as if it was trying to squeeze through a tiny crack.

'"It's just as I suspected," said the commandant. "The man you describe is clearly not an Englishman."

'"How did you find that out?" I blurted.

'The commanding officer grinned. "We asked him politely to undress. He is circumcised, and besides, he doesn't speak a word of our language."

'"But he won't admit it in front of the others," I protested, "and he's circumcised because he got himself circumcised not long ago."

'"Nonsense! An Englishman does not get circumcised. What I'm more interested in is what you're after with these lies." The commanding officer's voice was worse than any threatening gesture. "We will have to find out what you're up to." I thought I was done for.'

58
THE INVINCIBLE

Death lodged in everything. The few, scattered fields were covered with a thin layer of white ash that cast an inexplicable glow, and the few, scattered plants sprouted like dots of stubble on an old man's wrinkled chin. All the water had evaporated from the riverbeds, leaving stinking ooze. The trees were bone-dry. Mirza Abdullah was resting, like the others. It was cooler in his room, his body heavy after an excellent lunch. He heard yelling or something. His mind followed a blurry trail in his drowsy state. The noise thickened like fog. It was too loud for a nightmare; it was coming nearer. The door burst open: a group of men stormed in, grabbed him by the arms, threw him to the floor and started kicking him. A blow to the back of his head. Before he passed out, he could feel hands searching him. The ground beneath him when he regained consciousness was slippery, cold under his head. It took a while before he could feel his legs in the darkness.

'Who's there?' His voice scared him. It sounded as if it were coated in something.

'Aha. Our friend is awake.'

'We've been taken prisoner.'

'Who by?'

'Do you hear him? How blessed are foreigners in their ignorance. Who do you think? By the Angrezi.'

'The Angrezi!'

'Yes. There's one piece of good news. Mirza Aziz got away. He was the only one not resting when they stormed the house.'

'Mashallah.'

'And there's one piece of bad news. Because Mirza Aziz got away, the English want to know where he's hiding. And they'll torture us until they find out.'

'Do we know?'

'No. None of us knows. That won't spare us the pain, though. Things are a little different for you. You could try to explain that you're just travelling through, you're from Persia and only happened to be in Mirza Aziz's house by chance.'

'What good will that do me?'

'Not very much, I'm afraid. Even if they believe you, they'll have grounds to assume you're connected to the shah.'

'Time to pay the price of friendship with Mirza Aziz.'

They relapsed into silence. They couldn't even pray properly: the ceiling was too low to stand up straight, and they had no idea of the cardinal points.

There was a creaking noise, then a gleam of light; a torch illuminated the room they were in for the first time. A cell. Thick walls. Soggy rice on a tawa, which a sepoy set down in the middle of the floor. They had to eat with their dirty hands. His fellow prisoners scrutinised Mirza Abdullah intently, probably wondering whether they could trust him. The torch quickly burned down. It wasn't long before one of them was taken out. He was gone for a long time. They didn't know whether it was day or night. When he was brought back, he couldn't tell them what had happened to him. Fear made the cell grow even smaller.

59

NAUKARAM

II Om Durjayaya namah I Sarvavighnopashantaye namah I Om Ganeshaya namah II

'The commanding officer nodded to the sepoy behind me. He would definitely have hit me, if I hadn't taken any precautions. I had brought proof. That was one of the few times in my whole life when I had my wits about me. "Please," I yelled, "one moment, please, I'll show you something," and I reached into my bag and pulled out Burton Sahib's uniform and a few other bits and pieces. "Believe me, I'm not lying," I said. "You can ask me questions. I know all about the 18th Infantry; I know the names of the other officers. Please, take him out and ask him when he's alone."

'"All right," said the commanding officer, "but you're coming too." Two new sepoys accompanied us into a room with a bare floor which didn't have a single piece of furniture. Soon afterwards Burton Sahib was brought in. I was scared by how he looked.

'"Do you know this man?" the commanding officer asked. Burton Sahib didn't react. The commanding officer had the question translated by one of the sepoys. "No," Burton Sahib said without hesitating. The commanding officer looked at me suspiciously before turning back to Burton Sahib. "This man claims to know you. He claims to work for you. He even claims you're a British officer." The sepoy had to translate again, so it took a while before Burton Sahib's answer reached us. "I don't know what you're trying to achieve with this story. I have already told you I am a merchant from Persia and I have nothing to do with this business." The commanding officer thought for a moment. Then he ordered me to leave the room with the sepoy. I don't know what they talked about. Burton Sahib never spoke to me about that day afterwards. They came out after an hour. Both ignored me. The commandant went back into his office and Burton Sahib walked out through the massive gate, hailed a tonga, got in it and disappeared. He didn't wait for me. When I got back to our house, he had already gone to bed, still in his dirty clothes. I prepared a bath. I was afraid of his anger, which I didn't understand. But when he woke up, he treated me just as usual. Not antagonistic at all. I didn't dare bring up the episode and he never said a word about it. Not even a hint.'

'You didn't find out anything else?'

'I did, once, by eavesdropping. When he was talking to one of his teachers. "You should have made yourself known immediately," the teacher said. "It's not your fight! Do you think you can change sides so easily? You did what you did purely out of vanity." To which Burton Sahib answered, "You only ever think in crude patterns: friend and enemy, ours and theirs, black and white. Can't you imagine that there's an in-between? If I assume somebody else's identity, then I can feel what it's like to be him."

'"You're deluding yourself," said the teacher. "You don't take on his soul with your disguise."

'"No, of course not. But I do his feelings, because they're determined by how others react to him, and I can feel that."

'I was touched when I heard this, I have to say. Burton Sahib was practically begging, he wanted what he said to be true so badly. But the teacher showed him no mercy. "You can disguise yourself as much as you want but you'll never learn what it's like to be one of us. You can take off your disguise at any time: that's always there for you as a last resort. But we are imprisoned in our skin. Fasting is not the same as starving."'

60

OF THE MONSTROUS FIGURE

Then they came and took him out. He assumed the others expected he'd betray them, but he had sworn to himself that he would remain true to his disguise. What was it worth if he turned tail at the first confrontation, the first real test, and slipped back into the safe harbour of the empire's protection? That would have been shabby, low. He wouldn't have been able to look any of his adopted friends in the eye afterwards.

The room where he was to be interrogated was huge, with an uneven floor and recesses let into the walls at points. He recognised the Englishman sitting behind the solitary desk: one of Major McMurdo's men. Later he would remember how the officer hadn't got up once, but had sat by the window throughout, studying documents and occasionally making a note of something. He had instigated all the pain, and yet it was almost as if he remained uninvolved.

A sepoy questioned him: name, background. His relationship with Mirza Aziz. He answered in a way that could have been true. As expected, his interrogators started to listen intently when he said he was Persian. The Englishman looked up after the squat translator at his side passed on the information. Mirza Abdullah recognised in his expression the hunger for an unanticipated success, for advancement. Had he stumbled on a conspiracy that extended beyond Baluchistan to Persia, and so definitely took in Afghanistan, and, who knew, perhaps even Russia? Uncovering something that big had to mean a handsome reward in promotion and pay. The officer started to encircle this notional conspiracy with his questions. He wanted to hear whatever came closest to his expectations, impatiently sweeping aside any answers that pointed in other directions. Mirza Abdullah resolved to report this officer, who had now lit a Manila cigar, for incompetence. When the brazen obduracy of his questions became intolerable, he cursed the fellow. The translator watered down his insult, he noticed, but the interrogator had gathered the tone and looked up again. Mirza Abdullah recognised something else he was familiar with: indignation that a native should have the nerve to contradict one, to cut up rough. The sort of impertinence that cannot be tolerated, that can make a man livid with rage. The next moment a pail of cold water was poured over his head from behind.

'I've heard prisoners used to be stripped naked,' said the senior sepoy. 'I don't understand why. They freeze more in wet clothes.'

'I am certain you won't reveal what you know of your own accord,' the officer said from behind his desk. 'So we will not waste any more time on polite conversation. We will show you what we have planned for you.'

The translation was barely finished before he felt the blows to the backs of his knees, his back, his kidneys. Every sensation except pain vanished. He twisted over and fell on his side on the cold floor. He started shaking. One of the torturers put a boot on his face and stayed like that for a time before quietly saying, 'We will torch your father.' Everyone was silent for a spell, then the officer asked another question, but it was so densely and nonsensically phrased that Mirza Abdullah couldn't have answered even if he had wanted to. He doubled up on the floor. Something tore in his left shoulder as he worked himself into a sitting position and tried to explain why he couldn't know what they were asking of him. He was just a bazzaz on his travels.

He heard a voice just behind his ear. 'We can do other things to you. We can change you into a woman and ram –' Sheikh Abdullah felt a stab of pain in his anus – 'this stick up your Khyber Pass. You like that though, don't you?'

At that moment Mirza Abdullah realised that the senior sepoy was a Bengali, probably a Hindu. And he recognised the fateful connection between the British officer's ambition and his right-hand man's loathing. He smelled the cigar as if he were holding it in his own hand, that smell of rotten forest floor. The last thing he felt was his ear and later all he could remember was the stench of burning flesh.

61

NAUKARAM

II Om Vikataya namah I Sarvavighnopashantaye namah I Om Ganeshaya namah II

'He recovered from his wounds surprisingly quickly, but he was worn out. He had lost all interest in the country. Sometimes he lay in bed for days. Occasionally he read the paper. Otherwise nothing. He lay there and didn't even close his eyes. It is terrible when someone goes against their own nature. I didn't know he was there one day when I was attending to some task in his room, and suddenly I heard his voice: "Naukaram, we must get away from here."

'"Back to Baroda, Sahib?"

'"That's not possible. If we want to get out of here, we have to go back to England."'

'What was he supposed to do as an officer in England?'

'I was confused too. At first. Then I quickly understood when Burton Sahib began to pretend to be ill. At first he acted as if he was sickly. If other people were there, he moaned about how bad he felt. He didn't appear for morning muster; he stayed away from the mess. He went to the garrison doctor supported by two strapping Baluchis who were at least six foot tall. The doctor seemed concerned. He asked whether he drank, whether he smoked. "Not one cigar," Burton Sahib swore. "Now and then a glass of something, but I rarely finish it."'

'Was that true?'

'He was draining a couple of bottles an evening by then, but he didn't smoke: that was true. He couldn't stand the smell of Manilas since I had got him out of prison. Don't ask, I don't know why. He hired someone to stand guard outside his door and announce visitors in good time so that they would always find Burton Sahib in bed. He sent word wishing his comrades a good night as early as eight. And of course all this trickled back to the doctor. Burton Sahib began to talk about the corps very nostalgically, how his life would be ruined if he had to leave it. He forbade me to tidy up his room. Or even clean it. Cups lay around everywhere, soggy toast on the table. It was sickening. I hardly had anything to do for weeks. He gave me money to go and enjoy myself in the city. I only had one job, late in the evening, when no one would see me, which was to take him a tray of salad, curry, ice cream and port. One of his friends he could rely on prepared it. He blacked out his room all day, and never lit a lamp at night. He drank something that made him ill and then sent me out at two o'clock in the morning to fetch the doctor. He drew up his testament and asked the doctor to be the executor of his last will, as the Angrezi say. The doctor soon gave in; I think he valued his sleep. In a matter of moments he was convinced that Burton Sahib was unfit for duty. He gave him two years' sick leave. Two years! The Angrezi take care of their own. He continued to be paid. First we travelled about the country for a year, and we got as far as Ooty. You won't know it, it's in the mountains, in the south, a long way from here. That will tell you how healthy Burton Sahib really was. But then justice was done as it never fails to be, if you've got the time to wait. Burton Sahib fell ill. Really very ill. So ill, he almost died.'

Report to General Napier
TOP SECRET

You entrusted me with the task of finding out why, on what
is now a number of occasions, the rebel Baluchi chieftains
under Mir Khan have been informed of our plans and, thus
forewarned, have been able in good time either to flee or to
hide. I have been travelling for months looking into this
matter. I have gone to countless Baluchi meeting places, I
have lent every voice an attentive ear but nothing until
recently pointed to a traitor in our own ranks. At our last
meeting, you also ordered me to check whether, and to what
extent, British officers frequent the brothel called the
Lupanar. You probably didn't suspect that these two questions might be connected. I performed this task as well and I
fear I have the painful duty of informing you of certain
highly unpleasant conclusions. The Lupanar differs from
other brothels neither in décor nor hospitality but solely in
the fact that its courtesans are not women but youths and
men dressed as women. The boys cost twice as much as the
men, not only because they are the finest and most noble
creatures and love of them is of the purest form, a view the
local Sufis seem to have taken from the Platonists, but also
because their scrotums can be used as reins. This brothel is, I
can now definitely confirm, regularly visited by certain of
our officers. Curiosity and boredom takes most of them
there and we may assume that they are able to withstand the
temptations of this place. But some find precisely what
they've been looking for. Particularly noteworthy seems to
me the case of those who are constrained against their will
to perform acts of which they would not otherwise have
approved. The emir, to whom the Lupanar belongs, is a con-
noisseur of young, fair-skinned men and so, according to my

sources, he has on several occasions plied British visitors with spirits until they were completely submissive or unconscious and at his disposal. One might suppose he was thereby revenging himself for the humiliation our rule imposed on him, but in my opinion he simply lusts after the beauty of blond, hairless youths. It was reported to me that one of these griffins on the morning after expressed amazement that the local alcohol caused an irritation of the *postérieur*. All of which would be a trifle unsavoury, but certainly no threat to our security if information that should have remained absolutely secret had not been elicited from some of our officers in this Lupanar. I have promised my source who regularly visits this brothel and is related to the manager to name no names. He swears that on a number of occasions valuable information has been reported to the Emir after an officer has let it slip in the throes of intoxication or ecstasy, or the subsequent intimacies. And if we bear in mind that the emir in question, the Lupanar emir, is related by marriage to Mirza Aziz, we can see the links in the web that is causing us so many headaches.

63
NAUKARAM

II Om Mritunjayaya namah I Sarvavighnopashantaye namah I Om Ganeshaya namah II

This tale of mine is a necklace of choice pearls I should like to hang around the neck of your gracious and attentive perception, dear reader; this story of mine is a fragrant flower that I should like to press into your warm-hearted and compassionate feeling's hand, dear reader; this work of mine is a cloth of fine silk that I should like to spread over the skin of your perspicacious and far-reaching wisdom, dear reader . . .

The lahiya set aside his quill and read through the whole book once, and then a second time, as the sky outside turned light. The inviolability of the written word moved him deeply; he felt close to tears. Not that it was without weaknesses or misjudgements. If he could start again from the beginning, he would . . . Ha, nonsensical thought. The crucial thing was that the work towered over him, mighty and strange, as if he hadn't written it, as if he hadn't guided its every turn. He was reminded of the sentence the anonymous architect of the Kailash Temple in Ellora wrote on his building, the greatest phrase a creator has ever left: *How did I achieve this?*

There was one thing still to do. He mustn't write the ending, even if it was just one paragraph. No one should know the whole story. Just as no one could take in the Kailash Temple in its entirety. The lahiya called his wife, whom he'd heard moments before going about her early morning housework, and put his request to her. She was astonished and for a few wilful moments debated whether to rebuff him, but then she agreed. She hoped that as soon as this job was finished, their life would go back to how it was before, before this Naukaram had appeared and turned her husband's head. He thanked her effusively, then laboriously got to his feet and went out. He wouldn't go to the street of the lahiyas today, he wouldn't write anything. Perhaps not tomorrow either. And afterwards – who knew? According to Naukaram – an unmoored memory floated through the lahiya's mind – Burton Sahib had once expressed amazement that in Hindustani the same word meant yesterday and tomorrow. And? What could one conclude from that? Wasn't the word for the day before yesterday different from that for the day after tomorrow?

Naukaram wondered about the lahiya being late. That had never happened before. He saw a woman coming along the dusty street. Everything about her exuded strength. Some of the other scribes greeted her. She scrutinised him carefully before asking who he was. Then she introduced herself as the lahiya's wife. He wouldn't be coming today, she apologised.

He had sent her in his place because he didn't want to know the conclusion of the story himself.

'Why not?'

'It's an old tradition. Like not reading the whole *Mahabharata*.'

'I didn't know that. I heard something similar once from Burton Sahib. He told me the Arabs believed they would die within a year if they heard all the stories of the *Thousand and One Nights*.'

'A superstition.'

'Isn't he a member of the Satya Shodak Samaj? I thought he despised all forms of superstition.'

'He calls it tradition. Everyone is superstitious; some just give their superstitions other names. May we begin? I don't have much time. The grandchildren are coming to me this afternoon.'

'The fee? What did he tell you about the fee?'

'He didn't tell me anything. He probably forgot. You know, I'm sure he's got enough from you. Let's forget about it.'

'Not his fee, my fee.'

'Your fee?'

'He has to pay me.'

'I don't understand.'

'That's what we agreed. He pays me to finish telling him the story.'

'I don't believe it. He's lost his mind. How long has this been going on?'

'It didn't start yesterday. A few weeks now. Otherwise I wouldn't have carried on. You know what he's like, he's a nosy man.'

'He's completely mad. Who ever heard of such a thing? A lahiya who pays his customer. He's been behaving oddly ever since you came to him. But this makes him an utter laughing stock.'

'Only if you tell anyone. We've agreed not to breathe a word about it.'

'He'll hear a word about it from me.'

'Don't tell him. Please. It would ruin so much for him.'

'What are you now, his ally? You two have argued from start to finish. I know that for a fact; he's complained to me about it.'

'We've travelled the same road. That counts for a lot. Leave it be.'

'All right. And now, what are we going to do with the end of the story? It doesn't interest me, to tell you the truth, and as I don't have any money . . .'

'I'm not asking for any. It will be my leaving present to your husband. Not that he'll read it. Or who knows, perhaps he'll change his mind. Write it down. It's not much, but we can't swallow the ending.'

'All right. Has the ending got a title?'

'On the ship. Write: *On the Ship*. And then write: *Arrival in the Feringhi's Land*.'

'Sounds good.'

'Are you going to make as many comments as your husband?'

'No, I won't say anything from now on. Not even a sigh will pass my lips, you'll see.'

'The ship was called the *Elisa* and I thought it was a death ship. Burton Sahib looked terrible. His frame was wasted and stooped, his eyes sunken, his voice had lost its ring. He had been given permission to return home to recover there, if he was going to recover at all. Yes, I thought that ship was a death ship. I wasn't the only one. One of his friends in Bombay had told him: "It's written on your face that your days are numbered, take my advice and go home to die." We were becalmed soon after setting off. The water was so flat, Burton Sahib said it was a waves' graveyard. I nursed him as well as I could, thinking the whole time, what will I do in this unknown land if my master dies? Will I die too? My worries didn't draw breath. But then a wind got up and with the strong winds from the southeast we sailed into healthier waters. Burton Sahib turned the corner amazingly quickly and before we even reached the Angrezi's country he was restored to health. We were closer during that time than we'd ever been before or ever would be afterwards. He told me what happened in Sind, why he'd pretended to be sick without knowing that he would fall seriously ill. Rumours were going round the Angrezi about his visits to a brothel – forgive me, please – where men offered themselves. People claimed that Burton Sahib's reconnoitring was too thorough. That he didn't just investigate, he also sampled. His reputation was sullied. And his superiors, who knew the truth, didn't protect him. They were infuriated by his lack of unconditional loyalty. I felt his grief as if it was my own. Never in my life have I felt so close to that compassion for another being that our holy teachers demand of us. We landed at a port called Plymouth and finally I saw it. This England. I saw lush green and soft hills in the distance. The passengers, especially the ones who had served in the heat or the desert for a long time, were glassy-eyed. But I'm sure no one opened his eyes as wide as me. I couldn't believe how beautiful this country they called England was. I turned to Burton Sahib and I can still remember what I said, word for word: "What manner of men must you Angrezi be that you leave such a paradise and travel to a god-forsaken land like ours without compulsion?"'

64

INFINITELY CONSCIOUS

The general re-read this report more often than any other document in his life, searching for a way to shield this soldier from the consequences of having done his duty. Not only had he entered a mire which it was an indecent understatement to call 'a trifle unsavoury', but he had also exposed an intolerable breach of military security and so all the negative aspects of the case would reflect on him personally. To cap it all, he had refused, at least in writing, to divulge all the information in his possession because of a promise he had made to a native. That wouldn't go down well. McMurdo wanted a talk with this Burton, whom he'd already heard a lot of uncomplimentary things about. The lieutenant was called into the general's office, where he was surprised to find a handful of high-ranking officers. The general began speaking slowly. He looked tired.

'Major McMurdo wishes to pursue your investigation, and for this he needs the names of your sources and of the officers who frequent this place.'

'I can't give you the names of the officers because I don't know them. There were no officers in the Lupanar in my presence. I cannot reveal the names of my sources.'

'Why not?'

'Because I have given my word.'

'They're just natives.'

'I swore on my beard and the Qur'an.'

'He's joking. God, he's joking at the most inopportune moment.'

'I cannot break this oath.'

'You don't mean that seriously, soldier. Tell us you don't really mean that.'

'I'm quite serious, sir.'

'A promise to a common native means more to you than the safety of our corps?'

'I have contributed to the safety of our corps, if I may say so, sir, and I am confident that we will soon find out the entire truth through other means. I cannot betray this man's confidence.'

'You must decide, Burton. Him or us.'

'I proceed on the assumption, Major, that one can be true to various loyalties. You are creating an insoluble conflict.'

They didn't say another word, the assembled high-ranking officers, the general, his tracker dog McMurdo, their aides. They merely exchanged glances, with which they barred him from the army and their company for the rest of his life. He knew at that moment that he would never rise above the rank of captain. Not after the memorandum they would draft after this conversation, a memorandum about his unreliability, which would accompany him everywhere he went. You could change your nature, in fact you could change practically everything about yourself, but not your record. They would write something devastating along the lines of 'his understanding of the natives, their way of thinking, customs, language, is profound and could potentially be of great use. But the intimacy which feeds this knowledge has led Lieutenant Burton to a confusion of loyalties detrimental to the Crown's interests. We are therefore regretfully compelled to acknowledge that we are not in a position henceforth to gauge the extent of his loyalty.'

o

COLD RETURN

It was a grim reception. He and Naukaram were like two raisins tossed in a bowl of dough. The air was murky, thick with smoke and soot, unbreathable. The cold, grey sky made them shiver. Everything about the city was small, petty-minded and penny-pinching, the tiny, cringing single-family houses, the melancholy knotted in the public squares. And the food! Primitive, half-cooked, tasteless, the bread just crumbs or crust; to drink, a pungent tincture that went by the name of beer or ale. It didn't matter what they were served, there was no getting away from it: they had fallen among barbarians. The winter that followed was terrible. Every tree looked like a jangling candlestick. Swathes of cold fog settled over the city, bringing bronchitis and flu in their wake. The coal regularly ran out, the gas pressure often sinking so low that they had to forgo their main source of comfort – the chai that made many an afternoon bearable. Burton couldn't wait to leave this country again and visit his family in halfway bearable France. He was implacable. Nothing would make him conform with mediocrity. He wore clothes guaranteed to shock, kurtas in garish, screaming colours, freakishly baggy cotton breeches, tight puttees and golden gondolier's sandals – even though he froze in them. Thus attired he went about London and dropped in on clubs, accompanied by Naukaram whom, the moment he was sure he had the attention of the assembled members, he would talk loudly to in languages that only the two of them could understand. Occasionally he took things too far, exhausting the patience invariably shown a man who'd served in India; the club members wearied of his provocations and threw him out. Once he was almost given a thrashing. Only the wild look in his eyes restrained his outraged compatriots, who were already pretty drunk. It was an evening when stories were swapped from the different fronts of the empire. After much reminiscing marinated in nostalgia and overstatement, an elderly gentleman recited damp-eyed a couplet they all knew:

> 'Such is the patriot's boast, where'er we roam,
> His first, best country ever is at home.'

Then he raised his glass in a toast to queen and country. Burton clinked glasses with his neighbours. But he had barely put his glass down before his voice thundered out, reducing everyone else in the big circle to silence. 'Gentlemen, that toast reminds me of a grand joke. You have to hear it. You won't forget it, I guarantee. There were two tapeworms, father and son. They were shat out of a man's arsehole – sorry, this is how the joke goes – whereupon the father stuck his head out of the shit, had a little shake, looked around and said contentedly to his son: "Well, at least it's home."'

They crossed to France, to the continent. 'You'll see,' he promised Naukaram, 'life on the mainland is more bearable.'

'I didn't dislike your country, Sahib.'

His parents summered in Boulogne. They lived a modest life, the father's pension enabling them to rent a little house with a small outbuilding for the servants. An Italian cook called

Sabbatino had been working for them since Pisa, where they had lived for a considerable time. Naukaram and Sabbatino had to share a room. The cook had already occupied it with his smells, which did not agree with Naukaram. He and the cook had no common language, and their palates were instantly at loggerheads. Sabbatino was a man who set great store by his customs, which he considered inviolable, and was in no doubt that the position of cook was a privileged one amongst domestic staff. Other servants were employed to make his job easier.

Burton was rarely at home. He disappeared on long walks, and enjoyed the company of young women of his race. Naukaram wasn't clear about his position in the little house. The sahib's parents avoided him, and never gave him anything to do. He didn't dare go out on his own; he was afraid of getting lost. He had no alternative but to sit in his little room and wait. The cook, meanwhile, had things to do all day. Naukaram rarely watched him at work. If he ventured into the kitchen to prepare his own vegetarian meals – he couldn't trust anybody to do that, least of all that mlecha – the cook cursed him in his own language. He swore so much, he seemed to spice his food with his curses. Naukaram wasn't surprised that Burton Sahib had mastered the cook's language. He memorised some of the curses and asked Burton Sahib to translate them. Then he learnt them off by heart. *Corbezzoli! Perdindirindina! Perdinci!* They sounded soft compared to the ones he knew from the circumcised. Damn! Good gosh! Gosh almighty! One afternoon he got in the cook's way and the cook didn't even give him a chance to apologise or step back before screaming, '*E te le lèo io le zecche di dòsso!*' Naukaram couldn't say anything back because he didn't understand what insult had been hurled at him. Burton Sahib laughed. 'He wants to pick your fleas. He's threatening you with a beating.' Naukaram didn't know enough curses to repay the cook in the same coin. One evening when he was slow serving a soufflé – the cook was very proud of his soufflés – the cook's curses flew like sparks. '*Bellino sì tu faresti gattare anche un cignale!*' Naukaram could only remember half, so Burton Sahib had to ask the cook to repeat it. Then he explained it to Naukaram with an amused smile. 'He said, "You're so handsome, you'd make a wild boar vomit."'

'How dare he?' asked Naukaram.

'Don't take it to heart. That's the way he is.'

A few days later Naukaram was sure the Italian had intentionally stirred a meat dish with his wooden spoon that was kept in its own glass and was only to be used for vegetarian dishes. Burton Sahib had explained that to the cook in detail. Now the spoon smelled disgusting. Lucky he had noticed in time. The only language the cook understood was blows, so Naukaram hit him on the back of the head with the spoon. The cook spun around with a yell. He had a knife in his hand and stabbed the air with it, cursing. Naukaram turned and left the kitchen, clutching his spoon. He had to learn to swear in Italian.

Burton Sahib helped him. Belated repayment for the Gujarati, he explained. First the basics. *Stronzo. Merda. Strega.* Naukaram took to strutting about the kitchen ejaculating one or other of these words as spitefully and vehemently as he could. The cook replied with a whole battery of polysyllabic projectiles. *Cacacazzi. Leccaculo. Vaffanculo. Succhiacazzi.* Naukaram ceased to worry about translation; he knew he was still outgunned.

'If you really want to annoy him,' Burton Sahib told him, 'you should say, "*Quella puttana di tua madre!*"' Naukaram bellowed it at the mlecha at the first opportunity. It worked. More effectively than he'd expected. The cook fell silent, looked away. The next day Sabbatino gestured to Naukaram to come and join him at the stove; he wanted to show him something. He was emanating an unfamiliar friendliness. Naukaram carefully approached the cook. They both stepped up to a huge pot; the cook lifted the lid. A cow's head appeared, peacefully simmering away, its docile eyes trained on Naukaram. '*Ti faccio sputare sangue!*' Sabbatino hadn't

finished saying these words before he felt the dark-skinned foreigner grabbing him by the collar and forcing him down onto
the charcoal oven. He felt the heat singeing the hairs on his
underarms and retaliated by ramming his head into the
manservant's face. They fell to the floor, knocking over the pot,
and when Burton came rushing into the kitchen from the dining room, alarmed by the crash, he saw the cook, the servant
and a cow's head lying on the floor, and the Italian's yelling
was drowned out by a howling that came from somewhere
deep within Naukaram.

It was impossible to keep Naukaram on after that. Burton's
parents had become accustomed to Sabbatino's good cooking,
and, by comparison, Naukaram was superfluous. Burton paid
him enough money for his journey and to buy a little house in
Baroda. And he would have given him a glowing letter of reference if, utterly shameless fellow that he was, he hadn't
insisted that everything that had happened was his master's
fault. 'Why didn't you . . .' Burton shouted at him to hold his
tongue. That was the trouble with these people. They were
incapable of assuming any personal responsibility. Infuriated,
he confirmed in a short note that Ramji Naukaram of Baroda
had served him from November 1842 to October 1849. Then
he signed it with a flourish.

Arabia

Mediterranean Sea

Alexandria

Jerusalem

Cairo

Suez

EGYPT

Nile

ARABIA

Hejaz

Red Sea

Yanbu

Medina

Jiddah

Mecca

N
W · O
S

0   200   400 km

The pilgrims, the satraps and the seal
of interrogation

The Grand Vizier
Rashid Pasha
Topkapi Palace
Istanbul

Assalaamu Alaikum Wa Rahmatullahi Wa Barakatuhu
Peace be upon you, and upon those who enjoy your protection.

I should like to bring to your attention an affair that might not seem at first sight either to be of paramount importance or to pose an immediate threat to the caliphate's interests, but which nonetheless, in my humble opinion, demands the government's keenest consideration. You will, I am sure, remember my memo over a year ago concerning a British officer who had performed the Hajj, an event greeted with raptures of delight by the British press, which fêted him as the hero of the hour. A few weeks ago the publishing firm Longman Green brought out an account written by this individual, Richard Francis Burton, lieutenant of the British army, of his sacrilegious Hajj, which he performed disguised as a Pathan from India. All the newspapers have afforded this publication acres of space, falling over themselves to laud such a courageous exploit, glittering achievement and so on, and generally whipping one another up to ever greater heights of adulation. Apparently nothing in this age excites the imaginations of the British kingdom's reading public more than daring journeys of exploration to parts of the world of which they can form absolutely no mental picture.

The reasons for the book's success seem to me obvious and harmless, on the one hand, and mysterious and diabolical, on the other. The British empire's subjects long to participate in the adventure of world conquest; they crave a diet of modern-day legends with which they can vicariously identify. That apart, however, I also have a suspicion that these publications are preparing the ground for a not-so-distant future in which previously remote, unknown corners of the world will become part of the empire. This literature therefore serves to familiarise the public before the fact with foreign lands which the British empire plans to incorporate. Hence, to my mind, this apparently trivial affair reflects a disturbing development that requires close attention, particularly because the setting in this case is not the wilds of Africa or the jungles of India, but our most sacred shrines, the Holy Cities of Mecca and Medina, may God ennoble them.

I am well aware that Ambassador Viscount Stratford de Redcliffe enjoys your, as well as the sultan's, complete confidence, and I have no doubt his support is needed to see through those reforms that, with divinely blessed foresight, your excellency has initiated, but if I may, in all humility, be permitted to make a suggestion, I would advocate that with all due resolve – and the most thorough secrecy – an investigation be set in train to uncover the background of this case. The true intentions of Lieutenant Richard F. Burton and his sponsors (purportedly the Royal Geographical Society, a dubious organisation that professes solely to be interested in longitudes and latitudes) cannot be gleaned from his account, despite it being published in three volumes and running to 1,264 pages in total. From a close study of the material, we can gain a clear picture neither of the motives of this so-called adventure – with discoveries, generally the reward only goes to the first comer

and, as we know, several Christians have already performed fraudulent Hajj – nor of the actual results of this
alleged research trip. To allow you to form a clearer
impression, I enclose the three volumes, confident the
English will present no problems.

May the Blessings and Mercy of God be upon you.

Abu Bekir Ratib Effendi
Ambassador of the Sublime Porte in London

∾

'I know you!'

'Me?'

'Yes, you there, I know you.'

'How can that be, Effendi?'

'Stay where you are.'

'You must be mistaken.'

'It's not exactly run of the mill, your face, is it?'

'You must be mixing me up with someone else. We are all
looking the same.'

'Are you going to Alexandria?'

'No.'

'Where are you going?'

'I am going on the Hajj, mashallah.'

'On a British ship?'

'I was in the land of the Franks.'

'As a servant?'

'A merchant.'

'Long crossing, isn't it?'

'Yes, a long crossing.'

'Stormy today. Doesn't suit you fellows, does it? Still, you'll
soon be on dry land.'

'I don't mind . . . but yes, dry land, it's better that way, of
course.'

'Wait a second. You're from India, aren't you?'

'No.'

'Yes, yes, we met over there.'

'No, I have never been to India in my life.'

'But your English – you speak it like an Indian.'

'My English is not good.'

'Why are you so hot on us never having met?'

'Well, let us say we do know each other but cannot remember where from – surely that is the same as us not knowing each other?'

'What's your name?'

'Mirza Abdullah.'

'From Persia, isn't it? You're from Persia! Mirza? A Shia, eh?'

'And what is your esteemed name?'

'The nerve! That would be unthinkable in India . . . Captain Kirkland, if you must know.'

'If we're going to talk about my religion, we should at least introduce ourselves first.'

'Well then, Abdullah, you've got a noble face . . . I grant you that . . . and I never forget a noble face. We're not getting into Alexandria until tomorrow. I'm sure I'll remember where we've met before then.'

'Inshallah, Captain Kirkland. I would be glad to know the ties that bind us.'

∽

What an arrogant oaf. Unbelievable. He'd been very small fry in Bombay in his day; part of the stuffing at the bottom of the pile. A figure of fun in the mess, who could never remember his subordinates' names. Nondescript little blighter. How men's appetites – and self-importance – swell as their careers advance. The way he'd treated him – that puffed-up little failure thought himself infinitely superior. He needs a good kick up the backside, not that he can allow himself such a pleasure at the moment, not as Mirza Abdullah. It would attract too much attention. Damnation. He is trapped in his role, at the mercy of every imbecile. Donning the robes was easy, and remembering the codes of propriety and etiquette hadn't been that hard either, but now he will have to learn to endure the attendant humiliations.

Noble face? What did that castrated scarecrow, that miserable pipsqueak know about noble faces? Still, it was amazing that this barbarian from Wiltshire had recognised him. They hadn't seen each other for half a dozen years. How had he spotted him through the robes and the walnut oil and the full beard? Perhaps the way he walked, his bearing, had given him away. Someone like Kirkland, with all his days on the parade ground, would notice that. But he hadn't been as convinced of what he was saying as he'd made out. That was something you could take for granted with these birdbrains: the more they puffed themselves up, the more uncertain they were of what they were saying. But only with the natives, of course; only with the natives. It was a warning, though, this meeting – Fate tipping him the wink. Be careful, it was saying, be on your guard against chance; accidents will always trip up the overconfident.

∾

'I would like to apply for a passport.'
'Where are you from?'
'India.'
'Why do you need a passport?'
'For the Hajj.'
'Name?'
'Mirza Abdullah.'
'Age?'
'Thirty.'
'Profession?'
'Doctor.'
'Doctor? Aha, a doctor from India? Shouldn't I put "quack"?'
'I prefer "charlatan".'
'Have you the effrontery to contradict me?'

'Not at all. I am seconding your opinion.'

'Distinguishing characteristics, apart from insolence?'

'None.'

'That will be a dollar.'

'A dollar?'

'Which ensures you the protection of the mighty British empire. That is worth a dollar.'

'The mighty empire needs my dollar?'

'Hold your tongue, you old woman, or I'll have you thrown out. Sign here, if you can write. Or else just scribble some mark of your imbecility. There. Now you have to go to the zabit: the local police have to countersign the passport, otherwise it's worthless.'

∾

He won't simply be a doctor, he's decided; he'll also be a dervish. An excellent combination. As a doctor he'll win people's trust, if he can help them . . . only if he can help them, of course, but he's confident. He has been a dabbler in medicine for years and for the last few months he has been studying intensively, extending his knowledge book by book. Now he just needs practice, but there should be no lack of opportunities for that in Cairo. Local medicine has grown an ever paler shadow of its Golden Age with each passing century and, in any case, most people in those parts can be cured through suggestion, something in which he is a master. His dervish exterior, meanwhile, will protect him from zealots. It will afford him a certain licence, the privilege of fools. Unusual behaviour will be forgiven. A dervish can fashion his own wild piety out of a disdain for the laws. There, it's all thought through: his name is Mirza Abdullah, he is a dervish and he is a doctor.

∾

From the zabit he was referred to the muhafiz, at whose door he squatted for a long time until an official tossed him the scrap of information that the Diwan Kharijiyah was the place to apply for the authorisation he needed. He found his way to a huge building of confusing geometry, the walls of which were whitewashed to such a brilliant pitch it hurt to look at them in the dazzling sunlight. The corridors were crowded with nervously squirming petitioners. A door standing open proved not, as he quickly ascertained, to be an invitation to enter. Surrounded by stacks of files reaching almost to the ceiling, the official he spoke to leapt to his feet behind his desk to lend point to his yelling; Mirza Abdullah beat a dutiful retreat. The few trees in the central courtyard had been robbed of all their leaves. No breeze slipped past the guards at the gate. He stated his business to a police officer, who was sitting comfortably in a shady corner. Do not disturb, said the closed eyes, the outstretched legs, the chubby, contented expression. Even as he asked his question, he realised the futility of doing so. 'No idea,' mumbled the officer barely audibly, his eyelids motionless. Mirza Abdullah could have tried bribery, but that struck him as premature and not cheap, or threats, but they seemed undermined by his wretched clothes. All that was left, therefore, was the province of all supplicants, the sole recourse of the powerless: he could doggedly pester the officer until eventually, for the sake of peace and quiet, he did something. Mirza Abdullah took a step forward and repeated his question. 'Be off,' the reply rang out, the eyes opening. Mirza Abdullah held his ground with bowed head and unshakable humility. Leaning forward, he put his request for the third time.

'Get the hell out of here, dog!'

'But what about the brotherhood of Muslims?' whispered Mirza Abdullah . . . His plea died away as the officer tore himself from his dreams, a hippopotamus-hide whip in his hand.

Mirza Abdullah asked every possible source of information – other policemen, scribes, grooms, donkey boys, general loafers. He increasingly felt as if he had become lost in an encyclopaedia where every entry was a cross-reference. Finally, in weary despair, he offered a soldier some tobacco and promised him a handsome coin if he would help. Delighted by the smoke and the promised sum, the man took him by the hand and led him from official to official until, climbing a grand staircase, they entered the presence of Abbas Effendi, the deputy governor, a small man with tilted head and a pair of tiny, buttery eyes that scrutinised the new arrival expectantly, as he asked, 'Who are you?' All the appetite drained from his eyes when he heard the petitioner was a dervish on the Hajj. 'Downstairs!' he spat, an incomprehensible instruction to Mirza Abdullah but enough for the soldier to find an office that would attend to his case.

He waited outside the office with a group of men from Bosnia, Roumelia and Albania. They were barefoot and broad-shouldered, with dark eyebrows and furious faces; mountain farmers who wore long pistols and yagatans stuck in their sashes and suits of clothes slung over their shoulders. When an underling announced that his master, the official they needed to see, would not be attending to any more business that day, their seething discontent erupted. They grabbed the bearer of this disrespectful news by the collar and accused the both of them of being a pair of idlers. The curses rumbling in their throats forced the official into elaborate apologies, the conjurations of a tamer who has lost control of his wild animals.

The next day, Mirza Abdullah obtained permission to travel in any part of Egypt he pleased.

❦

It wasn't an easy business getting up to his room in the cara-vanserai. The narrow staircase was busy and so steep the porters staggered from wall to wall on their way down. They were fol-lowed by an imposing group of women intently pursuing their conversations from step to step, every gap in their ranks filled by children who ran their hands along the dirty walls. When the last of the women had passed, three soldiers appeared, sharing a joke in the confined stairwell. They stopped for the punchline, and then carried on in fits of booming laughter. Immediately they were gone Mirza Abdullah slipped onto the stairs. Halfway up he came face to face with a portly, middle-aged man who made no move to press himself against the wall. Mirza Abdullah introduced himself, and the man replied in turn: 'Hajji Wali, merchant, regular of this wakalah. May I invite you for tea?'

Mirza Abdullah accepted politely.

'I have to give some instructions'; the merchant indicated the courtyard with a self-possessed laugh. Below were the work-shops, shops and storerooms.

'And I'm on my way up,' said Mirza Abdullah.

'You're the younger man,' said the merchant, 'I'm sure you hardly notice a little flight of steps like this.' He laughed again. Clearly his gloomy eyes and talkative mouth were yet to come to an understanding.

The set of two rooms that comprised every guest's accom-modation were unfurnished. Stains the size of dead flies deco-rated the walls. Thick spider's webs hung from the black rafters; dusty air sneaked through the windows, past the jagged remnants of the original glass and the bits of paper pasted over their frames. Mirza Abdullah leant out. At least it was better than sharing the courtyard with its complement of tethered cattle, howling beggars and servants lying on huge heaps of cotton bales, scratching themselves pensively. He saw Hajji Wali picking his way through the throng; the merchant waved and repeated his invitation with gestures. Shortly after-wards a servant appeared and showed him to the merchant's comfortably furnished outer room.

'This city, this Cairo, is a pestilence –' Hajji Wali had lain down on the kelim but couldn't get his head comfortable on the round cushion – 'Who had the cursed idea to build a city here, between reeking water and blasted stone? Everything that creeps and flies in this place either bites or stings. I hate leaving Alexandria but business cannot make a detour round Cairo; its scourges are the price we pay for prosperity and good fortune. What about you? What has brought you here? You're not from

this dusty hole, I can see. I can hear it too. Smoke, smoke . . .
why are you hanging back, go on, smoke. I don't like the rose
taste, but the smell makes me forget I am here for a moment.
You don't look like most Persians . . . I understand, I understand. Ah, you have truly travelled the world. My journeying
seems merely like paying visits to neighbours by comparison.
But you're making one great mistake, if I may be allowed to
comment. I know my compatriots. As soon as their faith
wavers, they fortify themselves by turning on the misguided
Persians, sometimes with curses, and sometimes with blows as
well. You will be charged three times as much as other pilgrims,
I guarantee you, and you'll consider yourself lucky not to
receive at least one beating during the Hajj. Drink another cup,
come, drink. If I were you, I'd discard the title Mirza, no need
to present yourself in all openness. "Sheikh" will be safer. And
since you are versed in the mysteries of medicine, you should
put your knowledge to use. We are swarming with doctors, but
those who are successful quickly acquire a reputation and are
shown a respect that may be useful. I see you choose your own
path in life and I admire that, but alas, one so rarely has the
chance to explain one's path to others. Imbeciles lump everything into one box and then smash it, saying it's the wrong
shape. We will be friends, Sheikh Abdullah, but beware of candour and honesty. Always conceal, as the proverb has it, thy
tenets, thy treasure, and thy travelling.'

❧

The Governor of the Hijaz
Abdullah Pasha
Jeddah

According to our information the unbeliever who performed the Hajj and subsequently wrote an account of it
had already served as a spy in Hindustan. We can only conclude that the Royal Geographical Society is a façade for

reconnaissance missions to parts of the world not yet subject to the queen. Our primary concern is not the profanation of the Holy Cities, but the British empire's secret intentions. Disguised as a safarnameh, the report, a quarry of precise observation and calculation, is surprisingly learned; our ulema have confirmed the author's erudition, whilst adding of course that knowledge and faith are by no means the same. It is reasonable to assume that the author has not confided completely in the general reader. Our suspicion is that Lieutenant Richard Francis Burton spied on our positions in the Hijaz, our troop strengths, the nature of our defences. We also suspect that he sounded out the Bedouin's attitude to our rule and the likelihood of their taking up arms against us. We enclose all the relevant documents: a list of the persons who travelled with him; copies of the most important sections of his book with his often extremely illuminating commentaries, footnotes and the like. It is for you to conduct a thorough investigation into whether this man was travelling alone or with assistants or accomplices, whether he drew attention to himself in any way, and what, if anything, his behaviour can tell us about his intentions. The testimony of witnesses to his conduct during the Hajj may easily reveal the nature of his mission and the political aims of his superiors. The sultan suspects this affair could indicate a massive subterranean river that might wash away the foundations of our power in the Hijaz. Consider, therefore, how often Abdulmecid's astuteness has put the narrow confines of our reasoning to shame, and with God's help bestir yourself.

Grand Vizier Rashid Pasha

∽

Cairo waits for the sun to set and the moon to shrink before it opens like a mussel shell and reveals its beauty in a play of silhouettes. Scattered high above the invisible squalor, the summer stars bespeak a better creation. Strips of indigo separate the coping of the houses. It is as if he is sinking deeper into molten lead at every step. Is this what always makes him take to the road again – this temporary blindness? In soft, green, mannered England, everything is book-like, open. How can a country be so unmysterious? Here row upon row of heavy, wooden-worked balconies seem to interlace, while every alley suggests a dead end. The dimmest of oil lamps wrest everything he can see from the thick embrace of the night: passages, stairs with golden light falling over their steps. Not a line is straight; in these latitudes, the arch is preferred, even worshipped. The curve, it is universally acknowledged, buttresses faith more firmly than the right angle. Especially when elegantly inscribed with sacred quotations.

Buildings gnaw at the lanes; jutting pillars loom out at the last moment like discreet guards. At first he only sees the mosque's minaret above the roof ledge, and then, suddenly, the glowing invitation of its vaults. It is time for another prayer. He listens to himself breathing as he plunges his hands in the basin and washes each finger in turn. The splashing water lulls him. His feet dry a little at every step on the carpet. He finds a place near a pillar. Each word is meaningless unless it is preceded by a declaration of purpose, the compass needle that shows his prayers the way. A nearby candle casts its glow on his hands placed on top of one another. Behind his half-closed eyelids, all agitation has ceased. The last of his thoughts evaporate like the remaining drops of water on his eyebrows, his beard. He surrenders to the rhythm of the movements. All is forgotten except the regularity of the prayers. Pure self-evidence. Afterwards, leaving the mosque, he feels reconciled with all creation. A few palms lean their heads into the wind; the night is wondrous in all its parts, thanks to his, thanks to everyone's spirit. The lonely wanderer, he cannot imagine the dirty, rushed, dazzling, oppressive life that will resume at daybreak.

~

Sheikh Muhammad Ali Attar was recommended to him as a teacher, and sure enough, when this old man first came into the room, an entire lecture seemed to be written on his deeply wrinkled forehead. '*Aywa! aywa! aywa!* Even so, even so, even so,' he murmured before launching into his tuition, an exposition of doctrine equipped with every conceivable legal nut and bolt. Sheikh Abdullah let the teacher talk until he was exhausted, although nowhere near finished. Then he described the spiritual sustenance he had prescribed himself. Could the learned Sheikh Muhammad Ali Attar provide him with just this? Sheikh Muhammad complied, albeit in his own roundabout way; he was soon counselling and criticising his pupil on every aspect of his behaviour, roaming at will through all the areas of life.

'*Aywa, aywa, aywa*, what then is the meaning of Hajj? A striving! For what? For a better world. What are we on earth if not travellers to a higher goal? What are present tribulations compared to the eternal reward? And so, if a man is healthy, equipped for the journey and with the means to buy water and able to pay for the journey . . . you are always writing, my brave, what evil habit is this? You must have picked it up in the lands of the Faranjah. Repent before it is too late. Repent . . . *Aywa, aywa, aywa*, in ihram you may not cut or pluck your hair, not even trim it, neither the hair on your head, under your arms or on your genitals, nor the hair of your beard or any other part of the body. And should you be guilty of transgression, in expiation you shall give two handfuls of grain to the poor in Mecca – that is for one hair; you shall give double for two. Don't squander precious knowledge, my son, you have yourself and two servants to feed. Egypt's doctors never write so much as "Alif Baa" without recompense. Are you ashamed of your work that you ask no fee? What are you seeking to prove to yourself and us? Better go and sit upon the mountain and say your prayers day and night . . . *Aywa, aywa, aywa*, now take note; you must start from Safa and go to Marwa, and you must repeat this stretch seven times, the whole stretch, not a step less, and if you are not certain how many times you've walked it, start from the lower estimate reciting the Glorious Qur'an and when you reach the green marker in the middle, pick up your feet and run the few paces to the second green marker . . . I don't understand it, my dear friend, your servant wrote down two pounds of meat and you let him do as he likes; you don't reprimand him. Where is that supposed to lead? Do you never say, "Guard us, God, from the sin of prodigality!" . . . *Aywa, aywa, aywa*, you have to count out seven pebbles for the first pillar, the one nearest to the al-Khaif mosque, and you must throw them one after the other, aiming as well as you can, and if you don't hit the pillar, you must throw them again, and when you've finished, you go on to the next one . . . Have you a wife? No? Then you must buy a slave girl, my lad! Such conduct is not right. Men will say of you . . . Repentance: I take refuge with God . . . "Truly his mouth waters for the spouses of other Muslims.'"

Thus Sheikh Muhammad taught his pupil Sheikh Abdullah in the front room of a wakalah in Cairo, and yet, as he loudly and repeatedly declared at the end of their meetings, he would willingly have followed him anywhere on earth, even to the dark side of Mount Kaf.

It is a matter of patience, of learning to give his tongue time to acclimatise itself, to stretch and reach up for the consonants at the roof of the mouth, the asthmatic sounds at the back of the throat. He learns to rock his body to the fluent rhythm of stressed and unstressed accents in a recitation. To leave what is righteous and pure to the right hand. To drink sitting down, in three grateful gulps. To include his beard in every instance of surprise or reflection. To gird his every hope, his every thought of the future in an 'Inshallah'. To accustom himself to the fact that now, after careful reflection, he is a Pathan who was born and has grown up in British India and hence is more at home speaking Hindustani than the dialects of his Afghan forebears. This already seems familiar, almost second nature. How far he has come since the days of trying to learn the Arabic script on his own as a young student, the days when, proudly wanting to show a Spaniard how smoothly he could write, his attempts had earned only scorn. 'You start on the right,' remarked the señor, who had one of those Iberian names like folds of drapery. There were no Arabic classes in Oxford, no alternatives to the Latin mispronounced by old men who refused to listen to reason.

People's expectations of a dervish are far harder to satisfy. Deference is out of place; thoughtful, restrained behaviour equally so. He has to be rough and ill-bred, utterly unsubmissive to civilisation, despising petty human cares, liberated from the rational order. Proximity to God cannot be measured by weights one finds in the bazaar. He chants zikr after morning prayers until his devotion comes to the boil and his cries scald his neighbours' sleepy ears. If anyone crosses his path, he cuts him a dark look full of coded threats. He never misses an opportunity to hypnotise volunteers, who, once they are biddable, he puts in situations that reveal their ridiculousness. A dervish's lessons are painful for the petty-minded, for shopkeepers. But then he is equally quick to bring them round and ask them to tell the crowd of onlookers how much better they feel. He must always find a balance between magic and healing.

∽

It was amazing how quickly he became a sought-after doctor in Cairo. Shortly after arriving he had sat with one of the porters in the rear courtyard of the caravanserai and dripped some silver nitrate in the man's bleary eye, whispering that Sheikh Abdullah never took money from those who couldn't afford it. You understand, a dervish deserves richer pickings. The next day the porter knocked on his door to thank him –

his eye was much better – and behind him stood a friend with another complaint. Sheikh Abdullah administered various pills, the sick man's condition improved, and the new doctor's reputation with it. Henceforth the door to his outer room – he didn't let anyone into the inner – was thronged with indigents who, once they had been cured, came back to ask the doctor for the means to preserve the life he had saved. This drove him into a tremendous fury, and the importunate hurriedly took their leave before the dervish remembered he could not only prevent harm but also conjure it up.

After the people had made him famous, patients from wealthier backgrounds began to make appointments to see the truth of the rumours for themselves. Summoned to his first patrician house, he was on the point of committing a grave faux pas when Hajji Wali bumped into him in the rear courtyard and wondered where he was off to on foot. 'You owe it to your position to insist that a servant comes and fetches you with a mule and takes you to the patient's house,' the merchant exhorted him, 'even if it's just round the corner. One of my people can deliver the message,' he offered, and immediately called over an idler.

Sheikh Abdullah soon learned the use of sounding out on the way to a patrician mansion the servants, who were unable to refuse to answer a severe-looking dervish's questions. Knowing about the family, its habitual ailments, was half the cure. He would make a humble entrance, bowing to the assembled company and raising his right hand to his lips and forehead. When asked what he would like to drink, he would call for something they were certain not to have, before eventually settling modestly for coffee and a pipe. He would start with the patient's pulse, then examine the tongue, finally look into the pupils. After questioning him at length, he would parade his learning. His expositions had sometimes a Greek, sometimes a Persian gloss, or at least, if his knowledge wasn't up to it, his terminology was spruced up with Greek and Persian suffixes. The patient would run through all his complaints without drawing breath, finally eliciting a diagnosis that would identify a temporary enfeeblement of one of the four elements. The doctor from India would then prescribe something suitably substantial and robust – a dozen huge pills of bread dipped in a solution of aloes or cinnamon water for the rich man's dyspepsia, for instance – and he would never fail 'in God's name' to add 'one of the All-Merciful's' more painful treatments – the regular rubbing of the 'penitent's' skin with a horse-hair brush, for instance. After which the visit would culminate in the inevitable haggling over the fee. The doctor would ask for five piastres; the patient would complain. The doctor would be unyielding until the patient threw a few coins on the floor, cursed the boundless avarice of the Indians, furiously questioned his cure and concluded finally that the world is a carcass and they who seek it are vultures. Such unseemly behaviour couldn't conceivably be left unchallenged: the dervish would threaten never to treat any future sicknesses, to shun that house for ever, to inform all the other masters of the healing arts of the spiritual corruption he had endured under its roof.

Eventually, after all was said and done, the moment would arrive for him to leave a prescription, so he would ask for quill, ink and paper, and then write in a script that could barely control its flourishes . . .

In the name of God . . . Praise to the Ruler of all worlds, the Curer, the Healer . . . and peace be with His family and His companions . . . Let the patient take honey, cinnamon and *album graecum*, of each half a part, and of ginger a whole part, and let him pound them and mix them with the honey, and form them into little balls the size of a fingernail and daily let one of these dissolve on the tongue, the effects will be wondrous . . . and let him abstain from meat and fish, vegetables and sweetmeats and all foodstuffs that cause flatulence or acidity . . . so shall he be cured with the help of our Lord and Healer.

Peace be upon you – *Wassalaam!*

The doctor's ring seal would then be applied to the prescription, beginning and end, after which the visit would be deemed to have come to a successful conclusion and farewells could therefore be conducted in an atmosphere of the greatest mutual respect.

∾

The Sharif of Mecca
Abd al-Muttalib bin Ghalib
and the Supreme Qadi
Sheikh Jamal

I wish to inform my esteemed brothers in Islam as to the progress of our investigation into the British officer Richard Francis Burton, who completed the Hajj two years ago with the intention, we suspect, of reconnoitring the Hijaz and the Holy Cities. From his detailed descriptions, we have been able to trace some of the men who travelled with him, spent days and months at his side, and even went so far as to open their houses to him and show him their hospitality in al-Medina and al-Mecca, may God the Almighty exalt them! We intend to question these men about this desecrator. We have no doubt you will wish to be present at these interviews and we would value all such counsel as your wisdom can vouchsafe us.

Abdullah Pasha
Governor of Jeddah and the Hijaz

∾

His skills as a practitioner received ringing endorsements. He graduated from constipation to gallstones; he opened his first abscess, he cured insomnia and backache. This Sheikh Abdullah, people were soon saying, reads afflictions' tracks, he can recognise illnesses by touch. Soon it was patriarchs sending for him, obese men with firm voices plagued by gout and discontent; dignitaries who greeted him like a king and paid him like a forger; fathers who put the lives of their children in his hands.

One day one of these clients sent for him to enquire with many pious circumlocutions whether he would be prepared to treat the mistress of the house. The doctor, who had long imagined what it would be like to gain access to a harem, the last of the forbidden realms, hid his joy behind a solemn statement of a doctor's duty to put himself at the disposal of every living person, regardless of their standing, means or sex. The patriarch then described his wife's complaints, her pain and nausea, which could have been symptoms of almost anything. 'Only examination', replied the doctor, 'can reveal the true nature of the illness.' He had already treated women once, shortly after his arrival in Cairo – some slaves from Abyssinia. Their owner, who lived opposite the caravanserai, had asked the doctor for his help in a matter that was driving him to despair. Sheikh Abdullah had feared a terminal illness, a failure on his part. Crowded into a miserable little room, the slaves openly stared at him, giggling. The slave trader pointed to one of the young women. 'She's beautiful,' he said, 'worth at least fifty dollars. But her affliction is pushing down the price. I didn't notice the fault when I bought her, not that I could have.'

The doctor couldn't see anything out of the ordinary about the woman either, apart from a prodigious behind, but that was probably one of the characteristics that made her valuable. 'Perhaps you could explain the nature of her affliction,' he suggested.

'Of course; after all, it's not something you can notice during the day,' the slave trader said, smiling unpleasantly. 'She snores. Like a rhinoceros!'

Sheikh Abdullah burst into relieved laughter. 'A rhinoceros?'

'Unusual, isn't it? The others make a joke of it; they're young, they can sleep through it.'

'This little defect will not be a challenge for me. I am renowned in my country, and one of the names I am known by, you will be amazed by what it means, is Gharagharesha: the conqueror of snoring.'

It was the slave trader's turn to be relieved. A bout of hypnosis and the young woman was cured, or at least so the doctor claimed; the slave trader promised to pay after the following night. One of his easiest successes.

The discussion with the patriarch concluded, one of the servants asked the doctor to follow him, and he set off towards the woman of his imaginings: long, curly ink-black hair, velvety skin, slender arms – a continuation of the smiling eyes that addressed him in the street. Not that he knew the patient's age; perhaps his excitement was premature. He followed the servant up some stairs and along a balustraded gallery to a door. The servant stopped, turned to the doctor and asked him which was his stronger eye. Taken unawares, the doctor didn't know which of his eyes to give preference to. The servant stood behind him, put a black blindfold over his left eye and tied it in a tight knot at the back of his head. He checked the blindfold was on properly and only then opened the door before them. If women are only worth half as much as men, the thought flashed through the doctor's mind, then it's only fair men should just see half of them.

His first impression was that they were alone, but then he heard whispering. Some women were standing behind the partition dividing the room, he guessed. In front of him was a low bed, with a few big, thick cushions beside it. 'Sit down, Sheikh,' the servant invited him. The doctor did so, assuming the most dignified position he could, and sensed someone approaching from behind. He moved his head slightly, almost imperceptibly, to the right and out of the corner of his eye he saw three women enter his field of vision, three pairs of slippers, three shawls. Two of the women seemed to be supporting the third. 'Sheikh,' he heard the servant say to his left, 'would you use this, please?' The doctor looked at the object that had been put in his hand. It was a kaleidoscope. 'Put it to your eye,' said the servant. 'Call loudly if you need me; I'll be outside the door.'

The doctor pressed the tube to his right eye. Colours dissolved, fragments jumbling together and spinning apart. He tore the kaleidoscope from his eye. 'How am I supposed to do anything with this?'

'Don't take it off,' the servant's voice reproved him. 'Patience, you'll see quite enough.'

He put the running mosaic back to his eye. He heard the rustling of fabric, and sensed the sullen disaffection engendered by a chronic illness. Someone touched the kaleidoscope. Colours scattered; he saw a small hand, a tapestry, a nose that, as he pulled back, resolved itself into a face, the uncovered face of a girl whose amused, curious gaze was trained on the half-blind, half-monocled doctor.

'I am not at all ill,' said the girl, 'it's my mother.'

He smiled and directed the device at the girl's moving lips, and then round to the woman who lay on the bed. Everything about her was hidden except her pain.

'How am I supposed to examine her?' the doctor asked with a harsh laugh. 'I might as well have stayed at home to diagnose her.'

'We can do what we've done with the other doctors,' the girl said. 'You tell me what you need and I'll help you.'

'If we can start with the pulse,' the doctor said, 'that would make a good beginning.'

The sick woman's arm was held out to him. After the wrist, the eyes, the throat. He held the kaleidoscope with his left hand while tracing with his right the lines of pain that ran across the woman's back, over her kidneys and her liver to her creased belly, where his examination ended. He had to put the kaleidoscope down once to feel a swelling with both hands. The women didn't say anything.

The examination gave him no delight. The woman uttered bearish grunts of pain now and then, which her daughter responded to with cooing reassurances. Nothing about her suffering aroused his sympathy. The doctor wanted to get his disappointment over with as quickly as possible, especially since he had no idea how he was going to bring the patient any relief, let alone cure her. He talked about diet, explaining he would write out a prescription and give it to the head of the house, and was on the point of taking his leave when the third woman, who had thus far remained silent, asked him to stay a little longer, seeing he was already there. She had a complaint too, a minor one. But first they had to take their mother back to bed.

The doctor agreed. He sat down, savouring the aftertaste of the last voice to have spoken. The third woman was older than her sister, no longer a girl; slender, proud, dignified, she was clearly a self-assured woman. The two daughters returned.

'I am married,' said the elder of the two.

'Please put that thing back on,' interrupted the younger.

'My husband expects children from me –' every word the elder daughter uttered seemed to be an effort of will – 'and patience is not one of his strengths.' She drew back her veil and took off her shawl.

'Everything is in God's hands,' murmured the doctor.

'That is true, Sheikh, but perhaps there's something wrong with me, something that is in your hands?'

She wore dark red.

'If a doctor as renowned as you could just assure me that I can give birth.'

He couldn't take the kaleidoscope off her face. 'Of course,' he murmured, losing himself in her grief-stricken features. 'May I look in your eyes?' He moved as close to her face as the kaleidoscope permitted. Her deep, dark pupils were two fish swimming in an unfathomable sea. High up on her cheek, under her right eye, was a birthmark, as if she'd forgotten to wipe away a black tear. Close up it seemed excessive but in her face it was part of her perfection. She lay down.

'Start, Sheikh.'

He hesitated. How was he supposed to examine a woman's fertility? He checked her pulse to gain time, but the delay only amplified his misgivings. How could he promise her a child? A few harmless questions about appetite and digestion won him a bit more time. It wasn't for him to apportion blame in a couple, even as a doctor. How could he make her a promise of such magnitude?

'You are self-conscious, Sheikh,' she said, very close to him, interrupting his thoughts. 'You must examine me properly; it's more than just a matter of my life. I know you don't feel comfortable, but I beg you, steel yourself, examine me.'

Her sister knelt down next to her and began to undress her.

'If that's too much in your way, put it down. We can disregard rules in emergencies, don't you think?'

She gave him a look he would have gladly gazed at for hours. He saw her light-skinned, gently curving stomach. Her sister took his hand and placed it on her navel. He saw his hand through the kaleidoscope as if it were part of an anatomical still life. He didn't dare move. Her skin was cool, like satin. As he had expected. With a start of horror, he realised he was getting aroused. Did anything show under his jellabiya? He couldn't look down at himself with the kaleidoscope in his hand. The embarrassment was excruciating. She would carry on getting undressed and he would only be able to respond to her distress with his instinctive lust. He had to get out. He drew back his hand.

'Forgive me, I must go.'

Both sisters looked at him in amazement. He jumped to his feet, dropped the kaleidoscope, looked to the door.

'It has nothing to do with you, forgive me.'

He was at the door already.

'I have no excuse.'

'Wait,' the older sister called. 'If it doesn't suit you, you can take off your blindfold as well.'

The doctor wrenched open the door and rushed out. He walked away with the taste of his own inadequacy on his tongue.

∽

In the month of Muharram of the year 1273
May God show us His Blessings and Mercy

SHARIF: We are most grateful to the governor for his kind invitation. Clearly this affair . . . there seems no other way to express this . . . is of such weight and urgency that it demands to the very highest degree our keenest, our most undivided attention.

GOVERNOR: Before we turn to it, perhaps we should first, while we're relatively fresh, consider the Naib al-Harim's statements of account.

QADI: Of course, of course. The familiar before the unknown. The sharif and I went over all the accounts of the attendants of the Kaaba this morning. Revenues have increased, thanks be to God, by twelve per cent.

SHARIF: This file details the size of the purse we shall be sending to Istanbul this year, and as usual we are furnishing you with all the relevant records, not just the final balance but also a summary of all incomes, fixed costs, exceptional expenses, renovations and so on, so that no suspicion of irregularity may fall on us. Full and open accounting, as initiated by you.

GOVERNOR: Excellent. They appear reliable, the eunuchs. Our collaboration in this field is gratifying, most gratifying.

QADI: Gratifying to you because in the end it is us who have to pay. You have cause to be content, we the duty to be joyful.

SHARIF: What the qadi means . . .

GOVERNOR: I understand perfectly what the qadi means. He forgets, however, how expensive the Holy Cities are. Their protection costs us each year the equivalent of a military campaign, and this year, when we are forced to wage a costly war, the caliphate's finances are extremely strained.

SHARIF: They have been magnificent, the victories on the battlefield, if I may say. Our prayers have been answered. The infidels have been taught a stern lesson.

QADI: Admirable. News has reached me, though, that

Moscow's defeats were essentially the work of the British and French.

SHARIF: And of God Almighty . . .

QADI: Thanks be.

SHARIF: All the more reason to value the peace we now enjoy.

GOVERNOR: The qadi is too young to remember the grim times when we were unable to guarantee the protection we provide today. When forty thousand savages fell on Mecca, may God the Almighty exalt it. Sharif Ghalib, son of Sharif Massad, had underestimated the Wahhabi. They looted and killed and ransacked the holy places, which they said they were fostering heresy. What lesson do we draw from that? That we should never again be as weak as we were then. Our troops were forced to barricade themselves in the fortress; they were ready to fight but they were in no position to defend the city.

QADI: What about Sharif Ghalib?

SHARIF: I was a child, so I cannot trust my memories, but I have been told that my revered father, peace be upon him, hurried to Jeddah to organise the resistance from there.

GOVERNOR: I have heard that too. Although certain stubborn rumours maintain he went there to hide.

SHARIF: The nobler a family, the more enemies it has. Certain enmities outlive generations.

GOVERNOR: I consider our protection to be worth more than these dues. The Wahhabi have a large appetite, as do the British. Boundless greed surrounds us on all sides; we should all be on our guard – if we don't want to lose everything.

QADI: Some of us have more to lose than others. The Wahhabi are excessive at times, I grant you, but their faith is strong, and that is rare in this age.

GOVERNOR: Now, let us attend to the matter at hand. Have you read the documents I sent you? This British officer describes the people who accompanied him on the Hajj in great detail. He even gives names. False ones, we thought at first, but that proved not to be so: we have been able to find most of them. We will question them over the following months, God willing. Two live in Egypt, however, and so we asked our brothers there to question them for us. We received word today. The good news is that both men are alive, and were happy to provide information.

QADI: The bad news?

GOVERNOR: You'll see. I don't know what their testimonies tell us. But read them for yourselves.

SHEIKH MUHAMMAD: *Of course I remember that man. I am proud to have been his teacher. Aywa, aywa, aywa. Sheikh Abdullah was a cultivated, noble man and a wonderful doctor. I didn't need his help myself, thanks be to God, but stories of his talents were on everyone's lips. He was a doctor who actually cured people. A good Muslim, he immersed himself almost completely in religious questions; he had so little time for practical matters, I often had to set him straight. If it weren't for my vigilance, he would have been cheated and robbed blind. There was just one thing, since you ask so insistently, which didn't seem right about him: he was without a wife – do you know if he's got married in the meantime? I have prayed ever since that he may find a good wife; I didn't like the looks women gave him. He was a tall man with a handsome countenance, full of light. No one can resist temptation all his life. The Prophet, may God bless Him and grant Him peace, knew that the best way to ward off sin is to remove temptation. But apart from that? No, no. You are sowing doubts for which there is no justification; that is not only improper, it is also dangerous. He was the most serious student I have ever had; you can't believe how conscientious he was. Sometimes, when I couldn't avoid one of the Glorious Qur'an's difficult passages, we would read it over several times and he would press me to explain it to him. At such moments, I have to admit, a teacher may occasionally feign a knowledge he does not possess. So, not exactly blindly, but with old and weak and screwed-up eyes, I would hazard an approximation of its meaning. I expected, as with every other pupil, that my harmless deception would be*

accepted and allowed to pass quickly into oblivion so my hon-
our would be left intact. But this pupil listened too carefully to
every word. He saw through my deception, and losing his tem-
per, he exclaimed in a loud voice, 'Verily, there is no power nor
might save in God, the High, the Great!' I was gripped with
shame, and recovering the humility that behoves us all, I whis-
pered, 'Fear God, O man! Fear God!' Now tell me, would an
unbeliever defend the sacred book from the arrogance of an
old teacher like that?

∾

He had felt from the start he shouldn't trust this character, but
now the man was bellowing as loudly as only a barrel-chested
Albanian bashibazouk can bellow, it was too late. What had
driven him to this madness? At any moment the whole caravanserai would know the eminent doctor had become friends
with a boorish oaf. And, worse, far worse, that the esteemed
dervish had taken part in a drinking bout. He was allowed a
great deal of leeway as a dervish, but not that much – even if
he wasn't so drunk as to have lost all control and reason,
unlike the Albanian, who was flailing around, as if he was trying to defend his sister's honour after personally selling her to
a brothel.

They had met the previous day. Sheikh Abdullah, passing by
Hajji Wali's rooms to wish him good day, had found Ali Agha
ensconced, a broad-shouldered man with tremendous eyebrows, fiery eyes, thin lips and a chin sharp enough to moor a
boat. He had noticed him on several occasions already, swag-
gering about the caravanserai with a military mien, one hand
stuck in his belt as if he were wearing a gun. His gait was
impeded by a slight limp, and he sought to conceal his cultivation behind an affected gruffness. Conversation with the
Albanian was a halting business. He only used Arabic when he
had to make himself understood; otherwise Turkish poured
from him in an unbroken stream. When Hajji Wali was called

out into the courtyard, Ali Agha leaned over to Sheikh Abdullah and whispered, 'Raki?'

'There is none in the house,' the sheikh answered cautiously, whereupon the officer of Albanian Irregulars grinned scornfully and called him an ass.

The next day, however, Ali Agha called upon him in his rooms as if it were the most natural thing in the world. He launched into a monologue, only pausing occasionally to draw breath or take a deep drag on the hookah, accompanying his flood of Turkish with an array of gestures that sliced through the smoky air. When he finally stood up, and the sheikh likewise, he immediately put his arms round the doctor's waist as if he wanted a trial of strength. The Albanian clearly didn't think the Indian would be up to much, so loose and careless was his grip. The next minute, however, he was flying through the air; his head hit the mattress, his bottom thumped down onto the stone floor, his legs just missing the hookah. He jumped up and for the first time looked at his host with real interest.

'We shall get on well together, you and I! You should offer me another pipe.' He rested his hands on his hips. 'I'll stay a while.'

Out of a sudden new respect for the sheikh, he switched to Arabic and began jabbering fervently away in an equally broken, although now comprehensible, mishmash of languages about the heroic deeds he had performed in his life. By way of illustration, he rolled up his sleeves and his trousers and, pointing to an assortment of wounds, traced with his finger the topography of old scars, which lent themselves to any number of explanations.

'At home in the mountains,' he said, 'even children risk their lives. Whoever provokes a Turk earns unanimous respect, and yet still that Turk had never seen anyone as bold as I, let alone aimed at him. I knew no fear; the bullet shattered my shinbone.'

After three further eulogies to his courage, he declared the doctor was his bosom friend, and hence he needed to ask a small favour. Could he supply him with some poison, a discreet dose that never lied? He had an enemy who needed quieting.

He showed no surprise when the doctor immediately opened a casket and gave him five grains, simply dropping them carefully into the little pouch that hung round his neck. Had he asked, the doctor would have told him truthfully it was calomel or, if this were a more familiar term, horn quicksilver: it stimulates the urine and the gall bladder and is a laxative without parallel. In parting, the bashibazouk clasped the sheikh to his bosom and insisted they drink together . . . not now, this evening, late, come to my room.

When the caravanserai was quiet, Sheikh Abdullah crept along to Ali Agha's room with a knife in his belt. No one would notice anything; in any case, he could leave at any time. He would just stay for a glass and a few of those stories the Albanian would be such a master at telling. It was high time he had some honest enjoyment.

He arrived to find everything prepared for the banquet: in the middle of the room stood four wax candles in front of a solitary bed. Next to them a tureen of soup, a cold terrine of smoked meat, a few salads and a bowl of yoghurt. The dishes were arranged around two receptacles, one thin and tall, the other flat and small, like a flask. Both were wrapped in wet cloths to keep them cool.

'Welcome, my brother. Does my table surprise you? Do you suspect an Albanian of not knowing how to drink? Sit down by me.'

He took off his dagger and flung it in a corner, the sheikh following suit before sitting down. Then Ali Agha picked up a little glass, inspected it intently, wiped the inside with his index finger, filled it to the brim with spirit from the long, thin bottle and offered it to his guest with the hint of a bow. Sheikh Abdullah praised his host as he took the glass, emptied it in one, and then set it back down upturned to show that all was in order. Thus the ceremony proceeded, glass by glass. Draughts of water soothed the burning in their throats; brandishing their spoons, they tucked into the different dishes. The Albanian officer had started the feast on his own; he had cast anchor a while ago and was now sailing on high seas, but still he threw down glass after glass without any obvious loss of self-control or any diminishment in his epic storytelling. 'At home in the mountains,' he declared, 'when two men quarrel, they each draw their pistols and place them against each other's chests.'

Ali Agha paused dramatically.

'They thrash it out until they come to an agreement, but if one should pull the trigger, bystanders immediately shoot him down in turn.'

The bashibazouk inspected his drinking companion's face for any inappropriate traces of horror or contempt. Seeing Sheikh Abdullah's look of amusement, he reached for the flask in high satisfaction, filled his cupped palms with perfume and slapped it on his face. Sheikh Abdullah followed suit, and then exclaimed, 'Wait, no more stories for the moment!' He had had enough of brutal deeds; he desired enchantment, poetry – some respite from the executioner's decrees and the heady fragrance. He declaimed the first verse like a volley of cannon fire so the Albanian would give him his full attention.

> 'Night has fallen, friend.
> Stoke the fire with wine
> That in darkness, as the world sleeps,
> We may kiss the sun.'

The last two lines were like a declaration of love.

'What a poem!' Ali Agha's face lit up. 'There are such poems in the world, damn it all!'

He kissed the sheikh repeatedly on both cheeks, until the latter took his face in his hands and amicably pushed him away. Then they emptied another glass and leant back on the cushions, mouthpiece in hand, puffing thick clouds into the air with relish. Ali Agha surveyed proceedings and pronounced himself well satisfied with their commission of this, all things considered, respectable sin. But his satisfaction soon waned; the bashibazouk was restless, he needed further highlights. He sat up, pressed his palms together and exclaimed, 'That's it, brother. We need a grand project. Something truly grand.'

'What could be grander than this?' the sheikh asked disinterestedly.

'We have to convert our friend Hajji Wali. He doesn't know how to enjoy life.'

'What a facetious idea,' remarked the sheikh.

'Do you know a more rewarding victim? No!' The bashibazouk was determined. 'It must be Hajji Wali and no one else. We will teach him drinking as if we were teaching him multiplication. He will thank us when he feels as good as we do.'

Why not, the thought reeled through Sheikh Abdullah's mind. With his girth, who knows, maybe he's ready, a convert in disguise waiting for the invitation, our invitation.

He stood up and announced with extreme dignity that he would go and fetch Hajji Wali.

The merchant had already retired for the night. Wondering about the pungent smell clinging to Sheikh Abdullah and the surprise his younger friend promised him with such childish enthusiasm in his voice, he reluctantly followed the Indian doctor to Ali Agha's rooms, where he had never set foot. The bashibazouk leapt to his feet, seized the merchant by the shoulder and forced him down onto one of the cushions. In no time he had a glass in his hand, in no time the glass was full – to his horror, Hajji Wali realised the Albanian officer was giving him alcohol. He pushed the offer away with disgust. The bashibazouk grimaced, deeply offended, and persevered with his invitation. Hajji Wali refused steadfastly. Screwing up his face in contempt, Ali Agha brought the glass to his lips. He tossed back the contents, licked his lips emphatically, forced a pipe on his guest and gathered himself for the next assault. The Hajji protested in vain that he had avoided this sin his whole life; he promised he'd drink with them tomorrow, he threatened to get the police, he quoted the Qur'an. He had hardly reached the end of the sura in question, when Ali Agha drew a deep breath.

'Sin is sin and tomorrow is tomorrow, but I know what's in

the Qur'an too, even better than you.' He flung his arms out as if he were strewing gifts among the assembled company. 'The Qur'an', he pronounced as self-importantly as an alim at al-Azhar university, 'sits in judgement on alcohol on a number of occasions. Three, to be precise.' The Albanian gathered together three fingers and raised his hand. 'And on all three occasions something different is said. How so? The first time: God warns against too much drinking. We ask ourselves: when was that? That was before he has supped. The second time: God has supped, God has . . . let's say, he has drunk a few glasses, he is not feeling extraordinarily well, so he strongly advises us . . . under no circumstances . . . to drink. That's what everyone thinks who can't take what he has drunk. Then, the third time: God forbids drinking completely . . . categorically, and when was that my brothers? That was the next morning, when God woke up with a terrible hangover. Hah! Are you going to respect the rules of a drinker with a terrible hangover before you've even tried a drop yourself?'

Before Ali Agha, swept up in his disquisitions, could get to the point, Hajji Wali had jumped up and, cutting his losses, run out of the room, leaving behind his kepi, slippers and pipe. The bashibazouk didn't dare give chase. Instead he began sprinkling perfume on the merchant's abandoned possessions and calling him a mule in more languages than he knew. Then he invited his honoured guest not to let the rest of the supper go to waste and they applied themselves liberally to the soup and smoked meat, before aiding their digestion with a fresh pipe.

Peace descended again until the bashibazouk sabotaged it once more. Uncertainly, but with no shortage of drama, he announced a yearning for beautiful dancers, for a spectacle to delight the eyes.

'They are forbidden in wakalahs,' said Sheikh Abdullah.

'Who,' Ali Agha screamed furiously, 'who has forbidden them?'

'The pasha himself,' answered the sheikh, 'the pasha in his great wisdom.'

'If it is as you say,' Ali Agha declared solemnly, his fingers twisting his tapering moustache into two vertical spikes, 'then the pasha himself will have to dance for us.' And with that he stormed out of the room.

Sheikh Abdullah got to his feet, groaning. The evening was getting out of hand. This is your last chance, a woozy inner voice said to him. Go back to your room, shut the door and go to sleep. But the Devil never deviates from his course and the sheikh persuaded himself that it was his duty to help the bashibazouk in his confusion, so he followed him through the gallery, pulled him away from the edge, and grasping his crumpled red fustan firmly, implored him to go back to his room. Ali Agha paid as little heed to him as he would a wife. Taking umbrage at such cheerless counsels, he became greatly irritated. He lashed out like a blind boxer, hitting only air over and over again until he stopped and bowed his head as if he were listening for something, waiting for inspiration. Sheikh Abdullah let him go. Perhaps the storm had passed and he could say goodbye. No, the next moment the bashibazouk rushed at the nearest door, shouldered it open and burst into a room where, lit by a half moon, two elderly women were sleeping next to their husbands on the floor. They woke with a start. Who knows what they thought they saw, but whatever it was, it didn't intimidate them in the slightest; sitting up, they defended themselves with a torrent of the bitterest curses that impressed even an officer of Albanian Irregulars. Beating an orderly retreat before the vituperation of these disgruntled women, he stumbled down the stairs and tripped over the figure of the nightwatchman muffled in a blanket, whose snores turned to screeches. Among the servants sleeping in the courtyard, who were starting to stir, was Ali Agha's, a young, thickset Albanian who asked the sheikh to help him take his master back to his room. But the bashibazouk was not to be calmed; he kicked and spat and lashed out and screamed, 'You dogs, I have dishonoured you!' until other servants grabbed him firmly by his limbs. They carried him up the stairs and dragged him into his room, watched by all the occupants of the cara-vanserai who had slipped out of their rooms, worried and curi-ous, and now found themselves exposed to the Albanian's drunken curses: 'You Egyptians! You race of dogs! I have dis-honoured you; I have dishonoured Alexandria, Cairo and Suez!' Those were his last words before he flopped onto his bed and immediately fell into a deep sleep. In the tussle one of the helpers had knocked over the bottle of raki, and the ser-vants had to slop barefoot through the reeking pool of it as they left the room. Sheikh Abdullah picked up the flask of per-fume, splashed a good dose over the bed and floor, and then passed it through the door to Ali Agha's servant. 'To cover the traces,' he said. As he was going back to his room, he saw on the other side of the gallery, with a lamp in his hand, Hajji Wali, who looked at him for a long time. Not reproachfully, as he would have expected, just full of disappointment, with the saddest look in all of Cairo.

~

In the month of Safar of the year 1273
May God show us His Blessings and Mercy

HAJJI WALI: *There was only one counsel I could give my mis-guided friend: to set off on the Hajj immediately. I knew only too well what would happen. The whole caravanserai would speak of nothing but that night, about the Albanian bashibazouk who sought equals in wickedness and the Indian doctor who had revealed himself to be a boundless hypocrite. No one would remember that this foreign doctor had cured countless people without asking for a reward. His reputation was ruined. If he had stayed in Cairo he would have had to move to a different part of the city. Who can understand such a thing? Such a good man. And yet, when the Devil tempted him, he threw away his honour and reputation for a few glasses of alcohol with an insane Albanian. What a waste!*

QADI: That tells us quite enough. Vile – but still, if our esteemed governor is of the opinion such abhorrent material serves to establish the truth . . . Anyway, we don't need further proof: his faith was a complete masquerade.

GOVERNOR: If everyone who drinks on occasion is to be excluded from the true faith, the community of the faithful would be very small.

QADI: Is that the caliphate's official position these days? Sultan Abdulmecid is fond, so they say, of the red poison from France.

GOVERNOR: I am speaking realistically. Even here, in the Holy City, I have been told one finds raki for sale.

SHARIF: How can we stop it? Punishment is . . .

QADI: . . . not rigorously enough enforced.

HAJJI WALI: *Yes, it's true, I advised him not to tell people he was Persian. He would have only met with contempt and who knows, in the Hijaz they might have beaten or even killed him. He was very happy to follow my advice, certainly, but does it follow from that that he wasn't who he said he was? Although, I have to say, I was never sure who he did say he was. He shrouded himself in uncertainty. He talked in so many languages. But he couldn't fool me. I knew he was a heretic . . . no, not the way you mean, I can't believe that. He had another secret entirely. He always acted as if he were part of the Shafi school. But that couldn't be right. You see, at a certain point I realised he was practising taqiyya, as his tradition had taught him. As you know, the Shia think they are entitled to hide their faith in cases of necessity, where it is a matter of survival. So that is the cornerstone of truth with him: he was a Shia. He was definitely also a Sufi. As for everything else, I am not so sure.*

SHARIF: A Sufi, that's it. All of us know the Sufi sing the praises of wine.

GOVERNOR: As a metaphor, simply a metaphor. It doesn't mean they commit the sin.

QADI: Then why choose such a bad metaphor? But let's forget

that – what does it matter, him drinking, if he was a Shia anyway? One cannot be damned twice.

SHARIF: If he was a Shia and kept this not only from his travelling companions, but also from his readers, it doesn't change the fact that he performed the Hajj as a Muslim and not, as we feared, as a desecrator.

GOVERNOR: That is something he has to settle with God Himself. The principal question remains: was he a spy? Although, with all this, who can tell? Perhaps your supposition is true, perhaps he also gave his superiors false information.

QADI: Are we meant to admire the Shia for being born liars now?

GOVERNOR: That may have been in our advantage.

SHARIF: They love the Holy Cities too, that's undeniable.

QADI: They love them so much they want to take control of them.

GOVERNOR: We need to dig deeper. This Richard Burton is a master of secrecy and that disturbs me. Such men conceal their intentions from those closest to them. Even from themselves. Was he a dervish, one of those who follow a tangled path? Was he true to this path? At one point in his account he writes, I'm quoting from memory, 'And now I must be silent, for the "path" of the dervish may not be trodden by feet profane.' Is he telling the truth? Or did he only write that to make himself interesting? People are always hungry for secret knowledge. But think of it: he openly refuses to tell his countrymen something. Everyone knows the English are as avid for explanations as the Yemenis are for khat. He's leading his countrymen a merry dance. He is practising taqiyya!

QADI: I've a feeling he's leading us a dance.

SHARIF: God knows best.

❧

He can't believe his memory the next day. How could he have done such a thing? What devil had been riding him? He's a convoluted mixture: man and demon, carrying around a colossal saboteur, a high envoy of Satan, who always trips him up before he's barely taken three paces. No one gets to the middle of their thirties without being disappointed in themselves at least once. Why wait for others' mistrust if you can show them how well-founded it is yourself? How pitiful, and yet he's almost proud of it. He was feeling so confident, so fearless, and fear is what would have counselled him to steer clear of the devil within him. A difficult task. But now, the next morning, holed up in a room that seems besieged on all sides by a raging, furious city, he feels fear burgeoning like the pain of an incurable wound. Fear of his unruly, incalculable behaviour. A lot can be tolerated in Cairo but in Mecca he'd lose everything in one fell swoop. Make yourself comfortable, fear, you're a welcome companion. Hajji Wali was right: the wisest thing would be to leave the city as soon as possible. The entire neighbourhood will soon be amusing itself at the lapsed doctor's expense.

It took all of one long day in the desert to escape the city and its shameful memory. For hours he rode towards a horizon that seemed full of promise, his senses quickened by the air and exercise, sharpened like a knife. The desert was wounded ground, haggard, every rise grooved like walnut shells, but still it fired the imagination of Sheikh Abdullah, who felt more alive by the time they camped for the night than early that morning in the caravanserai's courtyard, when he had joined a handful of pilgrims leading their dromedaries on the road out of the city. Hajji Wali and Sheikh Muhammad had accompanied him to the gates and bid him farewell with such warmth that he regretted having to leave them. Their only request was that he pray for them at the Prophet's tomb, then they showered their friend and pupil with blessings. The arid landscape riveted his attention: the blue-black rocks that changed colour as you rode closer; the gorges where it seemed as if you were peering into a cliff's entrails, all the veins, layers and knots exposed; a cycle of growth invisible to the human eye. The earth appeared naked in the desert, the sky transparent. He enjoyed feeling his body again, the stiffness of his muscles, the pain that comes before you get used to riding. They crossed a few wadis, sandy riverbeds the width of the storm torrents that occasionally submerged them, that were empty except for a few dried-up memories. Suez was only three days away but these three days, Sheikh Abdullah guessed that evening, would revive his spirits. Even now he felt liberated. He was glad for the exertion, the sense of danger – not imminent on this stretch but ahead, in the Hijaz desert. Cairo had taken its toll. At last he could shed his hypocritical doctor's act and be the type of man he admired again: frank, generous, single-minded. He looked around at the spontaneous hospitality at every camp-fire. Civilisation had stayed back in the city, not daring to venture through its gates; after a few days, the stiff politeness, the narrow-minded behaviour would fall away. If it hadn't been so inconceivable, he would have climbed the hill at the foot of which they were camping and proclaimed his euphoria to the world, fully expecting to hear an echo, a confirmation. He drank a cup of strong coffee instead. That was all the stimulation he needed. Just the thought of alcohol disgusted him. Would the Albanian bashibazouk feel the same when he got back to his post in Hijaz, he wondered? His appetite had returned; he devoured a meal that yesterday would have seemed inedible. Then he lay in the sand, the best of all beds, in the desert air that would restore him to peak health. He kept his eyes open until the last light in the camp disappeared with a shudder and then the night took the earth in its mouth.

The next morning he had just saddled up when a young man ran up, grabbed the dromedary's halter and greeted him in a state of high excitement. 'Don't you recognise me?' It was an insistent character who had forced himself upon him in Cairo, in the market. 'He's looking for a strong pair of shoulders to carry him to Mecca,' Hajji Wali had warned, on the watch as ever for slyness, like a falcon for its prey. 'Soon he'll tell you how useful he can be to you in his home town.' Sure enough, the next moment the young man had said he knew Mecca as well as his own house. As it had done then, his expression fluctuated between insolence and flattery, like a misaligned swing. 'Yes, it's me: Muhammad al-Basyuni. It is a blessing, our meeting again like this.'

'Providence shines on you,' murmured Sheikh Abdullah, and then, more loudly, 'What brings you here?'

'How can you ask such a thing, Sheikh? I am on my way home from Istanbul.'

'Where to?'

'Ah, Sheikh, you have forgotten everything. To Mecca the beneficent, may God ennoble her. I have heard a lot about you, you have a great reputation. I have been watching you with delight since yesterday evening. Fate has decreed that I accompany you on your Hajj. I can be useful to you, especially in Mecca, the mother of all cities. I know its every stone.'

'And the people?'

'I know them even better than the stones.'

'Aren't you a little young for such far-reaching knowledge?' asked the sheikh.

The beardless young man, his bony face like a skull in the harsh light, wasn't thrown for a moment.

'I have travelled,' he said. 'And I am watchful when I travel. I know the value of men.'

Sheikh Abdullah was surprised by the lad's tenacity. Clearly he came from a well-to-do family. His self-assurance suggested a sheltered upbringing.

'Man proposes and God disposes,' the sheikh said pensively. 'Truly his wonders are many. All fame and honour to those whose knowledge encompasses them all. Now, if you would let go of my dromedary, I'd rather not be the last in the caravan.'

'We are bound to see each other again tonight, Sheikh.'

A little later, like the others before him, he rode along a fringe of palms that stretched out into emptiness like a triumphal way.

The next evening they would reach Suez, the sea. And there, sensed the sheikh, the Hajj would really begin.

∞

In the month of Rabi al-Awwal in the year 1273
May God show us His Blessings and Mercy

MUHAMMAD: I suspected him from the start. Anyone who has travelled as much as I have can smell a fraud into the wind. I have to tell you, I know Istanbul, I've travelled to India and that's where this man said he came from. Something made me suspicious straight away.

GOVERNOR: What? A little more precision, if you please.

MUHAMMAD: Nothing in particular, a feeling, a hunch. He was different somehow; he watched everything – not in a noticeable way, but I noticed – and he always spoke very slowly, carefully. Like a wise man, that's how many people saw it, but I thought, he's being devilishly careful not to say anything wrong.

QADI: Are your suspicions based solely on this sort of conjecture?

MUHAMMAD: It wasn't plucked out of thin air. You'll see how right I am.

SHARIF: Can I clarify something? Your father's name suggests your family is not from Mecca?

MUHAMMAD: We are originally from Egypt, but we have been here a long time . . . several generations. We are true Meccans.

QADI: A little more modesty, young man. The sharif's family has resided in this city since the days of Qusayr. A few generations hardly count.

GOVERNOR: Let him continue, please.

MUHAMMAD: When we first prayed, I stood directly behind him. To be able to watch him better. I know that converts can still make mistakes after years. If he was tricking us, I'd notice it in his praying.

GOVERNOR: And?

MUHAMMAD: No, nothing, unfortunately. He must have learnt well. But it's possible, isn't it?

QADI: What is possible?

MUHAMMAD: To learn the prayers off by heart and perform them blindly.

QADI: There are many ways to expose oneself to danger. Misusing prayers is one of them.

MUHAMMAD: I didn't miss out a single prayer, and I certainly didn't make any mistakes performing them either. Isn't it my duty to expose desecrators and hypocrites if I come across them?

GOVERNOR: You did the right thing. But now you must tell us a little bit more. You haven't fully convinced us that you were in a position to expose Sheikh Abdullah as a desecrator and a hypocrite.

MUHAMMAD: Well, why are you questioning me then? Would you be wasting your valuable time if he weren't those things? No. You know as well as I do that he was a snake. But he was sly, as sly as all Indians. In Suez there were lots of us in one room, it was terribly cramped, and everyone was bad-tempered because we had to wait days for the boat but he . . . oh yes, he made good use of his time. He lent generously to the others. They were misers; you couldn't get a more tight-fisted bunch. He'd barely given them a few coins before they turned tender and affectionate. They praised him to the skies. They gave him sweetmeats. They paid him pretty compliments even when he wasn't in the room, flattering him madly. 'That Sheikh Abdullah: what a great soul, what a wonderful man.' They even fought over who would have him to stay in Medina.

QADI: What about you: didn't he offer you any money?

MUHAMMAD: Some, a few piastres. How would it have looked if I'd been the only one to refuse his generosity? That would have aroused his mistrust. But I didn't let him lull me. A loan here or there, I kept my eyes open. One evening I found in his chest – he'd forgotten to lock it – an instrument. A piece of equipment no dervish from India would carry round with him, I was sure of that. It was a strange thing I'd never seen before. Some instrument of the Devil. I asked someone who would know.

GOVERNOR: What was it?

MUHAMMAD: A sextant.

QADI: What's that?

MUHAMMAD: A very complicated instrument for measuring the stars. Apparently it's useful on a ship, but the sheikh wasn't a ship's mate; he was meant to be a holy man. I waited for him to leave the room, then I told the others Sheikh Abdullah was an unbeliever.

GOVERNOR: That's news to us.

MUHAMMAD: They didn't believe me. I made only one mistake, and that was never in my wildest dreams to imagine they would close their minds to the blindingly obvious truth that he was an unbeliever. I had expected us to discuss what action we should take against him. Instead they attacked me. Dirty opportunists, every one of them.

What reason other than necessity can there be to stay in Suez? Civilisation is taking its revenge with this village bursting at the seams, it seems to Sheikh Abdullah; every lane and hut jammed with the thousands of pilgrims that have to be accommodated. Nothing is grimmer than a half-finished settlement, nothing more comfortless than this inn, which, for amenities, offers only a roof over one's head, which, as it never rains, is of little use. He'd be better off in the gutter than within these dirt-smeared walls, sleeping on this cracked floor with cockroaches, spiders, ants and sundry other insects nesting in its every crevice. He's been used to simple inns since he was a child. Every time they would have to move again, because his father couldn't stand the little Italian town or French health resort a moment longer. But he's never had to endure anything this horrendous. The noises are the worst: the pigeons cooing in the open wardrobe, their voices hoarse and scratchy from their amorous exertions, the huge cats hunting in the attic, howling with their inexhaustible lasciviousness. Even stray goats and mules come wandering in, and it is only when one of them goes too near to a figure on the floor and gets hit that they reluctantly back out. To cap it all, the mosquitoes sing a Stabat Mater all night over the outstretched bodies, which, in his case, never enjoy anything more than a jerky doze.

∾

The rooms were dormitories that had to be shared with other travellers. On the first day, eyeing one another mistrustfully, his fellow guests introduced themselves. Hamid al-Samman, ample moustache and quiet voice that was used to being listened to; Omar Effendi, chubby face and emaciated body; Sa'ad, just Sa'ad, the darkest man Sheikh Abdullah had ever seen; Salih Shakkar, unusually light-skinned and affected. On the second day they spent their time smoking and getting to know one another. The men came from Medina, apart from Salih Shakkar, who claimed the two metropolises of the world, Mecca and Istanbul, as home, as befitted a member of the high bourgeoisie. Sheikh Abdullah was the only one among them on the Hajj. Omar Effendi had run away from home when his father had tried to marry him off, despite him never making a secret of how much he despised women. He had managed to get to Cairo and enrol as a pauper student at al-Azhar University. The others were all merchants; they knew the world and judged a man by the stories he could tell of it. Sa'ad had travelled far afield, to Russia, Gibraltar and Baghdad. Salih knew 'Stambul' like the courtyard of his house. Hamid was an habitué of the Levant; he could recommend a caravanserai in every port.

On the third day they opened their chests and offered their valuables for inspection. Sometimes the young Muhammad would become smitten by a precious object and let it run between his fingers until finally he had to be loudly asked to return it, to the particular annoyance of Hamid, who preferred to sit on his box which was jammed full of presents for the daughter of his paternal uncle – his wife, in other words. Besides this chest, Hamid was poverty incarnate – his feet were bare, his sole piece of clothing a filthy tunic, the original ochre brown of which was only to be seen when the collar was turned up. He skipped prayers to avoid unpacking clean clothes. His eyebrows creased when the talk turned to alcohol, although the corners of his mouth betrayed a secret partiality. He preferred smoking other people's tobacco; the princely sum of three piastres clinked in his pockets, which he was actually able to contemplate spending. Omar Effendi, meanwhile, was utterly penniless, despite being the grandson of the mufti of Medina and the son of an officer, who commanded the escort of caravans to Mecca. He made up for his temporary penury with a rich store of prejudices and dislikes, which he pronounced in a soft, firm voice as if they were well considered and fair-minded. Sa'ad, who never left Omar Effendi's side, turned out to be the former slave, servant and factotum, and current business partner, of Omar Effendi's father. He had been sent to fetch the fugitive son home and was equipped with sufficient funds to provide for his charge. For his own needs he observed one strict principle: Be generous when you borrow, sparing when you pay back. It was his avowed aim to travel free and he came pretty close to his ideal. Because of his dark skin he was called al-Djinni, the Demon. Dressed in just a cotton shirt, he spent most of his time lying on his two chests, which mainly contained handsome fabrics for him and his three wives in Medina. The delicate Salih had set up his bed next to him. He used it abundantly, distrusting any physical activity. His dignity was protected lying down. Half Turkish, he followed Istanbul fashions whether he was in Suez, Yanbu or any other dusty hole of the caliphate. When he spoke, it was only about himself, as if he were a paradigm for all the others who were inferior to him in breeding, taste, education and, let's not forget, skin colour – he attributed almost magical powers to his light skin – quite apart from avarice and meanness. Before holding out his hand, he would say, 'The generous man is God's friend, even if he is the greatest of sinners.' And if no one gave him anything, he would remark, 'The miser is God's enemy, even if he is the greatest of saints.'

∿

In the month of Rabi al-Akhir of the year 1273
May God show us His Blessings and Mercy

OMAR: That spoiled little monster! The arrogance of Mecca pullulated in his veins. Puffing himself up, he made a great show of announcing that he, Muhammad al-Basyuni, had overwhelming proof that Sheikh Abdullah was an impostor. Worse still: an unbeliever. We were stunned. 'What proof?' we asked him. He showed us a device made of metal which he had taken from the sheikh's chest. It was used to measure distances. 'Why does a dervish need an instrument like this?' he asked. We thought in silence – I trust everyone thought as deeply as I did – and then I realised how groundless, how outrageous that youth's accusations were. Sheikh Abdullah was a man who showed respect and was offered it in return. We may have only known him for a few days, but we had become familiar with his goodness.

GOVERNOR: Would you say he was a generous man?

OMAR: Oh yes, certainly.

SHARIF: Did you benefit from his generosity?

OMAR: Ah, the whole world gains when a person is magnanimous.

GOVERNOR: We are not interested in the world in this case but in Omar Effendi and his relationship with this Sheikh Abdullah. So, what did he give you?

OMAR: Give me? No, it was only a loan my father paid back in Medina. Do you think that was the source of our respect? He was a learned man: that was why he was precious to us. I don't know if he was an alim, but he was versed in many things. Shortly before that incident, he had asked me to look over a letter to his teacher in Cairo, a very knowledgeable work in which he sought counsel about difficult problems of theology, problems that would only occur to someone who had attained a high level of faith. I studied at al-Azhar and there were even some things I didn't know.

QADI: A term at al-Azhar is not enough to make someone an alim.

OMAR: What I know now and what I knew then is enough for me to state categorically that Sheikh Abdullah was not only a true believer, he was also a very learned and honourable Muslim. Which cannot be said of all Muslims. Ask Sheikh Hamid al-Samman. You should talk to him; he is a very respected citizen of Medina. Ask him – his indignation knew no bounds.

HAMID: Muhammad? The young Muhammad, yes, how could I forget him? A naturally spiteful person. Despite his youth. Always looking for the worst in people. He was the camel that criticises the dromedary's hump. We all knew how learned Sheikh Abdullah was: a man of profound knowledge. Why shouldn't he have an instrument we didn't know about? The accusation was ridiculous: I didn't believe it for a minute. 'The light of Islam is upon that man's countenance,' I said. 'Anyone who can see that light can feel it.' Unfortunately that wasn't enough to silence young Muhammad – he was as vicious as a jackal. He had the nerve to tell me that someone who doesn't observe the prayers is hardly capable of recognising the light of faith. That was too much, and I would have raised my hand against him if the others hadn't restrained me.

∾

They were waiting, as if they had been consigned to a place of eternal torment. They had been told they were leaving early in the morning, and now, at midday, the sun gouged out their eyes if they opened them. Chests covered the beach – chests that had been heaved, dragged and shunted across the sand, then piled on top of one another with curses to form little barricades behind which the passengers sheltered, determined to refuse all requests for payment until the hoarse-voiced end. Suez's shopkeepers knew only too well this was the plan, and consequently, accompanied by slaves and intimidatingly armed servants, they had come in numbers and were determinedly clearing a path through the throng. They halted in front of the travellers who still owed them for the goods they had already packed away and tied up, while thieves lurked in the shadow of their quarrels, waiting for a chance to make off with any unattended possessions.

Sheikh Abdullah stood behind a mound of boxes, sacks and water-skins. Salih Shakkar's servant, whose assistance was needed at this exact moment, had gone to the bazaar to attend to his own affairs, and Salih was muttering resentfully about what madness it was to be kind and generous. They passed the time watching the ship that was supposed to pick them up and take them to Yanbu. About fifty tons, Sheikh Abdullah guessed, with a mainmast considerably taller than its mizzen. Suddenly, without any signal, the whole beach was in movement; everyone was rushing to the water's edge. Sa'ad immediately grabbed the bow of one of the boats, the boatman not daring to say anything, as if it was his collar this hefty black man had got a firm grip of, but still they weren't the first to reach the ship. It was undecked, except for a small, raised poop deck next to a handful of cabins which were already occupied by a dozen women and children. They forced their way through the scrum and clambered up to the afterdeck. The servants heaved their chests up to them and stayed in the hull. There was just enough room up above for the masters. The hours passed and passengers kept coming on board in greater numbers than either the captain had announced, or his boat could hold.

Sheikh Abdullah had barely voiced the thought that there

wasn't room for a single passenger more when a group of Maghrebis piled on board, tall men with large limbs, reproachful stares and roaring voices, all heavily armed, their heads and feet uncovered. They instantly demanded a party of Turks and Syrians in the hull make room for them. In no time everyone was fighting one another, indiscriminately scratching and biting, trampling and kicking; the hull was like a kettle boiling with rage.

The owner of the boat declared that he sympathised with the passengers' unfortunate circumstances, and so he was offering each of them the chance to leave the ship with a complete refund of their fare. That was an offer no one wanted to accept. The next boat would be just as full, the one after as well. When the sail was hoisted soon afterwards, they all leapt up as if silently following a pre-arranged choreography. They recited the first sura, the Fatihah, with their hands raised to heaven as if they wanted to catch a blessing falling onto the ship. After the amen they rubbed the blessing into their faces. Then an old man launched into another prayer. 'Subject unto us this sea that is Thine on earth and in heaven, in the visible and the invisible worlds, the sea of this life and the sea of the life to come. Subject all these unto us, O Thou in whose hand the power over everything lies.'

The captain's sole means of navigation, Sheikh Abdullah realised soon after they set off, was not to let the coast out of his sight. They slowly groped their way forward. Centuries ago, Sheikh Abdullah thought, progress would have been much quicker: the captain would have had the necessary instruments; he would have known the deeps, been able to instruct his helmsman day and night. The Sinai coast was a massive, overpoweringly uniform wall of granite, crowned by day by the pinnacle-like heights of the Jabal Serbal and the rounded silhouettes of the Jabal Musa, Mount Sinai. They anchored before the sun set behind Africa. For dinner they shared a sheet of 'mare's skin', dried apricot paste, which was easier to chew than the dry biscuits that could have been hewn from the cliffs on the shore.

They were discussing which of the group would take first watch that night when a disturbance broke out below, near the afterdeck. 'Help him up,' someone shouted.

'Who?'

'The old man.'

'Which old man?'

'Here, here he is.'

'What does he want up here?'

'He's a kaas, he has a story to tell us.'

Sa'ad leant down, grasped a frail old man under the armpits and lifted him up as if he was made of parchment. The old man sat on a chest and pointed down. 'My helper. Bring him up too.' Sa'ad was stretching out his arms to lift up the story-teller's companion as well when Salih asked suspiciously, 'Why do you need help?'

'Am I to collect the money myself?' the old man replied indignantly.

'He collects money? He should collect below,' Salih called out. 'He will be paid handsomely, with all those pilgrims.'

Sa'ad let the assistant fall.

When the old man started telling his story, everyone who could see him was amazed by his powerful voice. He recited a short prayer, during which silence like black ink spread from the afterdeck over the whole ship: 'O Guardian of the souls gathered in this hull, O Protector of this hull on this fathomless sea, watch over this boat, the Silk al-Zahab. Now, tell me all of you, what do you know of time? Tell me all of you, what do you know of age? At the dawn of our time, all the mountains and bays that we have seen yesterday and today and will see tomorrow were already created. The steep shores, the reefs, the sandbanks, the cliffs were all here; the gold, the blue and the purple in which the first king dressed and with which Paradise was hung. There were people who sought justice and people who wrought injustice. There were honourable leaders and sinful tyrants. There was Musa and there was the pharaoh. You all know the story of the flight of Musa and his people, of their pursuit by the pharaoh's army and the sea that parted before the true and closed over the false. But do you know that this story happened here? Between the mountain on this side and the desert on that side. In this water by the ship, and under it, where we will pass this long night. Here the pharaoh's army was drowned in the tides of Hell. A mighty horde, a hundred thousand men strong, more powerful than the caliph's army. Not one soldier among that number reached the shore, not one came home safe. They were all taken captive by the sea, and they have never been able to free themselves. If we could look far enough down, we would see the hundred thousand warriors on the bottom of the sea. They are still marching on and on, and they will continue until the end of our time; warriors in heavy armour who sink into the sand at every step. They have to march from one shore to the other. They are damned; they can never arrive, and never go home. That's why the currents are so dangerous in these bays. That's why the deeps of these waters are so uneasy. That's why the wind never ceases beating its black wings between these two shores. But do not be afraid. For God, who accomplishes and permits whatsoever He chooses, is the best of all guardians, the best of all helpers, and He has sent someone to watch over all travellers and sailors in these perilous seas: the saint Abu Zulaymah, of whom you all know. But do you also know that he sits in one of the caves in the mountains behind me? His every need is catered to; as recompense for his good deeds, he is served coffee – not just any coffee but coffee from the Holy Cities. Bright green birds bring him beans from Mecca in their beaks and sugar from Medina, and as they fly from the Holy Cities to his cave there in the cliff wall, these birds write the Glorious Qur'an across the sky and the coffee is given him by the ministering hands of angels who delight in nothing more than that Abu Zulaymah should ask them for another cup. So do not forget to say a prayer for Abu Zulaymah today, that we may continue to walk on this earth and not on the sandy bed of this dark sea.

There is no power nor might save in God, the High, the Great.'

∽

The day breaks on a huddled mound of humanity. He sits up; they took turns lying down and the late watch fell to him. For the first time he wonders if he hasn't made a mistake. A sleepless, uncomfortable night brings doubts in its wake. Muhammad is next to him, clasping his knees, his head on his chest, the arrogance gone from his eyes. He has warmed to him a little more since yesterday. Hamid is lying by the ship's wooden rail. Sheikh Abdullah doesn't understand how he managed to crawl there in the night with all the people lying in the way. He is clearly suffering from an upset stomach; he keeps leaning over the rail. Only a few people are faithful to the morning prayer. For everyone else it's hard enough lifting their heads and looking the day mistrustfully in the face, which is full of grim presentiment.

By midday the sun is scorching; the sailors abandon their posts and take refuge in the masts' spindly shadows. Any wind blows the heat of the glowing cliffs in their faces. All colour melts away, drawing a burial shroud over the sky; the sea is an unruffled mirror of exhaustion, the horizon like a line drawn under a balance sheet. The children haven't the strength to scream. Near Sheikh Abdullah on the afterdeck a Turkish baby lying silently in his mother's arms hasn't moved for hours. He consults with the others; they can't let this infant die before their eyes. A Syrian pilgrim produces a slice of bread and dips it in his tea, and the mother pops it in her child's mouth. Hamid passes her some dried fruit, and Omar offers her a pomegranate, which he peels and breaks into pieces. The mother opens her child's mouth, Omar leans forward and squeezes the fruit. A few drops fall onto the twitching tongue, then the juice becomes a red stream that spills out of the corner of the baby's mouth and down its chin. Moments later the

245

little one smiles for the first time with his blood-red mouth and Sheikh Abdullah is comforted by the tenderness reflected in Omar's face.

How many days and nights like this will they be able to survive? That evening the pilgrims who can still stand convince the captain to drop anchor near the coast so they can sleep on the beach. As Sheikh Abdullah wades to shore, he steps on something sharp and feels a piercing pain in his toe. He sits down, and in light that is an unending declaration of love, he examines the wound and pulls out a splinter. Perhaps he stepped on a sea urchin. He digs out a hollow in the soft sand. They have bested the ship lying at anchor before him, at least for a night.

∾

In the month of Jumada'l-Ula of the year 1273
May God show us His Blessings and Mercy

GOVERNOR: We have made progress.

QADI: Leaps and bounds. If I may sum up: Sheikh Abdullah is undoubtedly the British officer Richard Burton, a man of erudition, perhaps a Muslim, perhaps a Shia, perhaps a Sufi, but perhaps also nothing but a liar who pretended to be this or that solely to perform the Hajj, with whatever intention. Certainly we know more than at the beginning, but what is this knowledge worth?

GOVERNOR: A question has been bothering me from the start . . . Tell me: do you think it's possible for someone to keep up a pretence for months that he is a believer?

QADI: Rubies and coral are the same colour. If they are strung together on a necklace, they all seem precious stones.

GOVERNOR: There must be a way to tell them apart.

QADI: I can distinguish them by the shade. But of course I'd have to look at them very carefully and closely.

GOVERNOR: Through a loupe?

QADI: A loupe would be best.

SHARIF: The coral is the Christian?

QADI: No, the unbeliever.

SHARIF: That's what I meant.

QADI: There's a big difference. I think this man is outside faith of all kinds. Not just ours. That allows him to go where his will takes him, without attacks of conscience. He can help himself to others' faiths, he can accept and reject, take up and set aside as he chooses. As if he were at a market. As if the walls that surround us had fallen away and we were outside, on an endless plain, and could see in all directions. And because he believes in everything and nothing, he can, at least in appearance, although not in grade, transform himself into any precious stone.

GOVERNOR: It almost sounds as if you envy him.

∾

Haggling time. Men stand around every dromedary, their hands flat, outstretched, their shadows compressed as if they were trying to fit into the chests; the animals' halters are pulled tight. This is the Holy Land; they've arrived. Figures in white, figures in black; standing, squatting on their heels, slurping tea between the marks of hooves and patience in the sand. Here it is, the unmarked gateway to the desert. He must ignore the nagging pain of his swollen toe if he can. A boy comes up, offering him sweets. Muhammad is off proving his usefulness. Since sunset everyone has been engaged in the same sort of vigilant inactivity, swapping news, talking, endlessly talking, with the business at hand only ever appearing, as if inadvertently, on the fringes of their conversations.

Expectations are staked out, first offers laid in the sand. The boy is back with his brown, encrusted sweets. They agree on three dromedaries at an extortionate price. 'The camel drivers are all thieves and robbers,' Muhammad whispers. 'The dromedaries only obey them, they don't recognise any other masters.' The boy with the sweets again. He buys three and pays with a generous coin. The boy grins, as if to say: I knew you'd give in eventually. They agree a time to leave, and draw out their farewells to a respectful length. By dawn they're on their way.

~

He excited attention if he wrote anything down. If he wanted to avoid suspicion, he couldn't let anyone see him with a pencil in his hand. He had to go off on his own to write. This was easy in Cairo, but travelling there was rarely a chance to be alone. It was only advisable to write in the presence of others, particularly the Bedouin, if he pretended he was drawing up a horoscope or preparing a charm, abilities expected of a dervish.

At first he had written his notes, both harmless and secret, in English but in Arabic script, and made sure no one was watching before recording his impressions in his notebook. But with time, confident of his reputation, feeling himself beyond suspicion, he began to disregard these precautions. The script became Roman, and sometimes he jotted things down unobtrusively in daylight, on the back of his dromedary, hiding a scrap of paper in his palm. 'What are you writing in the middle of the desert, Sheikh?' asked Hamid, silently spurring his dromedary level.

'Ah, my friend, I am noting down a debt, so there's no embarrassment the day it will have to be repaid.'

'For a man like you,' Hamid said before riding off, 'everything has its use.'

On journeys such as these everyone was on intimate terms with his dromedary, that surly, wilful creature whose only friendly gesture was an occasional fart. Sheikh Abdullah was immediately at loggerheads with his, a malicious, uncontrollable, even dangerous character. It mistrusted everyone it didn't know, and the noises it made, snorting groans and bleats of self-pity and fury, were unbearable. It complained about every pound you loaded on its back. On the first evening Sheikh Abdullah made a few disparaging comments about it to the camel driver.

'You know how to handle people, Sheikh,' the man answered. 'Well, dromedaries are no different. When they're young, they don't know how to behave. As adults, they're violent and uncontrollable, and when they're in rut, the little man can scent a willing little woman five miles away – then they're stubborn, and their tongue starts quivering. And when they get old, they become quarrelsome, vindictive and moody.'

At that moment shots rang out – the valley they were riding through could have been made for an ambush.

'Bedouin, those dirty dogs!' Muhammad ducked as Sheikh Abdullah returned fire.

'No!' the camel driver screamed at him. 'If we kill one of these bandits, the whole tribe will rise up against us and attack the caravan before we can reach Medina. That would be the end for us.'

'But the others are shooting,' said the sheikh.

'In the air, just in the air, so the smoke gives us some cover.'

'Damned country, justice is turned on its head,' said the sheikh, loading and shooting again without aiming.

The firing soon died away. They reached Shuhada, the place of the martyrs, having lost several dromedaries and pack animals. Meagre spoils, for which twelve lives had been squandered, twelve men they had quickly to bury before they could carry on.

∾

As long as the caravan was on the move, he didn't have to keep an eye on his belongings; the baggage was the camel drivers' exclusive responsibility. But when they camped for the night, everyone had to guard his valuables himself, and it wasn't long before the first devious raids began. These were the work of the camel drivers themselves: guards by day, thieves by night.

'Those oxen of oxen' – Muhammad had insisted on taking first watch – 'those sons of flight, may their hands wither, may their fingers grow palsied.' Muhammad kept himself awake with his cursing. 'You heroes with your foul moustaches, you basest of all the Arabs that ever hammered a tent peg. Truly you dig in the mines of infamy!'

In the early morning the camel drivers shot him furious stares, muttering, 'By God! By God! By God, boy, we will flog you like a hound when we catch you alone in the desert.'

From then on, while the sun shone, Muhammad made sure his dromedary never strayed from the shadows cast by Sheikh Abdullah and Sa'ad the Demon's mounts.

On the second evening it was Sheikh Abdullah's turn to keep guard. He untied his bandage. His foot hurt so much he wanted to stick the infected part in the fire. Perhaps a wet bandage soaked in tea leaves would be soothing. He had to distract himself somehow, even it was just by naming the stars, Latin names first, then English. They would soon be reaching the fabled Medina, the city of refuge defended in countless legends by monsters, Amazons with goat's feet, Cyclops that had caused a wealth of geological faults in their frenzies. Once they'd arrived in Medina, the home – as was well known – of all gentle, kind people, he would be able to see with his own eyes whether the Prophet's coffin floated above the ground. In the crimson hamail Hamid had given him, rather than a Qur'an he carried a watch, compass, pocketknife and a few pencils. Anyone thus equipped didn't need to be afraid of monsters, only people. He stretched his legs a little. When he sat down the pain shot up his leg.

Sa'ad had got up. He slept badly too. 'When I've done everything I should,' he'd say, 'then I'll sleep well.' He put on some tea and crouched down next to Sheikh Abdullah. The uneventful night was dealt with in a couple of sentences. He must be happy to be going home, to be seeing his family, Sheikh Abdullah asked.

'I am happy, I am very happy, but this joy will pass.'

'Why so sombre, Sa'ad?'

'I am happy for a few weeks, and then I become restless, I think business is calling and I feel the urge to set off again.'

'I know the happiness of the way,' said Sheikh Abdullah.

'Yes, the way, nothing can take its place. Despite all the tribulations, it is what makes my heart knock louder. We are riders between staging posts; it is our fate to arrive and set off again.'

'And our hopes', Sheikh Abdullah added, 'stretch far beyond our short lives.'

'Tomorrow, if God the Great and Glorious so wills it, I will be at home, but you, Sheikh, you have a long road before you. I envy you. It is still early. Why don't you lie down, I'll take over the watch.'

Sheikh Abdullah dozed off thinking of the green cupola. When he woke, he realised everyone was already getting ready to go. Opening his eyes, the first thing he saw was Muhammad with his crimson hamail in his hand. He hadn't opened it yet. Muhammad sensed the eyes on him and slowly turned his head. They stared at one another.

'I . . . I . . . I couldn't find my copy of the Holy Book when I was praying this morning,' Muhammad stutteringly started to explain. 'I wasn't sure of a verse.'

'Which sura, my young friend? Perhaps I can help you.'

'The sura of mutual fraud.'

'The sixty-fourth sura.'

'Why do you number the suras?'

'It is a custom of ours in India – we love numbers. We invented them, after all.'

'I see.'

'What verse can't you remember?'

'It begins, *Upon the day that He shall gather you for the Day of Gathering; that shall be the Day of Mutual Fraud.*'

'Do you want to know how it continues?'

'No, I know that, but I can't remember the next verse. I wanted to look it up. I'm sorry I didn't ask your permission; you were asleep.'

'No need for excuses, Muhammad, it does you honour that you wish to correct your ignorance immediately. I will tell you the verse that escapes you. Better from the mouth of a friend than the page, don't you think? *And those who disbelieved and cried lies to Our signs, those shall be the inhabitants of the Fire, therein to dwell for ever – an evil homecoming.*'

'Of course, may God thank you, how could I forget?'

'Don't concern yourself. You are a conscientious soul. Now, if you would pass me my hamail, we need to pack up our things. The caravan will soon be on its way.'

∽

In the month of Jumada al-Akhirah of the year 1273
May God show us His Blessings and Mercy

GOVERNOR: Perhaps he was spying for another power.

SHARIF: You give speculation too much credence.

GOVERNOR: But why has he been shown so little honour in his own country? Why wasn't he in a hurry to go home after the Hajj? He stayed in Cairo, as you know, for months.

SHARIF: Who might he have served?

GOVERNOR: The French.

SHARIF: You mean the British spread the rumour he was Christian in revenge?

QADI: It might still be true.

SHARIF: Or a lie to expose a double agent.

GOVERNOR: He spent enough time here to draw up plans of the weaknesses of our positions in the Hijaz.

QADI: What interest could that be to the French?

GOVERNOR: Do I have to spell it out? The sharifs of Mecca are masters of the shifting alliance. They play Cairo off against Istanbul, seek allies everywhere, even the Yemen. What is there to stop the French intriguing with the sharif to set Saud against the sultan and the sultan against the British? Then the sharif will be left the sole ruler of Mecca, may God the Almighty exalt it, indulged and supported by his new friends, the French.

SHARIF: Do you suspect me of treachery? That is intolerable! My loyalty is beyond reproach, I can assure you.

QADI: You should take your father as an example. Everyone says he was a proud man. Not prepared to court another's favour. As befits a man whose duty is to watch over the holiest of holies.

SHARIF: He was a hero, a defender of the faith. I am perfectly aware of my duty.

GOVERNOR: Which of the many duties that fall to your family are you referring to? The duty of political expediency? Do you think we hadn't noticed how close a friendship you have with the French consul in Jeddah? Has he flattered you ? Persuaded you you can play a major political role in the future?

SHARIF: Our courtesy, the courtesy of the Qitadas, has always been renowned, and, truly, it has never excluded anyone, neither foreigner nor unbeliever. We treat everyone with the respect of a brother. Clearly, that can give rise to regrettable misunderstandings.

GOVERNOR: Extremely regrettable.

SHARIF: Why are we making such a mystery of this Burton? Perhaps he was just curious. You can understand, can't you? When somebody lives and travels in our lands and keeps meeting hajjis and hearing of the Hajj, why shouldn't he conceive a longing to see this wondrous event and these Holy Cities with his own eyes?

QADI: Almighty God has created all mankind, so all men may be drawn to Mecca, may God the Almighty exalt it.

GOVERNOR: I give up. You sons of Mecca are great believers in the good news you broadcast yourselves.

SHARIF: And you Turks suspect a scorpion under every stone.

∾

A surge of excitement sweeps through his companions. Previously motionless on their mounts, fused to their saddles by sheer endurance, they are craning their necks eastwards and urging their horses towards the sun rising over a familiar range of hills in the distance. For the first time Sa'ad spontaneously strikes up conversation with him, talking of his little garden and the delicious dates – his fingers cup a fruit – he will serve him personally, more delicious than anything he has tasted in his life. The idea of a palm tree sounds like a barefaced lie in this sea of lava. Nothing gives any hint of the flower of Islam that will soon offer itself to his eyes, apart from the general agitation. A jolt has gone through the caravan; it has picked up speed, the voices are louder. Riders press ahead without inhibition; there's no need to fear attacks so near their goal. A gentle ascent through a dried-out wadi, then they climb a huge flight of black steps hewn out of the basalt leading to an opening. 'This is Shuab el Hadj –' Omar says, passing him at a steep point – 'you'll soon see what you have yearned for all this time, Sheikh. You will soon love the desert and with it the whole world.'

The travellers stop at the top of the pass and leap off their dromedaries. He sees kneeling silhouettes, hears shrill cries, a purple and gold banner of euphoria floating above the ridge. He catches them up. Before him stretches a long stone table laden with gardens and houses, fresh green orchards and palm trees. To the left rises a mass of grey boulders that look as if they have been piled up by a huge avalanche. Shouts of rejoicing ring out on all sides; the Prophet is praised as no one else has ever been praised. May he live for ever, as long as the west wind blows gently over the Nijd hills and the dazzling lightning forks in the firmament of the Hijaz. Even the sun's rays, muted by the dew, seem to pay him homage. Sheikh Abdullah looks more closely and, although he can see nothing extraordinary in the view – the houses are simple houses, the palm trees simple palm trees – he longs to enter into the collective ecstasy. It's not the outward form that is moving, but the signs each of them recognises with his inner eye; it's not an inconspicuous little town, a tiny oasis in the middle of the barren desert, the settlement of al-Madinah that they see – it's the entire grandeur of their faith, its source and origin. Now he too looks down on the Glorious City and his shouts echo between the cliffs, and although he doesn't weep, like many of the other pilgrims, he suddenly falls into Sa'ad's arms and hugs this huge man tightly, murmuring words of genuine gratitude. 'The greatest happiness on earth,' says Sa'ad, 'the greatest happiness on earth.' He remains standing on the ridge for a long time, one in the one, caught up in the festive brotherhood engendered by the sight of Medina, and if someone were to ask him about his allegiance at this moment, he would fervently declaim the profession of faith. Without any of the reservations that flash through his mind moments later: 'Wait, you're not one of them. Why are you rejoicing?'

'Of course I'm one of them.'

'You must just observe.'

'I want to take part.'

The travellers move off down the winding paths, and his eyes begin to analyse the enchantment, scanning the little town, dissecting, memorising – the topography, the walls, the prominent buildings, the square gate, Bab Ambari, through which they will enter Medina, and as he looks away for a moment, he notices that his feeling of elation has disappeared.

Crowds of people had come out of Medina to meet the caravan. Most of the travellers were on foot to embrace their relatives and friends, kissing and shaking hands; no one sought to hide their joy. This was no time for self-restraint. Those who had stayed behind bombarded those who had returned with questions, without thinking they would be answered immediately. Riding together, Sheikh Abdullah and his party were constantly separated by the multitude. Hamid al-Samman was not with them. He had gone ahead to savour the reunion with his wife and his children alone, and to prepare the house for his visitor. After long evenings of discussions that had occasionally flared into quarrels, he had prevailed: Sheikh Abdullah was to be his guest. Omar had emphasised the gratitude his father was bound to show his son's generous benefactor. Sa'ad had concurred, adding that if the sheikh needed a second house, if he wanted to withdraw completely, his modest abode would also be at his disposal. But Hamid would hear none of it, claiming exclusive right to put up the sheikh and allowing no one to take it from him. They passed through the Bab Ambari and rode along a broad, dusty street. Omar and Sa'ad stationed themselves on either side of Sheikh Abdullah, assuming he would want to know the name of every corner of Medina. The Harat al-Ambariyah in Manakhah. The bridge over the al-Sayh river. Barr al-Manakhah square. Bab al-Misri, the Egyptian gate, straight ahead, and to the right, just a few yards on, Hamid al-Samman's house. The dromedaries knelt, the travellers dusted themselves down, and a man came out of the house, an elegant gentleman whom they barely recognised. Hamid had shaved, washed his hair, twisted the two tips of his moustache into commas and sharpened his goatee into an exclamation mark. He had put on a muslin turban and was dressed in layers of silk and cotton. He wore soft leather slippers and sturdy overshoes that in colour and cut followed the latest Stambul fashion. He looked transformed. And the tobacco pouch that hung at his belt was not merely embroidered with gold, it was also full to bursting. Clearly Hamid al-Samman was a tattered beggar on his travels and a proud master in his own home. His manners were equally transformed. Vulgar boisterousness had given way to measured courtesy. He took his guest by the hand and led him into the living room. The pipes were filled, the divans laid out, the coffee brewing on a coal stove. Sheikh Abdullah had barely sat down and been offered coffee and a pipe before the first friend of the family appeared. Hamid was a popular man, it seemed. A stream of visitors flowed through his house, all taking pleasure in chatting with the sheikh from Hindustan. The conversations would have enveloped the whole day if Sheikh Abdullah hadn't resorted to tactlessness and emphatically declared he was hungry and tired, whereupon his host was compelled to bid the visitors farewell, prepare a bed and darken the room. At last, the sheikh thought, a soft bed, I can be on my own. Shortly afterwards he heard women's exclamations of excitement in the distance. Perhaps his ungracious behaviour hadn't been so unwelcome to his host, who now finally had time to open his chests and distribute their treasures.

∾

He has rested, bathed and eaten. There's no other reason to defer the visit to the Prophet's Mosque. Night has fallen and night, according to Hamid, is when it is at its most beautiful. They form a little group almost before they leave the house, and a dense crowd by the time they reach the Prophet's Mosque. The call to night prayers rings out. The hurrying throng solidifies, finding its way to the sole entrance, through which it may course into another realm. Each pilgrim finds his place and position in relation to his brothers who surround him. It is not his way voluntarily to become part of a greater order. Only at prayer is it different, and for that reason alone, he feels he's not a fraud. Hardly have all the pilgrims formed up in rows, their feet in a straight line, than the muffled clamour gives way to a stillness in which the earth temporarily seems to stop, before it is launched on another orbit by the solitary voice of the imam. Soaring up out of the silence, his chant opens out the prayers above their heads. Before Sheikh Abdullah bows his forehead to the floor, his gaze falls on the soles of the feet of the man in front of him, a hand's breadth away. Everyone bows down to God, but they do so directly behind the callused, cracked soles of their fellow men.

∾

HAMID: All of you would have welcomed this man as your guest. All of you would have opened your house to him. Everyone held him in esteem. Even my mother, whose judgement is seldom favourable, praised his tact.

QADI: What is easier than gulling a woman?

HAMID: Not in my house. My mother has a nose for lies. She says they stink like old milk. If you doubt what I say, let me give you another example, which will convince you. In Medina we found out that Sheikh Abdullah had defended the true faith with his sword. In his country. In the fight he had actually killed some ajami. That's why he avoided their company. He didn't want to expose himself to their revenge.

GOVERNOR: How did you find that out?

HAMID: Everyone knew it, everyone who knew him.

GOVERNOR: This piece of news could only have originated with him though, couldn't it?

HAMID: You're right. None of us knew him from Hindustan. But I didn't hear it from him. Besides, he was a modest man, he wouldn't have bragged about that sort of thing.

SHARIF: So why did you believe the story?

HAMID: He was a warrior when the situation demanded. Besides, when we learnt of his heroics, we had all offered to stand by him if he were attacked and he gratefully accepted our offer. Would he have shown such joy and relief if he hadn't had anything to fear? No. You didn't know him. He was a rock of a man, and he knew how to fight. I thank God he was our friend.

QADI: You thank God for your own credulity.

SHARIF: We shouldn't be so hasty to judge. We have never met this man and we have no way of knowing how he had the effect he did on his companions. Perhaps it was charisma?

HAMID: The light of faith, I've already told you, nothing else.

GOVERNOR: You can't know this, because you haven't read his

book, but this British officer is eager and quick to judge. Sometimes he does so after reflection, sometimes purely at the promptings of an uncontrollable aversion. I don't know if you would recognise your friend in these judgements. He writes at one point that a day will come when political necessity will force the British to occupy the source of Islam by force. One of his opinions, which he expresses in the chapter on Medina, interests us particularly. An astonishing thesis; I'll read it out to you: 'One needs no especial prophetic gift to see a day coming when the Wahhabi, rising up in huge numbers, will liberate their country from its weak conquerors.' That's what your Sheikh Abdullah writes. You share my horror, don't you? Could you explain how he arrived at this conclusion while he was enjoying your hospitality?

HAMID: I don't know. I never expressed such a thought, nor did anyone in my family, I can assure you.

SHARIF: What did he do in Medina?

HAMID: What all pilgrims do. Performed the prayers in the Mosque of the Prophet, may God bless Him and grant Him peace. Visited the holy places, the mosque of Kuba, the al-Bakia cemetery, the martyr Hamzah's tomb.

GOVERNOR: Who did you introduce him to?

HAMID: No one in particular. I am a well-regarded man, many people know me in Medina; I have many visitors when I return from a long journey.

GOVERNOR: Did he have a chance to talk to everybody?

HAMID: He was my guest; he sat in my living room. He was a personable, good-looking man.

GOVERNOR: What was the subject of conversation?

HAMID: If my memory doesn't deceive me, because it was a long time ago, the war had just broken out. We were all agreed our army would rapidly defeat the Muscovites. Some even proposed we should turn it against all the idolaters, the English, French and Greeks, afterwards.

GOVERNOR: And Burton?

HAMID: You mean Sheikh Abdullah?

GOVERNOR: They're one and the same.

HAMID: I don't know a Burton.

GOVERNOR: Well, Sheikh Abdullah, if you insist!

HAMID: He was the soul of good sense. He said that no one could match our faith, but that unfortunately the Faranjah had developed powerful weapons to compensate for their weak faith, and that if we wanted to leave the battlefield as victors, we had to learn as much as possible about these weapons. We had to acquire them and make them ourselves one day. And then, both strong in faith and admirably equipped, we would be invincible.

QADI: Do you think God is on the side of the better weapons?

HAMID: You know better than I what side God is on.

SHARIF: On the side of the righteous, of course, and we are putting our shoulder to the wheel, isn't that so, we are putting our shoulder to the wheel. But tell me, when he was staying in your house, was he often on his own? Did he go out ever without you knowing where?

HAMID: Never. Certainly not. Muhammad, the young lad from Mecca, never left his side. I had him to stay too, even though I had a feeling Sheikh Abdullah would gladly have been rid of him.

GOVERNOR: Why?

HAMID: He took exception to his loose ways.

QADI: Loose ways?

HAMID: You would be amazed to hear the liberties he allowed himself. He was impertinent and frivolous. He neglected the ceremonies, had the nerve to go into the Prophet's Mosque without his jubbah, and one day, during prayers, he jabbed me in the ribs. Naturally I ignored him.

SHARIF: A little high-spirited, as he still is. Boys are at that age.

HAMID: He crowed about coming from Mecca.

SHARIF: One can't blame him for that. But tell me, what happened with the loans this sheikh so readily gave you all?

HAMID: His generosity, exactly, his matchless generosity. At our parting, which drove a knife into our hearts, he said he was writing off all our debts to further honour our friendship and so we would think well of him.

GOVERNOR: There is one question you haven't answered. Where could Sheikh Abdullah have got the idea that the Wahhabi are soon going to bring our rule over the Hijaz to an end? It must have been based on some observations or conversations.

HAMID: No matter how many times you repeat your question, I still won't be able to give you an answer. I don't know!

GOVERNOR: Is that what people are saying in Medina's bazaar?

HAMID: Not that I know of.

GOVERNOR: Have you friends or acquaintances . . .?

HAMID: It's not impossible that one of my visitors expressed such an opinion. When I wasn't in the room. There are so many different opinions in Medina, no one can take them all in.

SHARIF: But tell us, we consider each other friends, I think: is this or similar opinions shared by many others?

QADI: You can be honest with us; you have nothing to reproach yourself for.

GOVERNOR: You're not the accused.

HAMID: Well, if I must be frank: in our town, the Turks have never been loved. But they did at least used to be respected.

Sheikh Abdullah goes to bed exhausted – not drained so much as surfeited – and asks his host not to wake him the following morning. When he does wake, he thinks the incredible noise that has roused him can't possibly be coming from the little town he walked through the day before. He opens his eyes reluctantly, then tentatively pushes back the wooden shutters. Baghdad or Istanbul or Cairo has moved overnight. The adjoining square, formerly a dusty, yawning waste, is so densely packed with tents, loads, people and animals, it is as if it has been covered with a chequered kelim. The tents are neatly lined up like pilgrims at prayer, in long lines where the traffic has to circulate and densely packed in corners where thoroughfares are unnecessary. Men emerge with a relaxed saunter from round tents; children charge about between square tents; loads are shunted around on invisible backs. Peddlers tout their sherbets and tobacco; water carriers and fruit sellers fight over customers; herds of sheep and goats are driven through lines of snorting horses that churn the dust and dromedaries that tread and stamp. A group of old sheikhs has taken over the last bit of unoccupied ground to perform a war dance. Some of them fire their guns skywards or shoot into the ground dangerously near the nimble feet of others who brandish their swords and throw their long spears tufted with ostrich feathers high into the air, not caring where they land. The spectacle constantly shifts as he stands at the window, trying to sketch everything he sees. Servants seek their masters, masters seek their tents; guards clear a path for grandees through the throng, accompanying their warning shouts with blows; women protest furiously as their litters are bumped. Swords sparkle in the sunlight, tents' brass bells ring. A cannon booms from the top of the citadel. The Damascus caravan has arrived overnight.

One by one, they joined the expedition to the Martyrs. At first Hamid was supposed to accompany Sheikh Abdullah with just a few relatives, but there was no way of getting rid of Muhammad; Salih was bored in the provinces, Omar wanted to enjoy Sheikh Abdullah's company again, and that also gave Sa'ad a good reason to come. This would be the last time they rode together. The following day, they knew, the caravan would set off for Mecca, taking the foreign sheikh with it. They slipped out of town to avoid the tentacles of the caravan, and headed for Jabal Ohod at the foot of the mountain, where the great battle was lost. Hamid rode ahead with his relatives;

they still had plenty of catching up to do. 'When's the marriage then, Omar?' asked Sheikh Abdullah.

'I managed to talk my father out of it.'

'He has seen the beneficent influence of al-Azhar on his wandering son,' added Sa'ad, 'and he has decided to send him back to Cairo. But not as a pauper student this time.'

'If you want to learn, come to Mecca,' said Muhammad.

'That's not far enough from his father's mood swings.'

Laughing, they rode up to the battlefield. Behind them, covered in a dusty haze, the mountain looked like a fortress. Only arrogance would make one leave its cover to fight on open ground, especially when outnumbered. One of the dromedaries bleated and pawed the ground. Hamid and his relatives had come to a halt.

'Here, right here –' Omar pointed excitedly at some nondescript stones '– is where the betrayal took place.'

'How do you know?'

'My grandfather showed me the place.'

'How did he know?'

'That's what I asked him too. He gave me a surprising answer. One of our ancestors was part of the three hundred who abandoned the Prophet to His fate. "Can you remember that?" I asked him. "No, my grandfather's grandfather couldn't have remembered it. I dreamed it, though." "And how did your dream end?" I asked him. "We fled the battle-field heading towards the town; I felt terrible; I had to turn around, I kept stumbling, but I couldn't tear my eyes away from the Prophet. He calmly stood His ground and in a voice that drove down on us like a thunderbolt, He shouted after me: 'Fear has never saved anyone from death.' I woke up and rode out in the dark while the blood of my dream was still fresh. And then I recognised this place."'

'Did your grandfather say it was here?'

'Right here.'

They rode on in silence towards the steep sides of the mountain that rose up like charred, serrated masses of iron. They came to the Mustarah, the resting place where the Prophet had spent a few minutes in contemplation before He rode into battle. A rectangular, white-walled enclosure where pilgrims could pray. 'Let us offer two raka'ah,' proposed Sheikh Abdullah.

The battlefield was reached by a little rise, a slanting memorial to the lost battle, the blood spilled by senseless, vengeful souls. An army of unbelievers had attacked on this barren plain. Mecca's warriors had charged up from that riverbed winding away into the distance.

'They obviously knew nothing about strategy.'

Everyone looked at Sheikh Abdullah in surprise.

'Why? What do you mean?'

'The battle could have been fought differently. In country that offers so much natural cover, this is an especially unfavourable spot.'

'You Indians must be shrewd fighters.'

'The bowmen could have taken up position behind the rocks, on a broad front.'

'Do you hear that? Our brother is retrospectively winning the lost battle of Ohod. What misfortune that Medina had no Indian advisers!'

'Whether the strategy was good or bad, things boded well for us at the start. Despite the women of Mecca goading on their men. Their shouts carried to our warriors. "If you fight," they screeched like peacocks, "we will twine our arms around you, we will lay soft covers under you, but if you give ground, we will never give ourselves to you again." We are seven hundred, the unbelievers are three thousand, and yet we will drive them before us. Were the enemy giving ground intentionally? No, they were resisting with all their might. If only our bowmen had obeyed the Prophet's orders. They barely reached the enemy's camp, however, before they thought the battle won. They broke ranks and started pillaging. And now the enemy could fall on us from the rear.'

'Strategy, you see?'

'Even the greatest general cannot do anything to counterbalance the disobedience of his comrades.'

'We were pushed back, but we fought as Muslims, united and unyielding. We didn't scatter in all directions, we regrouped before the tent of the Prophet, peace be upon Him, and despairingly fought on. The Prophet was wounded. Five of the unbelievers had sworn to kill Him. One of them, Ibn Kumayyah, may all God's curses be upon him, threw stone after stone and two rings of the helmet of the Prophet, peace be upon Him, were driven into His face; blood fell from His cheeks over His moustache. He wiped it with a corner of His cloak so that not even a drop fell on the ground. Another unbeliever, Utbah bin Abi Wakkas, may all God's curses be upon him, throws a big, sharp stone that hits the Prophet in the mouth. It splits His lower lip and knocks out a front tooth – several teeth.'

'That is not recorded.'

'Do you doubt the word of a mufti?'

'No, not when the mufti is also the grandfather of the allegation.'

'Let's agree on two teeth. Our standard-bearer has his right hand cut off; he seizes the flag with his left hand, his left hand is cut off, with his two stumps he presses the flag to his chest. He is run through by a lance, he passes the flag to another before he falls to the ground. The battle is lost.'

'And this dome? We should pray two raka'ah. This is the place where Hamzah was killed by Wahshi the slave's spear.'

After the prayer, they stood next to one another and in their mind's eye beheld the horrors that had taken place between these rocks and the Holy City now shrouded in haze. Their thoughts continued to the end of the story, but no one could speak this part aloud. It was bad enough to have the horror of it stalking their minds. Hamzah's stomach slit open, his liver torn out – she takes a bite to honour her vow – then the nose, the ears and the genitals are mutilated. What a monster, this Hind, Abu Sufiyun's wife, part Amazon, part sphinx. Incarnation of all men's fears.

Sorrowfully they set off home. The battle of Ohod was lost once again and all around them the enemy's wives were desecrating the bodies of their fallen ancestors.

❧

The sky was an empty blue, the desert a flat infinity, and yet still too small to accommodate this caravan. The size of it was inconceivable – by the time the last dromedary set out, the first had already arrived at the evening's camping place. An entire society was on the move through that scarred terrain. From the richest pilgrims rocking in litters attached by wooden struts to dromedaries, and surrounded by a crowd of servants and flocks, to the takruri, the poorest of the travellers, whose only possession was a wooden bowl for collecting alms. They had no animals to ride on and even when they were lame they hobbled on, propping themselves up on heavy sticks. There were coffee brewers and tobacco sellers and an escort of two thousand Albanian, Kurdish and Turkish bashibazouks who inspired even less confidence in Sheikh Abdullah than the officer in the caravanserai in Cairo. All these soldiers were idiosyncratically armed, as if to claim a little individuality amidst the universal filth and neglect. The Syrian dromedaries towered over their counterparts from the Hijaz, which looked like dwarves next to them. Sheikh Abdullah would often climb a little rise and let the caravan pass in a dense stream of images, some of them flabbergasting – a servant running in front of a dromedary, holding a water pipe on which his master in his wicker litter comfortably puffed through a long tube – and some wretched – the first animal dying in the heat and the takruri fighting with the vultures over the carcass.

The richer a caravan, the more often it was attacked. 'This one', Sa'ad said, 'is like dragging roast meat on the ground after you. Ants, jackals, everything will try and get a piece. We are going to be attacked by the Bedouin, treacherously of course, without us having any chance of an equal fight. At night thieves will steal through the camp, jump onto the dromedary of a sleeping hajji from behind, gag the beast's mouth with their abba and throw down anything they can find of value to their accomplices. If they're discovered, they'll draw their daggers and fight a way out.'

On the second night a young Bedouin was caught. He didn't protest, but simply hunched over, motionless, awaiting the punishment he knew would follow. Before the caravan set off, the thief was impaled and left to die of his wounds or be eaten by wild animals. Sheikh Abdullah surprised everybody by expressing indignation.

'But even that', said Sa'ad, 'doesn't frighten the Bedouin. They are proud of their courage, their skill as robbers. They always try again.'

∾

Dust, noise, stench – the town drags itself into the desert and the desert accompanies its every step. Despite his companions' warnings of marauding Bedouin, and despite the pain – his wretched toe is still inflamed – Sheikh Abdullah climbs a hill at sunset. He slips once, grabs hold of a stone which comes loose from the scree, then manages to break his fall on a thorn bush. It takes a few minutes for him to get all the thorns out of his hands, but still he savours the brief moments he has on the hill. Otherwise he isn't alone for a minute. His companions have adopted him without mercy. Muhammad is like a bustling young cousin, always dancing attendance on him. Even Sa'ad seeks out his company, his taciturnity superseded by an inexhaustible chattiness. The closer they get to Mecca, the more urgent Salih's advice becomes. As soon as Sheikh Abdullah sets off somewhere, they ask him sternly where he thinks he's going, as if it was incumbent upon him to account for his every movement.

The tar of night covers the last traces of sun. Campfires flare up here and there, dotted over the valley like stars. After a while, he walks back through the camp and sits by one of the fires. Much of what he hears is vain and stupid, but now and then he listens intently, anxious to remember every word. The recollections of a faceless man from Egypt, for instance, who used to be in Muhammad Ali Pasha's service and was sent south to explore the slavers' routes. He had pushed far into the blacks' lands, past the desert to regions that never saw drought, to vast lakes whose extent he hadn't seen himself, but he had met blacks who knew the further shores of these lakes, which they called Nyassa, Chama and Ujiji. The largest was the lake to the north called Ukerewe, a circular sea in the middle of the continent. Sheikh Abdullah draws his cloak tighter around him. That evening, despite Muhammad's fitful sleep, he'll have to write all this down on scraps of paper, which he will then hide in his medicine box under granules. Who knows, maybe it'll be useful information some time.

The pilgrims had to endure many small, skirmishing attacks but it was only after they'd taken off their clothes and donned the pilgrimage attire – the two white cotton cloths, one wrapped round the waist, the other draped over the shoulders – that the attack which they had feared since leaving Medina came. At al-Zaribah they had their heads shaved and their beards trimmed; they cut their nails and performed their ablutions as conscientiously as possible. They set off again with a feeling their journey was over. For the first time, the cry went up that would henceforth accompany them until the day of witnessing on Mount Arafat: '*Labbaik Allahhuma Labbaik*: Here I am, O God, at Thy Command!' – the cry echoed on all sides. Sheikh Abdullah's group had ridden with a great assortment of pilgrims for the past few days. Now they fell in with a party of Wahhabis led by a kettledrum and a green banner that bore the profession of faith in resplendent white letters. They rode in double file and were the picture of wild mountain men in the imaginations of coastal dwellers: dark-skinned, fero-cious stares, hair twisted into thick braids, each armed with a long spear, a matchlock or a dagger. They sat on rough wooden saddles without cushions or stirrups. The women emulated the men, riding their own dromedaries or sitting on little saddle cushions behind their husbands. They spurned the veil and gave no suggestion of being the softer sex.

With this intimidating troop bringing up their rear, they came to the entrance to another pass. To their right stood a steep buttress, along the base of which wound a tiny stream, and to their left a sheer precipice. Up ahead their path seemed barred by a mass of hills stretching ever higher into the far blue distance. The peaks were still lit by the sun but down below, between the rocks and cliff where they had to ride, a curtain of grim shadows was spreading. The voices of the women and children grew quieter; the shouts of *Labbaik* gradually died away. A small curl of smoke appeared on top of the precipice and the next moment a shot rang out. A dromedary trotting close to Sheikh Abdullah folded over onto its side. Its legs twitched once or twice, then the animal froze. The configura-tion of the caravan exploded even before the next gunshots were fired, which were inaudible among the screaming and bellowing. Everyone spurred their mounts to escape from that place of death; reins became entangled, dromedaries butted heads, no one could move as the gunfire tore into the frenzied throng, picking off individual animals and people, who fell dead to the ground or were trampled underfoot. The soldiers rushed back and forth, shouting contradictory orders. Only the Wahhabi reacted in a considered, brave way. They galloped ahead, their locks tossing in the wind. Some took up a position and fired at the attackers on the heights, while several hundred began climbing up the rocks. Soon the firing thinned out and finally ceased completely. Sheikh Abdullah had only been able to observe it all. 'The closer you get to your life's goal, the more dangerous it becomes,' Salih said, standing at his side. 'Imagine having to die a day before you reach the Kaaba!'

They said a short prayer and remounted. Blind raging darkness threatened to swallow the caravan. Without anyone giving an order, the dry bushes along the way were set on fire. The deeply fissured cliffs loomed over them like brooding monsters. Ahead, the path plunged deeper into the gorge. The smoke from the torches and burning bushes hung over them like a canopy, the glow of the fires dividing the world into two dark halves, separated by a Stygian red. The dromedaries stumbled, blind in the darkness, blinded by the dazzling torchlight. Many of them skidded down the slope to the stream. If they were hurt, there was no earthly way of getting them back up – the bags were unloaded, if friends were there to help, and the journey continued on the back of another animal or on foot. When they emerged from the gorge early the next morning, they were tired to the bone; too worn out even to feel relieved.

The next day they rode into Mecca.

∽

In the month of Shaaban of the year 1273
May God show us His Blessings and Mercy

QADI: We are getting nowhere. We should devote our time to more valuable matters and leave this to take care of itself.
GOVERNOR: On the contrary. What we've learnt so far makes it imperative we continue. I've never known a murkier business.
QADI: Who shall we question now?
GOVERNOR: Not who, but how.
SHARIF: It's quite possible that one or other of them hasn't told us the truth. Ask a polite question, you generally get a polite answer.
GOVERNOR: We could be more insistent.
SHARIF: We should be careful who we want to subject to such an interrogation.

QADI: Omar Effendi is out of the question; he's the mufti's grandson . . .

GOVERNOR: We know.

SHARIF: Salih Shakkar, perhaps?

GOVERNOR: He's Turkish; he respects the sultan and loves Istanbul.

QADI: An infallible guarantee against hypocrisy.

GOVERNOR: Hamid al-Samman is a good candidate. He shared his roof with the foreigner.

SHARIF: He struck me as being very upright.

GOVERNOR: He was guarded; the information he gave us as miserable as smoked meat.

SHARIF: No, not Hamid.

GOVERNOR: Why not?

SHARIF: Well, if you really must know, I've learnt he is related to one of my wives, and relations with her family are extremely important to me.

QADI: What about Sa'ad?

SHARIF: A former slave.

GOVERNOR: The black.

QADI: The Demon. Not a good nickname.

GOVERNOR: He travels a great deal, including among the unbelievers – even as far as Russia. That must prompt suspicion. Who knows where his allegiances lie?

SHARIF: He won't have any powerful protectors.

GOVERNOR: His business often takes him to Mecca.

QADI: We will see how much of the fear of God there is in him.

He has been prepared for everything, even to be exposed and killed, but it has never occurred to him that he might be overwhelmed by his feelings. He can't go on; he has to stop at every step. Nothing in his heart or mind resists the joy welling up in him. Awe seethes in every face. Before him stands an idea, the Kaaba, a brilliantly vivid idea draped in black cloth like a bride's wedding veil, its gold embroidery like a love song. 'O supremely blessed night.' He repeats the enchanting phrases, understanding every word. 'Bride of all the nights in life, virgin among all the virgins in time.' The whirl of pilgrims spins anti-clockwise. Sheikh Abdullah is gripped by elation, as if all the dreams being fulfilled around him are a charge flowing into him. He gives himself up to the whirl to circle the immovable cube seven times, as duty prescribes. At a gentle run at first, as the guide urges him, keeping to the outside; the crowd clogs and jostles towards the middle. He oughtn't to look at the Kaaba – the ungraspable epicentre – but he can't take his eyes off it. Later, when he is so close that, like the other pilgrims, he can touch the veil with his outstretched arm, he dissolves into the throng, a tormenting feeling until he stops fighting against it. The current of the crowd determines everything, their direction, their speed, the pauses when they stop to receive the blessing emanating from the black stone and call out, 'In the Name of God, God is great.' After the last circuit he pushes his way through to the stone with Muhammad's help, stretches forward as close to its gleaming surface as he can, touches it, is surprised to see it so small; they say it was once as white as chalk before all the sinful lips and hands kissing and stroking it turned it black. The legend suits his mood; he will write it down that evening with, as a coda, his hunch the stone may be a meteorite.

As one of the multitude whose thoughts and prayers circumambulate the Kaaba, he is part of a circle rippling out to join other circles, extending beyond Mecca and the desert and its staging posts, past Medina, Cairo and on to Karachi and Bombay and on still further. A stone has fallen into the ocean of mankind and the waves beat against its furthest, most desolate shores. His seven circuits completed, he recites the prayer at Abraham's footprints, and then drinks the water of the Zamzam well. Pilgrims from India congratulating one another include him in their embrace. He says little. Muhammad watches him. Of course, it's beautiful to picture all mankind as brothers and sisters, but a suspicion had started turning round the Kaaba, growing with every circuit. If every person were close to you, who would you care for, who would you suffer with? Man's heart is a receptacle of finite capacity, whereas the divine is an infinite principle. The two don't go well together. Suddenly the order of things promised by the Kaaba seems suspect. Turning his back on those closest to him, he drinks another glass of Zamzam water. Why does there have to be a centre? Because of the sun? Because of the king? Because of the heart? 'Show me the direction where God is not,' the guru had said when he was reproached for pointing his feet disrespectfully towards Mecca. Surely that embodies the spirit of the great inventor, or rather the spirit of the uninvented, the uncreated. The external form is only necessary for those who lack imagination. Who can only imagine omnipresence when it is caught in stone, embroidered on cloth or rendered on a canvas? The water tastes brackish, of sulphur. But the well never runs dry. Water has given this place life and consequently has become part of its mythology. He won't drink any more, if he can help it, not like the man on the pavement outside the mosque who Muhammad points out, an invalid who has sworn to drink as much Zamzam water as he needs to recover his strength.

'And what if he doesn't recover?' he asks Muhammad.

'Then he can't have drunk enough water,' the answer comes back, and as so often he's not sure whether this young lad is parroting a piece of ancestral foolishness or making fun of it.

'There are many hajjis', Muhammad adds, 'who have pails of Zamzam water brought to their rooms and poured over them, because it purifies the heart as well as the body. From the outside in. We in Mecca do it the other way round.'

The scepticism of Sheikh Abdullah grows with every step he takes away from the Kaaba.

༄

In the month of Ramadan of the year 1273
May God show us His Blessings and Mercy

GOVERNOR: This is unacceptable. You overrate your authority. We will compel you to withdraw this fatwa.

SHARIF: I am confident we can come to a compromise that both sides . . .

GOVERNOR: God's curse on your fetid compromises.

QADI: We shall not submit our legitimate verdict to the whim of a pharaoh.

GOVERNOR: You are suffering delusions. You are doubting the caliph's rights.

QADI: He too is subject to the laws of God.

SHARIF: Try to understand us, please, Abdullah Pasha. All the most prominent merchants have come to me as well as the qadi to complain. None of them approves of the measures you have taken.

GOVERNOR: On selfish grounds.

SHARIF: They fear the complete abolition of slavery.

GOVERNOR: You know perfectly well that it is only trading in slaves that is forbidden.

SHARIF: The end of slave trading in the long term means the end of slavery.

GOVERNOR: Even if we are of different opinions, the qadi cannot publicly proclaim that by this decree the Turks have become unbelievers.

QADI: What else do you want to reform? Do you think we don't realise what is going on elsewhere? If we don't defend ourselves, what are you going to ban next? What unspeakable novelties are you going to permit? Will a volley of gunfire replace the Azan? Will women be able to show themselves bareheaded in public? Will they have the right to pronounce divorce?

GOVERNOR: You are exaggerating wildly. We have only forbidden trading in slaves.

QADI: Why?

274

SHARIF: I have my suspicions the caliph is under pressure from the Faranjah, who are claiming their side of their bargain for helping him win the war against Moscow.

QADI: Haggling in Istanbul cannot be the measure for the welfare of the Holy Cities.

GOVERNOR: You cannot shut yourself off from the course of history.

QADI: The course of history? Even if there were such a thing, it would be our duty to resist it. If this continues, one day unbelievers will take residence in the Hijaz, marry Muslims and end up infiltrating all Islam.

GOVERNOR: The Arabs are seeing to that themselves. They have no honour. They do not respect the caliph. We try to behave amicably and what happens? We pay taxes to the clan chiefs in corn and cloth, and they arm their men and raid the caravans.

SHARIF: Perhaps slightly thoughtless to feed your own enemy.

QADI: Since you have conquered our land, there has been no justice. You are only reaping what you have sown. When a thief is caught you don't dare behead him. And that sends signals. You have appointed capriciousness the supreme judge.

GOVERNOR: The Hajj has become safer, and if we combined our efforts, we could then impose the rule of peace on the Bedouin in the interior.

SHARIF: We are supporting you as well as we can but our hands are tied. You cannot fail to see that we do not have as much influence as before.

GOVERNOR: What has changed?

SHARIF: The ship is an enemy we had not reckoned with. How glorious were the days my ancestors watched over, with six caravans and hordes of people following their rulers on the pilgrimage. Did you know that the last of the Abbasids camped with 130,000 animals on Mount Arafat? And what is it like today? Pitiful. Only three caravans still come to our city, may God sanctify it, with a few tens of thousands of pilgrims, and the caravans from Istanbul and Damascus will soon just be ceremonial. If it continues like this, we will soon not have enough money to fulfil our obligations.

QADI: Poverty might be a blessing. The Wahhabi wouldn't be tempted by all those treasures any more.

SHARIF: The Wahhabi would try to subjugate us even if we dressed in rags.

GOVERNOR: Aren't you exaggerating your distress? You receive a quarter of the taxes. And if I'm not mistaken, all those who travel by ship bring presents for the Great Mosque, may God render it even more honoured and illustrious. And what about the licences you give to the guides – isn't that still a profitable business? The sultan is hardly thrilled by the rights you still possess.

SHARIF: If your soldiers could at least keep the roads safe. The caravans are robbed so often it's as if we're transporting ice cubes through the desert. There are only a few drops left for us at the end.

QADI: We must restore the faith. If the renegades are ruling the world, then we must find our way back to the path of pure obedience.

GOVERNOR: Enough chit-chat. Let me tell you a story our sultan prizes highly. A lion, a wolf and a fox go out hunting together. They kill a wild ass, a gazelle and a hare. The lion asks the wolf to divide up the bag. The wolf says without a moment's hesitation: 'The wild ass goes to you, the gazelle to me and the hare to our friend, the fox.' The lion reaches back and with a great sweep of his paw, he severs the wolf's head from his body. Then he turns to the fox and says, 'Now it's your turn to divide up the bag.' The fox bows low before the lion and says in a soft voice, 'Your majesty, the division could not be easier. The ass will be your dinner, the gazelle your supper. And as for the hare, it is bound to make a welcome tidbit for you between meals.' 'What a display of tact and good sense,' the lion says with a satisfied nod. 'Tell me, who taught you that?' And the fox replies, 'The wolf's head.'

By day, the colours of the desert seem as if they've been swept away, and Mecca is the desert, despite the high buildings and the narrow lanes. The transition to night is brief, a fleeting reconciliation between colour, returning in all its nuances, and the harshness of the day. It seems to Sheikh Abdullah, who has found a good place under the colonnades, as if a palette of colours has fallen from the hand of a figure dressed entirely in white. He is amazed by the different shades of white that suddenly appear in the ihram. Moments later torches are lit, the Great Mosque gleams with light and the sky goes black. The prayers of the other pilgrims all around him are infectious. He would like to lose himself too; he just doesn't know what in. Reciting the Qur'an, he keeps stumbling over thoughts of the meaning of a sura. He tries to pray but soon breaks off as he realises he can only accept prayer as a communal act. He cannot force himself to pray on his own. He stands up and seeks a place higher up from where he can look out over the heads of the pilgrims circling the Kaaba. His tongue has baulked at the prayers, so he will pray with his eyes instead. The throng rotates round the supposed centre at a steady pace, as though it were on the turning wheel of God. He could observe this circling for hours. At times it seems like a *perpetuum mobile* of devotion, at others a blind dance.

He feels Mecca has taken him in, made up a room for him, given him a peace far removed from all the snares and villainies of the world. He has grown into al-Islam quicker than he'd expected, bypassing penitence and privation and finding this heaven instead. No other tradition has created such a beautiful language with which to say the unsayable. From the song of the Qur'an to the poetry of Konya, Baghdad, Shiraz and Lahore, to the accompaniment of which he would like to be buried. God is relieved of qualities in Islam, and that seems right to him. Man is liberated, not subjected to any original sin, entrusted with reason. Of course, this tradition is no more capable than any other of making people better, of raising up what is broken. But man may live more proudly within it than in the guilt-laden, joyless depths of Christianity. If he could believe in the particulars of the tradition – it's not necessary to believe in the general, that is his great realisation – and if he could decide freely, and was allowed to serve freely, then he would choose Islam. But it is not possible, there's too much in the way – the law of his country, the law of al-Islam, his own reservations – and at moments like this he regrets it. The paradise that surrounds him fills him with delight, but even with the best will in the world he cannot accept the notion of a life after death, any more than he can the balance sheets God is supposed to fill out before peopling His kingdom. God is everything and nothing, but He is not a book-keeper.

∽

That evening the new moon rose over Mecca. They were sitting close to the footprints of Abraham the forefather. 'What do you feel now?' asked Muhammad. He gave the anticipated answer: 'This is the happiest new moon of my life.' Then he weighed his words, and realised what he had said was not so untrue. And he added in the ear of the young guide who was relentless in his efforts to catch him in error: 'May God in all His strength and might cause us to express our gratitude for His goodwill, and make us aware of all the privileges He has shared with us, even unto accepting us into Paradise and rewarding us through the unfailing generosity of His charity and the help and support He so mercifully extends to us.'

'Amen,' Muhammad murmured in a meek voice. Then Sheikh Abdullah closed the book of questions with a fervent 'Amen' that rose up into the air as if it was one of Mecca's doves.

Later, when Muhammad went to drink some Zamzam water, he sketched the mosque and tore the paper into tiny little strips, which he numbered and then hid in his hamail.

In the month of Shawwal of the year 1273
May God show us His Blessings and Mercy

GOVERNOR: Are you prepared to help us in the search for the truth?

SA'AD: I came to your city in peace. To trade. You have locked me up. You have dishonoured me.

SHARIF: A little honesty is all that separates you from your freedom.

SA'AD: How have I deserved this torment?

GOVERNOR: You have refused to help us.

SA'AD: I am refusing nothing.

GOVERNOR: We would like to believe you, but you must come some of the way to meet us.

SA'AD: There is something I didn't say before.

GOVERNOR: That you hid from us.

SA'AD: I didn't know it was important. He wrote on his ihram.

QADI: On the cloth itself?

SA'AD: Yes.

GOVERNOR: What did he write?

SA'AD: It was impossible to read.

GOVERNOR: You couldn't see it, or you couldn't decipher it?

SA'AD: I didn't try.

GOVERNOR: And you didn't consider this information important enough to tell us?

SA'AD: He was strange sometimes, like all dervishes. I thought it might be a prayer, a blessing that had come to him in front of the Kaaba.

GOVERNOR: Did you only see him write something down in the Great Mosque?

SA'AD: I did one other time.

GOVERNOR: Where?

SA'AD: In the street.

GOVERNOR: Where? Specifically?

SA'AD: Near the barracks.

GOVERNOR: What were you doing there?

SA'AD: We went for a walk.

GOVERNOR: Why there in particular?

SA'AD: We didn't just go there.

GOVERNOR: And? What else have you hidden from us? Speak!

SA'AD: He killed a man.

QADI: What?

SA'AD: In the caravan from Medina to Mecca. I saw him cleaning his dagger. Next morning a pilgrim was found dead, stabbed.

QADI: A murderer!

GOVERNOR: Did you help him?

SA'AD: No!

GOVERNOR: But you didn't tell anyone either?

SA'AD: I just saw a bloodstained dagger. He might have been attacked; it might have been justified self-defence.

SHARIF: Did you ask him about it?

SA'AD: That wasn't for me to do.

GOVERNOR: How much did he pay you?

SA'AD: Nothing. Why would he have paid me anything?

GOVERNOR: For your services.

SA'AD: I accompanied him a few times of my own free will.

GOVERNOR: That's even worse, a traitor through conviction.

SA'AD: Who have I betrayed?

GOVERNOR: The caliph and your faith.

SA'AD: I haven't betrayed anybody.

GOVERNOR: You are lying.

SA'AD: I haven't betrayed anybody.

GOVERNOR: We'll knock the lies out of you. Take him away.

GOVERNOR: They say you're sorry and want to confess everything.

QADI: Let's get this over with.

SA'AD: I helped him.

GOVERNOR: In what?

SA'AD: He asked me questions and I answered them. If I didn't know the answer, I tried to find it out.

GOVERNOR: Questions about what?

SA'AD: Everything. He was very curious.

GOVERNOR: Examples, give us examples before we return you to your suffering.

SA'AD: Our customs, our habits, the secrets of the caravans and trade.

GOVERNOR: Weapons?

SA'AD: Yes, he was very interested in weapons.

GOVERNOR: What sort of weapons?

SA'AD: Gold worked daggers.

GOVERNOR: You are making fun of us.

SA'AD: No, believe me. Old daggers with intricate handwork made him very excited.

GOVERNOR: When did he talk to you?

SA'AD: Just before we got to Medina. He was on watch; I got up early. He started the conversation.

GOVERNOR: Why did you do it?

SA'AD: I didn't have a reason.

GOVERNOR: Did you want to take revenge?

SA'AD: On whom?

GOVERNOR: On us all.

SA'AD: What sort of revenge would that have been?

GOVERNOR: You must have had a reason, damned negro.

SA'AD: Money?

GOVERNOR: Yes, it must have been the money . . .

SA'AD: My business was going badly.

QADI: I had a feeling from the start you would sell your loyalty and honour to the highest bidder.

GOVERNOR: There, you see? You can tell us everything with a little goodwill.

SA'AD: I am full of goodwill.

GOVERNOR: Did he say who sent him?

SA'AD: He never said anything. He didn't mention Moscow once.

GOVERNOR: Moscow? Why Moscow?

SA'AD: I mean his masters, he never talked about them.

GOVERNOR: What! Did he hint that he was Russian?

SA'AD: No, he was Indian. But if he spied, then it would be . . .

GOVERNOR: For Moscow?

SA'AD: Not for Moscow?

GOVERNOR: Tell us the truth . . .

SA'AD: I've told you, all of it's true, I'm testifying he was a spy . . . I don't know exactly what sort of spy. If it wasn't for Moscow, I thought, perhaps, for the viceroy?

SHARIF: He doesn't know anything!

GOVERNOR: I beg your pardon.

SHARIF: It is obvious he doesn't know anything. Everything he's told us is a figment of his imagination.

GOVERNOR: Is that true? I'll have you flayed, you filthy dog.

SA'AD: The pain demanded it. You forced me.

GOVERNOR: You have lied to us twice!

SA'AD: So you say. So you say.

GOVERNOR: I want to know the truth once and for all.

QADI: The truth is not deaf, Sheikh.

GOVERNOR: Oh, this makes you very happy, doesn't it? Gloating over our difficulties.

QADI: Finding the truth is a difficulty we all share, Sheikh. Without exception. And none of us can take pleasure in this regrettable situation.

SHARIF: His confession is useless.

QADI: It was a clever piece of fabrication, if not of thinking. A real Meccan revelation.

GOVERNOR: What does that mean?

QADI: Ah, I had forgotten that knowledge of the classics is no longer required for high office. It means that his confession is so one-sided that only he and God can understand it.

SHARIF: It is time for the Zohar prayer.

QADI: What about this man?

GOVERNOR: What shall we do with him?

QADI: I insist that he is bathed and given decent clothes. How is he supposed to pray like this? We do not want to incur any guilt.

GOVERNOR: I doubt whether he is physically in a state to perform the prayers.

QADI: He will have to decide that. We only have to make sure that he can pray if he wants to.

∽

Labbaik Allahuma Labbaik. The call repeated itself day and night; it was on every lip, it rang out on every occasion and in every place. The pilgrims called it as they approached the Great Mosque, as they went into the barbers', as they greeted their acquaintances in the street; *Labbaik* was the fanfare that echoed on the smaller and larger pilgrimage routes, a sound that illuminated even the pauses between itself. But on the eighth day of the month of Zuul Hijjah, the calls swelled to resemble the marching songs of an army. A vast exodus left Mecca for Mount Arafat, the pinnacle of the pilgrimage, where they would stand before God and behold His presence, regardless of the heat or their frailty.

After his time in the Great Mosque, after the sight of the Kaaba, Sheikh Abdullah anticipated further peaks of experience on the slopes of Mount Arafat and in the dusty village of Mina where the world gathered, a heightening of everything he had already felt, but in fact events in the desert outside the Holy City made him regret leaving Mecca. On the advice of young Muhammad, his party set off in the early hours in a comfortable litter. 'If you reach Mount Arafat too late,' Muhammad had warned, 'you won't be able to find anywhere for miles to put up your tent.' The dead animals dotting the roadside were impossible to ignore; masses of carcasses had just been thrown in the ditches. The Bedouin in their group stuffed their nostrils with cotton wool; others held handkerchiefs over their mouths and noses. They came to Arafat, a hill in the Atlas, a great metaphysical mountain. Pilgrims had scratched the surrounding desert raw. They pitched their tents at the foot of the hill and gave themselves up to those low conversations that would be their guides throughout the day. Some pilgrims murmured, others moved their lips in silence, going over in their minds every failing and every error, correcting the catalogue of their faults, adding stragglers, sins they had just remembered. Were they frightened by the array? Did they strive for honesty? Surely enough not to make God a promise they couldn't keep on this day of honest settling of accounts.

A cannon burst in upon this collective act of self-examination, announcing the midday prayer. Soon drums and gleaming trumpets could be heard. 'Come on,' Muhammad shouted, 'the sharif's procession is arriving.' They pushed their way to the front so they could see the procession as it wended its way up the mountain. First came a group of janissaries and mace-bearers, unceremoniously clearing the way. Then came horsemen, wielding long, tasselled lances with which they urged on the sharif's stud horses, pure Arabs clad in old, threadbare caparisons. Behind these marched black slaves with matchlocks, apparently shielding a mass of green and red flags from the wind as they guarded the high dignitaries, the sharif of Mecca and his courtiers and family. Muhammad could identify every member of this illustrious group. The sharif was an old man, an ascetic with dark skin which came – Muhammad appeared excellently informed about his family – from his mother, a slave from Sudan. 'There is nothing special about him to look at, but no one can match him for cunning,' he added admiringly. Alongside the sharif, whose eyes suddenly scurried over the crowd like a scorpion in the sand, walked a man who was at least a head taller than him and whose ihram barely covered his heavily-built frame. His fashionable little goatee contrasted with the sharif's full beard. 'That's the Turkish governor,' said Muhammad. 'No one likes him. I think that's how he prefers it.' Unlike the sharif, the governor seemed to ignore the assembled throng. A few steps behind these two walked a younger man with a chubby face and soft features, whose femininity was emphasised by an uneven growth of beard. He was the only one of the group who seemed oblivious to everything, part of the procession and yet removed from it. Muhammad had nothing to say on his account except that he was the qadi, a protégé of the city's most powerful alim, the recipient of honours at a young age that far surpassed destiny's usual allocation. The procession was swallowed up by the dense press of people behind whom rose the granite mass of Arafat, a stark reminder of the occasion. The pilgrims climbed the flanks of the hill. Suddenly complete silence fell, the sign that the sermon had begun, although it didn't reach to where they were standing. Sheikh Abdullah saw an old man on a dromedary who occasionally used his hands to back up his words. As every year, he learned later, the sermon recalled Adam and Hauwa, the tears Adam had shed on this spot in a prayer that lasted for months until a pool was created whose sweet waters the birds came to drink. Parts of the sermon were emphasised by the calls of the standing pilgrims, scattered *amins* and *labbaiks*, quiet and reflective at first, which gained in strength and intensity until they caught up even those a great distance from the preacher. By the end, everyone standing round Sheikh Abdullah was on the verge of tears – Muhammad had buried his face in his white cloth – and many were sobbing, despite not catching a word. Everyone knew the emotional import of the sermon. A gentle kindling blazed up into a fervent conflagration; the fiercer the afternoon sky became, the more ardent the pilgrims' pleading. They prayed for forgiveness, for the fear of God, for an easy death, for a positive report on the Day of Judgement, for the fulfilment of prayers as long as they lived. Of all that number, barely a handful could have remained aloof from the prayers at that hour; Sheikh Abdullah was not one of them.

As the sun set, congratulations rang out . . . 'Eid kum mubarak . . . Eid kum mubarak.' The Hajj was considered completed at the end of the day. Their sins forgiven, the pilgrims were like newborn children and they could call themselves hajjis from that moment on. Sheikh Abdullah embraced Sa'ad, Muhammad and his uncle. He felt an unalloyed pride that filled him with simple exhilaration. Everyone looked elated, as if they were floating. Some were already starting to leave. On all sides people were hurriedly packing up, tossing the loosely rolled tents onto their pack animals and beating their flanks. 'We call this the race from Arafat!' Muhammad said, relishing the exegete's role as ever. The pilgrims ran down the hillside, yelling passionately. 'Here I am, O God, at Thy command!' Although everyone in the party helped, their dromedaries were only ready at sunset. A great tide of men and animals streamed out onto the road to Mina. The ground was studded with abandoned tent pegs. Sheikh Abdullah saw a litter being crushed, pedestrians trampled under hooves, a dromedary knocked off balance, pilgrims defending themselves against other pilgrims with sticks. He heard voices searching for an animal or a wife or a child. The pilgrims forced their way through the valley, which looked narrower and deeper as darkness fell. They reached the defile called al-Mazumain, marked out by hundreds of torches that burned fiercely, as if they were stoked by the crowd's excitement. Sparks flew high over the plain like earthly shooting stars. The artillery fired volley after volley and the soldiers celebrated with their muskets, as the pasha's band played somewhere far behind. Rockets shot up into the air, let off by the sharif's procession and rich pilgrims who wanted the sky to know they were hajjis and perhaps hoped their explosions would be visible as far away as the places of their birth. The animals moved at a fast trot and there were as many reasons for the haste as for the deafening clamour with which the crowd marched through the Mazumain pass on their way to Muzdalifah and Mina. They had to ride for two hours before they reached a ramshackle camp. Everyone dropped down on the first unclaimed spot. No one put up tents except the pashas, who had tall lanterns that burned all night. The artillery fired constantly, a crescendo without end. Many pilgrims had lost their dromedaries in the confusion of their hurried departure from Mount Arafat, and as Sheikh Abdullah, wrapped in his ihram and a scratchy blanket, sought in vain for sleep, he heard their hoarse voices roaming back and forth.

∾

In the month of Dhu'l-Qaadah of the year 1273
May God show us His Blessings and Mercy

MUHAMMAD: I didn't take my eye off him for a moment. I was sure he would make a mistake one day and I wanted to be the one to unmask him. I asked one of my uncles to come with me to Arafat and Mina to help. That was a clever thing to do. I lost sight of our group on Mount Arafat. I had moved closer to the preacher because you couldn't hear him where we had pitched our tents, but Sheikh Abdullah was afraid we'd leave too late and so he sent the laden dromedaries on ahead. When I came back, there was no one left. I had to walk to Mina. I looked for the others for hours and then gave up and slept on the sand. It was cold in just the ihram. But my uncle was in the litter with Sheikh Abdullah, watching him. And something very strange and surprising happened. Sheikh Abdullah started tossing about as if he was suffering from the sins he had just confessed. He muttered and convulsed, and his thrashing about became so violent the litter was about to topple over. My uncle tried to talk to him and calm him down, but there was no way of restraining Sheikh Abdullah. He started yelling, as if someone had spat in his face, 'It's your fault, by God, it's your fault. Put your beard over the side, give me some room and God will make it easier for both of us.' My uncle did as he wished, looking out, straight ahead, listening to hear what was happening behind. Sheikh Abdullah writhed around a little longer, and then his thrashing about calmed down. I always doubted Sheikh Abdullah was a dervish. But this episode made me even more uncertain.

GOVERNOR: Your uncle is clearly not as sharp as you. The sheikh's fit was put on.

MUHAMMAD: How do you know?

GOVERNOR: It's in his book. He feigned the fit to be able to look back in peace and sketch Mount Arafat.

MUHAMMAD: So my suspicions were founded, from the start. Why didn't I catch him? I should have caught him.

QADI: At least he was forced to be more cautious.

GOVERNOR: More cautious? He seems to have moved about with complete freedom. In his book he goes so far as to give measurements and exact distances. It would seem he measured the Great Mosque, may God sanctify it. Can you explain how he could have done that?

MUHAMMAD: I've no idea.

SHARIF: Perhaps he counted his steps?

GOVERNOR: Not precise enough, and difficult with the crowd.

SHARIF: Think, you're an intelligent lad, think.

MUHAMMAD: Oh God, he must have measured everything with the stick he used as a cane. He had a slight limp; he said he'd fallen off his dromedary travelling between Medina and Mecca. I didn't see it but he was a truly wretched rider. He often dropped his stick, and then sat down and played with it. He wanted to spend a whole night next to the Kaaba. We prayed for a long time and talked to two merchants. I shut my eyes. I woke up when someone stumbled into me and Sheikh Abdullah was nowhere to be seen. I got up, looked round and finally I saw him right by the Kaaba; he was carefully moving closer and closer. He kept touching the kiswah, at the bottom, where it's already all frayed, as if he wanted to tear a bit off. He was constantly looking at the guards, but you know how watchful they are; they want to do any business themselves, and one of them came over, brandishing his lance in a threatening way. I pulled Sheikh Abdullah by the sleeve away from the Kaaba. I know, lots of people tear off little bits of cloth, it is not that serious, but all the same, how could a respected man do such a thing?

QADI: The only thing I find surprising is that this foreigner should write in his book that you gave him a piece of the kiswah.

MUHAMMAD: He wrote that?

QADI: Yes. He wrote rather a lot about you.

MUHAMMAD: I did, it's true, but later, when we parted.

QADI: Where did you get this piece?

MUHAMMAD: I bought it from an officer.

QADI: So you had that much money?

MUHAMMAD: My mother gave it to him. She wanted us to give him something that would last as a present.

QADI: And so she spent all the money this visitor paid to stay in her house on a farewell present? Extraordinarily generous.

MUHAMMAD: She was very taken with him. I've just remembered something else I should tell you; I'm sure it's important. One day, on the main street of Mina, we saw an officer of irregular troops who was completely drunk. He was elbowing anyone in his way and insulting them if they complained. When we passed him, he stopped, let out a yell and embraced Sheikh Abdullah, who pushed him away. 'What is it, my friend?' the drunkard exclaimed, and Sheikh Abdullah immediately turned on his heel and hurried away. He denied knowing him but I thought it was strange.

GOVERNOR: He knew him.

MUHAMMAD: You're sure?

GOVERNOR: From Cairo.

QADI: They got drunk together once.

MUHAMMAD: I knew it.

GOVERNOR: Things aren't so simple, alas. This man clearly has so many strong points that his weaknesses aren't enough to expose him. You may go, young man. You have served God and your ruler well. We will reward you correspondingly. Now, another matter: has Sa'ad the negro been arrested again?

SHARIF: We don't know what to do with him. I am afraid his mind has become too muddled. The guards picked him up in the Great Mosque, where he was circling the Kaaba day and night, which is extreme but would not be so bad in itself if he hadn't been screaming like an animal at every step: 'I have defiled the truth, I am no longer a man,' he kept yelling. No one could dissuade him from this highly inappropriate behaviour, which disturbed the other pilgrims. He was yelling in agony, His Excellency Sheikh al-Haram told me, and believe me, the head of the eunuchs was very troubled. The negro was yelling in agony, he said, as if he'd seen Hell itself.

∾

'It's today,' Muhammad announced joyfully after the morning prayer, 'today's the day we're going to stone the Devil.' The stones he had collected the previous night lay in front of them in seven little piles, and Sheikh Abdullah had to conceal a smirk when he saw the size of the missiles Muhammad had selected. From the start he had found it hard to take the stoning of Beelzebub seriously. With it, the clarity of the rituals disappeared; instead they suddenly found themselves plunged into the joyous hubbub of a country fair, with a shy as the main attraction – seven throws at a cloven hoof made of stone.

'Don't lose the pebbles on the way,' Muhammad instructed him, 'and if you do, don't pick up ones that have been thrown by other people.' Of course not, pebbles that have been used before can't harm the Devil, thought Sheikh Abdullah while staring at Muhammad with the wide eyes of the good pupil. Presumably the twelve months between pilgrimage seasons gave the pebbles time to recharge, because how could there be a brand new crop of pebbles every year? Even in the desert, the supply of pebbles is not infinite.

'Make sure', continued the young slave driver, 'that you hit the column with each throw. Hold the pebbles between your fingers like this . . .'

Even before meeting him in the vicious, narrow Mina pass, Sheikh Abdullah had almost felt a twinge of sympathy for this

Devil whose form was battered every year by hundreds of thousands of pebbles. But the Devil was made of stone, so it was like against like, and there was no danger of any fundamental change. The balance of power would remain the same; the pebbles could no more strike the Devil than the desert could be irrigated by a handful of water.

'Well, let's go,' he said eagerly, and Muhammad rewarded him with a satisfied look.

Because Muhammad was determined to adhere to the pilgrim's timetable with pedantic exactitude, they were soon caught up in a human avalanche; Sheikh Abdullah would learn later that those who struck compromises with God, the Devil and themselves set off before the appointed time or got up at night to perform their duty by the peaceful glow of the moon. But for Muhammad it would have been unthinkable to bend the rules, although Sheikh Abdullah had long suspected him of secretly plunging into the undergrowth of compromise now and then. A man barred their path, delicate-featured, the ecstasy bursting from his eyes. He grabbed Sheikh Abdullah by the arm and shook him. 'You can save yourself the trouble, brother, I've already put the Devil's eyes out.'

'Even blind, Shaitan puts temptations in our way,' replied Sheikh Abdullah, 'just as a blind man is not immune to sinning.'

'This is a great Indian dervish,' added Muhammad; 'his wisdom holds Shaitan at bay.'

'Both eyes,' screamed the man, 'both eyes!' Then he plunged into the crowd.

When the hajjis drew close enough to see the column, they were like a landslide falling on the valley. Sheikh Abdullah felt beleaguered on all sides. The crowd bucked like a ship in the swell, rolled uncertainly forward as yelling rose over yelling and the last remnants of caution and patience were crushed, not least by the dignitaries' dromedaries and mules. The column was a disappointment; it looked as threatening as a marker stone on a Roman road or a Huns' stone or a nameless headstone. But it enflamed the imaginations of the hajjis all around him; their faces twisted into furious grimaces as they started throwing their stones from far too far away. Many of the hajjis hit their brothers and sisters instead of the Devil. Sheikh Abdullah quickly used up his ammunition. Instead of saying a prayer before every throw, he murmured: 'We take refuge in God from the violence and assaults of the crowd and the excesses of unbridled passions.' But there was no refuge. Not in a crowd where each was the other's mortal enemy, where everyone's sole concern was to escape the ritual alive. He kept on being pushed further and further forward before he realised the danger. He was foam on a wave that was going to dash him on the column. Stones rained down on him, one of them missing his eye by a brow's width.

As soon as they had thrown their seven stones, the hajjis sought a way out of the mass, forcing and thrashing their way through regardless of resistance. They shoved the man or woman in front with all their might, not letting anyone through who was trying to pass in a slightly different direction. A blow on the back of his head revealed the ritual's deeper meaning to Sheikh Abdullah: after the elevation of the purification, the stoning was an exercise in the all too human. Everyone approached the Devil within; the pilgrims' hearts turned to stone again, and so there was no mistake the pebbles should hit the pilgrims. Quite the opposite: in their fellow men they hit the Devil, not the column that he had put there purely as a distraction. On the Hajj Sheikh Abdullah had experienced the *perpetuum mobile* of devotion, and now he was being dragged through a *perpetuum mobile* of violence; here, at the heart of Islam, Upanishe's words came back to him when he had explained the lesson of Adavaita: as long as we see our fellow men simply as other people, we will never stop hurting them. Seen from this perspective, the Devil was in the differences people created between each other. A jet of saliva landing on his face confirmed the thought.

After only three days of the Hajj, Mina's square, the nooks and corners between the tents and houses, the pilgrim camps – everything is overflowing with filth. Excrement, remains of mouldering vegetables and rotting fruit cover the ground. It nauseates him to pick his way through the detritus, especially today, when the air is poisoned with the stink of the great sacrifice. Hundreds of thousands of goats and camels have had their throats slit. The meat is distributed, roasted and eaten, while the remains are strewn over the ground – organs, entrails, bits of fleece and fat scattered among the rivulets of dried blood. Sheikh Abdullah cannot imagine a more horrific place on earth than the Mina valley. If someone dies, they are left lying where they are; once the body starts to decompose, it is thrown in one of the ditches dug for the remains of the slaughtered animals. There it festers, a pestilential, fleshly compost. The number of deaths increases inexorably, thanks to the hardships of the Hajj, the flimsy clothing, the bad accommodation, the unhealthy food, the lack of nourishment. Some pilgrims have been victims of the stoning when they took on the Devil a second time: he has grown three cloven hooves overnight, so they have to throw thrice seven pebbles, and the stoning is three times as unbearable and dangerous.

For him, the time at Mina is a test of endurance, but it's no better for the other pilgrims. The fresh food has run out, as has their inner fire. Dusk hangs like a pall over the whole day. Anyone who moves drags himself through the hours that lethargically spread themselves over duty's discarded cloak. The ranks of the dead keep swelling – group prayers now never end without a Salat al-Janazah for the most recently deceased. Sheikh Abdullah decides to travel the last stage to Mecca by donkey. He arrives to find that the order of the day, sickness and death, has filled the Great Mosque with corpses and invalids who are set down in the colonnades, either to be healed by the sight of the Kaaba or to die at peace in that holy place. Sheikh Abdullah sees emaciated hajjis dragging their helpless bodies along in the shade of the pillars. If they can't stretch out their hands to beg, compassionate souls put a cup next to their mats to collect the meagre alms. When these wretches feel their last hour approaching, they cover themselves with their rags, and sometimes, Muhammad tells him, their deaths are not discovered for a long time. The next day, after a further tawaf, they stumble over a curled-up figure, not far from the Kaaba, who, clearly dying, has crawled into the arms of the Prophet and His angels. Sheikh Abdullah stops and leans down to him. In a croaking voice and with a feeble but intelligible gesture, the man asks to be sprinkled with some Zamzam water. As they are carrying out his wish, he dies; they close his eyes and Muhammad goes off to tell someone. Soon after, slaves are carefully washing the spot where he was lying and it won't be more than half an hour before he is buried, the unknown pilgrim – however laborious and slow a person's arrival on earth, the world quickly rids itself of him when he is reduced to mere matter. The thought troubles Sheikh Abdullah but he feels that if anywhere, this is the place where he might accept it. He sits upright, his eyes fixed on the Kaaba, and imagines himself as the man lying there, dying. Can he still feel the drops of water falling on his face? What will he have to bid farewell to?

❧

In the month of Dhu'l-Hijjah of the year 1273
May God show us His Blessings and Mercy

GOVERNOR: Forgive me for inviting you to a final meeting at this hour, but I will be leaving for Istanbul straight after Eid al-Adha and I must take the complete report with me.
SHARIF: Almost a year has passed since we began occupying ourselves with this affair, which is certainly important, but we have done what was possible and yet, if I may venture an anal-

ogy, we have searched the sky for the new moon of truth in vain.

GOVERNOR: We still have a last witness to listen to; perhaps he will help us unravel the knots. It's Salih Shakkar. We have finally found him: he returned to Mecca with the large caravan. A dozen of my men were given the job of keeping him under watch. I have already questioned him a little, and learnt nothing new, but perhaps something will emerge if we question him together.

QADI: Even if the sky were pitch black, we would continue searching for the new moon.

SHARIF: One last time, as the governor says, one last time. I'm going to miss our discussions, you know; they were a diversion, so instructive and entertaining.

QADI: Entertaining?

SHARIF: In their own crooked way.

GOVERNOR: I'll send for our man.

GOVERNOR: Think. He must have expressed some opinions. Everyone passes judgement from time to time.

SALIH: He had a sharp eye for the world's injustice; he showed amazing sympathy for the poorer pilgrims. As if he was related to them.

GOVERNOR: Yes . . .

SALIH: He could get worked up, fly into a rage. Once he even started cursing the caliph.

GOVERNOR: Yes?

SALIH: He cursed the wealth of the grandees, the largesse afforded the guides of the big caravans. The corruption he saw everywhere. While the poor pilgrims, he often said, were completely left to their own devices, were given no support; no one did anything for their safety.

QADI: What should have been done in his opinion?

SALIH: Improving the wells wasn't enough. The poor pilgrims should have free access to them. It was a crime that well water was sold and that people without money were driven

295

off by the guards. No one should go hungry or thirsty.

QADI: Spoken as a true Muslim.

SALIH: The sick and dying by the side of the road preoccupied him greatly. I remember, because I asked him if no one suffered in India, to which he replied that yes, of course, it had its fair share of the poorest of the poor, but none of its rulers – either the British lords or the Indian kings – would ever have thought all men were equal. But in the country of the true faith, especially close to the House of God, such a state of affairs was well-nigh blasphemous.

QADI: Robust words. Bold. Some of our ulema give similar pronouncements.

GOVERNOR: Are you suggesting a connection?

QADI: No, I'm just saying it's not difficult to imagine a man arriving at this line of thought and following it to its conclusion.

SHARIF: Carry on.

SALIH: He thought hospitals should be built, half a dozen between Mecca and Medina alone. And public inns, in sufficient numbers. It wouldn't be expensive, he said.

GOVERNOR: It's never expensive when others are paying.

QADI: And what else?

SALIH: Waste troubled him a great deal. He often used the saying: God despises the prodigal.

GOVERNOR: And what else did he criticise?

SALIH: The disease . . .

GOVERNOR: The disease?

SALIH: Yes, he was a doctor, as I am sure you know.

GOVERNOR: That is interesting. What did he say about disease?

SALIH: He said pilgrims should be seen by official doctors when they arrived at Jeddah or Yanbu, and water should be available everywhere in sufficient quantities to guarantee proper conditions of hygiene. The sick should be immediately separated from the other pilgrims, and bodies and corpses quickly removed. And a lot of other things of that sort which I cannot remember in every detail. As I said, it's a few years ago, all this.

GOVERNOR: Very interesting. Thank you, Sheikh Salih Shakkar. We will compensate you for your trouble. You may go.

SHARIF: What was so interesting about that?

GOVERNOR: The vizier in his last letter communicated his concern that the British and French will use the threat of disease as an excuse to further their interests in the region. They've already said that epidemics originating in the Hajj are spreading worryingly in their countries; that Mecca, may God the Almighty exalt it, is a hearth for countless infections that the hajjis transmit to all parts of the earth.

QADI: In which they're not completely wrong. Cholera has become an inseparable companion of the Hajj.

SHARIF: And who has brought it, where has it come from, this cholera? From British India. We didn't have this disease before. Nowadays some pilgrims arrive sick, others are severely weakened, the weak get infected by the sick – and this is supposed to be the fault of Mecca, may God the Almighty exalt it.

GOVERNOR: The British have often claimed they have the right to intervene in Jeddah because of this threat to public health.

SHARIF: Couldn't their knowledge be useful to us if we didn't reject it immediately just because it comes from unbelievers? It is a matter of the well-being of our sick brothers and sisters.

GOVERNOR: I know how much you'd like to come to an arrangement with the Faranjah. You imagine that will allow you to keep your independence. You are utterly deluded! The British will swallow you up, you and your privileges. If their ambassador is well-disposed, you might be allowed some compensation, a modest retinue and a trivial role. You would soon have to say goodbye to your magnificent palace of Maabidah though.

SHARIF: What are you saying, I don't understand what you are alluding to. I respect the caliphate and harbour none of the intentions you impute to me with, I must add, a conspicuous lack of goodwill.

GOVERNOR: And the Sublime Porte respects the sharif of

Mecca. We should see we preserve this mutual esteem. In any case, as proof of our goodwill, we have resolved to increase the Jeddah garrison.

SHARIF: We should continue this conversation after your return. Convey to the caliph, I beg you, our deepest respect and equally sincere thanks. And to our old friend the vizier, of course.

GOVERNOR: And what should I tell them in conclusion about this particular case?

QADI: Especially in these days of purification, we should not forget that if God blesses anyone who visits the Holy Cities, then He also blesses the unbeliever. He opens his heart so he will be touched, and He opens his eyes so he will see. The grace of God is infinite and certainly does not limit itself purely to birth or intention. Who are we to measure His mercy? We do not know when or how this Sheikh Abdullah, this Richard Burton, became a Muslim, whether he remained a Muslim, whether he performed the Hajj as a Muslim, whether his heart was pure and his intention sincere. But there is no doubt that he will have experienced many things on his journey that will have touched him, and changed him. He will have experienced God's infinite grace.

GOVERNOR: We were less concerned with the welfare of his soul than his secret mission. I think we can say with certainty that he didn't receive any help or complicity from the inhabitants of the Hijaz. That should be a source of satisfaction. But despite all our efforts we haven't managed to find out if he gathered any information that could harm us.

SHARIF: And because we will never be able to do so, we should let reason have the last word. This foreigner was a solitary figure. Whatever he might have been able to learn, what can one single man do? Even if he were a spy, a particularly deft and cunning spy, what can a simple pilgrim observe, how could he endanger the future of the caliphate and the Holy Cities, may God render them ever more honoured and sublime?

QADI: Glory to God who shall preserve their honour until the day of the Resurrection.

GOVERNOR: Let us hope you are right, Sharif. For if the caliphate were to lose its influence in the Hijaz, powers would intervene that would be considerably less understanding towards your traditions.

QADI: We will be able to defend ourselves.

GOVERNOR: By arms or prayer?

QADI: By arms and prayer, just as our Prophet, may God give Him peace, did. Such a fight would rejuvenate the Faith.

SHARIF: Better if it doesn't come to that. We should beware of overhasty rejuvenation.

GOVERNOR: We should never forget how much we would all have to lose.

∾

The full moon relieves him of the vigilance Mecca's unlit streets have constantly demanded of him. Now he can lose himself in his thoughts without being distracted. He leaves Mecca with a mixture of relief and regret. Muhammad's insistent company he certainly will not miss. Yesterday evening he had again tried to make him confess he wasn't who he claimed to be. 'Have I ever claimed to be a good man?' he had replied. Muhammad had flung up his hands, crying, 'You dervishes, no one can ever get the better of you with words.' No, he will miss the calm of the Great Mosque, where he would have liked to stay longer. Not for eternity, like the other pilgrims, but for a few more days or weeks. Ahead lies the journey back, which, like all returns, won't have any highlights. A fast ride to Jeddah. There shouldn't be any danger on the way, although Muhammad, knowing best as usual, warns him against the customs men: 'They taught mosquitoes to suck blood.' Then the crossing to Suez, which he hopes will be more comfortable than the rigours of the Silk al-Zahab. He is planning to stay in Cairo for a while, there quietly to cut the Hajj's cord. He will decipher his notes, stick the torn pieces of paper together, write up his observations. If there is something he is looking forward to, it is this recollection in writing. He won't write everything, confide everything to the manuscript. He won't stint on external details; natural science will be given plenty of scope to eliminate his predecessors' mistakes. Factual errors are a thorn in his side. But he won't reveal his feelings, not all of them, especially because he hasn't always been sure of what they are. He doesn't want to bring more uncertainty into the world. That would be inappropriate, and he can't allow himself such openness. Who in England will be able to follow him into that twilight; who will be able to understand that the answers are more heavily veiled than the questions?

East Africa

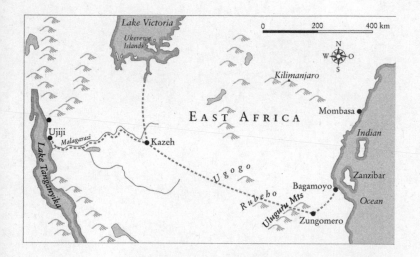

Writing blurs in the memory

SIDI MUBARAK BOMBAY

The island of Zanzibar was a victim of its own harbour. The harbour mouth opened like a gate in a wall of coral; invaders simply had to lower their sails and run up their flags. The sails were patched and furled until the next voyage, and then the flags flew for a spell before being in turn chased away by other flags. Now it was happening again. The Sultan's standard was being hauled down, and Sidi Mubarak Bombay, sitting in his usual spot on the quay, laughed to himself as if he couldn't grasp how much stupidity he had come across in his life. Everything comes to an end, said a voice in one ear. Nothing will change, countered an older voice in the other. A new flag was hoisted with a brisk snap – a statement of intent. Red abdicated and, in its place, the rays of a white sun raced like arrowheads across a blue sky, and next to these, presumably in honour of the big, heavy ships anchored off the harbour, fluttered a black cross, the standard of the ruler the whites knew as the kaiser. 'Truly,' murmured the old man, 'no day sits where another has sat before it' – then took his leave of the men with whom he had shared his amazement. He returned to the old town with its narrow, intertwining alleys that retracted the invitation the reef had been so quick to extend.

Landing in Zanzibar, a person was still far from having arrived. That took time, and the whites never had any time at all. They lost their curiosity long before they lost their appetites. They were more at home in the wind and waves than among that labyrinth of façades. The old man trawled slowly past the encrusted coral buildings, jostled by hurrying figures in the late afternoon sun. He steered round the bustling salt market, took a shortcut through the meat market, deserted save for its habitual stench. Thereafter the lanes became emptier; people greeted him as he passed. He reached his neighbourhood's mosque. The chorused recitation of a sura came from the next-door madrassa. The old man stopped and leant both his hands against the wall of a house. The stone was wrinkled, cool, as soothing as a familiar face. He shut his eyes. They were reciting the Ikhlas Sura, a beautiful lapping sound, although an empty promise: there is nothing eternal, even if it is invoked in children's voices. Every morning you have to search afresh for the truth that vanished overnight. Someone came up to him. 'High time you saw the mosque from the inside, don't you think?' The imam's voice was hoarse. The old man didn't open his eyes; that would unsettle the imam, who prided himself on the hold of his luminous gaze.

'Aren't you ever afraid, Baba Sidi? Death will soon be coming to fetch you.'

The old man rubbed the palms of his hands over the rough wall.

'I am confused,' he said after a while, speaking slowly, as if every word were timidly making its entrance, 'I don't know if I will be turned into a corpse or a spirit.'

'Your thoughts are blind, Baba Sidi; they are leading you into the abyss.'

The old man opened his eyes.

'I know the inside of the mosque.'

'How?'

'I prayed in it when you were still in Oman. But then I had to go on a journey, I was away for three years, I crossed half the world on foot . . .'

'I know; everyone knows your stories, Baba Sidi.'

'No, you don't know the story, not really, and I am not going to tell it to you either.'

'What are you afraid of, Baba Sidi?'

'The dullards' language you and your kind translate everything into. All the things I've seen will never find any space in your tiny, bare rooms.'

The old man turned and went down the lane leading to his house.

'The unbelievers have turned your head,' the imam shouted after him, 'everyone knows that! You were with them too long, you became too close to them. You were at their mercy; it's done you no good. Your left shoulder is heavier than your right.'

The old man carried on until he was out of earshot. To all life's other obscurities now this could be added: why was the imam constantly lying in wait for him as if he were the only outstanding account in his congregation? Distracted, leaving greetings unreturned, he mulled this over until he reached an arched door, which stood half open. Across its wooden panels fish swam among waves, carved by a hand as steady and unruffled as a windless sea. Palms decorated the frame, and at his youngest grandson's eye level, a lotus bloomed. Every one of the child's questions revealed the door to him afresh. From the arch hung scraps of paper, which his wife covered with prayers every morning, as if she didn't trust the unchanging calligraphy on the wood to ward off djinns. The old man called his request into the courtyard, the repository for everything that wasn't pure enough for the first floor, then sat down on the stone bench along the outside wall. It was still early; his friends would arrive later, but he didn't feel the need to lie down as he usually did and doze a little before the evening's exertions. Salim would soon bring him some coconut milk. He would pull his youngest grandson to him and enjoy his cheekiness for a while. Then he would stretch out on the bench and lay his head on the stone armrest.

The day called for the next prayer. The old man on the baraza outside his house trained an eye on the stream of events trickling through his mind. Thoughts bobbed drowsily past: the ceremonial exchange of flags, the lowering of the sultan's blood-red banner which he had once followed into the unknown. He had been infected by the conceited assurance of those two foreigners – one light-haired and ruddy, the other with an Arab's colouring and a warrior's scars – both blindly certain that their treasure and the sultan's flag would have the effect they desired on the rulers of the interior. And to his belated amazement, their confidence had been proved justified. He had survived that trip, and three others. He had survived.

And then much later, just after he had become a grandfather for the first time, another mzungu had appeared, lighter-skinned than the others, drawn, he supposed, by the fame he had accrued in old age. A harried man, as clumsy as Bwana Speke, as ambitious as Bwana Stanley. He had asked Sidi Mubarak Bombay to guide him into the interior. They had sat in the courtyard – the wazungu thought it impolite if you received them in the street, but when you asked them into the courtyard, you could see the disgust on their faces at the dogs and chickens roaming about and your servant dozing in a corner, spittle dribbling from his open mouth – and his thoughts had toyed with the idea of another trip, a fifth, when he heard a voice crash from the first floor like a cudgel, 'If you leave me again' – the mzungu couldn't understand the words, but the tone was unmistakable – 'I'll scratch every last bit of happiness out of your life!' A fear, sticky as an overripe mango, had suddenly gripped him. Not because of his wife's threat, but because, for the first time, he was scared of not coming back. The mzungu was asking for information that smelled of blood, tasted of disaster – everything about him was excessive. He seemed to believe the world was as he pictured it in his mind. So if the world disappointed him, would he change it? 'Don't worry,' he had called up to his wife. 'You won't get rid of me that easily.' He had thought for a moment of misleading that madman, inventing directions, but he quickly gave up the idea: it wouldn't have come to anything. He had played his share of games with the wazungu, but they had always reached their goal. Half blind sometimes, or half crazed, crippled and in agony, but always fully aware of their success. And now they had raised their flag over Zanzibar. The old man hadn't been surprised today to see his caller from before, the excessive Bwana Peters, standing stiffly by the main flagpole amid all the leading wazungu, aglow with pride in his lavish uniform. The world now did look exactly as he had imagined it.

'What are you shaking your head about?'

'I am shaking my head about a certain gentleman who insists on pestering me with stupid questions.'

'You wouldn't understand any other sort.'

'How do you know? You have never tried.'

'*Assalaamu aleikum.*'

'*Aleikum is salaam.*'

'Is all right with the world?'

'It is and it is not.'

'Is the family well?'

'The house is full of health.'

'And gold?'

'Full of gold, full of coral, full of pearls.'

'And good fortune?'

'*Hem!*'

'*Marhaba.*'

'*Marhaba.*'

'I have a hankering for strong coffee.'

'You are welcome.'

'If it is to my liking, I will tell you what I have learnt about the sultan's treasurer.'

'The sultan's flag will soon make a good duster.'

'Which is why the treasurer has offered his services to the wazungu.'

'Birth alone isn't enough to impress them. All that counts with them is what you can do.'

'They need their leeches too, and who better suited to that than the long-serving treasurer? He who has served yesterday's masters well will be able to serve tomorrow's even better.'

'You're right; I bow to your wisdom immediately. But will

you sit down now, finally, otherwise people will think we've had an argument and next thing they'll start believing all your tales.'

'Your kindness shines like a beacon.'

'An old habit I can't seem to shake off. I was just thinking – don't say anything, don't interrupt immediately – I was just thinking about the wazungu's self-confidence, how little I knew it at the beginning, how poorly I understood it, and now here they are today, showing us their flag from the highest pole on the island. Everything was a revelation on that first trip . . . Ah, Salim, come to me, come here little one, sit here with us . . . not completely unexpected, because that was what made me go with them in the first place, the confidence the darker mzungu instilled in me that you could go anywhere at their side – I only realised later that they needed us to get wherever they wanted to go – but still, they were so sure of themselves. Do you understand?'

'Did you know Grandmother then?'

'No, Salim, I didn't know your grandmother yet, but you can believe me, I did not set off to find her. It was more as if the ancestors had called me back to the land I was from, which I had never returned to. I was about your age, my morning star, the age you are now, when they hunted me down and caught me and carried me off, Arabs with heavy robes and loud guns whom we had already heard of . . . oh yes, we had been warned about them. But do you believe in the djinn you have never seen? Have you ever seen a djinn? And what will you do if it attacks you, my sunlight? You don't know! They fell on us, swifter than death. They were everywhere, firing their loud guns, bellowing their orders that branded my ears, raw orders that mingled with the screams of our mothers and grandmothers and sisters, branding my ears. And even now if I hear yelling like that – a pedlar cursing his boy, a pearl diver coming home tired and bad-tempered – then I hear it all again, all the screaming, and I see it all again. I see the soles of our feet running to the lakes, the soles of my fear. Who knows why we sought refuge at the lake instead of hiding in the woods like the others – I suppose that's what they did, because when we were lined up and our hands chained to a beam, some of my brothers were missing, and that was my only joy, that they were not with us. I was as young as you, coming up to the age to be eaten by the knife, but still a bird that could land wherever it wanted, a bird that didn't have to go to the madrassa yet or stay in a courtyard, that could hop through the forest and the savannah, and jump into the lake if someone was watching for crocodiles and was ready to slap the water when they were coming. And then the day dawned that wore the mask of an unknown, the day my wings and legs were broken until I did not know if I was anything more than a piece of meat to be dragged across the baking ground. The masks spoke in the tongue of the whip. You've never heard the tongue of the whip, sweetheart. You don't even know the stick – your father forgets all about anger when he is with you – so you don't know how the whip humiliates you before it causes you pain, how it punishes you before it threatens you, how it cuts through your senses, forces you to your knees, leaves you reeling. It is a tongue that cries out to be cut out, but our hands were tied, and sometimes when we rested at night, because we often had to walk through the night, our feet were tied too. And even now, after three other lives, if you look at your grandfather's wrist, there, you can still see the scars from when my first life died, my life as a child, the life with my ancestors and relations. After that I never saw anyone who knew my village again, who addressed his prayers to the same ancestors as me, and it was many rainy seasons before I met another person who spoke my language.

'From that day on I was alone. The nights were the worst. At night the hyenas prowled round us and we heard them, the Arabs heard them too. They threw stones into the darkness, sometimes they stumbled and sometimes they yelped, and then the Arabs lay down to sleep around their safe fires, and we screamed. Our screams were the only weapon we had against the hyenas sniffing around, a blunt weapon that only made our fear grow as the hyenas crept closer. You can't believe, my friend, how a man can scream until his voice is bitten off and then you hear something that you have never heard and you should never hear. We couldn't look the next morning in its ragged face. Our brothers weren't human any more, the flesh torn off their bodies in strips. They were carrion, and their spirits walked on their heads or darted like lightning between the trees, blasting them and anyone who came in reach. By the time we reached the coast all of us were dead: dead spirits, the living dead, dead people with working legs, dead people with eyes like squashed fruit. I didn't smell the sea, I didn't smell the rotten seaweed, I didn't hear the clamour of the waves, I didn't taste the salt air . . . Here in this town, on the square where the wazungu have built their house of prayer, I was put on show and three pitiless suns passed before someone, a banyan, bought me for a few coins. He took me to his house, where others like me, whom I couldn't say a word to, gave me something to eat and showed me where I could wash.

'The man who took ownership of my second life was a nobleman, my little one, who was forbidden by ancient laws of his own to trade in animals, among many other things. He lived surrounded by a mass of invisible laws that were supposed to protect him like the iron wires we stretch above our gate to protect the house from thieves. But the only protection his laws gave him was to lock him in. They were silent like cheats caught in the act when he bought a person as if he were meat. His laws forbade him to use cowries in case he caused the death of a shellfish, and he obeyed them then, but he traded in rhino horn and hippopotamus hide and ivory, even though that was breaking them. But when he bought human beings, he wasn't even in the wrong, because his laws said nothing about that. This banyan didn't sell me or make me work on a plantation; he kept me in his home. He gave me work which allowed me to recover my strength, and one day he took me to the city where he was born, on the other side of the sea, many days of damp food and mouldy dreams away, and if you want to know the name of this city, my talisman, you just have to say Grandfather's name . . . No, the last one! Bombay, exactly. Thanks be to the ancestors for this blessing, for this gentleman with the strange laws, because otherwise I wouldn't be here today, on this baraza. We sailed in a big dhow, not one of these pitiful mtepe, you know, one of those tubs that sail to Tanganyika, no, on a big, proud, powerful ship that rode the waves . . .'

'As if astride all the horses of the world!'

'*Assalaamu aleikum*, Baba Ilias. We have been waiting for you.'

'Ah, Baba Ilias, horses made of water – is that your latest invention?'

'Ships don't ride on horses and horses don't gallop across the sea but you can say it. I say it and others have the taste to appreciate it, all except Baba Ishmael, whose ears are shod with iron. You need nails, not a tongue, to get through to him.'

'What a talker you are, Baba Ilias, it's almost a pity you don't deliver the khutbah.'

'God keep me from such temptations.'

'Sometimes he can seduce us with his words, our Baba Ilias, but words themselves just won't conform to his will.'

'Perhaps Mama Mubarak would conform to our will and bring the coffee we were promised?'

'Perhaps, perhaps.'

'Weren't you sad, Grandfather, when you lost your name?'

'Sad? Why should our Baba Sidi have been sad? He just gave himself a new name.'

❦

Burton stands in the water up to his ankles and waits – as he has been waiting for over six months since arriving in Zanzibar – for the journey to begin. They must at long last set off into the interior, the most ambitious undertaking of his life.

The highest recognition beckons; rewards of a title, a life pension, will go to the man who can solve the mystery of the source of the Nile that has gripped and amazed the world for over two thousand years, and thereby open up the entire continent. His ambition doesn't scare him. What other aim can there be except to find a meaning for the white patches on the world's maps? This damn waiting will be over soon; all these laborious negotiations must surely be done with any moment now. And then in the blink of an eye all the fetters of habit, the burdens of routine and the slavery of settled life will be shaken off!

It would hardly be possible to prepare an expedition better. They've done everything – no, he has done everything in his power. So far his partner, John Hanning Speke, has elegantly refrained from contributing. Lack of expertise, apparently. An aristocratic soul. Things won't be simple with him. The incident in Somalia, when they were attacked in the night and only just escaped with their lives, had been a warning: Speke reproached everyone except himself. But he's a tough lad, an excellent shot and, in general, he seems to respect Burton as the more experienced traveller of the two, the leader of the expedition. He won't question his authority. Moreover he's well-to-do; he's paying a good part of the expenses out of his own pocket. The money's terribly tight – what a laughable state of affairs: the work of filling in the white patches in jeopardy over small change. That's what happens when you leave conquering the world to shopkeepers, though. They always economise in the wrong place.

He walks along the beach. The sun sets into the water. The sand looks like finely ground sea salt steeped in gold. He dips his hands in a long wave and wets his face, then runs his fingers through his hair to the nape. He is standing in the Indian Ocean up to his ankles, and his gaze travels over the crowns of foam, the bluish ridges that dissolve into the immateriality of a promise, the curvature of the earth, and on to the ports of Bombay and Karachi, the bays of Khambhat and Suez, the

Arab Ocean. He has experienced so much, written so much – for his superiors and for the public. And how has he been rewarded? The judges of a British subject's merits have passed over him and his achievements in silence.

Grey spreads across the beach in the sun's wake. He realises he is no longer alone as he approaches a pack of dogs whose paws are being washed by the sea. Their muzzles are smeared with blood, and before he can wonder why, he sees the rotting body they have pounced on, grateful for such a gift. Suspicious eyes turn towards him, anxious lest the interloper is a threat to their prey, as pale as tuna. The slave traders throw damaged goods overboard, he thinks. Death and the distribution of the legacy are left to the sea. Everyone they land is healthy enough to make them money; their calculated losses are eventually washed ashore somewhere. Burton turns away – it is high time he left Zanzibar.

On the terrace of the Africa Hotel sits, as expected, John Hanning Speke, Jack to his friends. Sundowner in hand, he observes the little town with an air of enjoyment. No doubt he's amusing his circle of fellow countrymen, businessmen – arms dealers – mainly, with hunting tales from the Himalayas. Amazing, all those adventures he's had in Tibet, when you see how happy he seems sitting here on this terrace. From here, the dogs on the beach look like children playing. Were Burton to point them out, Speke would earnestly reply: 'Zanzibar is too small, there's not enough game: why should I go and slog my guts out in the heat?' Burton has almost reached the oval table by the balustrade, the servants standing stiffly in the background – their outfits suggesting a cursory reading of the *Thousand and One Nights* – when Speke turns his head and sees him. He immediately breaks off his conversation and calls out far too loud a greeting, as if he wanted to draw the attention of everyone at the table to the unexpected visitor.

'Are you the bringer of good news?'

'We heard the expedition is ready to go.'

'That's the problem. It's high time it finally got going.'

'Well, good luck.'

'When you come back to Zanzibar, gentlemen, I'll throw a party such as you have never seen before.'

'Knowing his tight-fistedness, he's wagering on you not coming back.'

'I can smell the Arabs' mistrust already.'

'We have the sultan's personal protection.'

'That's only provisional, Jack. In the Orient, a solemnly given word of honour is a pure declaration of intention; it only guarantees a possible course of action.'

'How true, how very true! If I were you, gentlemen, I wouldn't trust those Baluchis the sultan is sending with you an inch. Even if they are good soldiers, which I heartily doubt, I can't think what fit of madness prompted the sultan to put muskets in their hands. They're all working on their own account.'

'One of my informants, by the way, reports a great deal of intriguing against you at the court. Some of the sultan's closest advisers have persuaded him your expedition is merely a pretext for the British Empire to get a foothold in East Africa. As part of a long-term strategy culminating in his overthrow.'

'They're afraid for their trade monopoly.'

'They're most afraid for their lucrative slave trade. They follow all the news from Europe, you know; they're better informed than we think.'

'Let them be afraid. I am a great believer in fear.'

'Richard, we have all heard a great deal about your extraordinary exploits. We are full of admiration, believe me. But you should be careful nonetheless. Until now, all things considered, you've travelled in civilised parts. There have been people who knew how to write, buildings that predated the last rainy season. This time you're about to embark on a journey into virgin wilderness, possibly even among cannibals.'

'Is there such a thing as virgin wilderness?'

'You haven't been in this part of the world before. Don't be deceived by Zanzibar. There is no mysterious city waiting for you beyond the wastes of the mainland, no Mecca or Harar or whatever you want to call it. Just a savage land that has never been tamed by human hand.'

SIDI MUBARAK BOMBAY

'Is everybody who comes from that place called Bombay, Grandfather?'

'No, some chose the names of the places they came from, the places they remembered. They called themselves Kunduchi or Malindi or Bagamoyo. I decided to take the name of the city where my third life started: Bombay. Before then some people had called me Mubarak Miqava because I come from the Yao, which was something I didn't know myself. I was Yao without knowing it. As a child I never heard about the Yao. Grandfather never said, "We are the Yao people"; Father never said, "We are the Yao people." I only found out I was Yao when I was a slave, just when it was no use to me. It sounds beautiful, Yao, but I didn't want to be reminded all my life of the land I had lost. I didn't want to be reminded every time someone called my name that I had already died one death. The path that lay ahead of me was more important than the one that lay behind, if you understand me.'

'Of course we understand, it is like the direction of prayer.'

'At the sun's rising, no one thinks of it setting.'

'Baba Ilias, your proverbs are as ill-fitting as Baba Ishmael's clothes.'

'The other slaves stayed in Bombay and took wives there; they were happy with their life as Sidis.'

'Sidis? I didn't know you had conjured up a whole people out of your name.'

'Over there Sidis meant anyone with dark skin who came from across the sea. That included people who were as unfamiliar to me as the inhabitants of Bombay, but the locals saw us as all having one skin colour and face, no matter where we came from.'

'Were they all true believers?'

'If I knew what the true faith looked like, I could answer your question, Baba Quddus. They observed the prayers, not very regularly, they read the Glorious Qur'an, on occasion, when they felt the need, and on feast days we all met in a house: in the main room of the house there was a man's tomb covered in green cloth, and on the wall there were clubs, gourds like the ones I knew from my village, the tools of a holy man who has protected the Sidis for a very long time. The festival began with drumming – only the saint's descendants were allowed to play the drums – and we danced in a circle round the tomb and sang, and then we crowded out into the narrow street and carried on dancing and singing, and it had the sound of childhood to me. It sounded like my first life, and suddenly I felt at home in that strange city.'

'What about the prayers?'

'We said prayers but they weren't prayers addressed to God; they were addressed to someone who I am sure you have never prayed to, and whose name you won't guess either, even if I gave you the whole evening, although it's obvious if you think about it.'

'Do you think our memories are that bad?'

'Don't tell me. It'll come in a second.'

'How could you forget it? A little while ago Baba Sidi couldn't think of it himself and you whispered it to him.'

'That was a little while ago.'

'Tell us!'

'We prayed to Bilal, because to us Bilal was the first, most powerful ancestor.'

'That's shirk!'

'Ah, Baba Quddus, what is shirk and what isn't? What was true at the beginning and what will remain true for all time?'

'The Glorious Qur'an, as you well know.'

'Bilal doesn't replace the Glorious Qur'an, he adds to it. He is the companion of the people who are slaves or were slaves; people who need some of their own verses of encouragement and consolation. You shouldn't forget that it was with the Sidis, the people who you say commit sacrilege, that I learnt prayer; I learnt the suras with the Sidis, I met people who explained parts of the Qur'an to me with the Sidis.'

'How did you come back from there, Grandfather?'

'The banyan fell ill. One day his sickness had barely touched him, the next day death had seized hold of him, and the day after that he was burnt on Bombay beach. I insisted on being there, even though it was a sad sight, and I thanked him as the flames devoured him. I thanked him despite everything, as he shrivelled and burst and was slowly turned to ashes – it took from midday until almost sunset. It lasted a long time, that final service I did him, and even then he wasn't completely burnt, his pelvic bone was still left.'

'That's revolting!'

'Imagine him wandering around Hell, just a pelvic bone, ash trickling off him whenever he moves . . .'

'How is he supposed to move if he's only a pelvic bone?'

'Mad!'

'May God give these poor people more sense.'

'I don't know if you're right. Howling with hyenas only seems mad if you're not a hyena.'

'Baba Ilias, perhaps you could explain to us what hyenas have to do with burning bodies one evening.'

'And I still don't know how you got back to Zanzibar.'

'My master had instructed in his last will that after his death I should be given my . . .'

'Coffees, how many coffees?'

'Only one person would interrupt me like that.'

'You get enough turns to speak. Let's offer our guests something they can enjoy with a light heart for a change. Madafu, who wants madafu? Our son brought fresh coconuts today.'

'Go on, tell her what you want. I won't get any peace until she's got answers from all of you.'

∾

The fishing boats have put in and lie close together on the beach like goats in a kraal. A few strands of cloud straggle across the sky; voices tussle for bargains. Women's hands clean the little mackerel, tossing the guts next to the drying nets and the rest of the fish into baskets. A few men mend their boats with slow movements, as if everything needed to be checked again by daylight. In the middle of it all stands Burton. He stands perfectly still; he must have been doing so for a while, because the fishermen and market women have ceased to pay him any attention, as if he were part of the scenery. Only a few children cling to him, trying to fold back the tail of his jacket to find shortcuts to his many pockets. He is like a sponge, absorbing everything; taut, full of avid attention. He passed an agitated night, his last on the island, then left the house early, that greyish brown box that contains the British consulate and reeks of the consul, who can't bring himself to sail away from his own death. His voice had detained Burton as he was on his way out. The consul was lying on the veranda, swaddled in blankets.

'A very good morning to you, Dick.'

'The best thing about it being that it's brought the night to an end.'

'Bad dreams?'

'No dreams at all.'

'Perhaps that's a good sign.'

'Sign? I prefer to be the one giving those. By the way, I'm glad you've decided to go home.'

'Home? Oh I'll certainly do that, one day.'

'One day? Last night you were ready to give the orders to start packing.'

'We did talk ourselves into ecstasies last night, didn't we, my dear fellow. I have to see you get off safely first.'

'The only thing you have to see to is that you recover your health. There's no better remedy than home leave.'

'Health, ah . . . not entirely at one with the tropics, is it? By the way, do you know what the rich Zanzibari die of – when cholera, smallpox or malaria don't get them, that is?'

'Poisoning?'

'No, old man. You do have a yen for the dramatic. Constipation. Several years ago a French friend, a doctor, explained it was because of their indolence. They die of laziness, something they are only able to indulge in because of their wealth. They fall victim to their station. A sign of divine justice, no?'

'Perhaps there's another explanation. A more prosaic, morally less suggestive one. The aphrodisiacs they take in astronomical quantities may not be entirely blameless.'

'Your speciality, Dick, your speciality.'

'The rich on this island? Addicted to stimulants, every last one of them. As if Zanzibar were under a bell-jar of impotence. Their favourite preparation? A pill three parts amber to one part opium, the opium to be regulated according to the level of dependency. They all take it, whether they need to or not.'

'Idleness and desire, there you have it. Between those poles, they meet their deaths.'

'Go home, Consul. Go home, won't you.'

SIDI MUBARAK BOMBAY

'Tell me, Baba Sidi, I've never understood, what exactly did you do on that journey?'

'Good question.'

'You didn't carry . . .'

'True.'

'You didn't fight . . .'

'True.'

'You didn't cook . . .'

'True.'

'You didn't wash clothes . . .'

'There were others to do that.'

'So what did you do?'

'I guided them.'

'Say that again, my brother.'

319

'I guided the expedition.'

'You? But you had never been to the lake they were looking for.'

'No.'

'And you guided them there?'

'If no one knows the way, anyone can be a guide.'

'I didn't know the way, it's true, but it wasn't hard finding it. There was only one route through that country: the route of the slave caravans. You mustn't think that just because you don't know something, no one else does. There were Arabs who travelled that route as often as our merchants go to Pemba. There were porters who supported themselves and their families by taking bales from the coast to the interior, fifty or a hundred days' march there and back. The route people take every day doesn't need signposts, don't forget. I had plenty of things to do, more than my fair share: I had to act as go-between, I had to scout ahead, I was Bwana Speke's right-hand man, I was Bwana Burton's binoculars . . .'

'What's that?'

'An instrument that brings what's far away near.'

'Like time?'

'Can you put time to your eye?'

'Imagine Bwana Speke reaching with his right hand for Bwana Burton's binoculars and, oh, oh, oh, there's our lump Sidi . . .'

'Couldn't you be the target for your gibes for once?'

'How can I? You know the razor cannot shave itself.'

'Ah yes. I had another very important job; I had to translate, because Bwana Burton and Bwana Speke couldn't make themselves understood by the porters. We only had one language in common, the language of the banyans, and I was the only person in Zanzibar who could speak it . . .'

'Why did the wazungu know the language of the banyans, Grandfather?'

'They had both lived in the city where I . . .'

'The city that has the same name as you.'

'Yes, my heart, you have been keeping up very well, the city whose name I bear. Bwana Burton spoke like a banyan, quickly and well, he could twist his tongue the way the madmen who run around the country of the banyans naked can twist their bodies. Bwana Speke was like a tottery old man, he groped for his words the way you grope for a coin that's been lost in a trunk, and when he found them, he didn't know how to string them together. You can imagine how slow and painstaking conversations were between Bwana Speke and me – at least at first, until he made progress and I did too and we had a richer stew of words to share. He was difficult to understand; his Hindustani was even worse than mine. I translated what I thought I had understood him to say into Kiswahili, and then, in the interior, we had to find someone who could speak Kiswahili and could translate Bwana Speke's questions into the local language. Often it was someone who showed a lot of goodwill but didn't necessarily understand everything. So he would leave out whatever he didn't understand, or make guesses, and so the answers we got after a long wait were sometimes only distantly related to the questions. On and on it went, and a traveller who lacked patience wouldn't have been able to stand those slow, cautious conversations. It was a lonely expedition for Bwana Speke: he could only talk his language to one person, Bwana Burton, and when a quarrel drove them apart, they didn't speak for months. Then he was silent, Bwana Speke, and he just let his rifle talk.'

'Did he shoot people?'

'How many?'

'He shot animals, only animals, my little one. Vast numbers of animals. If there's a kingdom of the dead for animals, it is now as full as the mosque at Ramadan.'

'Perhaps it was because there was no one for him to talk to that he had to kill so many of them.'

'If that were the case, Baba Adam, the dumb would be the worst murderers.'

'He was often lonely, it is true, and he got lonelier, the longer

321

our journey went on. Bwana Burton found a common language with almost everybody: with the slave traders he spoke Arabic; with the soldiers, the Baluchis, he spoke Sindhi; it was only with his friend, Bwana Speke, that he didn't have one. He even learnt Kiswahili, but only in small steps because he didn't like our language.'

'What fault did he find in it? It is the most beautiful of all languages.'

'That's always what people say when they don't know any other language.'

'The most beautiful of all languages is Arabic.'

'Kiswahili is like a world composed entirely of beautiful landscapes.'

'What do you mean by that, Baba Ilias? That the rivers are from the Persian, say, the mountains from the Arabic, the forests from the Uluguru . . .'

'More or less. You're starting to get the hang of it.'

'And the sands from Zanzibar.'

'And the sky?'

'The sky isn't part of the landscape.'

'Wouldn't it look naked without the sky?'

'It's like a kanga draped round the earth's hips.'

'At sunset.'

'What did I say? Haven't your ears heard how beautiful Kiswahili can sound, even in the mouths of chatterers like you?'

'We're talking about his taste, not yours. He didn't like putting things in front of words; it was like a muzzle, he said, which stopped words being what they were at the beginning. But even so he learnt it; he learnt a fair amount, and by the time we got back he spoke as much Kiswahili as he needed.'

'And the other one?'

'Not a word. Not even "quick" or "stop".'

'Two very different men.'

'Completely different. How can one understand two such different people setting off together on a journey that would force them to put their lives in each other's hands? They even looked different: one was powerfully built and dark, the other slim and lithe and pale, like the belly of a fish.'

'Some fish.'

'Their natures were different: one was loud, outspoken, stormy, the other quiet, reticent, cagey. They behaved differently: one was insulting but quick to forgive, the other self-controlled but prone to bear grudges. One was hungry and lusted after everything, and always yielded to his lust and hunger, the other had desires as well but he hobbled them – sometimes they tried to break free but they were always reined in.'

'But if they could travel across country together for years, they must have had something in common, mustn't they?'

'Ambition and obstinacy. They were more stubborn than the thirty asses we left Bagamoyo with. And they were rich, immeasurably rich. Over a hundred men were needed to carry their riches, men with bare feet and nothing to their name.'

∽

Everyone has assembled at Bagamoyo, the starting point for all caravans into the interior, a place where, as its name indicates, innumerable slaves have laid down their hearts. They are waiting for the signal to leave. The shoeless porters are wretchedly clothed, even on this, the day of departure, attired in just a few strips of goatskin and bunches of feathers. Some have tied bells round their calves which jingle, to the hilarity of the children who have broken off their games of hide and seek among the bulbous trees. The cloth for trading has been rolled into bolsters five feet long and secured with branches, loads weighing seventy pounds apiece. That's the most the porters can be expected to carry, especially because they have a few measly little possessions to manage of their own. The chests are slung between two long poles – the lighter ones at the end, the heavier in the middle – which are carried by two men.

Burton speaks to the kirangozi, Said bin Salim, who will lead the march, the expedition's master of ceremonies. A garrulous man, this representative of the sultan; not someone who would dream of underestimating his own importance. His job is simply to transmit orders, but he manages to do so as if they come from him. Loyalty in his case is a simple equation: always respect the hand that feeds. The kirangozi calls out an order; the kettledrum sounds for the first time. The gang of porters uncoils itself from the shade on the square and, like a corpulent python, winds its way down the avenue that leads towards the interior. Closely planted mangoes line the thoroughfare, their entangled branches forming a canopy under which it is never completely light. Burton joins Speke, who is keeping the bedridden consul company under a nearby awning. Instead of going home, he has accompanied them to Bagamoyo. To see everything goes off all right, he claims. To say goodbye for ever, Burton presumes. As if he wanted to say: You are heading off into the unknown and I into death.

'Look at that dancing-jack,' says Speke, indicating the kirangozi. 'Does he have to wear that purple robe? And all those furbelows on his head?'

'It looks like a griffin's nest,' remarks Burton, and they laugh in unison, a short, incongruous laugh. 'No sense of camouflage. We'll be spotted miles away downwind.'

'That's the point,' the consul says. 'That's why he's holding up the sultan's red flag, so everyone will know at a distance that this caravan comes from Zanzibar and enjoys the sultan's direct protection.'

'It's not him I'm worried about,' Burton says, 'it's our escort.'

The thirteen Baluchis pass before them, equipped with muskets, sabres, daggers and cartridge pouches, which each of them has distributed about his person after his own idiosyncratic fashion. They follow their commander, the one-eyed, pock-marked, long-armed Jemadar Mallok.

'I promised them a reward if they brought both of you back safe and sound,' says the consul.

The Baluchis shoulder their muskets and perform a rough approximation of marching in step, as if they're parodying a military parade. They remind Burton of the company of sepoys he had struggled to drill in Baroda, and the bashibazouks he had such a job of commanding in the Crimea. Compared to this crowd jiggling past, though, the sepoys were a model of discipline, and the bashibazouks were infinitely more belligerent desperadoes than these descendants of fakirs, sailors, coolies, date-gleaners, beggars and thieves – sons of an arid land that had driven so many of its own into exile, and yet still they sang its praises in their melancholy songs. In their memories the barren valley, which their forefathers turned their back on, was in perpetual bloom.

The consul gives Burton the sultan's letter of introduction. 'It'll be important,' he says, 'at least at first. After that you'll push on into places where no one knows a sultan exists; at the most, you may find someone who has heard vague talk of him, as of some figure in an exotic legend.' Burton carefully folds the letter and puts it in his leather bag next to his two passports, Cardinal Wieseman's letter of blessing and the certificate from the sheikh of Mecca confirming his Hajj. Something for every eventuality. He takes leave of the consul with a quick handshake, and immediately feels ashamed because he has to admit that the touch of that liver-spotted hand made him nauseous.

For the first few miles all he can think of are things they might have forgotten. Have they brought enough goods to trade? If they are short of beads and cloth, how will they get food? His gaze alights on the bolsters on the porters' heads, the rolls of merikani – unbleached cotton from America – and kaniki – indigo-coloured cotton from India. Those had better be enough, otherwise they'll starve. The sea is already a thing of the past, now the short avenue has turned off into the formless bush and they have been swallowed up by grass that reaches to their shoulders. They follow a river, which they rarely see. The ground is hard; the bush stretches endlessly ahead. The natives clearly avoid the caravans. Passing a dilapidated hut, they reach their first village, where the only signs of life are little fish drying outside huts and piles of freshly picked fruit. Coming out the other side, the atavistic landscape swallows them up again, that intimidating formlessness, which alone is enough to instil a slight sense of dread. They are going to have to assert their existence every day, Burton thinks. No one had warned him about that. Not even Tulsi, one of those servile Indians in Bagamoyo who had claimed to be helping them while exorbitantly taxing the expedition's purse. A prophet of doom of the highest order, he had dispensed a steady stream of terrible news, as if it were an effective prophylaxis against the horrors of the interior. The night before in his house in Bagamoyo, he had served up gulab jamun accompanied by sticky tales of savages sitting in trees who fired poison arrows into the air with such dexterity that, when they came down, they drilled through the skull and into the throat. The unsuspecting traveller died with his mouth nailed shut. Burton asked how they were expected to protect themselves.

'Keep away from the trees!'

'In the forest? Are we meant to avoid the sky too?'

Tulsi was volubly seconded by Ladha Damha, another Indian, who collected customs for the sultan. According to him, some of the chiefs had sworn not to allow the white man to enter their territory. Kill the first locusts, a seer had warned them, if you want to avoid the plague. That was just the start of the list of dangers awaiting them: an enraged rhinoceros could kill a hundred men; armies of elephants were known to attack camps at night; there were scorpions whose bite barely left you time to call out God's name; they would in all likelihood be without food for weeks.

The Indians were convinced the British pair wouldn't even get halfway. They had spoken openly in front of Burton, thinking he wouldn't understand their Gujarati dialect. 'Will they reach the sea of Ujiji?' asked Ladha Damha. 'Of course not!' his clerk replied with a disdainful sniff. 'Who are they to think they can cross the country of the Ugogo alive?'

'You Gujus,' Burton said as he was leaving in the cultivated Gujarati Upanishe had taught him, 'you think you're very clever. I'll cross the country of the Ugogo, I'll find the great lake, I'll come back, and then I'll pay you another visit.'

He lets himself fall behind. He can allow himself to do that now everybody seems to know his place in the column. He slows his pace until he can hear but not see the last porter. One hundred and twenty people at his command. It has to succeed, this expedition: that's all there is to it. He only has to stretch out his hand to touch the glory that is rightfully his, but to reach this point, he has had to disobey his superiors in the East India Company, he has got himself heavily into debt, and he has risked taking a loose cannon as his companion. The consul was right: the auspices could have been more favourable. The friend of his who was meant to come, an excellent doctor, had been incapacitated at the last moment; Sultan Sayyid Said, a staunch ally, had died just days before they arrived at Zanzibar; and the consul, who could not have been more helpful, was at death's door. If he fails – but he can't think that; if all other fear is alien, the fear of failure has to be similarly suppressed – the regiment in India is waiting. Go back there? Never.

They cross the verdant bush at a brisk clip, but they won't be able to keep it up for long. Legs will tire; the country will throw up obstacles. They will stumble, slip, sink, wade through mud. Their feet will catch in lures. There's another hour or so of today's march left, then the signal to halt will ring out. He quickens his stride.

Said bin Salim has chosen well for the site of their first camp. Notched trunks, charred branches, an enlarged clearing – people have camped here before. When they have unpacked everything and gone over the inventory again, they discover one of the compasses has been left in Bagamoyo. Burton is the only one who knows where it is: he'll have to go all the way back. To his surprise, Sidi Mubarak Bombay offers unprompted to come with him, even though this means a march of roughly six miles. Bombay – as he calls him in his head, and when he addresses him – is no stranger, they've already talked a few times, but this forced march, which will triple their daily stint, will be the first time they have been alone together for any length of time. A private conversation, thinks Burton: a rare event in the Orient. For the first half an hour they walk side by side in silence, Burton taking long strides, Bombay shorter, quicker ones. Then Burton strikes up conversation by regretting that his insufficient command of Kiswahili prevents him conversing with Sidi Mubarak Bombay in his own language. 'It is not my language,' says Bombay, 'my language is lost,' and then he breaks into a friendly smile. When his features are in motion, regardless of the direction, it is as if they have put out from the harbour of ugliness. With every smile, Bombay seems to be repairing his face – all apart from his jaw; his teeth are condemned to eternal decay. He's a stocky fellow, and he cuts an anomalous figure among these people; the idle part of his nature seems to have been mislaid somewhere on his travels abroad. Of course slavery is a nasty business, utterly intolerable in point of fact, but without it Sidi Mubarak Bombay would still be one of those apathetic figures squatting by the side of the road who can just bring themselves to give you a weary wave of acknowledgement.

SIDI MUBARAK BOMBAY

'There are questions that crowd to the front, questions that drag their curiosity after them like firewood. "Where do you come from?" That was easy to answer. From Zanzibar, from the coast, from Bagamoyo. But questions are always followed by other questions, the path has no end, and Bwana Burton and Bwana Speke didn't even know how to answer the second question: "Where are you going?" In the shade of every mbuyu and every mtumbwi and every miombo, that was the question that met us. It flew up like a flock of startled birds, it followed a greeting as naturally as one wave follows another, as inevitably as kazi follows kaskazi. Some questions are like barking dogs, like thorns you can't get out from under your skin.'

'Questions wives ask their husbands.'

'If you want to take over the story, Baba Burhan, by all means, go ahead.'

'No, no, I am just adding to it, as the ears add to the tongue.'

'When you've finished adding to each other, can we hear what happens next?'

'Don't you know, Baba Ali? Have you only just moved into the neighbourhood?'

'The story is different every time.'

'"Where are you from? Where are you going?" These were the questions that were waiting for us in the shade of every mtumbwi and every miombo. Such simple questions, you will say. Even children know where they are going. Or at least they know where they want to go.'

'Children can answer those sorts of questions, certainly, but grown-ups?'

'"To the great lake!" That's what the wazungu answered, if they gave an answer at all, but the people asking the questions didn't know of any great lake, and those who had heard of a great lake couldn't believe someone would cross the land with a hundred porters and twenty soldiers and face all the dangers of the forest just to get to the great lake. "What do you want from this lake?" they asked next. "We don't want anything from the great lake," answered Bwana Burton. "We just want to see it with our own eyes, because we want to know where it is and how big it is." The people in the shadow of the mbuyu, the mtumbwi and the miombo shook their heads. They could recognise the face of a lie; suspicion swelled in their minds. "These strangers", they muttered, "are bent on no good." "These strangers", they hissed, "have come to steal our land." They were afraid; eh, they were scared of us. But they were even more scared of what our coming would lead to. "These strangers will bring calamity," they worried. In one of the villages, a man died shortly after we had pitched our camp, a young man who had been working in his field just the day before. "You see," complained the villagers, "admit it, that is the first misfortune you have brought upon our land by coming here." This was how they complained, and as their complaints grew louder, their fear gradually vanished, and Bwana Burton was wise to hurry our leaving the next morning. Between the villages only children kept us company. They ran along beside us shouting, "Mzungu, mzungu," and "Wazungu, wazungu," laughing and swinging their arms. "What does 'mzungu' mean?" Bwana Burton asked me. "Someone who wanders about," I answered, "someone who goes around in circles." "Is that what they think of us?" He was surprised. "But we are heading straight for our destination," he said. "To these people," I said, "it looks as if we are lost."'

'What about you? Did his surprise surprise you?'

'The caravan of the surprised!'

'Why were there a hundred porters? Didn't you have enough pack animals?'

'Baba Ishmael would have sold you his three long-legged mules that chew more khat than he does.'

'We had animals; of course we had pack animals. We had five mules and thirty asses – thirty half-lame, stubborn, hopelessly unreliable asses. After three months only one was left, all the rest were dead. But I tell you, the men were even more ill-suited to the journey. Starting with the kirangozi who led the way and only served two people: himself and the sultan. Behind him came the Baluchis who were supposed to protect us, but how they were supposed to protect us when they were such cowards was a mystery to us at the start and was still a mystery to us at the end. We soon learnt not to trust the Baluchis: they would have sold their mother to the highest bidder. Then came the porters – eh, the honest porters who Bwana Burton and Bwana Speke couldn't trust either. They carried a lot, it's true, and they endured everything, but only until darkness fell. Then their blood refused and they ran away, or tried to run away. They were from the Nyamwezi people, who, as you know, used to be elephant hunters before they decided to earn their living crossing the land carrying loads on their heads.

They knew that only half of those who set out would see their homes again, and when they did, it would be with a wage in their pocket that meant they would soon have to set off again with a bale or a bundle on their head and a good view of death. And they couldn't always stand that view. So they fled, some of them with the bales they had been carrying; they ran away, they *deserted* . . . that's what Bwana Burton and Bwana Speke called it, although it puzzled me – I couldn't see any connection between the desert and running away. When they were caught, they were whipped in the name of justice on the first journey and on the second journey too. But on the third journey, on the orders of a man who condemned everything that stood in his way to death, sometimes they were hanged.'

'Just because they ran away?'

'"Anyone who runs off into the jungle is endangering the whole caravan," we were told by the man who condemned everything that stood in his way to death. "Running away is an attempt to murder the others," said Bwana Stanley. "And staying with the caravan is suicide," we whispered behind his back. I stayed – I had to stay. After I had survived the first and the second journey, I knew I could survive any journey. But the porters from the Nyamwezi people, who were proud of their work and proud of their reputation, were not so confident. They ran away in the night, and sometimes we went after them and sometimes we let them be, and sometimes they were caught by another caravan and brought back to us. Then they were whipped with a koorbash, a scourge plaited from hippopotamus hide, a terrible weapon, especially when it was new and as honed and sharp as the blade of a knife. They were whipped until their whole back was bleeding. Or they were hanged. I tell you, whoever invented that punishment couldn't tell cleverness from stupidity. There is no lash of any whip in this world that can prevent you taking the path your heart has set you on. When your fear or despair or anger or longing grow too strong for your reckoning, weighing mind, then you do what your heart tells you to do, even if all the torments of

Hell in this world and the next are waiting for you. Whoever invented that punishment didn't know a man's worth.'

'Baba Sidi, of course you know a man's worth, none of us would ever doubt it, but sometimes you don't recognise a truth that is there for you to recognise. Without the threat of the punishments of hell, man would practise neither honour nor moderation.'

'I have seen with my own eyes, Baba Yusuf, how men who have been punished do the same thing they were flogged for the first opportunity they get. The whip cannot leave lasting marks when a skin is shed. And believe me, my friends, man sloughs his skin like a snake. There is only one way to be certain of preventing him doing something: you have to kill him.'

'Bwana Stanley understood that.'

'But what good did it do him? All it meant was that he had one porter fewer.'

～

From Kingani to Bomani, from Bomani to Mkwaju la Mvuani. Every evening he carefully notes down the place names, the primer of his report. *From Kiranga-Ranga to Tumba Ihere, from Tumba Ihere to Segesera.* They are still in the region of established names, confirmed by his documents and by informants along the route alike; near the coast, harmony reigns as regards nomenclature. *From Dege la Mhora to Madege Madogo, from Madege Madogo to Kiruri in Khutu.* Every place captured geographically and hypsometrically – his methodical tables eradicate ambiguity, ward off malefic influences. The journey is still just beginning: he faces up to every problem, confident it can be resolved with a little manoeuvring, a few minor adjustments. Everything can still be put right. The country offers its share of discoveries meanwhile. He distinguishes three varieties of the miombo tree that is so well adapted to the long dry season: *Julbernardia, Brachystegia* and *Isoberlinia,* the latter's leaves a favourite food of elephants. The tall trees with the straight trunks and yellow bark are *Taxus elongatus*, or a member of the family, at least. The dwarf fan-palms: *Chamaerops humilis*, definitely. The Chinese date palms: *Zizyphus jujuba*, commonly known as jojoba. The indigenous varieties of *Hyphaena* and *Nux vomica*. The various broad-leaved trees: *Sterculia* with bright yellow bark and thick, bowl-like crowns; the kapok with its big pods, dark brown on the outside and white and fleshy inside. His observations aspire to a clinical rigour: 'The yellow fruit is not picked,' he writes, 'but eaten only as windfall; their flesh is similar in colour and taste to the mango's, while their seeds are, if not poisonous, certainly bitter – bitterness often being a natural warning? – and promptly spat out.' In those first weeks green is the colour of cultivation; plots lining either side of the river are heavily planted with rice, maize, cassava, sweet potatoes and tobacco. This is fertile country and Burton can see it progressing in leaps and bounds; all that's lacking is an organising hand.

The more familiar he becomes with the country, the more he fathoms its strangeness, the easier it is to defuse its threat. He grows accustomed to the relentless drumming in the distance, which suggests to the jemadar every conceivable horror, thereby prompting him to put his thirteen soldiers through a series of abstruse manoeuvres. He grows accustomed to the circumspection of the village headmen, old men with names like slips of the tongue. At Kiranga Ranga, it rains for the first time; at Tumba Ihere they see their last mango tree. At Segeresa, the Baluchis fight for the first time and have to be pulled apart before their daggers claim tribute; in the forests past Dege la Mhora, they see Guenon monkeys catapulting so nimbly from tree to tree that Speke's shots clang off branches, and with every echo he loses a little more respect – first because he raises his rifle to Guenon monkeys, and then because he misses his target. In Madege Madogo the first donkey dies; others follow over subsequent days. The first porter disappears; the expedition's mood drops like the barometer. They have to load up the mounts unexpectedly early, and soon even the head of the expedition is forced to walk.

Although Burton's progress on foot is barely slower than it was on his donkey, his perception alters as soon as he dismounts. His attention focuses on his steps, hundreds and thousands of steps strung together in an endless sequence. After the cool of early morning, in which he directs his gaze at everything and his mind seems to take in everything, gradually, hot and reluctant, his field of vision narrows to his steps until everything is blanked out except the pebbles and thorns and leaves that crunch and rustle under his boots, the tiny markings on the path that lend the wilderness something approaching a mutable face, the minute variations he watches out for – purely so as to have something to watch out for – the putrefying fruit that has fallen from the trees: neither completely round nor completely yellow; the splattered, rotting fruit with its brown blotches and heavy stink of fermentation.

In those first weeks when he isn't checking or observing, his mind cleans itself out, sweeping up everything that has left hooks or taken crooked root in his memory. He doesn't know if Speke, who has taken over the head of the column while he brings up the stragglers, experiences the same thing – such subjects are too intimate for them to discuss. Wounds he has suffered in the past now seem freshly inflicted. He blazes with the fury he felt when he found out about his superiors' treachery in Sind; fanned back into life, this rage gets him over the next chain of hills. He mourns Kundalini's death with the same grimly suppressed anger as before, grieving until he reaches the next horizon and a baobab that stands like a thick-skinned memorial to her name. He fears exposure as a desecrator as if he were back in the desert between Medina and Mecca. His steps drag him through anger, through sorrow, through fear, and as they do so, hours and days and weeks pass. Everything in his life that has ever sunk down inside him rises to the surface again: every humiliation, every disappointment, every wound. He feels as if he were adrift on the high seas in a rud-

derless boat, forced to lean overboard and grab every piece of
the flotsam that passes by, even if it is snagged with seaweed or
corroded by salt. He holds it in his hands for as long as he can,
turning it over to see if any of the sides has become unrecognis-
able, and only lets it go when he cannot feel it any more
because it has dissolved – but not into oblivion, only indifference.

SIDI MUBARAK BOMBAY

'At the beginning, none of us knew what was in store for us,
none of us could imagine what we were going to experience,
and if we had been able to, none of us would have embarked on
that path of scars and suffering. We were full of gleaming expectation at the beginning when our scars were still wounds, when
every enemy was still our brother and our hopes were richer
than our experience. None of us was prepared for what overtook us, not even the porters from the Nyamwezi people who
had already marched through that country at least once. They
had borne the weight of caravans seeking profit, but those caravans weren't driven by the ambition to reach what no human
had reached before. The porters had endured orders from brutal, greedy, cunning men, but those men weren't mad. None of
us had ever bowed under the weight of a caravan commanded
by wazungu, and the wazungu, my brothers, are strange creatures. I can recognise them, I can tell them apart, but I will never
be able to understand them. They think a person's highest calling is to go where his ancestors have never been before. How
can we, who are afraid of going where no one has been before,
understand that? How can we understand their happiness at
performing a task they have set themselves? You should have
seen the expression on their faces: they were as happy as a
father holding his newborn child, as happy as someone who has
just fallen in love when he sees his sweetheart coming . . .'

'Like Baba Ishmael's face, when he pulls his boat full of fish
out of the water.'

'Like the faces of children when they see rain for the first time.'

'How about: like the expression on Baba Sidi's face when he can regale his friends with his triumphs?'

'So you know this happiness, good, I don't need to describe it any more. That was the look on their faces when they reached a goal that no other wazungu had reached before them. But everything casts its shadow, and you cannot imagine how their faces darkened if they found out they weren't the first, if someone had been there before them. The darkest clouds gathered on their faces at the slightest threat that someone might have outrun them. I will never forget Bwana Speke and Bwana Grant's amazement on the banks of the largest of all the lakes the day they met another mzungu who had been trading there for years, a merchant by the name of Amabile de Bono, who wasn't from the same country as them but from an island their queen had conquered. You cannot imagine the anxiety on Bwana Stanley's face all through the long months when he believed Bwana Cameron was racing ahead of him with another caravan and might be the first person to cross the country from where the sun rises to where it sets. There was a tautness inside him that made him curse every evening and say the foulest things about a man he had never met. I tried to calm Bwana Stanley. "Does Bwana Cameron pick everything that grows by the path?" I asked him. "Won't he leave anything for you?" He answered me roughly: "You don't understand." I was annoyed by his answer back then, but today I'll happily admit: I don't understand the wazungu.'

'I know exactly what you mean, Baba Sidi, there's always someone who has woken up before you. When I was young, my father worked for an Arab who travelled with two other Arabs and forty porters to the great lake you are talking about, far to the west, and when they reached the lake, they built a boat and sailed across the lake in it, and then visited a country called Muata Cazembe. I remembered the name, Muata Cazembe; it sounded like a shout of encouragement. And then after another six months those three Arabs reached the far end of the country, the other coast, where the sun set in front of them, and there they found some wazungu who had set up a trading post. Those were different wazungu from the ones in Zanzibar, men from the Portuguese people, and the settlement they had founded was called Benguela.'

'Eh, so they crossed the whole country. If Bwana Stanley or Bwana Cameron knew that, the news would poison the well of their pride. They wouldn't be able to brag about being the first to cross the country from east to west any more; they'd have to learn to be just footsteps following in other footsteps, to accept the idea they were stragglers. For them, every village, every river, every lake and every forest was a virgin and they were like giants who could only be satisfied if they possessed them all. To satisfy their lusts, they exposed themselves to everything: they endured cold, they endured fever, they endured the bites of the ticks and flies and mosquitoes that swelled up overnight until they itched so much we thought we were going crazy. And everything the wazungu endured, we had to endure too. That was the terrible realisation that struck me, my friends, soon after we left. We were prisoners of a caravan that was at the mercy of the madness of two wazungu, a madness that meant marching through hell to no one exactly knew where or how or what. And there was no prospect of release for us, only our wages, our meagre wages that had already been paid in half, and those of us who had family in Zanzibar had left them behind with their wives and children. Every time the thorns of the acacia tore at me, I saw more clearly what I was caught up in. And there was no way out for me. The porters could try to run away because they knew the way home. We were heading towards their villages and no one there would take them to task for doing so. But even if I managed to get back on my own across the forest and plains, if I did not die on the lonely journey, if I was not torn apart by wild animals and did not fall into a slave trader's clutches, I would still never be able to show my face again here in Zanzibar. The sultan in person had chosen me to accompany these wazungu and stay with them until they returned or everything ended. I had to carry on, I had to endure the thorns – I had only one way out: the way leading straight through Hell.'

'Playing the hero again, you old braggart? Piling it as high as ever?'

'What did you hear, wife?'

'If you would pay attention for once in your life to something other than your stories, then you would notice that you and your friends are blocking the lane.'

'You're going to crack the shutters, ranting on like that. What are you talking about?'

'So many people are glued to your fairy tales, no one can get through the lane. There's a cart – if you stood up, you could see – the poor man's been waiting for an eternity for your yakking to end.'

❧

Everything changes when they approach a village. Muskets are fired into the air, even the most exhausted porters take hold of themselves, proudly falling into line with the caravan which is the cynosure of all eyes, children's, women's and men's, even though the latter keep out of sight in the background. As they march in, Burton feels everyone is putting on a performance, a dramatic scenario that disintegrates as soon as they turn their backs on the village; shoulders slump, feet drag, spirits crawl along the ground.

Compensation comes at night around the campfire. Sometimes he can't understand a word of his conversation with Speke for all the singing and laughter. Drums are played, bells are rung, old iron banged. One of the Baluchis, Ubaid, produces a sarangi and draws all the scamps of the caravan with his playing that sounds as if he's scraping the scales off a huge fish. Hulluk, the caravan buffoon, plays the part of a nautch girl to bawdy perfection. After a generous dose of contortions and grimaces, he appears to decide to try something more demanding, to give his character more depth. Standing on his head, he starts to waggle his hips and shake all over, his heels bulging out of his thin ankles like freakishly risen loaves of bread. Then he crosses his legs, still standing on his head, and imitates the yelp of a hungry dog, the sad miaow of a cat, the outraged bark of a monkey, the stubborn bleating of a camel and the calls of a young slave girl enticing all the men of the camp with her lascivious promises. Finally, he rolls over the ground in one amazingly fluid movement until he is sitting in front of Burton and, twisted over like a picture of embarrassment, starts imitating him too, doggedly bawling out orders until he receives a dollar for his shameless pains. Burton gives the money willingly, because the camp has forgotten the day's march in its peals of laughter. But when the fool demands another coin, he gets a good kick and rushes off with such exaggerated squeals of unrequited love that everyone's laughter chases after him like stray dogs.

SIDI MUBARAK BOMBAY

'Those were back-breaking days, my brothers, conniving days that inflicted the wounds whose scars we still bear, then led us into even more agonising nights. The air was still, the mosquitoes buzzed, the cold felt us over with its rough hands like a thief searching its victim again and again. It was as though the night wanted to rob us of our insides. Once armies of black ants drove us out of our tents: they stung us between our fingers, between our toes, on every tender part of our body. The donkeys, which were even more thin-skinned than Baba Ali, bellowed and bellowed until they lost their minds and all of us thought the next sting would tip us over into madness too. The jemadar, who normally swaggered about as if he was the wazungu's little brother, stole through the camp like a forgotten ancestor. Everyone lost their heads, not just him – all the Baluchis and the porters too. They whispered around the fire, giving and taking counsel, and the verdict that always crawled out of the whispering was: run away. I said nothing and turned my ears away because I didn't want to join them and I didn't want to lie to Bwana Burton. When sleep finally came, sleep tasting like cold, bitter chai, we knew what was waiting for us. Another morning breaking on fresh despair, fresh loneliness.'

'The loneliness of a widow.'

'A widow whose second husband has just died and she has resolved never to marry again.'

'What is this fit of inspiration, Baba Ilias? An image of yours that I can actually picture.'

'It's not mine, it's a Somali friend's.'

'Well, please call on your friend's sayings in the future rather than relying on your own.'

'How is this possible, Baba Sidi? Did you suffer the whole time? Do I know you so little? I can't imagine you not finding some pleasure somewhere.'

'Of course, you're right. We couldn't have survived the sufferings of the day and the night without the joys of the evening. I don't mean the food – eh, the food was all right at the beginning, no better than that, but anyone who walks as far and carries as much as we did will eat a lot and not turn his nose up at what's on his plate. No, I'm thinking of the time after the meal when we caught up on all the happiness that had been denied us in the day. We danced and sang, and when we realised how little Bwana Burton and Bwana Speke thought of our dancing and singing, we took to making fun of them. One of the porters was a man with bandy legs which he shook all over the place when he danced, and we laughed at him, so gawky and nimble, and his crooked songs that went something like:

> 'I am the Frij, I am the Frij,
> My brother Spek-e, my brother Spek-e,
> What does he seek-e, what does he seek-e
> Let's give him . . . a nice fat cow
> That will calm him down somehow.

'And at the end of the song we'd all roar, "Amiiiiin!" as if we had heard a prayer that could vanquish every djinn. When he heard our song, which of course he didn't understand, Bwana Speke thought it was a song of praise in his honour, so he got to his feet in front of his tent, came over to us and sang one of his songs, a song leaning on a mourner's shoulders, a song that would have been well suited to a funeral. But he sang it with all his might and all his heart, and at the end of the song we gave such a loud show of our enthusiasm that he started to do a dance, but just a little one, sadly . . . I suppose he heard us laughing. Eh, I tell you, my brothers, that gave us strength when we realised how ridiculous the wazungu could be.'

~

They plunge into the rainforest and everything is transformed. The horizon is swallowed up; lianas as thick as cables bar their way. The spreading treetops intertwine to form a dark green roof supported by grey pillars, as if this were a sacred grove to which only shadowy sounds had access. The black, greasy ground under the thick vegetation sucks at their every step. At the boggiest parts, tree roots provide the only footing they can rely on. The grass is like sharpened knives, the trees beset by epiphytes, parasitical plants that coil round their trunks and cluster in the canopy like birds' nests. Creepers and climbers strangle the paths – 'that which kills the way', mutter the bearers, 'kills the wayfarer' – and there is a constant, terrible stench, as if the corpse of some poor wretch lay behind every tree. The asses throw their loads, which the Baluchis, cursing their misfortune, leave to the others to strap back on. If they see anything more than glimpses of the sky, like strips of a dirty winding sheet, it is dense and grey and low, a pall of smoke that cannot clear. A sort of miasma forms on their skin, a film of dirt that couldn't be washed away, even if they were to find water and scrub themselves vigorously.

They knew from the outset that it was only a question of

time before the first sickness struck, but they hadn't anticipated malaria would lay both of them low at the same time.
They stop just on the edge of the trees, where clearings are
already opening out onto the plain. Burton lies on the ground,
unable to move, and he feels another person inside him, a hostile being bent on thwarting his every plan. 'Before I go on,' he
cries out, 'I need to know what's at stake. You can't subject me
to this endless struggle without promising me something.'

Voices reply without giving him any real answer: heads protruding from chests lick him with their hairy tongues, grisly
witches start to whip him. He screams they've got him confused with someone else, and they grin malevolently and croak
a song he doesn't understand at first, but then starts to, in
snatches. The words plummet down onto him like butterflies
without wings; he tries to catch them with a net growing out of
his fingers, and when he has caught all the fleeting words, he
has to stare at the net for a long time before he can pin them to
their meaning: 'There is no greater delight, there is no greater
joy than the crack of the bones we break from dawn till dusk.'

He raises his eyes, the witches nod rapturously: 'You have
understood us, good. Now give us your limbs. We are going to
drill holes and spit in them. They are so lovely and hairy; we
will pull out every little hair. Give us your limbs, we promise
you complete pain.'

He wakes up. He feels he has sweated out everything he has
ever drunk in his life. His tongue is like a caterpillar wrapped
in a cocoon of bitterness. His legs obey him only reluctantly.
He stretches them again. He calls Bombay, who brings him
water, and then enquires after Speke. Bombay tells him he is
already up.

Burton drags himself to the entrance of his tent and looks
outside. The sky is overcast. He feels as if he has been relieved
of a great debt. Speke is there. It is comforting to see him, he
thinks, as he greets him. The words trickle viscously from his
mouth. Speke's face is drawn, as if his skin has been stretched
on a drum to dry. He comes over to the tent and bends down

to Burton. 'We've seen off the first attack,' he says. Then he stretches out his hand and gently touches Burton's cheek. It's a clumsy gesture, but it is a sign of attachment nonetheless. Burton draws hope from it. 'I am going to rest a little,' he says. 'Then we can go on. I will see you in a moment.' Then he crawls back into his tent.

'Speke, my baffling enigma, Speke,' he says to himself in the fragile silence that follows the fever. He must not judge him unfairly just because he is so hard to judge. He has proved himself so far. He has done everything that's asked of him; he never complains about the hardships of the journey – if there is a Spartan and an Athenian type, Speke is undeniably the former: reserved, calm, equable. He is rarely good-humoured, it's true, but nor is he short-tempered or morose. Of course, there are certain things about him that annoy Burton. The total disinterest he has evinced in his surroundings from the start. He has found every type of country they've been through so far dull; the people he finds uninteresting – the only thing that stirs his passions are the wild animals he can kill. As if he can only get near life by taking it.

Burton had been forewarned: shortly after they had got to know one another, Speke had returned from the Somali interior with porters so heavily laden, it was as if they were carrying another Noah's Ark. An ark in reverse, wherein each species was represented by just one magnificent specimen, which was not only dead, but already gutted and flayed. 'I am a hunter,' explained Speke as he came on board, 'and a collector. That's why these latitudes suit me so well.'

Unfortunately this enthusiasm seems to have quickly faded. It is not a good sign that he is already bored after a few weeks. What will he be like in a few months? Speke had smiled at him though; he had really smiled at him. That's good, he has proved himself, everything is fine . . . so why does Burton feel something gnawing away at him, why does he only foresee disappointments that will expose his knowledge of human nature once more?

The fever boils up again. He drinks a few sips of water and steels himself for the next onslaught.

SIDI MUBARAK BOMBAY

'There were days when we woke up early in the morning, long before sunrise, and the first thing we felt was the pain the day would bring. Getting up on a morning like that takes courage. Your own hopes mock you in the cold; you feel the weight of the bales hoisted onto the shoulders of your fellow sufferers; in the confusion, you fight for the lightest load; you feel how misshapen your feet are; you want to curl up like a poor, defenceless wretch who can't take the day's blows any more, and you dream of an abyss that will swallow everything up. On mornings like that, it was clear to us how far we were from the journey's beginning and how much further still we were from its end. We saw how stunted we were; we realised how badly we needed help. Now the earth no longer smiled on us, the time had come to consult a mganga.'

'God preserve us!'

'No, Sidi, not that story again, not that shame!'

'Eh, I don't know why you are getting so worked up, Baba Quddus. I have a feeling our brothers here enjoy a little shame, especially when it is someone else's. Besides, it wasn't my suggestion; I didn't know anything about mganga in those days. It was the wish of Salim bin Said and all the Nyamwezi. "You want to see a witch doctor? Can't it wait until the end of this stage?" The wazungu reacted as many of them would, as I expected them to. Especially Bwana Speke, who knew almost nothing and understood even less, but still believed there was nothing he could not see through. Even Bwana Burton was disparaging at first. "A complete waste of time," he said, but then he thought it over. He was a person who could sometimes check over his opinions, the way people in villages check over their houses after the rainy season, and sometimes he'd change his opinion afterwards, sometimes he'd even build a completely new house. "What harm can it do?" he said in a low voice.

"'I don't see any harm it can do," I answered.

"'On the contrary" – his voice drew itself up to its full height – "it may be useful." So then he addressed the whole caravan and greeted this suggestion with fire in his words. Once we had found a mganga, he took me aside and, suddenly producing one of the rattan caps from India, a beautiful, white cap, which he rubbed between his thumb and finger as if he enjoyed the feel of it, he asked me to promise the man a present if he gave us a favourable prophecy. The mganga we entrusted ourselves to was a man of noble birth; his dignity rose far above him. A brightly coloured cloth was knotted around his forehead, and he wore a mass of necklaces round his neck, each strung with different beads and shells. He was a man I wanted to have on our side, because I felt a power contained in him that could break out at any moment. When silence had fallen on us all, he took a big pinch of snuff, brought out a gourd that contained his medicine and began to shake it with a rattling sound, as if it were full of pebbles. His voice boomed out from somewhere far below, as though it had taken root in the ground. I had never heard such a voice. It was his voice, and yet it didn't belong to him. It grew brighter as it slowly came up into the air. I tell you, my brothers, I had never experienced anything like that before. I was amazed, but it all seemed familiar somehow, like a man you meet for the first time yet you know his face anyway. I was spellbound. When his voice was so high and light the birds themselves could not have kept up with it, the mganga put his gourd on the ground. It rolled to the side a little and stayed there, wobbling, and I felt an urge – I don't know why, I didn't know myself at that moment – a need to soothe the calabash, I wanted to take hold of it. I stretched out my hand, but it was too far away and I couldn't move any part of me except my hand. Then the mganga took two goat's horns from his sack – a jute sack that I never expected to see there which I will tell you about later – two horns tied together with snakeskin and decorated with little iron bells. He grasped the horns by the tip and swung them in a circle. He pointed them at Bwana Burton, then he pointed them at me, then he pointed them at the porters and the Baluchis, and all I could see were those horns dancing in front of my eyes; all I could hear was the mganga's murmuring and whispering and spitting as he swayed back and forward, shaking the horns faster and faster and rattling the bells louder and louder. I began trembling. Later I found out that the others were trembling and paralysed just the same. If the mganga had stretched out his hand, I would have followed him. I felt he was in perfect communion with the spirits, in touch with the ancestors, and I felt a pain in me as if all the ancestors I had forgotten were cutting out my heart. The mganga was in touch with the spirit of his father and his grandfather, I thought, and I do not even know what my father and my grandfather looked like or their voices sounded like. Open me, I begged him in silence, show me the way back. But the mganga had finished; his eyes jerked up. You have never seen such terrible eyes; only a fool would not have felt fear at the mysteries glowing behind those eyes. He turned his head to one side and, as if a saint was speaking, he pronounced his verdict: we would have enemies, but our enemies would not be more powerful than us. They would not be more determined than us. Our journey would be successful. We breathed out slowly, as if we were not sure we were allowed that breath. There would be many quarrels but little blood. We would bring back plenty of ivory. We would return to our wives and families. Of those of us who had no wife, one would find a wife on this journey, another would reward the wife who had waited for him faithfully, and a third would leave the wife he would be given. Before venturing on a large, deep lake, we should sacrifice a hen of different colours – an easy task. The omens were good and we were relieved and happy.'

'The sack, what about the sack?'

'It was a jute sack like the ones we use for spices or rice, a jute sack from Zanzibar with a name on it, the name of one of

346

the biggest merchants in this town, which you all know – it was the name of the banyan who bought me as a boy at the slave market for a few coins.'

'The djinns took possession of you that day, Baba Sidi. But with time, your prayers have set your mind free again.'

'I have never prayed since then, at least not in the way you understand prayer.'

'In the prescribed way!'

'Not for me. I realised that when the mganga shook the horns at me. I submit to God, yes, but the five prayers were not pre-scribed for me. Perhaps for you, Baba Quddus, perhaps for the Arabs, but not for me. I have ancestors, and they are not called Muhammad or Abu Bakr or even Bilal. I have other ancestors, only I do not know what they are called. The true faith cannot reveal the name of my ancestors. It is helpless. The true faith promises me a better tomorrow, but I want to find the way back to yesterday. The true faith claims there is only one direction, the direction of Mecca, because there is only one centre, the Almighty, but I saw another direction in the mganga's eyes, many other directions, and you are right, my mind may have been possessed that day, but my heart was set free.'

'When the heart weeps over something it has lost, the mind laughs over something it has found. An old Arab proverb.'

'So that is why, brother, you shun Friday prayers. You have never explained it so clearly.'

'I need to tell you certain things this evening that I have been silent about until now, because they are important, even if they are also sad and hard.'

'Don't be angry with me, Baba Sidi, but I will carry on pray-ing for you. God must decide what we cannot make clear.'

'Pray in silence as much as you want. But curiosity settles in the hollows between prayers, so I'd like to know how the story continues. Were the wazungu impressed by the mganga's powers?'

'Bwana Burton smirked. He was pleased, pleased with him-self. He slapped me on the shoulder – a terrible habit of the wazungu – and said: "A well-timed gift speeds the traveller on his way." I tried to explain what needed no explanation, that a cap could not influence such a holy man, even if it was so beautifully plaited in Surat. "The mganga", I explained patiently as though to a child, "was possessed by a spirit, everyone could see that." "Even better," Bwana Burton said with a fat grin that I wanted to cut out, "we bribed the spirit with our present." "Spirits cannot be bribed," I said, and he replied: "If they can be conversed with, then they can be corrupted." He was wrong, Bwana Burton, I knew he was wrong but I could not prove it to him because I was ashamed: I had not even offered the mganga the cap for fear of offending him. Besides, it looked so good on me.'

'So Bwana Burton wasn't afraid of the spirits.'

'No. But he had his uses for them. After that evening he started threatening anyone who opposed him with dawa. His language has a strange name for dawa: they call it black magic. He would have liked to be a master of this black magic, I think. "Did you make fun of the mganga when you seriously believe in the power of dawa?" I asked him. He answered in the language of black magic in his country. "*Ignoramus et ignorabimus*," he said, and it sounded so good in my ears that I spent the next day swaying to the rhythm of his magic spell: *igno-ramus-et'igno-rabimus*.'

'What does it mean?'

'I don't know, I have forgotten.'

❧

Hongo. Constantly, at every turn. They've barely arrived at a place before the demand for it rings out, almost as if it were part of the greetings. What a welcome – pay us hongo or we won't let you pass – wherever they stop. Primitive tribal chieftains claiming the rights of princes. Hongo! The bastard child of every toll in the world. You have to pay for nothing; over and over again you have to pay these little tyrants of the bush, this almost endless swarm of bloodsuckers. Every village has its chief, who is called the p'hazi, or something of the sort: the titles change, the further into the interior they go, but not the insatiable greed. As he is still giving them their present, they're already peering to see if he's got anything else in his bags. The chiefs have advisers. Mwene Goha is the High Chamberlain – what an absurd name, Master of the Hut would be better, or Keeper of the Mud. He is the chief's right-hand man, his supreme glutton. Below him come three ranks of elders, a senate under the acacia trees. Entering their field of vision means more demands for gifts, in return for the caravan's safe passage.

Sometimes hongo dresses itself as a request, sometimes a threat. 'Strangers,' the greeting may go, 'what fine thing have you brought us from the coast?' And once the fine thing has been passed from hand to hand, they might say, 'Ah, we are still strangers to one another, but the sting of it has been removed.' 'That's blackmail,' curses Burton. No one translates. His presents are magnificent – forty rolls of cloth, a hundred necklaces of coral beads – but not enough, because they have to be divided between the first and second and third ranks, and the chiefs – one of whom has so much to carry with the imperial title of Headman Great Man of Precedence that he never appears before his people sober – all have villages full of wives and children to feed. Seen from this point of view, the presents appear almost modest, a token gesture of a dependent guest. 'How do these people expect to progress', storms Burton, 'if they rob blind the first peacefully intentioned visitors they get?' It must be in their interest to promote trade, and clearly the right way to go about that is not to hongo the whole wretched country.

Burton is worried. They are still a long way from Kazeh, and their supplies are already approaching exhaustion. If they can just get to Kazeh, that's all they need. From there he will be able to order supplies from the coast. He would have needed to take a thousand porters to satisfy these people's expectations of his generosity. It repels him, having to appease these parasites with such lavish gifts, while they oppress their own people. When their coffers run low, they raid the neighbouring peoples, abducting their women and children and selling them to the next slave caravan passing through – the price is added on to the usual hongo. Their own subjects can only be sold in cases of adultery or black magic, depending on the gravity of the crime. The mganga is the sole judge of a person's guilt or innocence, generally arriving at his verdict by means of a trial with boiling water. If a person's hand burns on immersion, their crime is considered proven. Witches thus exposed are instantly burnt at the stake. On a number of occasions already they have passed little piles of ash, with a few blackened bones and bits of charcoal. This is hongo too, paid by the unfortunates who live in these ill-starred latitudes. They will have to withstand every sort of hongo if they are to make it to Kazeh.

SIDI MUBARAK BOMBAY

'Nothing was more important to Bwana Speke than his guns. Every evening he cleaned them and oiled them and treated them with more loving care than the mules. During the day, he never let his rifle out of his hand, and he was always watching for one thing. Most of us looked at the path, or the sky, or the women beside the road, or the roots on the ground, but Speke just kept his eyes peeled for animals. Suddenly we would hear a shot, and if we turned quickly enough, we would see a bird falling from the sky or an antelope breaking through the bush. That happened several times a day, and after a while we got used to it; it almost came to seem natural. Bwana Speke didn't prepare at all. He didn't stalk the animals; at most he took a few steps off the path if he needed to, and then just fired. He always hit. The odd animal here and there at first, but then we came to country with vast numbers of animals. We didn't stay there, we hurried on our way, but still we left a country of dead animals in our wake.'

'How did you do that?'

'Are you setting us a riddle?'

'No riddle, my friends – or perhaps, yes, a riddle about what man is and what man does.'

'It's getting harder already.'

'Most of you, my brothers, do not know about hunting. You have never left Zanzibar, and in Zanzibar the wild animals roam through the air. You are master fishermen, but fishing is not hunting. When the Zanzibari hunt, they are only after monkeys to get them out of their fields. My ancestors were master hunters; they hunted with patience because the forest only rewards the patient hunter, and they used weapons that were no sharper than the teeth of wild animals. They performed devotions before they went hunting and they performed devotions when they came back from hunting. If they killed a big antelope, the village had a big feast. That is how my ancestors hunted and I am sure my brothers in my first life still hunt this way today.'

'Indeed, Baba Sidi, indeed. And? Do you want to teach us greybeards to hunt?'

'I am very glad not to have to know anything about hunting. Do you know the story of Hodja and the lion hunt? He was beaming when he came back from the hunt, so people asked him: "How many lions did you kill?" And Hodja said, "None." "Well, how many lions did you hunt?" they then asked him. And Hodja said, "None." "Well, how many lions did you see?" they asked. And Hodja said, "Not a single one." "Well, why are you so happy then?" they demanded. And Hodja said: "When you go on a lion hunt, not a single one is more than enough."'

'Oh, oh, Baba Ibrahim, that's a good one. I'd forgotten that story, it's wonderful.'

'Leave Hodja be for a moment and listen to me. When we reached the savannah, where the herds were stretched over the plain like carpets, I almost swallowed my tongue. Bwana Speke asked me to go with him, and we trotted over the plain until he had found a suitable place – a kopje, maybe, or a thick baobab. Then he took aim and started firing until my ears were sore, and anyone who could watch would have seen the animals falling one after another, like bales being tossed to the ground. After the first shot, the animals tried to escape, snorting with terror; they were a long way away but I could hear the fear roaring through their nostrils. They did not know where to run to, and the herds were so big, Bwana Speke had time to keep firing over and over. I counted the animals that were shot and fell in the dozens, and after a while I couldn't make them out any more, they were swallowed up by the dust raised by their hooves, and all I could see was a mass of living and a mass of dying and a terrible whirling between the two.

> 'Look at the steeds, how they race,
> Their hooves striking sparks.
> Storming through the early dawn,
> Spraying dust as they storm on
> To break the enemy's hearts.

'It goes on, Baba Quddus. They're glorious, the next lines, every word hits home like one of Bwana Speke's shots:

> 'Truly man on ingratitude feeds.
> Man is witness to man indeed.
> Truly his soul's only prompting is greed.'

'In the Name of God.'

'So long as Bwana Speke could fire a shot with death in its sights, he fired it. He was like an excited child: sometimes the excitement sent him running after the herds, chasing them with long, powerful strides, firing at them as they fled. He couldn't aim at one particular animal, that was impossible; he just aimed wherever his bullets could find blood. His face shone like Baba Burhan's at Bakri Id, delirious, overjoyed.'

'What about you?'

'I had to pass him the rifles and carry them and look after them. Those were terrible days, the days he hunted.'

'What sort of animals did he kill, Grandfather?'

'Anything, anything that moved. He wasn't proud in that respect. Even crocodiles and hippopotamuses – they were the most disgusting, because we had to wait on the banks until their bodies rose to the surface.'

'Why didn't they stay under the water?'

'Because their stomachs trap air, like the air that comes out when you fart, my little ray of light. You have to imagine thousands of farts blowing up a hippopotamus until it is as full and round as one of my best friends.'

'I know who you're thinking of, Grandfather. I know exactly.'

'Well done, sweetheart. But keep it to yourself.'

'Why? He knows too.'

'So you all had a lot of meat to eat then.'

'No! Listen, this will be another surprise for you. Bwana Speke wasn't interested in the meat. Or even the horns. We just hurried on, leaving the dead animals behind us, and I don't know if anyone ate them, because there weren't always villages near by. Only once, when he shot a pregnant antelope, did he tell us to cut her open and roast the unborn calf for him.'

'No!'

'We refused. He asked the porters first and they refused, then he aimed his order at me, and I refused too. How could I do such a thing? I would have brought ghosts into the world that would have tormented me all my life. He was furious; he hit me in the face.'

'He hit you!'

'I lost one of my front teeth . . . there. I have that to thank Bwana Speke for.'

'Did you let him get away with it?'

'What could I do? He was the head of the caravan. He abused us, told us we were mad to believe such foolishness.'

'What about the other mzungu?'

'He kept out of the quarrel. His words were often violent, but as a man? I never saw him kill anything. I don't know what he thought of Bwana Speke's hunting, but sometimes he

353

refused his wish to stop at a place because it looked so inviting for hunting. Then Bwana Speke would get angry, but he hid it from Bwana Burton. It was only when we were alone that he complained, and although I could understand almost nothing of what he said, I could hear the rage in his voice. The further we went, the worse they fell out. I think Bwana Speke found it hard to be subordinate. He saw the caravan as having two commanders, two leaders who were also rivals. I'd been mistaken. I had thought they were friends, but later, much later, when my English was better and Bwana Speke spoke more openly with me, I saw that for the first part of the journey he was constantly on the threshold of hatred – his ambition devoured all his feelings of gratitude and attachment – and then when it came to the quarrel that threw everything into doubt, his hatred slopped over and washed everything else away. Even before the end of the journey, even before we reached safety and the coast, he was accusing me of helping Bwana Burton to try to poison him. That is how powerful his hatred was.'

'But even so he took you on the second journey?'

'I don't understand how you could go with him again.'

'He came to his senses. He needed me, and he prized my services. We formed a partnership. I made him feel he was the leader. I had learnt how to contain my impatience, to wait until he rounded up his sentences in the banyans' language bit by bit, and then tell him what he wanted to know without him having to be beholden to Bwana Burton. He grew to trust me. On the second journey, I learnt everything that had been hidden from me on the first journey. Bwana Speke was a man of delicate feelings, and Bwana Burton had trampled on those feelings. He had showed him how stupid he thought he was. He knew how to treat someone condescendingly, Bwana Burton. And Bwana Speke had taken his revenge in secret; he had nursed a feeling of contempt for everything Bwana Burton had done in the past and everything he was doing on this journey. That was the way it was between them: Bwana Burton despised Bwana Speke because all he thought about was shooting animals, and Bwana Speke despised Bwana Burton because he was not the slightest bit interested in hunting.'

⌁

No matter what demands the day has made of him, no matter how shattered he feels, Burton sits down in the evening – after Bombay has unfolded a chair and table and set up a temporary study in a corner of his tent – and writes down everything he has observed, measured and experienced since dawn. It makes no difference if a storm is raging outside, if water is pooling under his boots and he can hear Speke's orders to cover the merchandise with tarpaulins, he writes – even when his feverish fingers can barely hold the pen and his inflamed eyes have trouble making out the inkwell; even when all he wants to do is lie down and forget the day as quickly as possible.

This is not just an exercise in self-discipline; he considers it his duty to waken the country to a new, written life. It is not in his nature to shrink from challenges, but when he stops and thinks of the potential significance of his notes, he feels slightly intimidated. He combats this anxiety with details, with all the details he squeezes from conversations, until there isn't another drop of useful information to be wrung out of them.

Bombay is his leading informant. With a wholehearted effort on both their parts, they can communicate virtually all their thoughts in a Hindustani shored up by columns of Kiswahili and the occasional pillar of Arabic. Bombay is a particularly valuable source about local customs and the all-pervasive web of superstition. After another exhaustive conversation between the two of them – Burton sits down for these sessions, listening closely and noting down anything he might forget, while Bombay stands behind him so that he can massage his neck and shoulders as he talks – Burton opens his notebook and adds:

Consequently the Wanyika, like our philosophers, consider Koma to have a subjective rather than objective reality, and yet sorcery is the sum total of their religious creed. All diseases are attributed to possession, and no one dies what we would call a natural death. Their rites are intended either to avert evil or to transfer it to other parties, and the *primum mobile* of their sacrifices is always what the mganga, the medicine man, considers his interest. At the decisive moment, when the spirit has been conjured to leave the patient's body, it nominates an object – technically called a keti, or stool, and worn around the neck, arm or other parts of the body – which it is prepared to inhabit without troubling the wearer. This idea forms the basis for numerous superstitious practices: to the negro, an 'auspicious remedy' can be an object such as a leopard's claw, necklaces of white, black and blue beads called mdugu ga mulungu (spirit beads) that are worn over the shoulder, or the rags taken from a sick person and hung or nailed to trees, which some Europeans call the 'Devil's Tree'. The ghost prefers the keti to the person of the patient and hence both parties are able to conclude a mutually satisfactory agreement. In many cases of possession, mainly of women, the unfortunates are haunted by a dozen ghosts, for each of which there is a specific talisman – one of which, ridiculously enough, is known as barakat, which means 'blessing' in Arabic and was the name of the Ethiopian slave Mohammed inherited.

Burton leans back, re-reads the paragraph and closes his notebook with satisfaction. That seems all there is to say on the subject for the moment. Clearly the most interesting field of study in these latitudes will prove to be anthropology, the business of comprehending and classifying all the different tribes. Their religion, however, if one can use the term at all in this context – Bombay has told him that none of their languages has equivalents for dharma or diin – is of minimal interest, and he doubts that future explorers who will venture along the paths he has opened up on this expedition will pay it any special attention.

In any case, once the missionaries have marched in, very little of the native superstitions will survive. Africa is not India, the keti carries far less weight than karma, and God's servants will swoop down like vultures on every heathen soul. All well and good, but there is one thing that bothers him: Bombay. Bombay who has got a head on his shoulders, whose name Mubarak contains a subtle, lofty promise, who is familiar with the riches of al-Islam – Bombay is clearly deeply moved by all the hocus-pocus; the quackery undoubtedly impresses him. Does the poison of his childhood run so deep that it can't be expelled, even though he has been exposed to so many more fulfilling truths? Or is this a form of madness, an instability of his own brought on by the hardships of the journey? Either way, he must keep an eye on him, because if Bombay falls by the wayside, he will have lost a good man.

SIDI MUBARAK BOMBAY

'Now listen, my brothers, listen carefully, because here comes the part you're all interested in; here comes the story of the women on the journey, the women of our caravan. When we set off, the caravan was almost all men, apart from a few of the porters' wives. Over a hundred men, and not one of us old, not one of us weak. It wasn't right that we should have to travel a path we didn't know and endure all that lies between life and death, and on top of that be expected to do without the company of women. It wasn't right that our nights should be lonelier than our days. So the caravan soon began to fill out and grow curves. Every evening there were more men who didn't join in the singing and dancing, and the longer the journey went on, the more women travelled with us, until Bwana Burton and Bwana Speke began to worry about what sort of influence they might have on the caravan.'

357

'Where did these women come from?'

'Most of them were bought from slave traders we met, but some threw in their lot with one or other of the men after he had convinced her or her parents with his money or his tongue. These couples lasted longer than the first sort, because a man who bought his wife had no idea what he was buying. But no one had as bad a time of it as the poor wretch who ended up with the woman called "Don't-know". She was built like a bull, a beautiful, gleaming bull that any man would have been proud to own, and so she had cost six cloths and a big roll of brass wire. Said bin Salim had bought her and he burnt his fingers on her immediately because she was worse-tempered than a lonely old buffalo. She came from people who pierced their upper lips with bones, so hers stuck out like a duck's beak. The sight of her inspired our respect, but the way she behaved filled us with fear. Said bin Salim passed her on to the strongest porter, a man called Goha, but even he was powerless against her. She treated him with contempt from the start, and I don't know if she kept him warm at night, but I do know what we all knew, that she was soon presenting poor Goha with first one, then a dozen rivals. She smashed every present she was given so she wouldn't have to carry it; she threw the whole caravan into confusion – we hardly talked about anything else. Everyone suspected his neighbour of secretly desiring her, because, however surprising it may sound, my brothers, the more arrogantly she behaved, the more we lusted after her. You should have seen her firm arms and her firm thighs – eh, we thought Paradise lay between them, and that thought, that sight, had all the time of our lonely, dusty steps to work its way into us. Nothing she did, none of her insults or roughness, could put out the fire that burned us. She ran away every evening, and there were always men who volunteered for the despised job of catching her, and she never showed any remorse or shame when they brought her back. She was so unique, so uniquely impossible that any boat she sailed in would have sunk. In the end Said bin Salim decided to trade her for some large sacks of rice with an Arab in Kazeh, and that was the worst bit of business he'd done, that shrewd merchant, because the next morning he came and complained bitterly to us that she'd cracked his skull. We laughed and laughed and were glad to be rid of her, but secretly our loins dreamed of what it would have been like to lie in her arms.'

'I know those dreams: they take as long to heal as burn scars.'

'Or a lump on the head.'

'New dreams have to take their place.'

'A new woman has to come along, and then the old one is wiped away like a leaf-print.'

'Show me the mark a leaf makes, Baba Ilias.'

'That is just what I was saying, you donkey, the memory of the woman suddenly becomes as faint as the print left by a leaf.'

'Something's not right with you, Baba Ilias, you always have to explain what you're trying to say.'

'That's the listeners' fault, Baba Yusuf. If a man doesn't want to understand, he stumbles over his own questions.'

'Come closer, my friends, come closer. Salim has gone to bed, and the threats that usually rain down on us have fallen silent, for whatever reason, so let's count our blessings for as long as we can. You all know that I returned from my first journey with a wife, a young wife who bound me with a spell the moment I saw her at the river washing our clothes with the other girls of her village. It was a morning; there was a smell of plants waking, of flowers in the dew, and I had nothing to do, no work, so my feet took me by a roundabout route down to the river. I pushed my way down a thickly grown bank and suddenly found myself standing by the water, and there, not very far away, were the young women of the village, bending over and beating clothes against a shelf of rock in the water as flat as a table. I say the women of the village but really I only mean one woman who took my gaze captive. I could not see her face, but what I could see pleased me so much, I wanted to carry on looking at her for as long as possible. I didn't move; I just stared at this woman whose body glistened with drops of water that caught the first light-hearted rays of the sun. Her skin was dark, as dark as my skin, and her movements were as strong and firm as my movements were then. I stood on the bank of the river for a long time, enchanted by the sight of this girl, until finally I mustered the courage to go nearer. It hadn't occurred to me that the girls might not have seen me, so I was startled when the first girl who saw me let out a shrill cry and all the others thrashed around in the water like fish snapping at a bite. I stopped, my hands trying to apologise, while all the women turned their heads so they could see me, and their backs to hide their nakedness, excited and frightened at the same time. The girl who had bound me with a spell covered herself modestly, but suddenly she looked at me with smiling eyes and at that moment I found myself facing the greatest test of my life. I wanted to be able to look at these eyes for ever – more than that, I wanted to possess this girl with the smiling eyes for ever.

'"Who are you?" asked an older girl.

'"I am Sidi Mubarak Bombay," I said, "the caravan guide."

'"Ah," said the girl who had bound me with a spell, "so these are your clothes we are washing here?" She lifted up the trousers she was holding in her hands and dangled them in the air, and the girls laughed and I laughed along with them – what else could I do? Besides, laughter makes a man more handsome, and I had to lend my worn-out face as much handsomeness as I could.

'"I don't wear that sort of thing," I said as the laughter thinned out.

'"Oh oh," called out another girl, "so you're not really that important, you're not yet allowed to wear the masters' clothes."

'"They aren't comfortable," I stammered.

'"So what do you wear, man of the coast?" asked the girl who had bound me with a spell.

'"A cloth, like this one, and when it is cold or on feast days, a kanzu."

360

'"Perhaps I am doing your washing now," called out another girl, and she held up a kanzu.

'"I am grateful," I said, "although that kanzu may not be mine."

'"Let's swap," said the girl I liked, and the two of them rolled their clothes into a ball and threw them at each other, and the shouts and laughter of the other girls became a boisterous hullabaloo that shut me out. "See if they fit him first," a girl called. And my girl opened the kanzu, held it at arm's length and squinted at me over the collar. "I can't tell from here," she cried. And the shouts of the other girls drenched me like heavy rainfall; challenges and shouts of encouragement jumbled together so I couldn't tell them apart. "Go over to her," I heard. "Are you afraid?" I heard. "Let her measure you," I heard. "He doesn't dare get in the water," I heard. And suddenly I was standing in front of the girl who had bound me with a spell and who was holding a white kanzu in her hands. I tried to smile at her, but she let out a wail, fluttering her tongue the way people there do at funerals, and the laughter flared up around me again as she called out in her loudest voice, "Oh, he is so small!" It was true: I hadn't noticed, she was taller than me, a good deal taller than me, and the kanzu almost came up to the tip of her nose, so it couldn't be mine. Eh, then my heart shrunk, because it would have been so lovely if she had handed me my kanzu.

'"Watch out," called another girl, "he will fall straight through that kanzu," and this time their laughter was like a waterfall, a river in spate. But the girl who stood before me – she wasn't beautiful, her nose was a little crooked, a little too long, and her chin too pointed; eh, no, what she was, that girl, was unlike any girl I had ever seen before, with eyes like two leaping, bounding, frolicking dik-dik – that girl had stopped laughing and was looking at me thoughtfully. The kanzu slipped out of her hands, and our eyes became entangled in a gaze that was like a roof of palm branches that sheltered us from the pelting laughter. We stayed there without moving, until one of the girls called to the others to get back to work, and the girl in front of me turned round, shaking her head, and then all the girls suddenly turned their backs on me and bent down to pick up the clothes out of the water. I couldn't stay there rooted to the spot as if I were a willow tree; I had to leave, even though I could have stayed looking at the girl who had bound me with a spell for hours.

'I slowly went back to the camp, a flame under my thoughts that neither brought them to the boil nor gave them any peace, and I realised how bad it was not to have anything to do in the village that day. Wherever I looked I saw the young woman in front of me, the smiling girl holding first a pair of trousers, then a kanzu; the serious look that suddenly replaced her laughter, and her behind – I know, I am talking like a young man who hasn't yet tamed his tongue – but her behind emptied my mind of all other thoughts. Eh, it was a curse or a blessing, depending on whether you ask me or you ask her, and when you ask me or you ask her.'

$$\backsim$$

'What are you writing?'

Speke again. Closing the tent flap is no deterrent. He has no idea how he's supposed to pass the time; in a moment he'll want to discuss some problem he's invented out of sheer boredom.

'I'm busy, Jack, writing up the last stage of the expedition.'

'What on earth is there to say?' Speke asks. 'It all looks the same, the same endless, monotonous gunge, regardless of whether it is forest or plain. And the people are even duller than the landscape: they all look identical, with the exact same leaden expression on their faces wherever you go. Why are we wasting our time drawing a map of this place? A white patch sums it up to a tee.'

Burton feels his self-restraint slipping. He has never learnt to hold his tongue.

'You know, Jack,' he says, 'it should have made me suspicious that you didn't learn more than a smattering of halting Hindustani in those ten years in India. But that's still no justification for such self-inflicted blindness. The people are precisely what's most interesting about this country. You'll see, anthropology will be this continent's science of the future.'

'You like rootling around in the mire. I've noticed that before. You have a perverse fascination for weeds and vermin, it's well known – so will you please explain what was so interesting about today, about the last village, where everyone was completely drunk. You noticed that, Dick, didn't you? Your piercing intellect didn't overlook an entire village being dead drunk? In the early afternoon?'

'I'm convinced a whole book could be written about that drunkenness. Take the brewing of the millet beer, for instance. Every villager is their own brewer, have you heard that? Often the women do it. They soak half the millet in water until it ferments . . .'

'I am not interested in how the beer is brewed, only in its effect. The chief already had a thick voice, fiery red eyes and the drunkard's pushy ways by midday, for goodness sake.'

'And the reason for this drunkenness? You gathered that?' asks Burton.

'Yes, I know the reason, but that does not make the whole thing any more acceptable. There was a funeral in the morning, an old man was put in the ground, and next thing you know, by the time we showed up, there wasn't a sign of mourning to be seen – quite the opposite: nothing but laughter and merriment and chatter.'

'Like in Italy,' Burton pointed out, 'where the biggest celebration of one's life is one's burial. There is a song in the Mezzogiorno, which goes something like: "Oh, what a time's to be had by my corpse."'

'Absolute rot, Dick! These savages have no control over their appetites, that's all. How can a whole village get drunk in broad daylight? No wonder they're poor.'

'Poor? Yes, they're that, but they're sharp as tacks with it. Do you know what they said when I asked why they were celebrating so exuberantly? "Because of the dead man," they said. "We are happy for his sake because he has finally reached the place he had been hoping to get to for a long while."'

SIDI MUBARAK BOMBAY

'We stayed on the outskirts of the village for a few more days because both Bwana Burton and Bwana Speke had come down with another heavy bout of fever and all of us needed a rest. So that meant I could go to the river every morning and look at the girl who had bound me with a spell, and the more I saw of her, the more I wanted her to be mine, until I decided I was not going to leave the village without her. So I asked the p'hazi of the village and he took me to her parents, and I squatted down in front of their house and spoke to her father. His first answer encouraged me, because he said he was prepared to give me his daughter, and his second robbed me of all hope, because he demanded a dowry I could not afford, even if I asked for the rest of my wages. I could not free myself from my longing for this girl, and yet I knew I would have to take my leave of her for ever. That night I was finally given something to do: I was put to guard the camp. I walked round it, listening for unusual noises, and then I sat on a tree stump. Now this tree stump, as the one who guides our destiny intended it to be, was right next to our store of rolls of brass wire. So there I sat and my gaze kept alighting on the wire, and after each of my rounds I sat back down on the same stump and I stared at the brass wire and I thought, "Why is the brass wire lying exactly where I am sitting?" And then I thought, "It's amazing how much wire there is. Who would worry if a little wire was missing? Who would notice if a tiny little bit went missing from so much brass?" I listened to the dark night and to my shadowy thoughts in turn, and I heard a suggestion that sounded so good and saw a solution that looked so simple. Of course, Bwana

Burton accused me of stealing afterwards, but he couldn't prove anything, and when he asked me how I got the girl who left with us the next day, I told him I had earned enough from a little business with the p'hazi to be able to pay her dowry, and although he did not believe me, there was nothing he could do because I gave him calm, confident answers – not because I was proud of what I had done but because I knew it was the right thing to do. Besides, the wazungu were completely dependent on me by then; if they lost me, they would have lost all connection to the country. And so I could take this girl with me whom you all know; some of you have known her since she was a young woman, others as a mother, and this girl who had bound me with a spell the moment I saw her proved a boon, not only on the long journey that lay ahead of us, but also in the house in Zanzibar that we built after we came back and filled with life, and I can tell you now that when I took that girl with me, I made the greatest conquest of my life.'

'Oh no, you don't believe him, do you? You don't believe his lice-ridden tales?'

'Oh, oh, my whispering had too long a neck.'

'Your ears are a disgrace. Gluttons, all of them, funnels for every sort of rubbish. Can't you tell the difference between the stories that drip with his pride – that pride that is bigger than the caravan that he is supposed to have guided across the whole country – and the stories that occasionally his modesty forces him to tell? Have you ever asked yourself what this conquest was like for me? Haven't you ever been amazed that this beautiful young woman – because if he desired me, then others must have desired me too – was prepared to go with him, this vagabond accompanying two mad wazungu to a great lake? Or two great lakes. Or the end of the world, as far as I am concerned. To go with a man who back then – you can take my word for this – looked no better than he does now. Far from it: the white hair that traps his face – yes, that sweet-potato field we call a face out of politeness – that white hair has given him some charm. Back then he was as handsome as a crocodile, and if I had known his character better, a hyena too. You should listen to me for once, all of you. Then you'd learn how pitiful it is only to know half the story. My parents had too many children. All my brothers and sisters were sturdy and healthy. We all ate a lot, and my father, who was frail, had trouble feeding us all. My father's brother helped us a little but it was barely enough. We wouldn't have starved; our village was not like this city we live in now. No one in our village would have been happy to be the only one with a full belly. But we were often hungry. And that is the reason, the only reason why this vagabond's offer seemed like a gift from our ancestors. If he paid for me what my father asked, the whole family would be able to get by until the next harvest and I would be in good hands as long as I lived. At least that is how my father saw it, and my mother did not contradict him. But I was frightened. When you see me now, you might think, how can that be, this woman doesn't know fear, because you only know the strength that I have made my own. But you have to picture it to yourselves: I was just a slim, delicate girl back then, and I was frightened of the weight this man would load onto me. I didn't want to be given to him as his wife. I told my mother. It didn't do anything. She told me to be quiet, to trust my father's decision. Then the next morning this strange, ugly beggarman paid my father the price he asked – of course, we didn't suspect how he'd come to afford me – and I had to say goodbye to my sisters and brothers and to the girls my age and to my parents. And I will tell you something else, because this man thinks he can talk about my behind in the middle of the street – he did not win me over with his shy gestures or the brass wire he gave my parents. I didn't let him win me over at all. I told him the first night, "You can only touch me when I say so. Until then we will sleep apart, and woe betide you if you do not respect my wish. I swear I will cut off what it is you imagine makes you a man.'"

'But if I may ask, Mama Sidi, was your father so wrong? Haven't things turned out well for you?'

'Now tell the truth, wife.'

'My father saw what no one could see. Although this man has continued his vagabond's life, he has always come home safe. But if you want to hear the truth, this is it: I have never had another husband, so I cannot compare how my life might have turned out with somebody else.'

❧

They have run out of water in the wastes of Ugogo, wild, rugged country with nothing to allay its severity. Above them, veils of cloud twine across the highest vault of heaven, far too high for any prayers to reach, while here below everything is scorched by an invisible furnace. This country is a beggar, Speke and Burton had realised as they looked out over its emaciated frame from the top of the Rubeho mountains – a beggar with jaundiced skin and jutting ribs streaked with dried-up watercourses, the scars left by the floods that lash its helpless body year after year. They had lingered at the top of the cliffs for a long time before eventually, by sheer force of will, scrambling down into that desert. Their most experienced porters had warned them it would be a month before they sighted another hill or valley. But, even given all these inescapable obstacles, there was nothing inevitable about the water running out; there was no need for it to happen. Some of the porters had left the last of the water-skins behind – intentionally, Burton was sure; they hadn't thought further than they could spit. They had blithely trusted the future would take care of itself, if they had given it any thought at all. The loss only came to light after two days' march, when the skins they were using started to run low. No need to worry, was his first reaction. We'll just ration it and get by on less than usual. How is he to know that they had stumbled upon a drought? Every village they come to, panting, they find the last well has dried up, the last pond has evaporated. They aren't even wells really, just hollows that have been dug out a little and shored up with rudimentary planking. The huts are deserted, the few people they meet crumpled figures, their lips as cracked as the ground, who stare aimlessly at the eternal acacias as they wait for death. Burton orders that the remains of the water should only be used for drinking. If they are sparing with their supplies, they should be able to last another three days, perhaps four. He orders them to take advantage of the full moon and march at night: anyone who protests will be left behind without a drop to drink.

Day and night they scratch a path across the plain. They cross deep riverbeds, sinking into the crumbly sand, pulling themselves laboriously up onto the other bank with the help of twisted roots – how they learn to hate rivers that carry no water. Only baobabs rise from the monotonous expanse. By nine o'clock, the sun is already snarling. The prickly little hairs of the buffalo grass jab them in the legs; tsetse flies bite them through the thickest material the moment their concentration lapses. Trees and bushes bear more thorns than leaves. Every hint of moisture evaporates from their mouths. At ten o'clock the sun starts to bark. They count the steps between pauses to wipe away the sweat. Grim presentiments have replaced the songs they normally hum. They are no longer able to moisten their lips with their tongues. After eleven o'clock, the sun bites. Before Burton can raise his heavy head, he has to fight off a mass of voices in his mind stubbornly questioning whether the effort is really necessary. Mortar flakes away from the roof of his mouth, falling in lumps onto his swollen tongue. They ought to rest, they ought to have rested a long time ago, but these trees that can survive without water cast only a skeletal shade. The next village they come to seems uninhabited, except for a whistling wind. Decapitated baobabs jut out at crooked angles – what can the fugitive villagers have used their branches for? It is a village of the dead, and the porters' murmuring carries the knowledge that they have arrived on the eve of the village's All Souls' Day, when its spirits will return to mourn the parched rivers after another year without rain. Suddenly there's a movement behind a mud-caked house, a rustling followed by a hoarse cry from a terrified cockerel, red as scorn, white as a solitary cloud. The comb flies over the cracked earth as it tries to flee. No one moves except Speke, who calmly levels his rifle and fires. There isn't much meat on the bird; none of the porters wants to touch it. Everyone takes the gulp of water they are entitled to, then stumbles on. Burton knows how futile it would have been to question their fear of that deserted village. Every head has dropped; their last hope of resurrection seems to have died with the cockerel.

Burton stops and waits for Speke to catch him up. They look at each other for a long time. There's nothing to say. Their uncertainty as to what lies ahead cannot be allayed by words. They silently agree and force their exhausted faces into an encouraging grin. 'You like putting yourself through hell, don't you?' Burton remarks, and Speke replies: 'It's something we have in common.'

SIDI MUBARAK BOMBAY

'My brothers, my friends, in the heart of the land of the Wagogo my ancestors almost came and fetched me back to them. They thought about it for a long time, and as they were thinking, a crust covered my tongue and the roof of my mouth and my gums. After a while I couldn't feel my tongue, and all the flesh in my mouth burst and split, but no blood came seeping through the cracks. I tried to bite my lips, at least to have the soft, round taste of blood in my mouth, but nothing came out – perhaps I was not biting hard enough, or perhaps all my blood had already evaporated. So this is how my third life ends, I thought. I was robbed of my first life; something was given back to me at the end of my second life; and now, in the heart of the land of the Wagogo, everything is going to be taken from me. Despair is a man, we say, and hope a woman. But perhaps hope is a mganga too, I thought, a mganga like the one we consulted, who gave us a different picture of our future. Why should he be wrong? My tongue may shrivel up but I am still going to get out of this desert. And as I was thinking that, we were saved! We were overtaken by our saviours, another caravan who knew where we could find water less than a day's march away.

'This was not just any caravan: it was the caravan of Omani Khalfan bin Khamis. If you have never heard of this man, then you should know one thing: he was the soul of cruelty and terror, plain and simple, even though he rescued us from the Wagogo desert after two days and two nights without a drop of water. When you hear the name Omani Khalfan bin Khamis these days, you think of trade and wealth, but in those days, if you were travelling, you trembled when you heard his name. He was in league with the lightning; he was the pharaoh of his caravan, and his heart – his slaves told us in a whisper after we had shared the terror of marching under him – his heart didn't live inside his body. It was wrapped in heavy cloths and kept in a trunk with his possessions, and only at night, after the last prayer – which he attended, like all prayers, without taking part – in the privacy of his tent, did he take it out, unwrap the cloths and look at it, because even a man, the slaves told us as they kept on looking over their shoulders, even a man who lives without a heart sometimes has to check that he has one.

'We travelled with Omani Khalfan bin Khamis's caravan for several days, and we had to keep up with it because we were dependent on its leader. He didn't allow any halts, didn't let anyone stop to catch his breath. He set a pace fit for charging bulls and hunting lions, not for men with narrow shoulders and legs like twigs on a thorn bush. He drove on his porters by every possible means, not just relying on the effect of his commands that pitilessly rained down on them, but using all the cunning a brain can devise. He would distribute three days' worth of the food, say, and tell the porters they wouldn't get any more rations until they reached a place a week's march away. Then hunger was the spur. The porters were dressed in shreds of animal skins and rags; they were at the end of their strength, and hunger drove them on. But the will can only do as much as the flesh allows. Many of them collapsed, and when they did, no one helped them back to their feet; their bundles were taken off and divided up among the others, and they were left lying on the path, no matter whether there was a village near by or if they shared the country with wild beasts. Some of them tried to run away – then he sent his men after them, who beat them raw. Omani Khalfan bin Khamis, remember this name if you do not know it already, and one day, when you are asked to name the monsters that make a hell of this earth, who take from people what the Creator gave them, say this name – and then say it again, in token of all the evil he has done.

'We owed him our lives though; when he caught us up and guided us to water, he saved our lives. But once we had recovered our strength, we parted ways with his caravan, because even Bwana Burton, who liked to act as if he were the Devil's younger brother, told me we should beware of men who we were not sure had a mother. Bwana Burton himself sometimes talked like a man who had no mother, but it was just talking; his actions were the opposite: he was a more lenient, sympathetic man than he pretended to be.'

'Some Wagogo have been coming to Zanzibar lately, and I've heard they always cause trouble.'

'That is how the Wagogo are. We were told so before we met them. We were given enough warnings to be on our guard, but still they turned out to be filthy liars and terrible thieves, those Wagogo from the forests without trees, who had heard as much about us as we had heard about them. They always greeted us with ravening questions, and only when those questions were exhausted would they give us a little goat's milk.

'"Is it true that the whites have only one eye and four arms?"

'"No," I said. "It is not true."

'"Is it true the whites are full of knowledge?"

'"No," I said, "they do not even know magic."

'"Is it true", they asked, "that when they travel through the land, rain falls before them and drought follows in their wake?"

'"No," I said, "they have to walk through drought just like us."

'"Is it true", they asked, "that the whites cause the pox because they cook watermelons and throw away the seeds?"

'"No, those are pregnant women's tales."

'"Is it true they make cattle sick because they boil milk and let it harden?"

'"No," I said, "that is not true either."

'"Is it true", they asked, "that these whites with straight hair are the rulers of the water?"

'"No," I said, "they travel the sea in boats large enough to take a whole village, but in storms they drown just as you and I would drown."

'"Is it true", they asked, "that they have come to steal our country?"

'"Nonsense! Complete nonsense!" That is what Burton said every time he got angry about something someone said. "These barbarians," he complained. "The less they have, the more they're afraid someone wants to take their pittance from them. They remind me of those gaunt figures in Somalia who were slowly starving before our eyes and yet still had the strength to suspect us, in the loudest possible fashion, of spying out the wealth of their country. 'What wealth would that be?' I felt like asking." I do not know why this subject sent Bwana Burton into such a fury. "You don't understand", he yelled at me, as if I were the source of all the mistrust, "what a sacrifice it would be for us to settle in your country, and what a blessing it would be for you."

'"This is not my country," I told him, "and I cannot translate the fears of these people." But now I doubt what Bwana Burton said even more; those flags the wazungu hoisted in Zanzibar today have outpaced his words. From what I know of the wazungu, they are definitely not going to sacrifice themselves for our sake.'

'And yet they have come here and seem to want to stay.'

'So the only question is: do they want to take from the poor the little they have, or are the poor not as poor as they seem?'

'The second, Baba Adam, definitely the second. Bwana

Burton must have had reason to say, as he did several times: "This country could be rich, you cannot imagine how rich it could be." I thought of the wealth of Bombay and the wealth of Zanzibar, then I looked at the ground, the cracked earth, and I did not believe him. It looks as if I was wrong.'

∾

After toiling across plain, jungle, desert and hopeless waste, Kazeh – tiny, dusty, parched Kazeh – seems like an oasis to them, a worldly metropolis. After a thousand miles, and 134 days, they sweep into the settlement as if they haven't suffered the slightest humiliation or injury getting there. Earlier that morning, the Baluchis had removed the elegant uniforms intended for such ceremonial occasions from their packs and donned them so that now, utterly transformed, they may take their places at the head of the caravan as it proudly parades itself before the assembled village, flags aloft, horns blaring, muskets incessantly repeating a deafening salute. The village's inhabitants, all of whom line the path down to the very last old man, accept the challenge, returning the uproar cry for cry, crash for crash, whistle for whistle. The entire village has come out to greet them, but Burton cannot at first see an official reception committee. Then he catches sight of three Arabs in voluminous white robes, who come forward and offer him the warmest of welcomes in their language – presumably Omani Khalfan bin Khamis has already reached Kazeh and given a detailed description of this foreigner who speaks fluent, flaw-less Arabic. They indulge this rare pleasure to the full, employ-ing every conceivable formula of greeting before asking whether, from the goodness of his heart, he would do them the honour of following them. From their purposefulness, the way all three wordlessly line up, Burton deduces that the question of who will be his host has already been settled. He stops. He has forgotten something. He turns and sees Speke a dozen paces behind him, his face cold and smooth. Burton hurries back to him, apologising. 'I've got to get on their good side,' he explains. 'They will be very important to us.'

'Go ahead,' Speke says with a feigned air of understanding, 'if it's so essential. I'll see to the camp.'

The Arabs show Burton the open ground where caravans can set up, and announce that he will be staying in the house of a merchant, who has returned to Zanzibar. On their way there, a matter of minutes, they apologise profusely for having to make him walk so far; Burton assures them it is no strain. They enter a house sheltered by a canopy, whose walls, he sees, have been freshly cleaned and its floor scrubbed. The staff is introduced to him, and then the Arabs take their leave, saying they will fetch him once he has rested and bathed. Burton bids them farewell, thanking them. A little later they return to invite him to eat, so that he may satisfy his hunger for a proper meal and they their curiosity about the expedition. The invitation is an open one, but Burton tells Speke, who in the meantime has set himself up in the second bedroom, that it would be best if he saw the Arabs alone. Speaking their own language, with someone who knows and respects their customs, they will relax, open up. 'But of course, Dick,' says Speke, 'I would only be in your way.' His tone doesn't change in the slightest.

Burton will always remember that meal of stuffed goat, succulent rice, turkey in a hot, spicy sauce, chicken giblets, steamed cassava with ground peanuts, omelettes with raisins and melted clarified butter. But, above all, because it is the first time he learns from a reliable source that there is not just one great lake, but two – one directly east, the other directly north. His hosts, the Arabs of Kazeh, do not know whether the Nile flows northwards out of one of these lakes. They promise to try and find out – they promise to help him in every way they can, but before they do anything, they say, he must wait upon the king, King Saidi Fundikira, who rules from his seat in nearby Ititemya. After the meal, they invite him to join them in prayer, presuming that someone who speaks such perfect Arabic must be a Muslim, and they are disappointed when

Burton declines. He has no choice though: Said bin Salim and the Baluchis have prayed early every morning, and they wouldn't understand how he could rediscover his piety in the grand surroundings of Kazeh when it had failed him throughout the trip. It is a pity: he suddenly feels a powerful need to chant zikr in a rapt choir of voices.

The next morning they set off to pay the king his customary respects. They find him lying in the shade of the royal tree, his body bloated beyond all measure, a leader who apparently abhors movement of any sort. Two huge drums boom by way of greeting, royal drums that can only be played by the initiated – the Arabs are experts, Burton notes with satisfaction. King Saidi, who in Europe would go by the title Fundikira I, does not look at them; he never looks any mortal in the eyes. A man whispers something in his ear, perhaps describing what he would see if he opened his eyes and turned his head. One of the Arabs, who has an impressive grasp of the Nyamwezi language, takes charge of the conversation, conducting what sounds like a refined, seemly exchange. The king, whose back has been weakened by years of good living, remains silent, merely raising and lowering his head with an air of deliberation – Burton can't tell if this nodding has any significance or is simply an unfortunate habit.

'His legs', explains the Arab next to Burton, 'can no longer bear all his different sicknesses. So he remains lying down and leaves all the decisions to the mganga – that young man talking at him now.'

The king shows no interest in the presents Burton gives him.

'It is our bad luck', the Arab continues in a whisper, 'that the mganga has embarked on another quest for the truth of the king's illness. This is elusive prey, and although he is a particularly powerful mganga, he will need all day to track it down. We will have to stay until he does, since it is incumbent upon guests to witness the moment of discovery. And because we are here, the mganga will put on a tremendous show. He has developed an infallible strategy for maintaining his position:

375

any of the king's relatives who incur his disapproval through ambition or obstinacy, he accuses of witchcraft.'

The Arab's prediction proves accurate. After a while they, the guests, also take their seats on the ground, from where they witness the mganga rattling off a long, muttered liturgy with disinterested haste. A hen is then produced, a splendid creature whose neck the mganga breaks with a fluid movement as if he were picking a flower, before cutting it open to study its entrails.

'Any blackness or blemishes on the wings will mean treachery on the part of the children,' whispers the Arab sitting next to Burton, 'whereas the spine damns the mother and grandmother. The rump indicates the wife's guilt, whilst the thighs denounce the concubines and the feet some of the other slaves . . .'

The muttering continues, the bird is cut up; apparently no blemishes are visible in the flesh; the only darkness is the shadow that after a long silence passes over the mganga's face. He leaps to his feet and in a raw, furious voice that spurts out like pus from a wound declares that dark clouds are blocking his view, thick, dark clouds; he won't be able to see clearly until the whites have gone.

Clever dog, thinks Burton, using our presence for his machinations. This way he can leave the king's relatives in doubt about the results of his investigations, if one can use the word, while at the same time putting pressure on the foreigners not to stay too long in Kazeh. The king gives them a barely perceptible nod of the head as they take their leave. At least this unexpected turn of events has had one good outcome: they will not have to spend all afternoon in the shade of the largest tree in the kingdom.

'That mganga is quite something,' Burton remarks. 'He knows how to make the most of his power.'

'He can't be bought,' says the Arab, 'that's the one good thing one can say about him. He still lives in the secluded hut his kind is entitled to.'

But he can sell himself, thinks Burton, his charisma must have won him plenty of admirers. At Leadenhall Hall, they would call him a careerist: as smooth as steel, more cynical than any brothel owner. No one can convince me he believes any of that humbug he peddles with such a song and dance.

SIDI MUBARAK BOMBAY

'In Kazeh, the place where we were able to recover from the storms of the journey, something wonderful happened, something that filled my heart so full happiness shone out of my eyes and my mouth and my skin. I met a man who could share with me what I had not shared with anyone for many long rainy seasons. He came up and spoke to me. He was not from Kazeh, not from the Nyamwezi people – you know how strangers seek out other strangers – but had been cast up in that place by paths as strange as those that had cast me up there, and he knew my language: he could speak the language of my first life, which, like me, he had not used since the days of his childhood. So we squatted down together under a broad acacia tree, as eager as young lovers, and began to talk, hesitantly and carefully at first, exploring each word with our tongues before we said it, feeling it as if it was a present we had just been given, rummaging about in our minds for those words we had forgotten as if in a trunk we had not opened since the days of our childhood. We let the sun pass over our heads as we talked, as we became children again, and soon we were chattering away as quickly and excitedly as if we were squatting on the shores of the lake at home, making fun of the crocodiles stretched out on the sandbanks. That man became my friend; it was as if we were both born on the same day, and each of our conversations was like a jewel we stored in a treasure chest that kept getting heavier until it was overflowing by the time we had to leave Kazeh. But the blossoming of my first language was not the only blessing this friendship brought me . . . No, my brother was also close to the most powerful mganga in the country, to whom he introduced me. He had sung his praises so highly and spoken of him with such reverence that I expected an old man whose experience had written itself in the silver of his eyebrows, a man who had long since taught his children to run and talk. You can imagine my surprise when instead a tall, perfectly upright figure pulled back his leopard's skin to reveal a face with eyes as clear as a stream. The mganga was my age, and I felt a brief stab of doubt. Had my new brother promised too much? That stab only lasted long enough for us to exchange a few words, and after that I forgot the mganga's age, I didn't take in his appearance – I just listened to his voice that sounded as if it had no age, to his words that were so weighty, it was as if he had carried them with him through several lives already. He felt my hunger to learn everything that had been hidden from me up until then, and later, when we took our leave of each other, he said grown-up pupils tear knowledge from their teachers, whereas young pupils waited for their teachers to smuggle knowledge into them . . . because as everyone knows, man can take by force, but he cannot give by force. So, during those long days we spent in Kazeh, he guided me through the forests of truth, forests I had never set foot in where herbs grew – real herbs, I mean, herbs of every sort to be used for every purpose. The knowledge of these herbs was sacred, because they could help women give birth, they could chase off headaches and staunch wounds, but they could also be dangerous, they could poison a human being, and much else besides.'

'The mganga was your friend.'

'He touched my life. Every day he spent some time with me and my new brother, despite his many responsibilities, and sometimes it was just the two of us alone with him. And we did not even notice how we drank in his wisdom: it was like sugar in coffee, pleasurable and lovely, and it was only afterwards that I realised how his words had embedded themselves in my memory, how valuable they were.'

'What sort of wisdom, Baba Sidi? Wisdom is a matter of details too.'

'He taught that raw lump the value of politeness.'

'Ah, Mama, mother of Hamid, how nice, you have not forgotten us.'

'He taught him to honour women. Because, until then, your friend was someone who only knew the world of men.'

'She's right. I had no memory of my mother, there were no women in the banyan's household, and in Zanzibar I lived with some brothers in a little house. I had already spent a life and a half without women.'

'I was grateful to that mganga. You cannot imagine how grateful I was.'

'He was so good at talking. I remembered everything he said: I couldn't forget it even if I tried, it was as if my head was writing down his words. He never said exactly what he meant: he used decorations that only made sense after you took a step back and thought them over. He would say things like: "If you arrive in a place where you are a stranger, you will be hungry. And if you meet a woman whom you do not know, you will want to ask her for food. So greet her and say: 'The way women bring their children into this world is the same wherever one goes: their sufferings are the same, and their joys are the same.' That, you will find, is the measure of politeness." That is how he talked, and he would always pause at the still point in the middle of what he was saying.'

'I listened too. I sat a few paces behind the men with my face turned to the ground, but I listened more carefully than everyone else and I tried out everything I heard straight away on this strange man who was now my husband. And so little by little all my uncertainties about how I was to treat him started to crumble away.'

'"That is much better", the mganga would go on, "than if you say: 'I am hungry.' The woman will give you something to eat because you have reminded her of her own children, of the love she feels for her own children. She will take the place of your mother and she will call you 'my son' and she will start cooking what she has right away."'

'And this fellow, who spends his time sitting with you, test-ing the stamina of his tongue – to my great, young woman's surprise, this fellow followed this advice, and other pieces of advice from the mganga. And so he began to discover me over the days we spent in Kazeh, he discovered me through the eyes of a new respect, and he treated me with the gestures of a new politeness. Thanks be to the ancestors.'

'Thanks be to God.'

'And thanks be to the mganga's mother too, because she gave me the gift of pleasure, and maybe life too, by giving me herbs that prevented a new life blooming in my belly. I still had not allowed that big mouth down there with you to do what he most wanted to do. I wasn't only protecting myself against his strangeness, I was also afraid of falling pregnant because I was convinced that in that caravan I could only give birth to a still-born child.'

'God preserve us!'

'Everything was fine. I boiled the herbs and drank the juice, and after he had shown me further proof of his newfound politeness, I allowed this man I was sold to to share my bed. And our first son, Hamid, wasn't born until we had a stone house here in Zanzibar.'

'Mother of Hamid, my wife sends you her greetings. Her joints are hurting again and she asks if you could go and pay her a visit.'

'I will go and see her now, Baba Ishmael, before dinner is upon us.'

'You have done well, my friend.'

'That is the truth.'

'Of course, but it is also a very timely truth.'

'This mganga impresses me, even this far away.'

'He gave me back my faith, my brothers; he showed me a faith that reached deeper into me than anything I had known before. Through him, I became aware of what I was missing. I was wandering through life incomplete, grieving because I had lost something that was close to my heart. One evening we were eating together and he asked me to put out banana leaves on the mat for everyone who would be at the meal.

'"But it's just the two of us," I said.

'"I invited my father as well," the mganga replied, "and my father's father."

'I stopped because I knew they were both dead. "Are we offering a sacrifice to the ancestors?" I asked hesitantly.

'"They will eat with us," the mganga said.

'We sat down with two leaves beside us, two places at which no one sat. The mganga introduced his father and his father's father to me. "What about you," asked the mganga, "don't you know anyone you would like to invite?" And all I could do was be silent.'

'What I don't understand, Baba Sidi, is that you talk of religion but not of prayer. What are prayers like in this other faith?'

'There is no prescribed prayer as you know it.'

'How can that be?'

'A prayer designed like a law is only needed when prayer is an exception, when you step out of your life to pray. But if each of your breaths is a prayer, if everything you do is a prayer, if you honour God because you are in God, then you do not need any other sort of prayer. Eh, you already have the highest form of prayer. In the mosque, prayer is no more than a declaration of intentions, well-meaning and visible to all. It is like a boat, which you make seaworthy on shore but is only tested at sea, when you hit your first storm. Who wants to know then how good the boat looked when it was still on shore? Do you think at our moments of weakness God counts up our prayers?'

'Baba Sidi is right. A well-lived life is the best prayer.'

∼

Burton can't understand why Snay bin Amir is being so helpful. Is he acting on the sultan's orders? Or is it because, since being in Kazeh, Burton has worn Arab clothes and behaved so much like an Arab that Bombay, when they recently crossed paths in the village, walked straight past him as if they had never met? The little fellow was deeply impressed when he heard his name and recognised Bwana Burton jokingly calling out, 'I've changed my name to Abdullah Rahman Bombay, we're related now.' Would Burton's natural way with the Arabs explain why Snay bin Amir had helped him in the dispute with Said bin Salim and the Baluchis? With his help, Burton had nipped their shameless demands for more wages and provisions in the bud.

But that still doesn't account for the fact that Snay bin Amir spends an almost limitless amount of time with him, entertainingly whiling away the hours explaining the basics of the Nyamwezi language, or sketching the northern lake, which the natives call Nyanza. Finally Burton cannot suppress his curiosity any longer. Snay bin Amir laughs, and after speaking of hospitality and mutual sympathies, he adds, 'Why do you think we merchants should have anything to fear from you British coming? It is the opposite, if anything. Our business would be greatly simplified.'

'What about slavery?' asks Burton.

'We are not so deeply attached to the trade in human beings as all that. We can deal in gold or wood or sugar. Who is going to drive us out? Look around you: do you really think your compatriots will flock in droves to dusty outposts like this to live a life that, although it makes us happy, will render them utterly miserable? No, they will prefer to work with us; it will be more agreeable for them and quite profitable enough.'

Or else, thinks Burton, you will pull out and leave the country to those who know no other.

Kazeh suits him. He sits at a little desk the Arabs have set up in his room for him and enjoys this restful break at an unexpectedly enchanting milestone on the journey . . . well, no, not exactly enchanting, but satisfactory at least, sufficient, and perhaps that is more important. He remembers a striking paradox about Buddhist students in India: the more they progressed in their studies, the smaller the cells they were entitled to. It was considered a privilege for them to give up their individual rooms and squeeze into a cell half the size with their fellow students. He has spent the equivalent of a term in the bush; now he is wise enough to be able to value a place like Kazeh. But with this unaccustomed modesty come doubts about the sense of the whole enterprise. He nearly died a miserable death; he almost lost his mind; his body has been plundered to the limit of its resources, and what is there to show for it? What success counterweighs these sacrifices? He has reached Kazeh, a village. No doubt the Buddhists would say such doubts are the expression of a persistent vanity, but isn't it something that having set out to conquer the world, he is now satisfied with a tiny, dusty nowhere? Even if it is just for a time. Oases only give pleasure when you have crossed a desert. Now he knows for sure that there are two lakes, and that the Nile may flow out of one . . . Or maybe there are four lakes? This indifference he feels can't last.

Later he sits at the little desk for hours and answers the letters that have been waiting for him at Kazeh, welcome communications that vouch for a world that is starting to recede in his pallid memory. Some, however, prove very hard to bear. One brings terrible news of his brother; another from Zanzibar informs him of the British consul's death. Burton had expected it, but still the news affects him deeply. That good man had not sailed back to Ireland. He will have to send the new consul a comprehensive report and hope he will respect his predecessor's promises. News also reaches him of another death, General Napier's. His son-in-law McMurdo was at his deathbed, and as the general was drawing his last breath, he had waved the flag of the 22nd Regiment over him.

'What are you doing?'

From his tone of voice, it sounds as if Speke is asking, 'You haven't found something else to write, have you?'

'Putting down some thoughts, Jack, just a few thoughts before they go.'

'Care to read any out?'

'Not at the moment.'

'You know I have a soft spot for your thoughts.'

'I received a letter from my sister. My brother has been wounded in the head in Sri Lanka. It's serious: apparently he doesn't know who anybody is. The doctors say he could live for another half a century without recognising himself or us.'

'I'm sorry, Dick. Your brother . . . Edward, isn't it? He was . . . a good man . . . That's the sort of fate I'm scared of. I wouldn't mind a bit being killed in Africa, if that's the way it has to be, but to be taken by fever, or imprisoned and tortured but not killed, that's a prospect that drives me absolutely out of my wits.'

'Come on, we have to get out; let's go for a walk. We'll imagine we're in Devon.'

SIDI MUBARAK BOMBAY

'After all our evenings together, Baba Sidi, your journey is as familiar to me as my own travels. But this mzungu, this Bwana Burton, was a mystery to me from the start and he's still a mystery to me now.'

'Because I can't resolve the mystery myself, Baba Ishmael. I can't describe him fully because he never showed himself to me fully. I always had the feeling he was on the other bank and there was no ferry in sight to negotiate the river between us. I didn't think he was a terrible man: it was the man he pretended to be that terrified me. I am sure he never killed anyone, but he liked to make us believe he was capable of it. Bwana Burton was driven by djinns no one else knew, djinns he couldn't explain to anyone – not to me, not to the porters, not to the Baluchis or to the banyans, not even to Bwana Speke. It is easier to live if people understand your djinns. That is also why, I suppose, he hardly ever sensed other people's despair: he was like an old elephant that has withdrawn from the herd and always drinks alone at the watering hole. Bwana Speke was different; he also kept his nature hidden, but when anything revealed itself, I saw who he was, what he felt. He could be terrible, but he was closer to me. At times he treated me like a dog and at times like a friend.'

'Didn't you say friendship with the wazungu was impossible?'

'It's true, I did say that. But Bwana Speke was an exception. We spent so many months together, he trusted me and by the end he didn't hide anything from me, not even what he thought. It's a strange thing, but he didn't see any harm in explaining to me why people like me were worth less than the wazungu.'

'People like you? Which people is that?'

'"The Africans," he said. I asked him if he meant the people of Zanzibar, or Wagogo, or Nyamwezi. He answered, "All of you." And when I asked him how so many different types of people could be worth less than him and his kind, he spoke about the Bible, the holy book of the people who wear the cross on their chest, and he told me the story of Noah – we know that story too, but we tell it differently, as you'll see. He was less interested in the prophet Noah and his exhortations and warnings than in his sons, his three sons who were called Shem, Ham and Japheth. Listen to this, this is amazing: all the people on earth are supposed to come from these three sons. One day Noah was supposed to have been lying drunk in his tent . . .'

'The prophet, drunk!'

'On his own wine. And as he was sleeping, without realising, he exposed himself, and Ham noticed. He saw his father's private parts and told his two brothers, who averted their eyes while they covered Noah with a garment, and that's why the prophet cursed Ham's children and his children's children to be the slaves of the other brothers for all eternity. A strange story which would have nothing to do with us, if Bwana Speke hadn't claimed that Ham was our forefather, our original ancestor, and so we must submit because he and the other wazungu were descended from one of the other brothers, I have forgotten which one. Isn't it strange: the wazungu, who have no ties to their immediate forefathers, claim to know exactly who their original ancestor was.'

'I hope you told him that there's nothing about this in the Glorious Qur'an?'

'I didn't say anything; I am experienced enough not to fight against holy books.'

'Will you please explain, Baba Sidi, why the wazungu are against the slave trade if they are convinced we are worth less than them as human beings?'

'The wazungu are against the slave trade?'

'Of course, especially Bwana Burton, he passionately rejected slavery, eh, oh yes, he despised it . . . and yet he agreed to slaves being part of the caravan. And when I asked him how he could be against slavery and use slaves at the same time, he explained that there weren't enough free men who wanted to work, he didn't have any choice, so he paid them a wage and treated them like free men.'

'He probably thought that if he treated slaves like free men they would become free.'

'It's like giving alms. If someone amply rewards a beggar, does the beggar become a man of ample means?'

'He said he had no power to prevent Said bin Salim, the Baluchis and the two banyans purchasing slaves. He raised objections. Raised objections! Do you hear that, my friends? The king of the caravan goes up to the men who are utterly dependent on him, who are under his command, tentatively taps them on the shoulder and asks them politely not to go too far with the slavery. "But our laws allow it!" his dependents reply, full of righteous indignation, and the king of the caravan walks away without even asking if it's true. He thinks, "I've done what I can." He soothes his conscience: "I've shown these savages how steadfastly we reject slavery."'

'Hypocrisy is thriving.'

'And its future is even brighter.'

'I told him: "You do not understand. Slavery is a condition

that has to be completely removed from the world. It is not just the suffering of a few people here and now. It is the suffering of their families and their descendants. When all that pain and fear has seeped into the ground, how will it ever come out? Who will clean the land? Who will protect it from the seeds of violence that will grow in their descendants, in their grandchildren and great-grandchildren who will have to see another sun than the one their ancestors have seen?"'

'What did Bwana Burton say?'

'"You're talking gibberish," he said. "The mganga has turned your head!"

'"Perhaps," I replied, "perhaps he has turned my head. But now I know I am looking in the right direction."'

He stands in the river, murky water up to his hips, and every time he puts his arm beneath the surface, he touches something slimy. It's not unpleasant, as a matter of fact, just unfamiliar. There's mud wherever they put their feet, a darkness they have to wade through, the queasiness rising in their throats, as it sucks at their legs. He stands in the water and wonders if they made a mistake when they were standing by what was at the time a broad, gently flowing river, debating where they should cross. Perhaps it would have been better back there: the water was deeper, it's true, but at least they could see the other bank. Here cannot be right: this inland delta is so overgrown they could get lost at any moment. The landscape seems completely untouched, as if this river they are following is flowing back to the time of original sin, as if they were returning to the dawn of the world when plants grew wherever they pleased and giant trees ruled over everything. As far as they've gathered, this river, which is called the Malagarasi, will lead them to the lake.

Snay bin Amir had sent them on their way with a guide, a young half-Arab, half-Nyamwezi who had seemed to be doing a good job, self-confident fellow that he was, until they realised he had forced them into a three-day detour so as to visit his wife. Not wanting to leave her, he had then offered them the services of his nephew, an equally self-assured soul who had also led them astray, although unintentionally in his case. Burton had decided to send the hopeless bungler back and simply follow the river, which at that point inspired more confidence: a lovely broad stretch of water lined with trees rustling in the wind, Palmyra palms that had been planted by the slave traders, according to Snay bin Amir, tall and fruit-bearing with dense fronds rising from their thin, perfectly straight trunks. It was an idyllic scene, animated by carefree birds wherever they looked, above and on the water, perched on every branch and twig: kites with their languid mastery of flight, wheeling through the air in perfect circles; sociable pelicans gathered as though at a garden party, every beak pointed down, every head tilted to the left; kingfishers diving perpendicularly into the water and then shooting out equally vertically, fish in their beaks; Goliath herons standing perfectly still, watching for their prey on rocks in the middle of the river.

Cries of colobus monkeys ring out, not far away – not a friendly sound. Speke lifts his eyes as if the faint light seeping through the canopy might relieve his suffering. It looks as if he has caught trachoma: his conjunctiva are inflamed, his eyelids severely swollen, especially that of his left eye, which he can't shut completely. Now he is virtually blind, he tries to stay as close to Burton as possible, wordlessly accepting his leadership. In the swamps he grabbed hold of him repeatedly, clinging on to his baggy shirtsleeves, slipping when he slipped, falling when he fell. A few days ago, irritated by his companion's superciliousness, Burton had wished the jungle would break Speke, would finally make him lose his composure, his lordly ways, his superior manners. Then, in the village where the guide wouldn't leave his wife, he had seen an old man who had gone blind: both his eyelids were ingrown, the cornea terribly scarred, the iris lost in a wad of what looked like red cotton wool. Burton had stared into the ruined eyes, unable to tear himself away. Ashamed – sometimes he grew weary of seeing himself – he instantly revoked his curse: let Speke's eyes heal, he prayed.

Lord, this exhaustion he feels; if he were to relax for a moment he'd fall asleep on the spot. He ducks under a willow, climbs over a rotten tree trunk that seems to have come down in a different age. He looks ahead. This isn't such a big river: the delta must end somewhere. Barely five yards away, emerging from the thick vegetation as if swinging through a vaulted window, a huge, dark baboon suddenly jumps over the rivulet without a sound, its movements seemingly slowed down because of the silence. Burton stops and signals to the others not to move. A female follows, a baby clinging to her, then a few youngsters, then a massive throng of baboons, one after another, flitting through the tangled opening in the foliage without even a twig snapping, without looking round, as if the human beings only yards from them do not exist. Burton is spellbound by the interlude. Pure movement. Perhaps a sign . . . definitely a sign: follow the apes. They have to follow the apes. He gives the order. After half an hour at most they find themselves standing on a bank, looking out over a broad, gently flowing river.

SIDI MUBARAK BOMBAY

'The long stay in Kazeh, my friends, had brought the wazungu relief and given them fresh vigour, but it had not really cured them. They recovered enough of their strength to get through the journey, but not enough to regain their health. In the swamps the fever returned and gave Bwana Burton a terrible beating. Back and forth he swung between attacks of sweating and shivering; he was sick constantly; he lapsed into fits of madness when the djinns would whisper more evil thoughts in his ear than a drinker imagines deep in his drink. He could not feel his legs, they were covered in ulcers, and he just lay there, paralysed. "I haven't got any muscles left," he said softly, his lips hardly moving at all, his lips covered in pustules. His eyes were bloodshot, as though the evening sun had burst in them like an egg. They burned and he kept groaning, over and over. He couldn't stand the shrill noise in his ears caused by the wazungu's medicine, a medicine called quinine that tormented him, but if he didn't take it, he said, he would have already died long ago. He was full of pain, and yet nothing hurt him as much as his weakness, his dependence. You should have seen the revulsion on his face when he had to be carried by eight of the strongest porters because he couldn't hold on to his donkey. As for Bwana Speke, who was almost blind, he tried to hide his suffering, but how could he fool us when he didn't shoot anything, didn't even unwrap his gun? He needed me in the morning when his eyes were as puffy and sticky as if they had been smeared with resin. I had to wash them out with water, I had to put on his boots – eh, he was testy and gruff then. The two wazungu were at our mercy in those days and more than once I thought how lucky they were to have fallen into our hands.'

'Baba Sidi, I'm sorry, it's getting late and I promised my grandchildren to tell them a story . . . perhaps I'll tell them one of yours . . . I have to go now, but I didn't want to leave without having heard – I have such beautiful memories of it – how you reached the lake.'

'Yes, the first great lake.'

'Fine, Baba Yusuf, I will leap over the Malagarasi swamps and land at our last climb. That hill was the death of Bwana Speke's mule: it simply lay down as if all its strength had been used up on one last wheeze. Bwana Speke was bewildered: he just lay there, stretched out on the ground on his side, digging his fingers into the soil, not saying anything. I suppose he didn't want to draw attention to himself, his undignified state. I helped him up and had to support him as we climbed that steep hill, the last hill we had to climb . . . I know now . . . but at the time it just seemed one more test among all the others.

He gripped my elbow painfully and begged me to describe everything I could see, the scattered thorny bushes, the foamy clouds, the stones like pumpkins – there was not very much to describe but he was hungry and impatient; the minute I stopped to take a breath, he told me to go on, and I had to swear I wasn't keeping any changes in the landscape from him. When we reached the summit, we drew breath and then I saw something unusual, something that pricked my curiosity – a metallic expanse shimmering in the sun. Bwana Speke sensed something too – he could barely see, but light and darkness still somehow penetrated his swollen eyelids – and he asked in an excited voice: "That strip of light, Sidi, do you see that strip of light too? What is it?"

'I took time over my answer, savouring my joy. "I think, Bwana," I said slowly and deliberately, "I think it is water." And as I said that, I realised everyone around me was rejoicing. I saw Said bin Salim talking ecstatically to Bwana Burton, who was sitting on the shoulders of the strongest porter, craning his neck, I saw the Jemadar Mallok smiling like a gambler who's just doubled his stake, I saw the Baluchis congratulating each other with deep, solemn bows. Sensing this joy, Bwana Speke let it infect him, but still he had to complain a little, grumbling about the mist before his eyes. Soon we had a clearer view of the lake; it lay below us like a huge blue fish basking in the sun. We were bewitched, we forgot all the toils, all the dangers, all the doubtfulness of return . . . oh yes, we forgot everything we had suffered, and for the first and last time, my brothers, we all shared one and the same happiness.'

It is February 13, an historic date in the annals of world discovery, he exults, when civilised eyes catch their first glimpse of a lake of unsurpassed beauty – although appearances, as they proverbially tend to be, are initially deceiving. At first it seems the lake is no more than a glinting line, a piece of radiant mockery. Is this poor prize all he is to get for his labours, this crushing disappointment? But then they take a few paces; the sun ceases to reflect off the water; they see the lake from a different angle . . . and suddenly they receive a first impression of the true size of the shimmering expanse of water stretching into the far distance before them. This holy lake – euphoria erupts in him like a long-delayed orgasm – surrounded by mountains as if it's lying in the lap of the gods, with its bright yellow sand and emerald-green water. The sun caresses his face, a gentle breeze gets up, raising tufts of foam on the low waves, canoes ply back and forth, and the water's alluring murmur grows louder as they climb down the steep path. The litter is uncomfortable, the porters slip occasionally, causing him to cling onto the struts at the side, but with such a view, what can concern him? Below them lies the Malagarasi, discharging its red waters into the lake, and a village that nestles so blissfully in the crook of a softly rounded bay that if it were provided with gardens and orchards, mosques and palaces, it would be far more beautiful than the most magical places on the Italian coast. Melancholy? Monotony? Every trace of them is swept away. Here is the reward for all the deserts he has toiled through, and the contentment he feels at this moment is so all-encompassing that he would have endured double the pain and troubles and hardship to gain this prize, and not have regretted it for a minute.

SIDI MUBARAK BOMBAY

'My brothers, I have been proud to tell you the story of my travels, and my wife is right, sometimes I have told you only what my pride wants to hear. So now I must confess, as we have reached the heights of that first trip, I must confess to you why I rued every one of my journeys. For I saw with my own eyes what no one should see: I saw the beginnings of slavery. I was forced to relive my death over and over again, and every time I said to myself that nothing could be worse than Ujiji, our destination on that first journey. But you know that if you give life time, it always produces something worse, and so I came upon a place on my second journey that was even more gruesome than Ujiji. Every time I saw a slave caravan, at Zungomero, Kifukuru, Kazeh or Gondokoro, I died my first death again, and believe me, the death that repeats itself is not a pleasant death.

'The wazungu I was with called themselves explorers, but the real explorers of the mainland were the slave traders. Wherever we went, they had been already. When villages were not burnt to the ground, they were orphaned; when the slave traders were not driving their spoils across country, they were filling boats so full that half their load had to be sacrificed – that was the hongo they paid death.

'The slave traders at that first great lake were the cruellest of the cruel; they were cannibals, and to my bitter shame I saw them again on both great rivers, the river they call the Nile and the river they call the Congo. From Ujiji the slaves were driven all the way across country to Bagamoyo; on the Nile, they were taken north by boat to a place called Khartoum, which I would see with my own eyes on the second journey, and from there to a place called Cairo, which I also saw, and from then on to every part of the world.

'These cannibals, these merchants of death, came when the wind blew in their favour. That cursed wind carried their fleet of ships south, reuniting them with the hunters they had left in groups living in camps along the banks of the Nile. And in the months when the wind wasn't favourable, these groups went hunting and rounded up their prey in their stockades, where they held them captive and waited to be able to move them north by ship. If they couldn't find anybody, if the inhabitants of the villages hid or the chiefs were not prepared to sell them prisoners or villagers in disfavour, they rounded up the village's cattle and blackmailed the elders: either they gave them slaves and the cattle would be returned, or they starved. Then the elders were forced to attack neighbouring villages.

'That is how those bands went raiding, and when the wind gave them its cursed help, the stockades at a place called Gondokoro were full of people who had suffered their first death. If there is one place on this earth that terrifies me, that fills me with a dread that torments me by day and tortures me at night, it is there, that place called Gondokoro, a place that knows neither mercy nor pity. The only women in Gondokoro were sick women selling their bodies, tattered sponges to mop up men's lusts. The only children in Gondokoro were herded together and locked up. Gondokoro was a place of death for everyone. For the people who lived there as much as foreigners, for Muslims as much as Christians. Even the lemon trees of Gondokoro had died. They had stood in two rows, planted by men with the cross on their chest from the land of the Germans. They had built a house for their God, and planted gardens for their health, and laid out a cemetery . . .'

'A cemetery! The madmen.'

'A handful of them lay close together in the graves behind the lemon garden. They hadn't been able to convince a single person about their religion. Everything they had built had fallen into ruins, and there was not a single person in Gondokoro who proclaimed his faith in the cross, but far too many to count who had been enslaved by drink.'

'Not one Christian? There, you see what a weak religion it is.'

'Perhaps, perhaps the religion of the men with the cross on their chest is weak, or perhaps people were satisfied with their forefathers' religion.'

'The true faith just had to reach them.'

'It had reached them. The true faith resided in the heart of the slave traders, the cannibals: it was brought by the same wind and it kept silent when they stole people's lives, like a father who turns a blind eye to his son's crimes because he is his son. But what is justice worth if it is not also – no, if it is not first applied to your own family? Our brothers in Islam were worse than the Devil. They wrought havoc again and again, and if a village defended itself, if it fought them and lost – because they had matchlocks that spread death faster than any spear – if everything was in upheaval and their trade in danger, then they took prisoners, hordes of prisoners, and bound their hands and feet, not to sell them, but to drive them over a cliff from the top of a waterfall. That would have been bad enough, if their prisoners had been shattered on the rocks and drowned, but this river was full of crocodiles, so they were torn to pieces as they floated on the surface, their broken bodies easy prey for the crocodiles, and the news of their death spread over the country as fast as a plague of locusts . . . And if the slave traders killed anyone in the fighting, they cut off his hand to steal his copper bracelets. They threw the bodies on a heap a good distance from their camp and next morning all that was left of the dead were bones.'

'Vultures!'

'I've heard the vultures start with the eyes . . .'

'Is this something we want to know?'

'Then they pick at the inner thigh, then the flesh under the arms and finally the rest of the corpse.'

'Are people who do such things human?'

'You know only another person can call you human, and I have never met anyone who called them that. But people who do not know them, who do not know them from their own experience, who are completely ignorant about them and do not think – they would call them brothers in Islam.'

'One of these brothers once took all the men of a village prisoner to get the ivory they had hidden. The elders and the women gave in and bought their husbands' freedom with all the tusks they had, but one of the men was poor, his family hardly had anything, so they could not offer anything for his freedom. The slave trader cut off the man's nose, his hands, his tongue and part of his manhood and tied them together and hung them round his neck like a necklace and sent him back to his village.'

'Did you see that with your own eyes, Baba Ishmael?'

'No.'

'So perhaps that story isn't true?'

'Do you think I could have invented a story like that? I saw the man with my own eyes, and I swear that his nose, his hands and his tongue hadn't grown back.'

'I am going to tell you what I saw, although it is painful to talk about and painful to hear. If I cannot forget it, then at least I can tell it. We were camped next to the slave traders; the wazungu had no scruples about seeking to be near the Devil. In the night we heard a shot, and the next morning we found out that someone had stolen into the camp, the father of one of the young girls who had been kidnapped. He had come to see his child again, and when the guard noticed him, his daughter had already wrapped her arms round his neck and both of them were crying. The guard dragged the man to the nearest tree, tied him to the trunk and shot him. Next morning I had to go into the slave trader's camp with Bwana Speke; he needed me to translate, there was some information he wanted. Before we saw the men, we saw the possessions that had been stolen from them: pots, drums, baskets, tools, knives, pipes, all scattered on the ground as if the slave traders didn't know what to do with them. The first person I saw was a young man who held up his arm even though the manacles cut into his flesh. He kept it up to lessen the pressure of the iron collar, and he reminded me of a bird trying to raise its broken wing again and again.

'There were many others like him, but when I looked at him more closely, I didn't just see a young man I didn't know crouching on the ground, I saw myself, at the end of my first life, I saw in this boy's face the boy that had died in me, and the scars on my wrists and neck suddenly started burning. I didn't want to see any more prisoners, so I kept my eyes lowered. But what a fool I was to think I could escape by making myself blind. I may not have been able to see but I couldn't close my nostrils to the awful stink, the fumes of people who weren't allowed to go down to the water, who couldn't relieve them-selves behind the termite mounds, who weren't given anything to eat but had to dig in the forests for food. That was the job of the women prisoners, and they happened to be driven back into the camp just as we were standing there trying not to see or smell anything. They had dug up roots, picked wild bananas, and what they brought was thrown to the others, chained up in the rancid fog of their survival. The food was all unpeeled and uncooked, as pitiful as the women who had dug it out of the earth and picked it off the bushes, but the prisoners threw themselves on it all the same, crawling across the ground, fighting each other for those raw roots and green bananas and letting out shrill screams as the collars and manacles and chains dug even deeper into their flesh.

'Suddenly the slave trader we had come to see was at our side, and after the customary greetings for which Bwana Speke did not need my help, a conversation began which I could not follow very well. I didn't understand what Bwana Speke was saying and I could see from the slave trader's face that he didn't understand what I was saying either: his face roamed through a long valley of astonishment. Bwana Speke started to speak louder, his words spoke of a conviction a huge ditch separated me from; his speech was a stream irrigating other men's fields.

'"Do you see these men?" I heard myself saying to the slave trader. "They need to drink just like you. What would it cost you to give them a tub of water?"

'His face darkened. "You gnome," he yelled, "do you think anybody listens to you if you're not translating for the mzungu? You are nothing, and if you don't shut up, I'll put a nice tight collar round your neck and throw you in with the others."

'His face distorted like soapstone and froze in a look of contempt. He turned to Bwana Speke and smiled a hideous smile to which there was only one answer: I had to scratch all the teeth out of that smile. I didn't think. The dagger was in my hand, my arm went up, I didn't hear anything, didn't see anything; Bwana Speke told me afterwards I roared like a buffalo when it's shot, and the look of contempt on the slave trader's face shattered as if the soapstone had fallen on hard rock. He was defenceless, as defenceless as anyone against the un-expected. I don't know if I would have wounded him or killed him, and I will never know, because Bwana Speke grabbed me by the shoulders, his long arms wrapped around me and he whispered "Shanti, shanti" in my ear, the word banyans use to wish each other peace. I couldn't stand it and I would have turned my dagger against him too but he was too strong, he was amazingly strong and my rage dashed itself against his strength, then slowly ebbed away. And while he was still hold-ing me, the slave trader jerked into movement, gesturing furi-ously to Bwana Speke that he wanted to give me a whipping to punish me, but Bwana Speke shook his head and uttered the only word he knew in the languages of slave-taking, Arab and Kiswahili. In a loud, calm voice, he said "*Hapana*" and then shouted a "*La!*" that whirled through the air and divided off everything that had happened from the rest of the day. He dragged me away with him and I saw, as I turned . . . I saw the people chained to the stakes again and I noticed they had stopped fighting over the roots, they were all looking at me in silence, and I could not see what their looks were saying, whether they approved of what I had done or whether they despised me. I only knew they were looks I would never forget. I wished I did not have eyes.'

He has to face it: he can't go anywhere in a leaking canoe; he isn't even sure he could hold on tight enough to stop himself falling overboard. He is lying in a hut on a camp bed, having taken a double dose of his secret medicine, ether mixed with brandy. The air of heaven. It calms his nerves, his nascent hys-teria, the convulsive vomiting. Speke brings him news of the outside world when he comes back from swimming in the lake or going to the market. 'My sunglasses, my grey French sun-glasses brought the whole place to a standstill,' he reports. 'I had to take them off before I could get out of there.' He is in a good mood, recovered. His job is to find them a boat so they can explore the lake for a river – the Ruzisi river – somewhere on the northern tip. They have to find out whether the Ruzisi flows in or out of the lake. To that end, Speke is now going to have to cross the lake with just Bombay. There's an Arab on an island close to the opposite shore, according to Snay bin Amir, who has a seaworthy dhow. 'I'll see to it, Dick.'

Speke leaves the hut, and instead of returning after a few days, he is gone for a month, four endless weeks in which he sees to nothing – nothing, that monstrous failure. If only Burton could move a little. Cold nights follow blazing days, cold, damp nights; he has rashes all over his legs, his arms. When he looks at his body, he hates himself. He has to stay here lying on this camp bed as surety. Of the two of them, one has to be sacrificed so that the other may be set free. It's harder for him to drink than it is to form a coherent thought: his mouth is full of ulcers. Eating is impossible.

The juice of my dreams, give me a little of the juice of my dreams. Pass me my flask. Where are you? Are you going to refuse me the soma that relieves all pain? A double dose, there, that's for you: pain is a letter of indulgence. Run away. Be caught. Over and over again. Why not turn round, go to meet it?

He leans into the pain, lets himself fall headlong into it.

Love thy enemy. Be grateful you are being slit open; embrace your pain. Let the flames that devour you become the flames that caress you.

He dissolves, dissolves into the arms of three beautiful women, laughter in their amber eyes, who look like the dancers on the relief of an Indian temple, which he had once discovered in a village that had produced nothing else save those three visions of pure promise. They move with sublime deliberateness; he circles around their eyes, around his yearning, each of their movements an injunction, summoning men back to the barracks of their inadequacy. He doesn't dare . . .

They break out in superior smiles: they know more than he does. Bronze melts over their skin as, holding his present in their hands, his offering of tobacco, they invite him to follow them and shrug off the cloth gathered at their hips. They are even stronger naked; they take him with them to a sheltered spot they know, a soft hiding place, and lay him down. Their fingers glide from one button to the next. The first hand that touches his skin caresses his chest as circumspectly as dawn: it feels like cool spring water he can drink; the second hand touching him massages his excitement; the third feels its way to his groans, no traps, no hesitations. He will surrender; he will feed on the sunset. He is at their mercy. He is no match for them. They want more, and he has nothing to give. He hasn't the courage to die.

He sees himself in front of a curtain. He is paddling with elegant, powerful strokes but he is going nowhere. On the other side of the curtain sit the spectators; they see the man's shadow, a freakishly huge shadow of a man paddling, and they're thrilled, but he is the only one who notices he isn't getting any closer to the mouth of the river. Rain pours down the curtain, dividing his shadow into strips; the man carries on paddling; the strips peel away from the curtain. He paddles northwards along the coast, and gradually he sees the audience and they see him in a village only two days from the river mouth. They are waiting for an explanation, but he cannot speak, he has ulcers on his tongue, so they stand up and tear away the curtain and look at the little man sitting in a canoe. Then they all open their mouths in unison and say matter-of-factly, in passing, as if they were shop assistants answering an enquiry about a price: 'It flows into the lake. It was all a misunderstanding. It doesn't flow out. You were misled. Anyway, no matter: the performance is over now.'

The river flows into the sea. Burton lies on his camp bed; the rain falls; everything gets wet – the guns are rusting, the flour and grain are soaked. The canoe must stink of their excrement; they must be having to sleep in the mud. Speke is going to come back with good news. No, he isn't. Burton lies in a puddle of disappointment. He hasn't the courage to die with dignity.

400

'What I still haven't understood, Baba Sidi, is why it was so important for them to know how big the lake was and which rivers fed it and which flowed out of it.'

'Because there is a river called the Nile, a vast river: I have seen it just before it joins the sea in the country they call Egypt, and I tell you it is as broad as the sea that divides our island from the mainland.'

'The wazungu wanted to know where this river came from?'

'Why was that so difficult? Why didn't they just travel up it?'

'They tried but it split into two rivers. They followed one, which they called the Blue Nile, to its source, but they couldn't travel up the other, which they called the White Nile, because swamps and waterfalls blocked the way. They had to find another route to the source. When the wazungu reached the great lake, they were still far from reaching their goal because in Kazeh they had heard there were two great lakes, so the Nile could flow out of Lake Ujiji, or out of the other great lake, or even out of neither of them. That is why Bwana Speke was meant to get hold of a dhow so we could sail the lake, a dhow belonging to a merchant called Sheikh Hamed on the other side of the lake. The Arabs in Kazeh had told us about it, but Bwana Speke was not the man to persuade a conceited, self-satisfied Arab to give up his only dhow for a month. Bwana Burton might have managed it but, as you know, death was holding him hostage. At first, when the merchant gave us a warm welcome, we were in good spirits; the dhow was not there, but we waited confidently for it to come back. But it turned out that our patience wore different clothes: Bwana Speke's was clad in rough wool that itched constantly, whereas mine was draped in pure silk. There was not much to do on the little island where the Arab lived apart from chat and gossip: the dhow was a long time coming, the conversations stretched out peacefully under the Arab merchant's wide veranda, and the less Bwana Speke understood, the more he hated them. One day he couldn't control himself any longer. He told me how revolting he found everything on the island, how filthy the people were, lying around like swine, as lifeless as piglets basking in the sunshine. He said that and more of the same, not noticing how he wounded me. I anticipated the worst; the coarse wool was rubbing the skin of his patience raw. After a while the dhow came back, gliding white-sailed along the channel between the island and mainland, and Bwana Speke seemed encouraged. For a moment, I hoped everything would turn out well, that after the dhow had been unloaded – far too slowly for Bwana Speke's liking, of course – we would set off straight away: one last conversation with Sheikh Hamed, hand over the rolls of cloth, eat a farewell meal and then hoist those large white sails and turn our backs on that island of chitter-chatter. That's how Bwana Speke imagined it: I saw it in his face, which was like a monsoon sky when a splinter of sun finally breaks through. But a man would do better to listen to a child's advice than to his own hopes. Sheikh Hamed told us the dhow was ours to take, but that he could not give us the crew to go with it; he needed them for another job. He had already started looking all over for another crew but, as we could imagine, it was very difficult in those parts to find someone who could sail a dhow. That was the moment I had dreaded, the moment Bwana Speke could not stand the chafing of his impatience any more. His face disappeared in a whirlwind of shouts and reproaches; he spat on his host's dignity, and although the Arab calmly denied any hidden motives, although he emphatically declared that we would soon be able to come to an agreement because he only expected what his guest would freely give, I realised how much harder our task had become. The next morning the Arab refused to say another word on the matter; he could give us the dhow and crew in three months when he had returned from his next trading trip. We should have done something dramatic, fattened up our generosity, but Bwana Speke was not a person to listen to advice from anyone else and so, ignoring my suggestion to offer the Arab twice as much money, he decided to leave the island.

'Destiny had struck us its blow; eh, there was no need for the storm that suddenly overtook us when we were in the middle of the lake, a storm that would have swallowed us up if we had not been washed onto an island where we waited it out, Bwana Speke in his tent, the others wrapped in tarpaulins. I was allowed to shelter in his tent with him. The storm grew stronger, ripping part of the canvas away from its pegs, and all we could do was wait. And when the storm dropped, Bwana Speke lit a candle to check if everything was all right and suddenly there were beetles everywhere, little black beetles. Bwana Speke should have given up on sleep that night or spent it in the canoe, like me, since there was no hope of getting all the beetles out of that tent, there was no way he could brush all the beetles off his clothes. But he fell asleep and one of the beetles crawled into his ear, and he woke up feeling a rabbit was digging a hole in his eardrum.

'"I couldn't stand it, I couldn't stand it," Bwana Speke told me the next morning. "Bats were flapping in my brain, their wings were bigger than my head, flap flap flap; if I could just have caught them, I would have crushed them with my bare hands. I begged them to leave me in peace, I begged God, but I did not know how to get into my head, Sidi, there was no way into my head. I wanted to pour hot oil in my ear but I couldn't make a fire, everything was wet. I beat my head with my fists, but the flapping wouldn't stop. It was worse than any pain: I could have cut off my hand but I still wouldn't have been able to forget the flapping. I couldn't think of anything else, hear anything else, feel anything else. I took a knife and pushed the tip of it into my ear. I knew I had to be careful but my hands were trembling and I didn't have any patience; there was a crunching sound, then pain, a sharp flash of pain like a scream. The flapping stopped. I dropped the knife and lay on the ground, and at that moment I was more afraid than I have ever been in my life, I was terrified I would hear the flapping again, that it would come back. But it had gone. My ear felt wet; I touched it and I felt blood on my fingers, but the flapping wasn't there any more."

'"Why didn't you call for help?" I asked.

'"What would you have done, Sidi, how could you have helped?"

'"I would have held the candle close to your ear; the light of the candle drew the beetle to your tent and I would have drawn it out with the same light. It would have crawled out by itself." That's what I told him. But instead he had wounded his ear, wounded it very badly . . .'

'Wait, what did that stupid man say when you told him a better thing to have done?'

'Nothing. He just stared at me with a strange expression I didn't understand. Things got worse. Inflammation set in, the ear became full of pus, Bwana Speke's face became contorted and his whole neck was covered with boils. He couldn't chew; I had to make him soup and spoon it into his mouth, like a little child. He was almost deaf in that ear. A hole ate its way through to his nostril, and when he blew his nose, his ear made a squelchy, popping sound which made us laugh, and that made him even more annoyed. Months later a bit of the beetle came out in some earwax. From the other ear!'

'No!'

'Baba Sidi, we know we've reached the part of the evening where you have your fun with us, but this is too much. Are you saying the dead beetle went through his whole head and came out the other side?'

'There are stranger things than that.'

'Of course, but whether we believe a lie doesn't depend simply on its size.'

'The journey back to Ujiji was very hard. Bwana Burton had escaped death, something very difficult, and so he expected we would have performed our task, which seemed much easier. He was disgusted; Bwana Speke was crestfallen. They did not speak for several days and then they decided to go and explore the lake anyway. So we got back in the canoes and travelled for thirty-three days just to hear from reliable sources that the Ruzisi flowed into the lake. And if one of us believed that was the end of our disappointments, our return to Ujiji taught him otherwise, because in the thirty-three days we were away, the loyal, kind-hearted Said bin Salim . . .'

'The one you said would have sold his own mother?'

'Exactly, him . . . He had eventually come to the conclusion that the wazungu must be dead, so no one would blame him if he sold most of their supplies. How were we going to get back to Kazeh without any food or anything to barter? Were we going to have to beg, rob? There was nothing to be done. The more we thought about it, the clearer our hopelessness became, until it was banished in an instant, or rather blown apart by the volley of gunfire that, as usual, greeted the arrival of the caravan. Eh, there it was, the caravan bringing the supplies Bwana Burton had asked for a month before. It didn't have the right ammunition, but at least there was enough cloth for us to get food for the journey back to Kazeh.'

They take another route on their way back. The Malagarasi swamps are something you only subject yourself to once. The idyll, Burton thinks, is a cup with a dirty rim. Tea in the cup, chicken broth in the saucer, specks on the tip of your tongue. Time is bitter, he thinks, and resolves to give up thinking, at least until they reach Kazeh. 'Did you see that mosquito?' Speke calls over. 'It was enormous, absolutely enormous, you've never seen such an enormous mosquito in your life.' This must be very poor country for Speke to be bothering himself about mosquitoes. At the edge of the path a hollowed-out tree with a mouth carved into its trunk, lips gaping in an oval scream, marks the entrance to a village. What strange sights are hiding under those freshly cut roofs? The first man they meet walks with a stick, for self-explanatory reasons; his affliction, his bad leg, has skin wrinkled like bark, you can't see the knee . . . my God, it is like an elephant's leg, while his right one is like a human leg. Look at him, he's only young, his face looks healthy, perfectly sound, not a trace of bitterness despite that misshapen leg he has to drag around that has made him the village pariah – who'd want to clap eyes on anything as repulsive as that? The next villager has a similar condition, although his leg is even more deformed. Only the toes have human proportions; the swelling starts at the arch; the skin is thick and infected, torn in places, burst in others. The third villager takes their breath away: he walks on a pair of elephant's legs, while his torso is brutally emaciated – how could it be anything else when his legs are so engorged? They're all the same, he suddenly realises, all the inhabitants of this village who sit in front of their huts or limp past them without a greeting. He sees the signs wherever he looks: elbows submerged in flesh; upper arms like yielding pumpkins; forearms hanging from the bone like gourds full of water; swollen left breasts almost reaching to the thigh; folds of flesh sliding away from the right breast down the left leg, or the other way round. Every permutation of deformity gathers in this village; the sickness, the diabolic, turned outwards, as if it were high tide inside their bodies.

He sees a man in a headdress, the only person sitting on a stool, who is surrounded by men and women squatting in the sand. That must be the p'hazi. He has a serene expression on his face and is saying something incomprehensible. He makes no attempt to cover himself up: his testicles are as big as papayas, his left thigh hangs down like an udder fit to burst, his right thigh is covered with ulcers that look like the worms winding around inside his body, and his leg ends in a club foot, without toes or heel.

I see, Burton thinks, that's the hierarchical principle: in this village the one with the biggest scrotum is the chief. He would like to stop and talk to these people, tell them, 'The gods love jokes. Sometimes they make mistakes, even with their own sons. You don't know Ganesh, but I'd like to tell you about him, if I may. His situation is not unrelated to yours.' But Burton is carried along by his footsteps, by the unruffled advance of the caravan as if the others haven't seen anything, haven't noticed that even the mules have thick, swollen haunches as though they have been crossed with elephants. A question nags away at him like a grain of sand in his shoe; something disturbed him when he was looking at the p'hazi . . . the penis, that's it, where was his penis? He says out loud: 'I didn't see his penis.' And Speke, who is walking next to him – how long has he been there? – replies: 'We don't need to know that.'

SIDI MUBARAK BOMBAY

'Do you feel it getting cold too, my friends? It is the season, of course, but it is more than just that. It is as if the cold is rising up from this stone and working its way into my body. There are evenings when I can't get warm, no matter how many blankets Hamid's mother drapes around my shoulders. The cold doesn't just cling to my flesh, no, it forces its way into my bones. No one told me how cold bones can get, how cold your knees and your skull can turn until you're so cold, you feel you're a fish lying frozen at the bottom of the sea that can only move its mouth, and in the end your tongue will become bone too.'

'Oh now you are exaggerating, Baba Sidi. Your tongue's a long way from going numb.'

'Even the unimaginable will happen to us one day.'

'We'll look forward to it.'

'And in the meantime, we'll carry on listening to you.'

'And I'll go on talking, don't you worry, don't go getting up any false hopes, although sometimes I suspect my words have outpaced my steps, that my stories of what happened have hidden the things that happened in their shadow. It reminds me of a boy in my first life, when I was little, who tried to catch my shadow. He told me to stand still and he scrabbled in the ground with his little hands where my shadow fell and just when he thought he had finished, he saw my shadow had moved. So then he started digging again, and he followed every movement of my shadow until his strength and my patience ran out. Then we took a step back to look at the shadow he had caught and all we could see was a big shapeless hole. It didn't look like any of my shadows. That made him sad, so I suggested we go and pick some fruit. I have never forgotten that boy; he wasn't one of the ones the Arabs caught at the death of my first life, and I often wonder about the shadows he cast in his life. When I dream, I dream of meeting that boy again, both of us as old men, and asking him to tell me everything about himself. Then I would see before me in flesh and blood the life that was stolen from me, the life lived by the man who couldn't catch my shadow, and who never will, because I never cast another shadow in my real life. Through him, I would see all the shadows I might have cast.

'It is a beautiful dream and an ugly dream, like all my dreams. They are like dishes cooked by two women – one who has been loved, and one who has been left – dishes as sweet as sugar and as sour as the pods of a baobab growing in a grave-yard. It's like another dream I cannot shake off, the dream of the lake and the heron, which is not a dream in fact, but the unmoving shadow of a memory. A memory of the second lake, and a beautiful bird. The second lake existed: eh, it was really there, just as the Arabs in Kazeh had told us it would be, and Bwana Speke and myself and a few porters reached this lake after half a month's march. Bwana Burton had stayed in Kazeh, perhaps because of his illness, and perhaps also because he preferred the Arabs' company to that of Bwana Speke. We stood on a little hill and there it was before us, the second great lake, and we felt less exhausted and less despairing and less excited than on the day we had seen the first great lake. All of us except Bwana Speke, that is, who suddenly seemed transformed. Our first sight of it told us that it was bigger than any other lake we knew, or Bwana Speke knew, and bigger than the first lake. We were standing on the bank, marvelling at the water that had no end, when there was a rustling near us and a heron flew out of the reeds, ponderously slapping its wings as if they had gone to sleep, a slender bird that didn't know the law that no animal could fly or run past Bwana Speke unpunished. The heron rose into the air before our eyes, it picked up speed, confidently gliding over us, grey, white and brown, its beak like the needle of a compass. Bwana Speke was thrilled, we could see that. His heart was only rarely allowed to show itself on his face; he hid it the way some men hide their wives, but there on that bank it cast off all its veils. 'This is what we've been searching for,' he said solemnly, and he stretched out his hand as if he wanted to lay it on the lake. He was truly happy, and we carried on looking up at the heron, which, for reasons that are forever carved in uncertainty, was wheeling above us, right above our heads, and then a shot rang out, just one shot, of course, and the heron fell like a stone. Bwana Speke shouted with delight, and waved his rifle like a gourd and did a little dance, the wazungu's misunderstanding of a dance, and shouted in triumph: 'I've reached our goal, I've reached our goal.' None of us watched the heron fall, we didn't want to bring disaster on ourselves. We stared at Bwana Speke, not knowing why he seemed transformed, why the second lake was better than the first lake and why a heron had to die to share Bwana Speke's joy.'

'Assalaamu Alaikum Wa Rahmatullahi Wa Barakatuhu.'

'Waleikum is salaam.'

'How goes it, brothers?'

'Thanks be to God, thanks be to God.'

'Come and sit with us, Imam Muhtaram, we are listening to Baba Sidi's stories, and this evening, I can tell you, they're rewarding our attention.'

'Don't worry, the stories don't bite.'

'I am not afraid for myself.'

'You won't regret it.'

'Just for a little while; the night is still young.'

'We always think the night is young, until it's suddenly over.'

'You must rest a little, Imam Muhtaram. Sit here on this baraza, it will do you good.'

'We will see what it does me. Well, all right, I will keep you company for a while.'

'We have just heard how Baba Sidi reached a lake almost as big as the sea.'

'God's miracles are manifold.'

'And how a heron was shot – you forgot to say that, Baba Quddus. It is as much a part of the story as the lake, that heron that fell like a comet. Bwana Speke was pleased, and his good humour increased after he had boiled some water and stared at his timepiece and noted down all sorts of numbers – since we had set off without Bwana Burton, he had become friends with the notebook too.

'"Do you know what we're looking at, Sidi?" he asked.

'"No, Sahib," I said.

'"We are looking at the sources of the river called the Nile. Somewhere to the north the mighty Nile must flow out of this lake." It is amazing how Bwana Speke could have known that.'

'He guessed.'

'Yes, of course he guessed. After all, he hadn't seen the sources, but he guessed wisely, because on our second journey his hunch proved correct. We both stood at the other end of this great lake and saw how the river flowed out of it.'

'The Nile?'

'We didn't know that then, not for certain. But another mzungu followed the river, and when I went on my third journey, I heard the mystery was solved, and that everyone now knew the Nile flows out of the second big lake.'

'So he was right.'

'Bwana Speke was right and also he wasn't. A river pours out of this lake, and it is the river they call the Nile, certainly, but there are also rivers that flow into the second lake, so a friend of argument could say that every one of these rivers has a source and that these sources are the source of the Nile, because the water that pours into the second great lake feeds the river they call the Nile. Bwana Speke wanted to explore the lake immediately. He wanted to recruit the man who had told us about the far end as a guide, buy his boat and then sail round the lake; the trip would have taken months. I begged him to think of our meagre supplies, the tired and reluctant porters, Bwana Burton waiting for us in Kazeh. "You don't understand," he said, his face glowing. "If I solve the question of the source beyond all doubt, the prize is mine. I will be the one who has solved the greatest of all riddles." And then, he meant, I won't have to share the fame with Bwana Burton.'

'Oh, the excessiveness of man.'

'Especially the wazungu's.'

'Of us all! It is excessive to think of yourself as an exception.'

'I managed to talk him out of it, mainly by assuring him the porters would all run away if we didn't soon return to Kazeh. But before we left the second great lake, he wanted to celebrate his triumph with a fitting ceremony. He called us together and asked us to get into the water with him until we were standing up to our knees in the waves – don't look amazed, that lake is so big it has waves, and when there is a storm, the man who knew the other bank told us, the waves become bigger than houses and anyone out in his boat is lost. "Go deeper into the water," Bwana Speke said, "deep enough to put your heads under, and when your whole body is under water, come out, shave each other's heads and then bathe in this holy water again."'

'Holy? What holy water?'

'That is what he said. I refused. "None of us can swim," I told him.

'"Don't be afraid," he told me. "Hold onto each other, I will watch out for you."

'I translated his scheme to the porters.

'"My hair," one of them cried, "what does the mzungu want with my hair?"

'"And what's he paying for it?" asked another.

'"We have to take him to a mganga quickly," said a third, "he's got more than just a beetle in his head."

'I explained to Bwana Speke that the porters refused to sacrifice their hair and dive into the water.

'"But it is such a beautiful ceremony," he implored me, "you must know it from India, Sidi, the sacred bath in holy waters."

'"You don't bathe in Zamzam water."

'"Of course not, but the banyan believe many rivers are sacred, and instead of praying they bathe in them."

'"But we're not in India," I said, "and how do we know this water is sacred?" I told Bwana Speke.

'"It is the source of the Nile," he said, "how could it not be sacred?"

'"Can we just decide which water is sacred?" I asked.

'"How do you think such ceremonies came about in the first place?" he answered. "Someone must have said something one day, done something, then others believed him and imitated him and now we tremble in awe before the tradition."'

'He has insulted our Prophet, may God grant Him peace.'

'Don't get excited, Imam Muhtaram.'

'I'm sorry? What are you saying? This blasphemer insults . . .'

'It was a long time ago.'

'Maybe Baba Sidi reported his words wrong.'

'He didn't insult the Prophet.'

'What? You repeated his words yourself.'

'As far as I am aware, he did not know the Prophet. I mean, I am sure he had heard of Him, he knew a little about al-Islam, but his knowledge had no roots. He just wanted to do something solemn at that moment, something that seemed impressive, something that corresponded to the deep feelings his discovery had awakened in him. He wanted to celebrate and he didn't know how we could celebrate together, how we should honour the moment.'

'I don't understand what it is you find to enjoy in these stories, night after night, that gives so much pleasure you neglect
your families. Dead herons, shaved heads, an unbeliever out of
whose mouth the Devil speaks.'

'We are learning about the world, Imam. What harm can
there be in that?'

'I think the imam follows the wise precept: the man who
knows nothing doubts nothing.'

'Are you trying to insult your imam as well now?'

'Are you going to object to everything that doesn't come out
of your own mouth?'

'Devote yourself to reading the Glorious Qur'an instead.
You'll find plenty of stories there, and they are far older, and of
eternal significance. I will now take my leave, my brothers.
Assalaamu alaikum.'

'*Waleikum is salaam*, Imam Muhtaram.'

'*Waleikum is salaam*.'

'He didn't stay long.'

'Longer than Baba Sidi in the mosque.'

'Your ways will never meet, you two.'

'Perhaps in the next world.'

'Tell me, my brothers, I've always wondered: does one read
the Glorious Qur'an in heaven too? Or is it only a guide to get
there?'

'You should have asked the imam.'

'I thought about it too late.'

'It's better that way.'

'What is the second great lake called, by the way?'

'Nyanza. That's what the man who knew the other bank
told us. But Bwana Speke wasn't satisfied with that name; he
wanted another. Every place he saw on this trip, the short trip
we took without Bwana Burton, he immediately gave a name,
as if he were giving gifts to the children of poor families. The
minute he decided on a name, he ordered me to tell the porters.
I would pass on the name to them, and they were amazed by
this custom. They couldn't make sense of it: perhaps he can

only remember what he has named himself, one of them suggested. Before Bwana Speke knew what the other shore of a lake or the other side of a hill or the other end of a valley looked like, he had already given it a name. While we were still gasping for breath after the steep climb, he called the hill on which we got our first sight of the second great lake Somerset. The little bay at our feet he called Jordan; one of the rocks that stretched out into the water became Burton Point and part of the lake Speke Channel. A small group of islands was given the name the Bengal Archipelago and the lake itself, this lake that seemed as broad as the sea, in a solemn voice, as if he was speaking in a council of the elders, he named Victoria. The wazungu still call this water Victoria, at least they did on my last journey, and now they have raised their flag over our port, who knows, perhaps it will be called after one of their women for years to come. Most of the wazungu are proud of this name because they think the lake is named in honour of their queen, but Bwana Speke told me a little later that evening that it was a happy chance: his mother had the same name as the queen of his country and so he could dedicate the lake he had discovered to his mother without fear of being accused of anything inappropriate.

'"But Sahib," I said, "the lake already has a name. The lake is called Nyanza."

'"Nonsense," cried Bwana Speke, and I felt the anger coming to a boil in him, "how can it have a name? I only discovered it today. Don't you understand, Sidi, it hasn't existed on maps until now?"

'His words bewildered me. I thought about them for a long time, and finally reached the conclusion that it couldn't do any harm if the lakes and mountains and rivers had a number of names, names from different mouths for different ears that spoke of different features and different hopes. But there was one thing I hadn't counted on; I had sown too close to the river and overlooked the danger of flooding, as they say. The wazungu would only accept one name for everything: they are stubborn as mules, and won't tolerate the different names a place can have.

'When we returned to Kazeh, where Bwana Burton was waiting for us, and talked about the lake to the Arabs there, Bwana Speke insisted on calling it Lake Victoria. I had to explain to the Arabs that Bwana Speke said Victoria but meant Nyanza, at which one of the Arabs said with a sharp tongue, "Why doesn't the mzungu say what he means? Does he want to hide something?" As always when things got difficult, Bwana Burton stepped in, soothing the waters with his Arabic that flowed from his mouth like melted butter.

'But there were also times, I won't hide this from you, when Bwana Speke asked me to tell him the local names so he could write them in tiny letters next to the names he had given the places. I found out the names and told him: Nyanza for the great lake, and Ukerewe for the islands on the great lake . . . And so his book would have contained his invented names and the traditional names side by side if we had not been invited to a feast where we drank banana beer. We drank so much banana beer, the taste was still sticking to my tongue days later, and the meat broth and sweet potatoes and everything else I ate tasted of banana beer. You know I don't drink but it was the only thing that could revive us. We had been invited by the men of the village; they had brewed the beer in our honour, and all the porters drank with me. We didn't hold back that evening: we licked our wounds and cursed the journey and the wazungu at the tops of our voices. Then another guest of the village told us about a man living on the other shore of the lake who called the lake Lolwe. When we asked him what that meant, he said it was the name of a giant who was so big he made a lake every time he relieved himself – a little lake or a medium lake as the case may be, and one night he let fly so much water, more than ever before, that the next morning people were staring at a lake without banks.'

'He had been drinking banana beer.'

'Eh, too much banana beer, far too much. It was a fine story and what we thought was a wonderful idea came out of it. Why not make up names for places like him and give them to the mzungu to take back to his country? We could give him names that would make fun of anyone who read them without them realising they were being made fun of – names like Great Emptying Of The Bladder for the lake on the bank of which we had drunk so much banana beer. It was a lovely idea and we got on with it immediately. We thought of names while we were drinking banana beer, and next morning our names found their way into Bwana Speke's book. "What do these people call this river?" he asked me, and I answered: "The people of the Wakerewe call this river Monkey's Tail Riddled With Lice." And when he asked me the name of a hill, I answered: "The people of the Wakerewe call this hill Rump Covered With Warts." And when he wanted to know if a gorge had a name, I told him: "The people of the Wakerewe call this gorge Where A Man Goes In And A Baby Comes Out." Don't give me such a horrified look, Baba Quddus, it was a crude joke, I know, but not as crude as the joke Bwana Speke permitted himself when he filled the whole world with his names. The reason I'm whispering is not because I am ashamed of this joke, it's because someone is watching on the first floor who doesn't like this joke either. Ah, now wait, I've remembered another one, the best: there were two hills that were alike and their name, I'm sure you've guessed, in the language of the people of the Wakerewe was The Flabby King's Tits. We were pleased with our jokes and forgot about them until the next journey, when Hamid, my firstborn, was old enough to walk. Bwana Speke showed me the maps he had had made in his country, and read me the names of the places we had seen together. I heard the name Victoria and the name Somerset, and then he showed me some small writing and said this was the names I had told him were used by the people who lived there. I asked him to read out some of them, and sure enough, even though he chewed up the words in his mouth, you could still understand them. He said: "Rump Covered With Warts" and "The Flabby King's Tits", and believe me, my brothers, I have never had so much trouble in my life controlling the laughter that was trying to burst out of me.'

'So if I went to the wazungu's country and bought one of these maps, I could read all of Baba Sidi's childish jokes?'

'Eh, yes, Baba Ali, but you've got to hurry. The wazungu are conscientious. Another wazungu may soon travel there, collecting fresh knowledge. Their maps are constantly redrawn, it is a favourite game of the wazungu . . . no, it's more than a game, people's pride depends on it, and in the end, Bwana Burton and Bwana Speke's friendship was dashed to pieces.'

'How is that possible?'

∾

A noise, like the prick of a needle. Then a crooked cry of pain grabs a whole octave by the throat. A pair of screams cut into the delicate skin of his sleep. At first he thinks the sound is coming from a dream edging into wakefulness, but then he becomes aware of the low sky of his tent and the tarpaulin walls close on all sides. The raw cries are coming from outside. He gets up, grabs his rifle, crawls out of the tent, but can't see where the danger lies. He can't make out anything in the sleepy dawn, until suddenly the sound bores into the back of his head; he swings his rifle round, ready to fire, but all he sees is a bird, an ugly bird that opens its beak and lets out the scream that stabbed his sleep. Burton feels uncontrollable rage at this tiny bird that has the effrontery to make so much noise. He grabs his gun by the barrel and swings it, but the bird can fly, and it flutters away, squawking indignantly, leaving Burton completely unsatisfied.

They had set out from Kazeh the day before on the last stage of their return. New porters had had to be recruited for the stretch to the coast. They stood before them, part of a new Nyamwezi crop brought in by Snay bin Amir, young men all spruce and impatient, overzealous, refreshingly innocent.

Some of them stood on one leg like the cranes on the Malagarasi, the soles of the suspended foot pressed against the other knee, their arms round their neighbours' necks, a nonchalant gesture that would barely last the first week, while others squatted on their heels, hugging their knees with both arms and looking expectantly at the expedition leader.

He had set off reluctantly. Kazeh had become an oasis again, and it is always hard to leave an oasis, to subject oneself to the Ugogo desert anew. He wasn't afraid; grim presentiments didn't plague him. It was worse than that. He already felt the pain that lay ahead, the torment. He didn't feel fear so much as disquiet he knew would be abiding; such knowledge is the curse of all return journeys. Especially because he couldn't look forward to their arrival with any pleasure. Speke was smitten by his clumsy, ignorant solution to the great mystery. His sketches, his cartographic speculations, couldn't contribute to any logical explanation. The water in his rivers flowed uphill; his lakes emptied in whatever direction he chose. It was laughable and yet – this was the disturbing suspicion that ruined the return journey – it was just possible that Speke might be right. It was possible that all the details were false but that the overall claim was right. The moment they set foot on British soil, the dispute between the two of them would escalate, fanned by public interest. His many enemies would be only too glad to seize on such an opportunity; the scope for conjecture would allow everyone staunchly to ally themselves with the side to which they felt bound. He couldn't stay in Kazeh, and the thought of going back to England, the only place in the world where he could not feel at home, was repugnant. Perfect conditions, he thought grimly, to set off into the desert again.

SIDI MUBARAK BOMBAY

'Bwana Burton doubted Bwana Speke's claim that the second great lake was the source of the river they call the Nile. Or if it was, he thought that that still had to be proved, and that proof was not established just by Bwana Speke setting eyes on a lake they already knew existed. While Bwana Speke and I were away, Bwana Burton had sketched his own maps in Kazeh based on information from Snay bin Amir and other Arabs, and when we got back, the wazungu compared the position of the lake and its outlines on their maps, and there were almost no differences between Bwana Burton's sketches and Bwana Speke's. So Bwana Burton said: "You exerted yourself for nothing, we knew the essential facts already."'

'Truly, there is no dagger as sharp as a man's tongue.'

'But after he had studied Bwana Speke's map more closely and listened to Bwana Speke's claim, Bwana Burton had to change his own map. You know that the size of the animal you kill always depends on the size of the animal your rival says he has killed. His map had to prove that the first great lake was the source of the river they call the Nile. One evening I went into his room in the house he and Bwana Speke lived in in Kazeh – I wanted to ask him something – and I saw him drawing. He seemed pleased to see me, and asked me a few questions about our short trip to the second great lake. Then he explained his map to me in detail, as if the truth needed my agreement. The names he read out were names like Changanyika and Nyanza, and he must have seen my surprise because he explained that he thought there was nothing more crazy than branding remote places in the heart of this land with English names. On his map, I could see not just these two lakes but also mountains, and I didn't understand everything he told me about them, except that they were mountains that none of us had seen, but he assumed they existed because his books talked about them. He called these mountains the Mountains of the Moon, and he had shunted them back and forth across his map until they stood in the way of Bwana Speke's claim that the second great lake was the source.'

'A behind can't sit on a horse and a donkey at the same time.'

'That's true, but when two people argue, both of them can be right.'

'Baba Sidi, my head has always been a layabed, and now I am getting old and this evening is too . . . the point is, I don't understand a word you're saying.'

'It's all right, Baba Burhan, he's just talking about two wazungu who shunt big mountains around as they please.'

'It's easy to move mountains one has never seen.'

'Bwana Burton had found one or two mistakes in Bwana Speke's maps; he had pointed them out to him, and Bwana Speke had changed his drawing. I saw them in his room; he made one of the lakes smaller, the other bigger, and moved the mountains further north. I was baffled because I couldn't understand why the wazungu, who in everything else were so conscientious, were so careless with these maps for which they had risked their lives. But when I discussed the wazungu's strange behaviour with the mganga, he told me the story of the mountains. They were three brothers who, to obey their father, the King of the Mountains, set off travelling through the world, and I understood what had remained hidden from me until then: the wazungu's maps were collections of fairy tales, and Bwana Speke and Bwana Burton were constantly changing their tales a little, as all good storytellers should.'

❧

Burton's open journal lists ten bouts of fever in the three months since they left Kazeh. Some evenings he is paralysed, others almost blind. It is no longer possible to keep the camp dry: the rain has been lashing them for days. When it breaks off for a moment, time seems to grow white wings that spread in the damp air until there are more termites than there are seconds. The nights keep getting colder. Even his nightmares are plagued by shivering fits.

Speke lies beside him, describing his agony. It helps him to put it into words, to gasp out the details between his fits of coughing and groaning. The rain splashes outside. He has been ill plenty of times before, but this breakdown is by far the worst. It started with a burning sensation, like a branding iron being pressed into his right breast. From there the pain spread in sharp, stabbing twinges to his heart, then to his spleen, where it concentrated for a while before attacking the upper part of his lungs and then settling in his liver.

'My liver! My liver!' Speke cries, then sinks back into a semi-conscious state.

Next morning he wakes from a nightmare in which a pack of tigers and other beasts harnessed with iron hooks had been dragging him over the ground. He sits up, clasping his sides, half stupefied by pain. 'Can I try something?' Bombay asks, and with Burton's agreement, he raises Speke's right arm and tells him to reach behind his head with his left arm to relieve the pressure of the lung on the liver. The excruciating pain diminishes. Burton looks admiringly at Bombay. The worst seems over until Speke suddenly has a relapse like an epileptic fit. Demons resume stripping the sinews from his body, chewing on them as if they were smoked meat. After the fit has passed, he lies rigid on his camp bed, his limbs wracked by cramps, his facial muscles drawn taut, his eyes glassy. He starts making a barking noise with a weird chopping movement of his mouth and tongue. He can hardly breathe. When his mind clears, he is convinced that he is close to death. He asks for pen and paper and, with a trembling hand, writes an incoherent letter of farewell to his mother and family. But his heart cannot give up. The scalding little irons gradually recede. Hours later, half asleep, Burton hears him murmur, 'The knives have been sheathed.'

SIDI MUBARAK BOMBAY

'Our suffering knew no bounds: barely had one pain worn off before another broke on us, barely had one burden been set down before another was loaded onto our backs, and I kept wondering how we endured it. How did the wazungu endure it when they came from a country where everything was different – the heat and the animals and even the sicknesses? It was only at the end of that first journey that I realised what I should have known from the beginning: without this suffering, the wazungu do not feel alive. Just before we reached the coast, I understood that they depend on suffering the way others depend on alcohol or khat or ganja. So it was no surprise when I saw the wazungu again, less than two monsoons later. Hamid had not been born by then. Bwana Speke came back to Zanzibar with a different partner this time – that was no surprise either – a silent man called Bwana Grant who made a dull replacement for Bwana Burton. Even the others, Bwana Stanley and Bwana Cameron, kept coming back, drawn to their own suffering; all of them did, except the ones who did not survive. They only had to get back on their feet and they were already planning their next journey. It did not have to be easier or more comfortable, the next one. Eh, far from it. They sought out more pain next time, they sailed even closer to death, like a fisherman who is not satisfied with surviving the reef but is compelled to try ever more impossible channels, channels where his boat can only be dashed to pieces.

'Bwana Burton was the worst of them all: he did not even want to interrupt his suffering; he did not even want to wait until he had returned to his country before setting out again. We had reached Zungomero, from where we knew it was only half a month more to the coast. We could already see our houses and families before us – those of us who had houses and families at least – they were just one last half a month's effort away . . . and then Bwana Burton told us we still had to find the route to Kilwa.

'"Which Kilwa?" I asked, because I was the only one who dared contradict him openly.

'"The old town in the south," he answered.

'"Is this you talking or the fever in you?" I asked. "If you have no desire to return, then you are a mystery to every other human being, and you will have to go the rest of the way alone because we all of us have only one goal."

'"You will do what I order you to," he cried, loud enough to sound as if it wanted to be a command, but his tone was full of despair. I looked around at the survivors, and at that moment we were all in perfect agreement: we would refuse immediately, without any discussion. Then the porters turned away, the Baluchis turned away, even Said bin Salim and Sidi Mubarak Bombay turned away from Bwana Burton, who was left alone, a madman who could not inflict his madness on anyone any more.'

꩜

The rain has stopped at last, leaving the earth sodden and heavy after days of constant downpour. He hears drumming – is that what it is? – a drumming he does not recognise, which sounds menacing amid the occasional report of raindrops bursting as they hit the ground. There's a hissing noise and then, before he can rush out of the tent, a sudden boom of something like thunder, which unnerves him all the more because he doesn't know what has caused it. Outside, in a darkness lit with incomprehensible sounds, before he can even look around to see what is happening, the ground is snatched away from under his feet. The earth lurches into movement. There's a roar as if the entire riverbank is collapsing. Burton is knocked over, and, lying on his side, his ribs bruised, his right leg sticking up in the air, he feels everything sliding. He scrabbles to his feet and tries to find something to hang on to, but his leg is a useless pump, a blunt anchor, and he keeps being dragged along in the grip of a monstrous force. A thought stamps itself on his mind: the camp, the whole blessed camp is going to be washed away. We're going to be buried under the mud. He screams: 'Jack! Jack!' Something heavy knocks him down again, pain boring into his right kidney, and rolls him over, his face jammed into the ground, his scream filling with mud, mud seething in his mouth like maggots. He tries to prop himself up on his arms but they plunge into thick dough. Something is pulling him under; he's going down; he's going to be buried alive – my God, it's not fair, it's not fair. His head bangs on a stone; he is knocked around, tossed up, spun around again, and then suddenly he feels air on his slimy, mud-caked face. He inhales; the air forces its way through one clogged nostril. He risks a cough, then shouts, 'Jack!' over and over, and then, 'Bombay!' In that whirling din, he can't hear a single human sound, not even a groan. Where are the others? That is his last thought before he tumbles into the water as if the slope has tipped him out.

He falls into another sort of coldness; he doesn't know which way is up or down, but surrounded by water, he feels a little calmer. The river is also moving, sweeping forward with the same determination but with less hysteria. He feels safer in it, and stretches his heavy limbs. His fear has gone. I can't drown, he thinks, as if all other threats have paled into insignificance now the danger of being buried alive in the mud is over. At times, the waves share a rhythm, like a choir in full crescendo; he can raise his head out of the water a little and look around, into inky, hopeless blackness. But then they tug at him, competing voices sucking at their prey, and he curls into a ball and waits to be flung against rocks or the bank. Suddenly his hands close around something, something long and fibrous; he seizes hold of it as the water shoots past him. The root – liana? – in his hand is like a spider monkey's dislocated arm. He hangs on tight at first, nothing more, just hanging on with his back to the pounding water, and then he gives it a pull, once, very carefully. He meets with resistance, so he pulls again, harder. Hand over hand, he hauls himself up until he feels something firm under foot, but he doesn't dare put any weight on it or let go of the root in case he sinks. He has the impression the sky is clearing a little. He can make out bushes, tangled branches, the bank he is pulling himself towards. He is only an outstretched arm away when something snaps and he is thrust back down; water gushes into his mouth, his nose. With his left hand he clings to the root and shakes his head to get rid of the water, barking hoarsely like a dog until it is out. His chest feels as if it has been sanded. He thinks the current has caught him until he realises something is anchoring him. The root is still attached to the chunk of riverbank that was torn away. He pulls himself back up and this time there are no surprises in store. He makes out the outline of a tree, and hungrily flings his arms around its trunk. When he lets go, he just has the strength to slide to the ground, gasping for breath. He lies there without moving, without thinking, until an instinct registers itself: you've got to do something.

Sitting up, he sees a miracle. The massed ranks of clouds are retreating, a gleam is spreading over the river and its banks, signalling the forgotten presence of a full moon. He stands up, holds onto the tree trunk and tests the firmness of the ground. He goes as close to the river's edge as the footing allows, scans the water and then ventures along the bank. Not far from where he climbed out, he sees a sandbank, above which, caught between two trees, glints the inside of his tent. He picks out all the tiny crooked thorns and rolls up the canvas. In the meantime the moon has brushed aside the obstacles in its path. The landscape that reveals itself bears only a distant relation to the setting of their overnight camp. The river is narrower, the vegetation thicker. The current is swift, steady; the hounding panic of the mudslide has subsided. A donkey drifts downstream, stretching its neck out of the water like a cursed swan. Moments later a chest is washed past, closely followed by more things of theirs, only a corner or an edge sticking out of the water so that he can't make them out. Is this how the expedition is fated to end, with him watching their belongings pass one by one, covered in mud, fragments of an order they fought so hard to preserve, each a perfect dose of contempt? With everything they have spent months collecting torn apart by a mudslide, and reduced to flotsam and jetsam? Random bits and pieces that will be caught in bushes when the river perishes after the brief glory of the rain season, or strewn across the dried-out riverbed for miles. They won't even serve as a warning: who will be able to make any sense of them, scattered to the four winds like that? Burton starts as he sees a figure hanging onto a branch drifting past in the water. He rushes to the tree where he had left the long root, grabs it and jumps into the river. In a few strokes he reaches the branch. With his left hand he clasps the figure from behind, puts his arm round his waist, and pulls on the root with his right hand, but it hasn't occurred to him that he will need both hands to pull himself back to the bank. He wraps the root around himself and the figure, and ties it in a knot, securing the pair of them. Two bodies, hanging by one rope. Slowly, to the rhythm of his dwindling energy, he reels them both in until they reach the tree. He heaves the body onto the bank and lays it down on the canvas. He parts the smeared hair and looks at Speke's unconscious face: feverish, half-drowned, but alive. Pallid amid its shock of blond hair. Burton can't do anything except cover him with the canvas and massage his limbs. After a while, with Speke's feet in his lap, he drifts off into a half-sleep, the final demand of his utter exhaustion.

The sun bursts through. There, it will put everything right; the sun doesn't nurse grievances. Slowly and deliberately it spreads its warm blankets over the fevers of the night, perfectly self-assured, as if it bore no responsibility for its disappearance. Burton squats at the river's edge and sees a grimacing face staring back at him like the ghost of a drowned man. The flesh hangs from the bones; the eyes bulge rabidly from the sockets, the lips peel back from the brown teeth, like swampy pools. Speke mutters something, his eyes wide open.

'How are you, Jack?' asks Burton, gently kneading Speke's right shoulder.

'Dead everywhere,' mutters Speke, 'make the dead go away.'

'What dead, Jack?'

'Somalis, dead Somalis. Not all dead, some are still dying, raising their arms, stretching out their hands, they want to touch something one last time, it doesn't matter what; make them go away, please.'

'Drink something, Jack.'

'No one's screaming, it's unbearable, no one's screaming, damned Somalis, how can anyone die so quietly?'

'I'll sit you up, Jack, I'll take this off. There, you see, it's wet, we have to take it off.'

'Everything's destroyed, all the tents, destroyed, all the equipment scattered everywhere, no one's in sight, everyone's left me, they've run away, I can't run, I don't have any legs, I can only crawl.'

'That's better, Jack, this'll do you good, warm you up.'

'I am going to die, the Somalis are coming, the Somalis raising their arms; I am going to die, I see the blood pouring out of me, I see the spears going into me, I have so much blood, I never knew, endless blood.'

'I'm going to rub you now to warm you up, Jack, do you understand? We've got to get you warmed up.'

'Useless blood. Useless. Put-downs from him, just put-downs, nothing but put-downs. Oh, he is always so much better, he's always God.'

'All right, that's enough, we're going to put my jacket on you now. It's almost dry.'

'He's a thief, that's all, just a common thief. My journal torn to pieces, a lamb to the slaughter, just for an appendix to his book, to his fame. My blood, all that blood for his fame. My collection just given away, he can do that, he's God, given away to a museum. He's a cannibal, I swear, a cannibal.'

'Calm down, Jack, calm down, you're with friends. What are you saying; who are you talking about?'

'He is not human. People only call him names. His gravestone, damn it, should just say: Dick. Nothing else on his grave, just Dick.'

Burton lets Speke fall back. He is dazed by all the hatred his companion has spewed forth. They have had misunderstandings, of course, differences of opinion, sometimes serious – but

427

raw hatred: he hasn't deserved that, especially because he was badly wounded in the attack in Somalia as well. The marks from the spear that pierced his cheek are still visible, but obviously they did not go as deep as the wounds to Speke's pride. His collection, the appendix: ridiculous reproaches! He just wanted to do the man a favour. No one would have printed an unknown officer's pedantries otherwise, whereas now his inkhorn observations have at least partly been made public; as for the collection, it is in far better hands in the Museum of Calcutta than it would have been anywhere else. Cannibal – totally absurd. He had to pay for publication, he hasn't earned anything, hasn't profited from the enterprise in any way whatsoever. What a hypocrite he is, that man lying there on the ground, and Burton is taking care of him; he's nursing this mean-spirited soul back to health when mankind would be far better off without him.

Speke has drifted off to sleep again and Burton decides to continue searching the bank. He has survived but what is the good of it if he can't find his notebooks? They were wrapped in an oilskin bag. He finds thousands of little things, most of them useless except a box of biscuits and some dried dates. And then on the other side of the river, which is now floating coyly, inconspicuously by after its hysterical outburst of rage, he sees a few monkeys. He pays no attention to them at first, until something at the corner of his eye jerks his head back: one of them is holding an oilskin bag in its hands. Burton doesn't know how many oilskin bags the expedition has, but he is certain that it's his the monkey is playing with, the one that contains everything he has been working towards for years. Burton howls at the top of his voice, louder than the monkeys. They notice him and the monkey drops the bag as if wanting to make fun of Burton, then another one grabs it out of the branches. Burton howls in no known language, howls threats that have no effect. The other monkey tries to reach into the bag, finds the opening, holds one of the notebooks in his hand. Burton was right. The monkey turns its attention to the notebook; the bag slips from its grasp. Burton rushes into the river, diving under the surface, arms thrashing, and when he reaches the other side, the bag is lying there in front of him as if waiting to be collected, but the monkeys have disappeared. He hears their calls for a spell, before they fade into the distance, and he knows nothing would be more futile than to give chase. He opens the bag, counts the notebooks. One is missing but the loss barely registers because he has noticed something else: the damp. He thought the bag was waterproof but he senses water everywhere, he feels everything has been soaked, and with a sinking feeling in his stomach he opens one of the notebooks: the writing is blurred. Not all over, there's a legible core; like a fruit rotting from the outside in, the moisture has worked its way in from the edges, blurring the tops and bottoms of the pages, chewing up the last letters of every line, ruining a third of the contents. It's the same with every notebook he opens: a third of his observations, explorations, descriptions and reflections have been wiped out. He should be able to reconstruct them partly from memory, but even in one's memory, he knows, writing blurs.

SIDI MUBARAK BOMBAY

'You say Bwana Burton never came back to Zanzibar after this journey, only Bwana Speke. But doesn't that contradict what you've already told us about him?'

'No, not at all, Baba Burhan, but I am honoured you pay me so much attention at this late hour, so I will gladly explain why. It was only on the second journey that I realised Bwana Burton was dependent: he was dependent on the masters of his country like all the other wazungu. He was not the rich man I had at first taken him for; he was a servant like me, serving the other wazungu who did not have the strength or courage or will or desire to undertake the journey themselves and so gave money to men like Bwana Burton and Bwana Speke to do it in their place. And since these two wazungu were sworn enemies by the end of the journey, peace could only reign between them if they were divided by a great sea. So it was obvious that their masters were going to have to choose one of them for the second journey, and even if Bwana Burton knew many things, he sometimes didn't understand the simplest of questions. Even the cleverest man can be stupider than a child. It was obvious the masters of the wazungu were going to prefer Bwana Speke because he looked like one of them, while Bwana Burton was worlds away in his appearance, with his thick, black beard, his skin that became so dark you couldn't tell him and an Arab apart, the robes he wore. He was worlds away from the appearance his masters liked – clean and handsome like Bwana Speke with his slender frame, his blue eyes, the light mane of his hair – there was no danger of anything about him being foreign. I saw for myself how his people respected him at the end of the second journey, when we got to Cairo and stayed in a hotel called Shepheard's Hotel – yes, my brothers, I stayed in the same hotel as Bwana Speke. That's how highly he prized me.'

'Ask him what sort of room he got! Then you'll hear how your great hero, Baba Sidi Mubarak Bombay, slept in a tiny little maid's room, while his friend with the light skin and the blond mane slept in a palace on the top floor.'

'Leave it, Mama, otherwise we'll never get to the end.'

'Do you think he would have given me his jacket as a farewell present if he hadn't prized me?'

'That old jacket? All tattered like that, it was easier for him to give it to you than throw it away.'

'I was given a silver medal by the Royal Geographical Society – you don't know who that is, do you? That is the council of high lords who commissioned my first and second journeys. I was photographed, presented in public.'

'You actually dare blurt out your shame! He was put on show like a wild animal they'd captured. He and the others had to pretend to run across the savannah, then he had to stand still, like a statue, for hours as people walked past and looked at that picture, a dead picture made by living people.

Worst of all – are you listening, you friends of this shameless old man – the worst thing of all was that all those inquisitive passers-by paid money to gawp at my husband as he pretended to have been turned to stone.'

'Oh, who's listening to you anyway? Why don't you spare yourself the effort? I know what it was like because I was there. I know how we were honoured at concerts and ceremonies where they introduced us to the people as the assistants and companions of the great explorer Bwana Speke. We were even invited to a reception in the viceroy's palace, which wasn't in Cairo, or on the mainland, it was on an island called Rhodes, and we were so important that we were taken there by boat and put up for days in the palace. And we ate better and we ate more there than we had ever eaten in our lives, and we also, I have to admit, drank far too much because the alcohol flowed like water. Only then did we return to Zanzibar by boat, a long journey on which we got to know other new places such as Suez, Aden, islands like Mauritius and the Seychelles where they gave us gifts of money, our fame had flown on so far ahead . . .'

'Bwana! Don't you see no one is listening any more? Baba Ishmael is snoring so loud they can hear him in the port, and everyone else has gone home; the last one, Baba Burhan, has just slipped away. You're only sharing your stories with the rats. Stop gabbling and come into the house, I want to make your food. And don't forget to wake Baba Ishmael, give him a proper shake, otherwise one of his sons will come looking for him again and complain to us.'

～

Speke is in a hurry. He has had his hair cut, his beard trimmed. Perhaps he did it himself. He comes briskly towards him with long, powerful strides. Burton is reminded of a hunter who has wounded an animal and is now on its bloody trail, determined to find it before nightfall. Perhaps that's unfair, though.

Burton holds out his hand and says something non-committal in parting, like: 'I'll be back there soon. Won't be long.'

Speke replies gaily – he can always count on the fellow's joviality; the jungle hasn't beaten it out of him, unfortunately – 'Goodbye, old man. No need to fret: I'm not going to look up the Royal Geographical Society before you get back. We'll go there together. You take the next boat and I'll be waiting for you. Don't you worry.'

When someone tells you not to worry, start doing so immediately: one of his mother's sayings. Burton nods and murmurs that he hopes he has a good trip. Then he turns and leaves John Hanning Speke behind on the port. He would not put anything past him; he trusts his promises as much as an exact date of the Apocalypse. No, their dispute does not stem from a lack of knowledge of human nature on his part. When fate throws you together with someone, when you have no other choice, what use is the best judgement of character? Fate has conspired against him, that's all, and he has been powerless before it.

SIDI MUBARAK BOMBAY

Sidi Mubarak Bombay's wife – his wife acquired with brass wire and retained with affection – grates coconut in the kitchen, puts the rice to soak and adds the pieces of fish to the pot where the curry is simmering, chilli-red. She hears his voice in the adjoining room, still talking – there's never a lull once Sidi Mubarak Bombay has set sail on a story; the winds are always set fair. She isn't really listening though as she drains the rice, concentrating instead on the throbbing pain in her left side, a pain that had at first discreetly announced itself, like a guest who sits humbly in the corner, happy with any crumbs you care to offer him, before gradually growing greedier as the months passed. Now her guest is polishing off more than she's prepared to give and none of the herbs, which the doctor gives her and she carefully pounds as instructed, bring her any relief. She focuses on the pain as she cooks and her husband carries

432

on with his story. Absorbed in what she is doing, suddenly something makes her prick up her ears, some words suggesting a story she hasn't heard before. After all the years they have spent together, this blustering, vain, gnarled tree knot of a husband can still dish up new stories, still add spices when the routine is threatening to grow stale. He can still surprise her after all these years – this time with the memory of a man who he met on his last journey, a journey he took immediately after Hamid's wedding, which he rarely talks about, his fourth, on which he came across a European who decorated his neck and head with the most incredible things.

'This strangely adorned man collected the future's cast-offs,' the tree knot was saying outside her kitchen, and she didn't know what he meant by these words that penetrated her tiredness, but even so she stopped cooking and went closer to the passage so as not to miss a word, just as before she had taken care not to waste a grain of rice.

'Every time', the tree knot went on, 'this strange man found some broken-off piece of metal or old cartridge case or empty bottle on the path, he couldn't help himself: he had to pick it up and look at it, and from then on, he couldn't be parted from it. He couldn't throw it away; he had to drill a hole in each of those objects he had picked up and thread them on a chain he always wore around his neck: a weird necklace from which dangled half a dozen medicine bottles, the key to a sardine can and some bits of metal.'

Now she understands: the foreigner, this adorned character, wore on his body bits of rubbish left by the caravans that had passed through the country. Sidi Mubarak Bombay, her husband whose peculiarities she will never get used to as long as she feels anything, went on four of those caravans. If his stories are to be believed, he even guided them, and that is why, in his own lopsided way, he is delighted by this foreigner who adorned his body with the skins of his old journeys. A smile spreads across her face; there truly is no one else like him, this childish old man who keeps surprising her afresh.

When she tells him the food is ready, he says conciliatorily: 'Let's eat together this evening.' They mix the curry with the rice and in silence shape the rice into balls with their fingers. He only eats a little but she can see he likes it. When he leans back from the table, she slowly heaves herself up and brings him a bowl of water to wash his fingers. Then she leaves him to go and tidy up in the kitchen and boil the water that she pours in a bucket and puts in the bedroom before calling, 'The water's ready for your bath.' When she sees him again, he's only dressed in a kikoi. She looks at his gnarled body as he sits on the bed, barefooted, and she remembers how strange the thought of being with a man shorter than her had struck her as a girl. She had even been scared his penis would be too small for her. When she had begun to trust him a little, she had ventured to bring up the subject of his height. He had laughed. 'Yes, but that's also why I'm strong and not so easy to knock down; I may be restless but I can't be torn up by the roots.' And that has proved true. 'Learn to know the tree you want to lean against,' her father had advised her once. She hadn't been able to choose the tree, but the man she had been sold to had always borne the weight she had put on him. 'Bwana,' she says slowly, savouring every word, 'I am your wife. Let us make love, bwana, I feel a great desire.' Sidi Mubarak Bombay sighs, looks up and walks deliberately over to her on the bed. It takes a certain effort these days but it still brings them joy.

Revelation

In the days following the funeral, the priest went over the events of that night at the dying man's bedside in his mind so incessantly he could hardly bear their memory. Among his many causes for reproach, one in particular allowed him no peace. The widow had forced him to administer *si es capax*, extreme unction, which is usually applied when someone has lost consciousness. But the Englishman was conscious. He had looked him in the eye as he bent over him. The priest hadn't tried to talk to him. He had simply yielded to the wife's urging, not even daring to ask if the dying man wished to receive the sacrament, let alone if he was entitled to it. And yet he hadn't known the man at all. What sort of priest was he? There must be some way to find out the truth; only that would restore his peace of mind. What if he asked the servants? Servants know everything, and they'd give more honest answers than the wife whom he couldn't trust precisely because she was such an ardent Catholic. Dumbfounding, the whole thing. It was agonising how little he understood it.

At Sunday mass, Massimo noticed one of the priests looking at him intently. An elegant-looking figure. He seemed more interested in him than the service. He looked like a servant of God who ministered to the rich. A young, closely-shaven man with a haughty expression. He must have come to this part of town by mistake. On a Sunday morning? And why was he staring at him so? After mass, the priest came up to him on the church steps.

'Are you Massimo Gotti?'

'I am.'

'Can I talk to you for a moment?'

'To me? Why, padre?'

'You worked for Signor Burton.'

'That's right.'

'For several years.'

'Nine years.'

'Did you associate with the signor?'

'Associate with him? I am a gardener.'

'Did you speak to him on occasion?'

'A few times.'

'Can you tell me anything about his religion?'

'He was a devout believer.'

'Are you sure?'

'Quite sure.'

'What makes you say that?'

'He was a good man.'

'Let's hope so for his sake. But even a heathen can be a good man.'

'A heathen? He wasn't a heathen.'

'He was rarely seen at mass.'

'There's a chapel in the house.'

'Did you see him praying there?'

'I work outside.'

'So you didn't see him praying?'

'He prayed. I know he did. Maybe he did it somewhere else. He was a very strong man. Definitely not a heathen. Heathens are different.'

∽

He hadn't learnt a thing from that idiotic gardener. What about the maid? he'd thought. Maybe she would know more.

There was nothing easier, as it turned out, than speaking to her in the market, but he hadn't anticipated that she would ask him about his motives. He hadn't known what to say. He couldn't confess his doubts, and so had lied instead, sinking deeper into error in the hope of shedding light on the original transgression. My God, what quagmire had he got himself trapped in? He told her he wanted to write an obituary for the diocesan journal illustrating the different aspects of Signor Burton's personality. 'Ah,' Anna the maid said to his stupefaction, 'so you want to know if he was a good Catholic?'

'That is one of the questions we are interested in, yes.'

'I would say . . . yes and no.'

'You're not sure?'

'Oh yes, I'm quite sure. He knew a great deal about religion. Sometimes he told me stories about saints I'd never heard of. Did you know that St Josaphat was Indian? He was actually called Buda or something like that.'

'You believed his stories?'

'Oh yes, you had to believe his stories.'

'But you also doubted whether he was a good Catholic?'

'With good reason.'

'I've heard there's a little chapel in the house.'

'There you are, that's just it. He never set foot in there. The mistress was the only one who went in the chapel, and me too sometimes. With her permission.'

'Perhaps he prayed in his room?'

'I never saw him pray.'

'Perhaps he didn't pray in your presence.'

'When he was at home, for the most part he didn't leave his study all day. And there wasn't anywhere in there to pray, padre. No cross or image of Our Lord.'

'I understand. Did you see him do anything strange?'

'He only did strange things.'

'Did you come across him in an unusual position? Sitting on the ground, or on his knees?'

'No. He was always sitting in his chair when I came in. Or

else he was pacing up and down his study. Sometimes he was reciting things.'

'What?'

'I didn't understand.'

'Of course, he was English.'

'They weren't in English.'

'Do you understand English?'

'No, not a word. Why should I? The master and mistress spoke perfect Italian. But they always spoke English to each other. After all that time – I worked for them for over eleven years – you get used to the sounds of a language.'

'What language was it?'

'That I can't tell you.'

'You never asked him?'

'As if, padre!'

'What did it remind you of?'

'A poem, or a prayer. It was something simple, always the same thing.'

'Like a refrain?'

'What's that?'

'The repetition of a central truth. The way we say: *gloria patri et filio et spiritui sancto*.'

'That sort of thing, yes, perhaps. It was a little like that.'

'Was it an ugly sound, in the throat?'

'No, it sounded beautiful, actually.'

'Listen, did it sound a bit like *Bismillah hir Rahman nir Rahim*?'

'No, that wasn't it.'

'Or like *Laa-illaha-ilallah*?'

'Yes, that's it. It sounded like that. Do you know what it is? Yes, I'm sure it was that.'

'Oh God!'

'Have I said something I shouldn't have, padre?'

'Oh God, what have I done?'

'What is it, padre?'

'He was a Mohammedan, he was a bloody Mohammedan!'

The evening sun was smoothing the roof tiles as he embarked on the course of action he had most wanted to avoid. He called on the bishop, his father confessor, and described the doubts that had sprouted in his mind like mushrooms and were now running rampant since his conversation with the maid. Having been dreading this conversation for days, he didn't dare openly express everything weighing on his conscience. But none of the reproaches he had anticipated could have unnerved him as profoundly as the complete calm with which the bishop reacted. He smiled with a superiority that comes from living in a palace, from being born to such a station. The priest had had to study hard, he had had to climb the stairs of education one step at a time, and now someone with more power, more self-assurance had taken him for a fool.

'I see I should have taken you into my confidence,' the bishop said nonchalantly. 'I must have forgotten to tell you that I once took Signor Burton's confession.'

'You did?'

'His wife had been urging him to go to confession. For years, I presume. She had gone on at him, implored him. "It will unburden your heart." The only thing that could unburden his heart, he had told her, would be the news that he didn't have to die soon. Witty character, Signor Burton.'

'Why did you hear his confession?'

'He was the British consul in our city, and his wife is a loyal daughter of the Church. Besides, between you and me, I enjoy hearing the confessions of those who rarely go to confession. And it did prove interesting in his case.'

'Interesting?'

'He claimed he had nothing to confess at first.'

'The arrogance!'

'Although an officer for over a decade, who had faced the most brutal dangers on every continent, he claimed never to have killed a man. "You don't know how highly that ought to make you think of me," he declared. I pressed him a little, whereupon he confessed to a small sin, *une petite bêtise*, as he put it. He had never killed anyone, but he had once spread a rumour that he had killed an Arab because he had caught sight of him relieving himself standing up. It was a terribly bad lie though, he had chided himself afterwards. "Try relieving yourself standing up in those robes," he told me, "it's absolutely impossible." I told him that that could not properly speaking be considered a sin; there must have been something more serious in his rich life. No, he claimed. Nothing he could think of.'

'Did you ask him if he had always been a good Christian?'

'Oh yes, and he reacted very vehemently. "You don't want to know that, Reverend Father. Believe me, that's something you want to steer well clear of." He did have something else to offer though, something truly shameful, he said after a while, when he saw I wasn't going to be so easily satisfied. He was still ashamed of it, a sin of his youth, in Sindh. It wasn't important where that was, he said, God would know, he had been there once, and then moved on in no time – I interrupted him; honestly, this was too much. "Sorry," he said, "this confession is making me nervous, as you can see. I hardly recognise myself."'

'I know where Sindh is. He lived there a long time. Among Mohammedans.'

'In Sindh, he told me, some amateurs lacking either knowledge or common sense had been digging for archaeological treasures. He'd be the last to dispute that archaeology – the word didn't exist at the time – is an important science, but he couldn't help having a little joke. So he had smashed a cheap red clay vase in the Athenaeum style, painted with Etruscan figures, and buried the pieces where those avid foragers were digging. Of course, they had then found the fragments, to their wild excitement, and gone around boasting about their discovery, claiming that the history of the Etruscans, even the history of ancient Rome, would have to be rewritten. Somewhat prematurely. He didn't know if it was his friend Walter Scott who had enlightened them, or if they had started having doubts themselves after not finding anything else, but one day they'd packed up their things and disappeared. He was still ashamed about it. Surprising confession, don't you think?'

'A stale lie. Is that all?'

'No, I got more out of him. He confessed that the day he was knighted by Queen Victoria, he had left the reception early and hurried off to a printer in a disreputable part of London south of the Thames to prepare a new edition of a book named the *Kama Sutra*. I wasn't much impressed by this supposed sin until he explained what was in the book. I can't repeat it; suffice to say it was sinful from cover to cover. And not only did he publish it, he also translated it. He then told me about the carnal desires he had succumbed to in Africa, with three women, an absolute Sodom, I had to stop him, I had heard enough. I gave him the *te absolvo* and quickly ushered him out. It had all begun so harmlessly and then suddenly . . .'

'If he had lied so much in his life, how do we know where he stood on the question of faith?'

'You worry unnecessarily. He was Catholic. *Basta.*'

'How do we know that?'

'He told me: if you were Christian, the thing to be was Catholic.'

'What a profession of faith!'

'Let's be realistic. No one believes of their own free will.'

'Yes, but the lack of freedom should be determined by God.'

'Ah, that reminds me. He said something else – he had a marked sense of humour, as you'll see. He was Catholic because unfortunately there were no Elchasites in Trieste. A longing for Elchasites, have you ever heard of such a thing?'

'What does it mean? What does it mean for me?'

'You should put the whole thing behind you.'

'Did he at least seek God?'

'Absolutely, and like most people he seldom found Him. He had an unusual point of view on this subject. "No one will ever really encounter God," he told me once at an official dinner.

"For what would happen if he did? His self would dissolve and he would merge with God. No more I, no more future, he would cross over into eternity. Who would want to remain a human if he could be a part of God?" Remarkable logic, don't you think?'

'What followed from that for him?'

'That we want to search, of course, but under no circumstances to find. That's exactly what he did all his life, he told me. He searched everywhere, whereas most people are happy just to look in the same pot. Having said which, he looked me frankly in the eye. Somewhat mischievously, I have to say.'

'You hold to him being Catholic?'

'Let's say he was an honorary Catholic.'

'This is too much for me. Why did you send me there?'

'Because I don't like being dragged out of my bed in the middle of the night. And now let's drop this matter before it begins to annoy me.'

∾

Richard Francis Burton died early in the morning before you could tell a black thread from a white. Over his head hung a piece of Persian calligraphy upon which was written:

This too shall pass.

1998–2003: Great Eastern Royale, Bombay Central, Mumbai, India
2003–5: Strathmore Road, Camps Bay, Cape Town, South Africa

Glossary

Aba: neckerchief

Aira, Gaira natthu Khaira: 'Tom, Dick and Harry'

Ajami: 'Non-Arab', mainly used to designate Persians – pejorative in some cases, neutral in others

Alif Baa: first and second letters of the Arab alphabet

Alim: scholar in Islamic studies

Angrezi (Hindi): English(man)

Anna: a penny in pre-decimalised Indian currency

Are Baapre: 'Oh God', exclamation of astonishment, delight, shock, etc.

Arti: Hindu ritual performed after sunset

Aste aste: 'slower than slow'

Azan: call to prayer

Baba: 'elderly man', respectful term of address also used for holy men

Badhahi: carpenter

Banyan: originally a merchant caste from Gujarat, used in East Africa as a synonym for Indians

Baraza: stone bench along the outside of houses in Zanzibar, where guests who are not members of the family sit

Bashibazouk (from the Turkish, meaning leaderless): irregular mounted troops in the Ottoman army

Bhai: friendly, respectful term of address

Bhajan: religious song

Bhakti: declaration of love for God in song

Bhang: alias cannabis, alias hashish

Bharat: India

Bhisti: servant

Bilal: the first muezzin (caller to prayer at mosque) in Islamic history, a former Ethiopian slave

Bindi: dot, generally red, on a woman's forehead – one of the body's energy points – which protects the wearer's aura. Originally a Tantric practice, it also indicates a woman is married

Birbahuti: red velvet mites (*Trombidium*)

Bol: literally, 'speak'; a tone on the tabla

Burkha: black veil covering every aspect of a woman that might arouse a man

Cantonment: British military quarters, temporary or semi-permanent, with broad, straight streets and hedges

Chai: tea with milk, sugar and spices

Chillum: hashish pipe

Chilumchi: large bowl, usually copper

Chowkidar: guard

Daaru: alcohol

Dervish: mendicant who has withdrawn from everyday life to live in a state of ecstasy; Muslim equivalent of the Hindu *sadhu*

Devadasi: literally 'servant of God'; in effect, servant of priests, ritual prostitute

Dhal: lentils

Dharma: the inherent nature of a person or object, duty in life, law

Dhoti: 'the washed', an unstitched loincloth worn by men in India

Dhow: traditional Arab sailing vessel, plying the Indian Ocean for the purposes of trade for centuries

Diin: religious belief and way of life

Dik-dik: smallest East African antelope

Diwan: chief minister

Diwan Kharijiyah: Foreign Office in Ottoman Egypt

Djinn: spirit, ghost

Dukaan: shop

Dupatta: long scarf covering women's shoulders and breasts in South Asia

Effendi: respectful term of address for men in Ottoman Empire, equivalent to 'Sir'

Eid al-Adha: The Feast of Sacrifice commemorating Ibrahim's (Abraham's) willingness to sacrifice his son Ishmael (Isaac), celebrated the day after pilgrims on the Hajj descend from Mt Arafat

Eid kum mubarak: 'May your Eid be blessed'

Faranjah: the 'Franks', which came to mean all western Europeans

Feringhi: foreigner, from 'Faranjah'

Fustan: fustanella, traditional Albanian pleated kilt

Gaekwad: literally 'keeper of the cows', family name of Baroda's royal dynasty

Gandharva: male spirits in Hindu mythology, which guarded soma, the drink of the gods, played music in the heavenly palaces and acted as messengers between the gods and humans

Gandharvavivaaha: love marriage contracted by mutual consent and without formality

Ganesh: Hindu deity, son of Shiva and Parvati, with a plump man's body and an elephant's head

Ganesh Chathurti: eleven-day festival in Ganesh's honour in September and October

Ganja: marijuana

Garuda: the half-man, half-bird mount of the god Vishnu in Hindu mythology

Goras: the 'white skins'

Gotra: literally 'cow-pen', a lineage or clan assigned to a Hindu at birth, which traces itself ultimately back to a saint (Rishi)

Gulab jamun: Popular South Asian dessert: doughballs, or milkballs, in sweet syrup

Hadith: 'report', oral traditions concerning words and deeds of the Prophet (pbuh), which serve as binding guides to action and thought

Hajam: barber

Hamail: a case for the Qur'an, slung by red cords over the left shoulder

Hapana: 'no' in Kiswahili

Ihram: two pieces of white, unsewn cotton cloth, the only garment a hajji is allowed to wear

Ikhlas Sura: The one hundred and twelfth sura of the Qur'an, declaring *tawhid*, God's oneness and absolute unity. God is without equal, without origin, without end and unlike anything else that exists

Imam: leader, spiritual exemplar, person who leads the prayers in the mosque

Inshallah: 'if God wishes'

Intezaar karna: 'to wait'

Iskander the Great: Alexander the Great

Jain: 'followers of the Jinas, the conquerors', a religion that privileges asceticism and non-violence

Jellabiya: long, full tunic, often with a hood

Jemadar: the most junior rank of Indian commissioned officer, equivalent to a lieutenant in the British army

Jubbah: long outer garment worn by more prosperous Muslims of both sexes

Jyotish: astrologer with broad area of responsibility

Kaas (Arabic): storyteller

Kaka: paternal uncle

Kala: time, which, according to Hinduism, is eternal and cyclical

Kama: love, desire – a central task of life in the Hindu belief system

Kanga: cotton wraparound worn by men and women in East Africa

Kanzu: long white robe worn by men on the East African coast

Kaskazi: one of Zanzibar's monsoon winds

Kayf: the capacity to savour the moment, much emphasised as an 'Oriental' trait in Orientalist depictions

Kazi: another of Zanzibar's monsoon winds

Kedmutgar: servant who waits at table and works in the kitchen
Kelim: woven carpet
Khabardar: 'watch out'
Khat: leaf of bush (*Catha edulis*) chewed for its stimulating effects
Khatarnak: 'dangerous'
Khelassy: servant who works the *punkah*, or fan
Khutbah: sermon at Friday prayers in mosque
Kikoi: East African cloth used for multiple purposes
Kirangozi: caravan guide, leader on the march
Kiswah: black brocade cloth, with a gold-embroidered Muslim profession of faith and band of ornamental calligraphy, that covers the Kaaba
Kobbradul: fine cloth
Kofta: meatballs, not always made of meat
Kopje: natural rises, rocky outcrops
Kurta: Indian Muslims' traditional dress, consisting of wide trousers and long shirt
Laddoo: sweet made out of flour, sugar and clarified butter
Lahiya: letter-writer, scribe
Madafu: coconut milk
Madrassa: Qur'anic school
Maharajah: literally 'the great king'; title of male Hindu rulers
Maikhanna: bar
Mama: maternal uncle
Mashallah: 'That which God has willed', often used when something wonderful has happened
Mast qalandar: '[spiritually] intoxicated dervish'; chant in praise of Lal Shahbaz Qalandar, the Sufi saint of Sehwan
Maya: deception, mistake, illusion – in other words, the reality we perceive
Mganga: traditional healer, medicine man
Mithaiwallah: sweet vendor
Miya: 'circumcised'; pejorative term for Muslims
Mlecha: barbarian, unclean, untouchable, low-born – hence, European

Mt Kaf: mythical mountain that marks the limit of the world.

Mtepe: small boat

Mubarak: blessed

Muhafiz: governor

Muhtaram: Arabic mark of respect

Munshi: teacher, scholar

Nagar Brahmin: 'urban' brahmins, a sub-caste that provided most of Gujarat's administrative officials under British rule

Naib al-Harim: vice-intendant of mosque

Nandera: sub-caste of brahmins

Nautch girl: dancer, cultivated courtesan

Neem: margosa tree

Oim aim klim hrim slim: 'abracadabra'

Paratha: unleavened bread with various fillings

P'hazi: village chief

Pratikshaa karna: 'to wait'

Pujari: priest

Punkah: large fan

Puranas: 'old texts', Sanskrit creation myths, divine biographies and saints' genealogies

Puranpolis: sweet filled pancakes

Purnamadaha/Purnamidam/Purnaat purnamudachyate/Purnasya purnamaadaaya/Purnameva avasishyate: 'That is full; this is full. The full comes out of the full. Taking the full from the full, the full itself remains.' Invocation of the Isa Upanishad

Qalandar: Sufi saint

Raka'ah: Islamic prayer cycle

Raki: eau-de-vie, generally made with aniseed

Sadhu: holy man, Hindu equivalent of *dervish*

Safarnameh: travel book, report

Sakuntala: heroine of the play of the same name by the celebrated fifth-century AD Sanskrit epic poet and dramatist Kalidasa

Salat al Jannazah: Islamic funeral prayer

Santana Dharma: 'eternal faith', Hindu term for Hinduism

Sardarji: Sikh

Satya Shodak Samaj: 'Society of Seekers of Truth', rationalist, progressive Hindu organisation founded in 1873

Sayaji Rao the Second: maharajah of Baroda, 1818–47

Sepoy: indigenous soldier under British command

Shirk: polytheism, animism

Shishya: pupil

Shivaji Bhosle: Hindu founder of the Maratha empire in western India in the seventeenth century; in competing Hindu and Muslim nationalisms, he is claimed as a hero or tyrant depending on point of view

Shivaratri: 'Night of Shiva', Hindu festival

Sircar: servant who carries the purse

Smashaana: cremation ground, cemetery

Soma: a mountain plant pressed to create a drink that, like the Greek ambrosia, both confers immortality and is conceived of as a god itself

Sufi: Islamic mystic. 'To find joy in the heart when care assails it' (Rumi)

Sulla: pejorative term for Muslims

Sutra: aphorism

Tabla: Indian double drum

Tapas: physical privation, which releases energy

Taqiyya: special, and controversial, dispensation whereby Muslims may conceal their faith when under threat, persecution or compulsion

Tarawih: recitation of the entire Qur'an during the evening prayers of Ramadan

Tawa: round metal dish

Tawaf: the seven rounds hajjis are required to make of the Kaaba

Thali: popular Indian meal, a selection of mainly vegetarian dishes

Tintaal: tabla rhythm with sixteen beats

Tonga: cart drawn by horse or mule

Topi: finely crocheted cap worn by Muslims

Ulema: plural of *alim*

Urs: celebration of a Sufi saint's birthday at his tomb

Vidhata: goddess of destiny who writes a child's fate on its forehead six days after birth

Wakalah: caravanserai

Wazu: ritual washing before prayer

Wazungu (Kiswahili): 'those who turn around in circles', meaning white people

Yagatan: sword

Yaksha: semi-divine beings ranging from benign nature spirits to ghosts and demons

Zabit: prefect of police

Zamzam water: water from the well in the Great Mosque at Mecca, credited with beneficent properties

Zikr: 'remembrance of God', form of meditation practised particularly by Sufis

Zohar: Islamic mid-afternoon prayer

Acknowledgements

Numerous people across three continents have helped me research this novel, so much so, in fact, that a complete list of their names would resemble a telephone directory. Rather than such a bald statistical summation, I would rather extend my deepest gratitude to them all in the same breath.